The Tales of Averon Trilogy:

Dawn of the Great War

A.M. Keen

 New Generation **Publishing**

The Dark Army

Part 1

The Stranger

1

The earth shook violently as the Dark Army thundered across the Great Vast Open. Each hunter in the battalion was tracking the musty scent of their target as it hung thickly in the warm air, leaving an invisible trail for their snouts to follow. Hundreds of paws shattered the silence as the hunters, overcome by the deafening rumble in their footfalls, knew nothing more than the instinct within them; to ignore the burning in their chests and the water seeping from their eyes, to ignore the aching and tiredness of their limbs, to keep sprinting forward, together, as a unit, and never look back until their target was apprehended. The humans were lagging further behind on their horses, trying in vain to catch their soldiers, to become one with them, to scream their war call and end this battle once and for all.

Ahead of the monstrous army ran their general. He was motivated, concentrated and evil. His gaze was fixed firmly upon his target, the fox they had tracked across many green, open miles, and who still pushed himself as fast as when they had caught his trail and descended upon him. In his wake the general darted right, then left, jumped ditches and avoided bushes, ignoring the burning, screaming pain of exhaustion coursing through his body. His focus kept firm, even as his limbs hung loose and his head swayed from side to side and up and down as he sprinted forward.

His prey kept distance ahead, but exhaustion was setting in and now he showed signs of fatigue. The general noticed and smiled to himself. The huge, grassy meadow they amassed was now diminishing, and a Great Forest loomed from nowhere ahead of them. It rolled slowly upwards from behind the incline they had unknowingly begun to ascend.

The war calls of his comrades seemingly subsided into nothingness and the thunderous rumble of their feet vanished. The general's eyes narrowed. His heartbeat thundered through his ears. The noise of his breathing disappeared.

There you are. I have you now.

The general ran faster, the bushy red tail of his prey no more than six feet away. Closing in. Closer. Four feet. The general opened his snarling mouth.

Jump!JUMP!

The bugle screamed through the summer afternoon, halting the general instantaneously. The war-calls of his comrades surrounded him once more and brought him back to consciousness. The burning, the aches, the sharp pains that had all vacated him now stabbed at him viciously and forced him to pant wildly. He now recognised the uncomfortable feeling of saliva falling from his chin and trailing warmly on the left side of his neck towards his shoulders. He turned back to see his army in the distance behind him, howling and barking, unable to stand still, the adrenaline surging through their veins. They looked to him with expectation. All of them were his, and would follow him to the ends of the earth. All were ruthless and savage, decorated with dark patterned fur upon their bodies. Whether it was black, grey or brown, they wore wonderful and intricate blotches of darkness, leaving only white fur on their underside and muzzles. They feared him yet loved him. He was their leader. Baal, the most vicious hound to ever lead the Dark Army...

One of the humans was shouting at him from behind the sea of darkness, commanding him sternly back to their ranks. He rolled his eyes in anger, and barked out in sincere frustration.

Without even noticing, he had stumbled upon the clearing to the huge forest that had appeared during the chase. He looked upon it in wonder as its density vanished into a blend of dark greens and browns behind the border trees. Each tree was huge, and to him somewhat unwelcoming. It appealed to him. Challenged him...

He span around, momentarily disorientated, his bearings confused and unfocused. Suddenly he realised how close he was to The Lodge where he lived with his hunters. This was the forest he could see from the pen he was caged inside way back across the field and across the Great Vast Open. His target had led them in one huge circle from where they found his scent miles away in the opposite direction.

Clever fox. Very clever...

He turned back to the forest clearing and watched his opponent's red body and tail vanish into a thicket and out of view. The smell they had tracked was still high in the air and was lingering long enough for him to be followed. The general turned to continue his challenge, to ignore the humans as he desperately dreamed of doing so, when his master's voice bellowed in disapproval and summoned him once more, and probably, for the final time. He looked at the thicket, back at his hunters and back to the thicket once more. "Not this time, my friend," he whispered, almost relishing the fact that the hunt would still continue. He smiled, turned, and trotted back to his comrades. He looked back over his shoulder towards the forest. "I'll be seeing you soon."

2

He felt the rush of waking from a deep sleep. He could feel himself rousing from the darkness, rushing to consciousness rapidly, and then stirred when his body took notice and started to respond. Some voices were way away in the distance. He couldn't hear what they said until they came closer...

"...Waking up..."

He opened his eyes to see he had come to rest in a clearing surrounded by vast trees, wild grass and thick vegetation at its border. The sun was beaming brightly down upon him, casting shafts of light between the trees beyond the clearing in all directions. He noticed parts of a dandelion dislodged from their stem and watched as they floated past in the gentle breeze. Where was he?

"Are you okay?" a female voice asked. He shook his head and steadily rose to his feet. After fluttering his left eyelid to remove the cloud that obscured his view, he saw that he had been joined by a vixen and male fox, known as a dog, the same as him. A puzzled look crossed his face for a moment and he shook his head as if to rid himself of the final cobwebs loitering inside.

"Um, yes, I think?" he said unconvincingly. The dog trotted closer to him.

"You even know how you got here?" he asked in a gentle tone. This took him by surprise as every other dog he had ever met had always been confrontational and derogatory.

"I don't think he's -" the vixen began, but he interrupted her before she could finish.

"No, no. I'm fine." He looked around, at the flowers and trees, at the vastness of the vegetation and how dark it made the forest look in the distance. "I just, just, don't know where I am?"

"Okay," the dog said uncertainly. He lowered his head and trotted over to within touching distance. "You are in Averon."

"Averon?" he asked, perplexed.

"The forest," the vixen began, "It's what we call the forest. Do you live here?" It took a moment for him to register. He was still groggy, but after a second or so he knew too well that he was just a visitor.

"No."

The two foxes looked at each other. "Then you're from the Great Vast Open?" the vixen asked, either worried or excited, he couldn't tell which.

"Vast Open?"

"Ha!" the dog laughed, almost enjoying the comedy of the situation. He looked over at the vixen and gestured his head to a clearing that almost looked like a track. "Let's take him back. He'd never make it back to where he came from in this state. Kedem can take a look at him; maybe he'll know what to do." He turned back to the visiting dog. "Come with us, we'll get you back on your feet again and ready to continue on your journey. You got a name?"

A name? He had one, but it took a moment to remember. It's what his mother hd called him when he was just a pup. It had something to do with the thin shard of white fur that ran up his left cheek, across his left eye, and then tapered away between his ears. That's it. He remembered.

"Streak."

"Streak?" The vixen asked. He nodded. He was unsure about a lot of things at that moment, but his name he was certain of.

"Streak," he replied once again in confirmation.

"Okay Streak," the dog began, "this is Tali and I'm Doran. We're going to take you back with us to our den, and maybe the leader of our community will let you stay a while until you get your head back. I wouldn't suggest wandering Averon while you're not thinking straight." Tali nodded in agreement.

"I don't know..." Streak began.

"Just come with us, if you don't like it we'll take you to the borders. Simple," the vixen said.

After a moment or two of convincing, Streak let himself be swayed and agreed to go with them, but only because he trusted them both, something he had never done so quickly ever before. Maybe it was his head. Did he bang it? Probably - it was beginning to feel sore somewhere around his right ear - in which case he decided it was probably best to go with the flow and see what happened. He'd already had enough for one day.

As they walked, Doran looked up into an elm tree not far away. "Well, would you look at that?" he said to Tali. Tali followed his gaze and saw a white barn owl perched upon a stretching branch.

"Cyrius is up early today," she replied. "Wonder if it has anything to do with our strange new friend?"

"Could well be."

Streak just let it all go over his head.

The skulk of red foxes walked for an age, or at least what felt like one to Streak. They passed through dense and light woodlands, crossed fallen tree-trunks over rivers, paddled through streams, through light thickets, over mounds and through colourful grassed openings. The sun rose high in the sky and was boring down a ferocious heat that was kept at bay by the covering leaves and branches that towered high above them. The breeze gently cooled him with every gust, but each one was few and far between. Mainly he remained in silence as his guides led him through the foreign lands, relying deeply on their goodwill, that they were leading him to a safe and welcoming place. His head stooped a number of times on his journey, and occasionally it ached or pounded inside.

Streak first focused on how much the pain throbbed when it arose, but soon found it more of an annoyance as the journey went on.He said very little to his new companions, just 'yes' or 'no' answers mostly. This was because he didn't really have a great deal to exaggerate upon with the questions that they asked, but also due to the fact that his memory had been returning to him over the course of the trip, and he was trying to remember what had happened. He remembered the latter part of his foray into Averon, but the beginning was still very much a blur. He remembered being scared and being chased, but he did not remember by whom. He remembered thinking to himself that the deeper he passed into the forest the safer he might be. He then remembered tripping or falling somewhere and rolling almost a thousand times across the grass, and then blank. Nothing else.

He had racked his brain, trying to force it at times to remember, but it was a lost cause. With the pain that seemed to arise and subside whenever it felt like, having nature return his memory in time seemed like the best and less stressful way for it to come back.

Doran and Tali had tried to engage him in conversation but had given up after a while. It was clear that the outsider had a problem, and it was in their nature to help, but they had soon realised that hurrying back to the den was the best thing they could possibly do for him. They knew he was injured when they met him, but his condition seemed to decline as the journey wore on.

They had both been raised to do the better thing in life, and this was just a part of that existence. The two red foxes were siblings, and had always prided themselves that they could do the right thing, when so many dens across Averon were alleged to be the opposite. Stories emerged from time to time about dens and families, particularly in The North, who would refuse to assist others, even their own in the time of crisis.

The forest of Averon was different. It was a world within a world, and most of the creatures had never strayed beyond its borders. The pheasants, well, they claimed they had entered into the Great Vast Open, but their statements could hold little credence when the matter was discussed deeper. The badgers; they were wise and superstitious. They believed in many things, but their strongest belief was that everything happens for a reason. They stayed within the solace and safety of the trees until they could understand the world beyond themselves. The muntjac deer were brave and intelligent creatures who had often been seen running across and through the Great Vast Open, but all too often suffered many losses of their kind. They came back with terrifying tales of humans and of roaring monsters who screamed before they attacked creatures who dared cross their path. The rabbits however were energetic and sociable, and enjoyed good relations with most of the forest's species. They were the eyes of anyone who would listen, and were trustworthy and honest. Finally, there were the foxes. Inside Averon, the foxes lived in larger communities than anywhere else. These were referred to as a host of different names; dens, communities, skulks or families were the most common terms used, and they were dotted throughout Averon's vast borders. Most foxes had been sociable with each other and each den but many disagreements had diminished relations somewhat in previous years, which had led to a tolerance between the communities, nothing more. The community that Doran and Tali belonged to was Shadow Oak, the biggest in Averon, and headed by a wise old fox named Kedem. Kedem had worked hard at improving relations with the other den and community leaders, but had gained nothing more than a tolerance. This in itself was a success after the many years of bickering between the communities, but he had reached the limit in regard to their relations. One day Kedem decided that this was as good as things would ever be, and chose to leave relations as they were, or potentially risk a breakdown in tolerance altogether. The leaders would talk when needed. He had done his part, and that was that.

Doran and Tali had discussed many things on their journey back, always keeping a watchful eye on Streak as he lagged a little behind them. Soon they entered the small opening that led to Shadow Oak. As they wandered further inside, the grass cleared to soil which hardened underfoot and subsequently became littered with woodland debris. They entered a vast opening that was surrounded by trees and heavily shaded from the sun. Further away to their left a lake resided, gently lapping at its bank as the current pushed it slowly outward. Foxes had appeared as the trio made their way to the huge oak tree that gave the community its name, all looking at the new face in tow. The old oak was huge and dark, its bark knotted and uneven. It leaned to the left as it rose from the earth, its branches swaying in the gentle summer's breeze drifting between them. The leaves it sprouted seemed bigger and darker than any of those seen anywhere and it stood ominous, its shadow almost completely eclipsing the entire community.

Streak had felt groggy most of the journey here, and definitely knew he was an outsider when he entered Shadow Oak. The eyes peering from the dens judged and studied him as he slowly passed them. When the trio finally came to rest in front of a larger-than-usual burrow underneath the oak, most of the community had surrounded them, their conversations mumbling into one murmur.

From the burrow emerged a large fox. He looked vibrant, but Streak, even with his fuzzy head, could tell he was ageing. Even though his coat was red, he bore patches of grey fur; the most common sign of what foxes called 'Becoming Wise.' It was easy to tell. This was the chief. This was Kedem.

"Well, well, what do you bring back to us?" he asked both Doran and Tali as he left the burrow, but didn't give them time to answer. "I don't think I recognise you from any other community here in Averon?"

"No, we found him in the Western Clearing, unconscious," Tali stated in reply. "He says he's from the Great Vast Open."

A sigh of excitement rippled through Shadow Oak as Kedem sat down in front of them, sturdy and firm. "The Great Vast Open, of all places?" he asked, studying Streak.

"We think he may have injured himself, a knock to the head or something," Doran began, "so we brought him back with us. He was quite prepared to carry on his journey, but we didn't feel it was safe for him to do so alone and in this condition."

Kedem switched his gaze to Doran and nodded. "Nor would it have been a wise decision, for yourselves or your friend. How would you feel now if you had left

16

him alone there, knowing he may be injured? I am glad to see you both thinking of the greater good." He turned to Streak. "What is your name, stranger?"

Streak raised his head, his eyes closing and opening as if struggling to keep conscious. "Streak," he replied in a weak, raspy tone.

"Streak," Kedem repeated and smiled. "You are not in the best of conditions, are you?" Streak shook his head. The blunt, thumping pain he received in return made him regret that decision. "No," he replied.

Kedem looked to Doran. "Help him into the burrow and find him a place to rest. We'll find out what we need to know when he's ready."

"Thank you," Streak mustered, and followed Doran past the leader and down into the den beyond.

Kedem began walking, and called Tali to his side. "I'll have Jinx look him over and keep a watchful eye." Tali nodded. Her mind seemed elsewhere, and Kedem noticed. "What's troubling you?" he asked gently. She looked at him bemused, as if something was happening that she didn't fully understand.

"Cyrius was there. We noticed him as we left the opening to come back."

Kedem turned immediately to her. "Cyrius, you say? How very interesting," he began. "He's not often known to take an interest in the business of foxes, nor many other creatures in Averon. Are you sure it was him?"

"Positive," Tali replied. "He watched us leave and followed us part of the way. I thought about speaking to him, but decided against it."

Kedem smiled and nodded once. "Cyrius speaks very rarely, usually because he has nothing to say. When he does speak though, it is worthwhile listening to him. He is wise and insightful. Don't worry yourself about him though, I would assume he merely took an interest in your companion as he is new to the forest. Had there been any danger to Shadow Oak, the forest, or anything else which would disrupt the land of Averon, he would have informed us."

"I'm not worried," Tali began, "It's just that he was there. We hear all the stories, and -"

Kedem stopped, prompting Tali to do the same. "Stories, Tali. There are many about Cyrius within Averon, not all of them true. One day you will see first-hand what effect he has on the forest, and you will see how each living creature in his presence reacts, but right now your thoughts and efforts should be with our guest and his speedy recovery." Tali sighed and slowly nodded. "Do not worry," Kedem assured her. "Everything will be fine."

He had no idea what would soon descend upon Averon.

3

The western entrance to the general's warren was guarded by Coinin, an experienced rabbit who was midway through his term of service as a Forest Guard. He'd been out on a number of patrols before, but today had been given the duty of guarding one of four major entrances that would lead directly to the intricate connection of tunnels underneath the earth, and into the huge warren where the largest community of rabbits lived. This entrance was also the closest, most direct entrance that lead to the biggest chamber within the warren, and where Lupus, their general, presided.

Coinin sat on his fluffy white tail, enjoying the sun as it broke through the leaves above and bathed his grey, ruffled fur. He always enjoyed how the sunlight illuminated the leaves in the sky way up above him, changing them various shades of green and yellow, turning the forest treetops into a canvas of mixed colour. His favourite part of the sunshine however was how it warmed his body, and made a distinctive difference from the cold season that would soon fall upon the forest. He raised his nose towards the sky, closed his eyes, and relaxed his ears so that they fell back and rested over his shoulders. He could hear some birds tweeting and chirping above in the trees, and the sound of the rustling leaves as they clattered in a breeze that seemed to exist somewhere up above him.

The warren's entrance had been scraped out at the bottom of an elm tree and disappeared into darkness deep down beneath it. The tree's roots formed an un-symmetrical but sturdy entrance as they poked out here and there, solid and dry. He started believing that he truly was the luckiest creature in Averon to be posted to guard duty on a day like today, when across the distance emerged the sound of trampling paws. He remained basking in the summer warmth, perking his left ear upright to gain better understanding of the footfalls. They were rapid and light, both telltale signs of other rabbits. Had they been slower and heavier he may have been alarmed, but he'd run the length and depth of western Averon a thousand times and knew exactly what a group of sprinting rabbits sounded like. He sighed, dropped his head, and straightened up to look as though he'd been committed to his duty, not a secret admirer of the summer season.

Through the long grass and daisies he saw a reconnaissance party of four rabbits hurrying towards him. He could hear their pants as they drew closer to the entrance, and tried to put on his best don't-mess-with-me face. The rabbits bounded over a small branch that had fallen from the elm and almost overshot the entrance as they hurtled towards him. As the leader stopped the remaining party failed to react in time and crashed into him, knocking them over into a heap on the woodland floor. The leader looked up. It was Wickett, the fastest rabbit in the forest, and newly promoted leader to the western border Patrol Guards.

Coinin shook his head as he looked down upon them. "Is it really time for you to ruin my day again?" he asked as Wickett jumped to his feet.

"Coinin! Coinin! You gotta let us in! Quickly!" he said rapidly.

"Quick! Quick!" came another voice.

"You won't believe what we saw!" came another.

"Really! It was huge. Huge!" came another.

All four rabbits were babbling rapidly and together all at the same time, so much so that Coinin could feel his head struggling to keep composure. They shouted and shouted and shouted...

"ENOUGH!" Coinin screamed, settling the party instantaneously. "What? What did you see? What's huge?"

"Well, we were over patrolling the western border as ordered," began Blits, still panting to catch his breath, "and we heard these almighty roars."

"Loud as thunder," chipped in Digby, also struggling for breath.

"Screams, howls!" shouted Apollo, who was becoming way too excitable. Coinin shot him a glare that told him to calm down or face the consequences. Apollo took note and said nothing more.

"Wickett," Coinin began, "What did you see?"

Wickett lowered his voice as though he was telling a secret he had sworn to keep. "We saw, from beyond the tall grass of the Great Vast Open, an army. An army of hounds, screaming and howling, and they were hunting."

Coinin couldn't tell if they were winding him up or telling the truth, but he was certain that this group of guards wouldn't tire themselves to the point of exhaustion and seek entry to the main chamber to speak with General Lupus all for the sake of a joke. The General, as amicable as he was, would not take too kindly to a joke at his expense.

Coinin spoke in a calm temperament in order to settle the young guards and promote them to think about what they were saying. If he did let them enter they wouldn't do themselves, let alone him, any favours with the hierarchy whilst they were in this state. "Did you see what they were hunting?" Coinin asked, but the entire party shook their heads.

"Not properly," Wickett replied, "just a glimpse. Blits got the best look at it."

"I saw a flash of red through a clearing not far from where we were. I'd say it looked more like a fox than anything else, but couldn't say for definite though," Blits informed him.

"One of the hounds hunting it carried on ahead of the army and almost reached the border, but didn't enter the tree-line," Digby replied, now a little more coherent.

"He didn't enter?" Coinin asked, piecing the event's together in his mind.

The rabbits shook their darkened heads. "No," replied Wickett.

"What's with all the noise? Coinin, are you guarding this entrance or holding a communal chat session?" A larger, older rabbit emerged from the burrow enquiring as to what was disturbing the peace. "You can be heard talking as far back as Willow Junction."

"Sorry, sir," came Coinin's stern apology.

"Sorry, sir," came four more apologies, all slightly out of time with one another.

"Sergeant Castor, the reconnaissance party for the western border has witnessed an occurrence that they would like to report back to the General in person, sir!" Coinin stated.

Sergeant Castor shifted his gaze from the warren guard to the western border Patrol Guards. "And what might that be?" he began warily. "The General is very busy. He doesn't have time to hold council with just anyone."

Apollo sensed a hint of sarcasm in Castor's voice. Not many of the rabbits serving duty as Forest Guards liked him. He had served for many years in the defence of the warrens, fending away attacks from hares mainly, and the power and prestige that came with his position had swollen his head more than just a little.

"Wickett?" Coinin said, prompting him to begin relaying the developments once again.

Wickett retold the story exactly as he had done with Coinin. The sergeant listened intently, and afterwards reassured his reconnaissance team.

"I will report this back to the General instantly," he replied after Wickett had finished. "However, I will say that if you boys are spinning a yarn, you will be severely punished."

"Yes, sir," came the general reply, as all four spoke simultaneously yet again.

Sergeant Castor turned to re-enter the warren, but stopped and glanced them over.

"Boys," he said. They looked at him. "Well done. Keep up the effort."

He turned back and vanished between the elm's roots, leaving them gracefully in the presence of Coinin once more. The group looked at each other.

Digby raised his eyebrows. "Wow, do you think he'll ever say that again?" he asked.

"Savour it, boys, that won't ever emerge from his mouth in the future," Apollo replied.

Coinin had re-established a partial guarding position. The rabbits looked at him sheepishly. He knew exactly what they wanted. He sighed and gestured his head towards the entrance. "Go on," he said, watching their eyes light up as they passed, "but don't bother the General. Let Sergeant Castor speak to him first."

"Thanks Coinin, you're the best," Apollo said full of false excitement as he hopped by. Apollo was always the joker of the group, and the warren.

"And don't forget to come back and tell me what happens!" Coinin shouted after them. He shook his head as the trampling sound of their paws vanished deep into the burrow. He stood a moment checking his surroundings for others, and when he was quite sure he was on his own once again he closed his eyes, relaxed his ears, and bathed in the sunshine.

4

Night crept across Averon as Streak slept, left tended to by the new group of foxes who had discovered him in their homeland and taken him in. Far from the burrow, from the den, beyond the borders of Averon, the Great Vast Open began. It was formed collectively of the fields and meadows that dominated the countryside for miles upon miles all around the Great Forest. Even through human eyes it was huge, expanding from horizon to horizon and engulfing the open lands, broken only at times by the occasional coppice or sturdy hedgerow. From the western border of Averon a vast, grassy meadow steadily declined for miles until it came to rest on a set of buildings built by humans. One was the dwelling place of those humans, the other a tremendous building known by its occupiers as The Lodge.

On the outside of The Lodge a huge pen extended its perimeter with steel fencing that surrounded a concrete surface littered with upturned bowls, splashes of water and remnants of food. The Lodge itself was built a foot or so from the ground and perched upon sturdy stilts, allowing a small gap between its base and the concrete ground it rested upon. Between the gap of the floor and its base a wooden skirt had been constructed around the perimeter to keep the building secure. It was flimsy and loose, a sign that the humans building it had been slack in their efforts to seal it securely. So vast was The Lodge that it could not be contained within the pen, its outer walls serving as part of the barrier between living quarters and the Great

Vast Open. Inside, the wooden slats that connected to make the first level of flooring had begun to be dismantled, in a darkened corner away from any prying human eyes that may fall upon it. When the humans entered, the slats were pushed back in place. When they left, teams of hunters worked to burrow out and into the freedom beyond.

Outside the great structure the weather was warm and pleasant. The slight breeze that had passed regularly throughout the day had all but disappeared, leaving the Great Vast Open with the cool breeze that the night-time always brought with it in the latter, summer months.

Sat inside the steel fencing,a scouring eye fixed upon the tall trees of Averon in the far, far distance. Their branches and leaves were beginning to diminish from sight as the night began to descend upon the world.

His vision was not impaired in his left eye, however his right eye was blind. He had lost its use years ago whilst hunting a vixen. There was no pupil left to see from; it had simply turned a shade of patchy whites and greys, giving him distinct character and confirming that the sight he once had was now indeed lost. The skin surrounding the lifeless appendage was black, the same colour as the scar that swirled from his paralysed lower eyelid and down towards the right side of his upper lip.

The scent of his previous target still lingered within his nostril, and sparked a hint of nostalgia that he was trying in vain to remember. It was useless asking his hunters, who by now were resting on the straw flooring of The Lodge inside. None of them had even come remotely close to the fox before it vanished into the forest and beyond his grasp, or had the intelligence to remember previous hunt's where he was sure they'd followed the same scent before. Cameo, his second-in-command, had been the closest to him out of the entire battalion today, and even he had stated that he hadn't caught the scent strong enough to remember. This fox was clever. Clever, and fast. He'd led them down through streams to dampen his perspiration and slow the trackers as they stumbled across. He'd led them past burrows and trails that belonged to other foxes, catching most of the advancing army off-guard and sending them in different directions, leaving only Cameo, himself and a few other intelligent hounds on the right track.

"Baal?" a voice asked from the diminishing light. Baal turned both his good and bad eye to the direction of The Lodge, where another hound emerged from its opening. The hound trotted slowly to Baal's side and gently sat down. Baal returned his gaze to the treetops of Averon.

"He was only the second fox to escape my jaws," Baal said in a low, gruff voice, still catching hints of the loitering scent within his nose. "This does not bode well for my reputation, Cameo."

"You're reputation is still strong and fearful within the ranks," Cameo began. "They believe you will become even more ruthless and aggressive."

Baal nodded. "Yes..." he said, trailing off into a line of thought. "There's something familiar about him," he began a moment later, breaking the silence. "I've tracked and killed hundreds of those filthy creatures before today, but not once have I ever felt a familiarity with them, with him..." His mind wandered yet again as he tried to place the nostalgia from the back of his mind to the front.

"Do you think you've maybe tracked members of his skulk before? Each group have their own distinct scent."

Baal turned and snarled viciously. "I'm well aware of the trends and habits of the foxes, Cameo. Do you disrespect my intelligence and believe I have not thought of this already?"

A quick flutter of adrenaline passed throughout Cameo's body. "I'm sorry sir, I meant no disrespect."

Cameo had grown up with Baal, been friends with him whilst they were training as pups, watched him grow into the fantastic leader that he was, and had been the only hound in the many ranks of hunters that Baal could say that he actually liked, but that had not stopped him attacking and maiming Cameo previously when he had felt challenged or disrespected. The last attack, now many seasons removed, had left Cameo so badly hurt that the human's had taken him away from the army to be healed. The look on Baal's face indicated that he would pounce any second, tearing and ripping him into a state beyond recognition. Cameo's heart began to pound faster and faster as Baal lurched forward, who instead this time gently turned his head back around and fixed his gaze across the Great Vast Open.

"I do not believe I have encountered him before, but I am not certain. I cannot place it though," he said calmly, as if he'd already forgotten about their confrontation.

Cameo sighed a breath of relief and started to relax once again. "Our warriors have been talking," he finally said once he had gained composure.

Baal turned back to Cameo. "Oh, and what do our warriors have to say?" he asked, genuinely interested.

"They are saying that the humans are scared of the forest, and that's why they ceased us before you could catch him. They believe that the forest is haunted."

Baal sighed and smiled. "Humans are superstitious," he began, noticing that the sky was becoming ever darker as the night rolled in. "They are a strange breed. The superstition within the forest has been created purely as a defence from intruders."

"Like us?" Cameo asked.

"Like us," Baal confirmed, before continuing with his explanation. "It's merely a story designed to keep us away from the borders and keep its occupants safe from harm. Nothing exists in there, except for the fox we lost today, and the foxes we have traced in there before."

Cameo studied Baal a little longer before asking his next question. He wanted to be sure that Baal was in the right frame of mind, and not one that would encourage his leader to separate his head from his shoulders.

"What about the ghost that was seen?" he eventually asked. Baal slowly closed his eyes and sighed.

"What ghost?" he asked, his tether showing signs of wearing thin.

"In the trees. When the fox disappeared inside the borders, a floating white shade was seen high in the branches."

Baal had begun to lose interest with the conversation. "What you and they saw was purely a shaft of light or a bird of some type."

"But..."

Baal's chest rumbled. The pupil in his good eye dilated. He frowned. "Imagination," he forcefully stated. Cameo nodded rapidly. "Yes, right. Imagination. I'll tell the others," he said, quickly disappeared towards the opening of The Lodge, and vanished.

Baal considered staying outside a while longer. The weather was fine, he would now be un-disturbed after his meeting with Cameo, and he wanted to remember where he'd met that fox before. After a moment's thought he decided instead to retire to The Lodge and get some sleep. After all, it had been a long day, and his limbs felt worn and achy. He rose to all fours, pushed his front two paws out as far as he was able, stood on his hind legs and arched downwards, having one final stretch before he slept. He yawned and shook his head from side to side. He rose back to his paws, feeling the distinct sensation of tiredness creep subtly over him. He gave one last glance over his shoulder in the direction of Averon and left, returning back to The Lodge to sleep.

'Sleep, my friend. We will meet again soon.'

5

Streak had been sprinting across a wet field during the middle of a thunderstorm. The lightning thrashed across the sky in thunderous shards of light, shaking the ground with every single illuminating flash. The ground continued to quake throughout the heavy rainfall, even as the thunder subsided. It followed rapidly from behind him, and carried with it the screams and howls of a million hounds, all searing towards him to rip him to shreds.

We'll tear your guts out!

Streak screamed as the snarling voice from behind surged above the rumble of hunters and bore deep into his mind.

You can't run forever!

Streak began to lose his footing as the ground became sodden. He saw that the Great Vast Open had turned from fields of grass and rape to a sea of freshly spilled innards and blood. His paws splashed fresh claret across his face and body every time they fell into the warm ooze. He looked up to see that it was flowing from the western borders of Averon.

We'll get you, no matter how long it takes, and the blood of your friends will be on your paws!

Streak woke with a start. He was alert immediately, and quickly pounced to his feet. For a fraction of a second he had no recollection of where he was. Tali jolted upright at the far end of the burrow where she had been posted by Kedem to keep watch over him. Streak's jolt had roused her from a light and restless sleep, her eyes

31

only slightly open. He span round in a circle, gaining his bearings and taking notice of his new surroundings. It returned to him now that he had followed Doran down here to rest, and that he was now staying with another group of foxes he'd fortuitously stumbled across.

"Streak?" Tali asked in a weary voice. She shook her head and rose to her feet. "What's the matter?"

Streak wore a look of fear upon his face. His unconscious mind had drifted into a nightmare while he rested within the vast den. His mind exploded with the reason he was here. He remembered everything instantly. He was chased by the Dark Army, the most feared predators in red fox history, and had only just managed to escape with his life. Worse, though, his scent had been tracked by one hound who did not fall for any of his tricks. That hunter would remember his scent, he knew it. His eyes looked over to Tali who now trotted over to him. "Streak?" she asked, with mild concern.

If the scent remained with any hunter, the next time they went to war they'd attempt to locate it and continue where they left off, following his trail.

To Averon. To Shadow Oak. To him.

"I can't stay," he replied in a nervous and unsettled voice as he walked past her.

"Streak?"

"Did you hear me? I said I can't stay here, I have to move." Tali looked on. Confused, Streak stopped and dropped his head, almost in shame. "I'll only bring danger to Shadow Oak," he said solemnly.

"What?" came a voice emerging from the entrance to the den. It was Doran. He had heard the minor scuffle and Tali's soft voice from his own lodgings, and come along to investigate. "I'm seriously interested to hear how much danger you think you've attracted to us after we have taken you in and nursed you."

"Doran -"

"What, Tali? We help this stranger back to our community, who ironically loses his memory, and only seems to remember the danger he's placing us in when he's taken our assistance and rested in our home?"

"It's not like that," Streak began.

"Then what is it like?" Doran snapped.

Streak sighed. "Show me the way out of here, and it will only follow me."

"Right this way!" Doran replied, and began leaving the burrow.

"Doran, stop it!" Tali snapped. He stopped in his track and looked at his sibling. Her eyes were fully open now and glaring at him intently. She was headstrong and at times very stubborn. He knew how she felt, deep down. She believed that they had done the better thing by returning Streak to the den, and whether she was right or she was wrong, this was a battle he may not win. He knew there was a line he could reach with her, but could not cross. They'd all be living together for a long, long time, and he knew she could make life unpleasant if she really wished to.

From the moonlight outside a skulk of foxes headed towards the ruckus.

"What is the meaning of this?" came the distinctive voice of Kedem. He had been joined by his fellow advisors Jinx and Delfin.

Doran and Streak left the burrow into the clearing to join them, quickly followed by Tali. Streak noticed that the clearing was circular in shape, and had many den entrances that housed the foxes of this community. Many of them were filled with the snouts of their owners, all looking out to see what the commotion was.

"Ah, I see our guest is up and about," said Jinx happily. He'd fed Streak a cocktail of berries before he'd slept to help with the headache he'd suffered. "How are you feeling? That was a nasty knock you took there."

Streak had all but forgotten about the headache. Jinx's magic berries had done the trick, although his head did feel a little tight where the swelling was.

"Better," he stated.

"Our guest seems to remember leading danger to our community," Doran interrupted, not really caring how Streak felt, just wanting to cut straight to the chase.

"Settle down, Doran," Delfin asked. "Let Streak explain what it is he remembers."

Delfin and Jinx were advisors to Kedem. They were both honest and trustworthy, and much loved by the foxes within Shadow Oak. They, as did Kedem, always thought of the welfare of the community above and beyond anything else in the forest. Sometimes the decisions they made were harsh, and tough on those who followed, but the greater good had always prevailed. Delfin had at times been known to lose his temper, and was sometimes clouded by what he thought best for them all, but had always spoken to Kedem and Jinx to discuss matters through. More often than not they had been able to argue their points for and against, and always collectively reached a solution.

Streak began pacing back and forth. He was conflicting with his own interests. Should he lie? Should he be honest? No matter what happened he'd be on his way, by dawn at the latest. He paced back and forth a while longer. Doran shook his head in disbelief.

"Streak?" Kedem asked sternly. Streak decided what to say, and answered.

"I was tracked here," he stated. The three foxes looked at him, eyes wide, shocked and somewhat misunderstanding.

"Tracked here?" Delfin shouted after a moment. "YOU WERE TRACKED?"

"SETTLE DOWN!" Kedem shouted, asserting his authority. Delfin did so, a little shocked that he had borne the brunt of Kedem's tongue. The foxes watching from the burrows were confused, as too were Doran and Tali.

"Tracked? What's that?" Tali asked inquisitively. Doran frowned in confusion.

"It's an old tale," Jinx began hesitantly. "It's what happens to red foxes outside in the Great Vast Open."

"Is it bad?" Doran enquired.

Jinx nodded. "I'm afraid it is." Murmuring emerged from the surrounding burrows as the rest of the community discussed the situation between themselves. "Far across the Great Vast Open, very, very far away, is a different land, different entirely from the existence we know here in Averon, our brothers and sisters who exist there were once maimed, tortured and killed in cold blood whenever they were found."

"What?" Doran whispered in shock and disbelief.

"Our kind was murdered," Kedem stated, "and we believe the slaughter still continues now." Kedem looked extremely dismayed. "We are still hunted in the Great Vast Open. Reports have suggested that our kind are now only be tracked by these creatures and nothing more, but we know of one rogue who still slaughters foxes when the opportunity arises."

"Who?" Tali asked. "Why would they do such a thing?"

Delfin moved from Kedem's side and began walking slowly back and forth as Streak had done previously. "Out there exists an army," he began. "A

Dark Army. It is an army so vast, so huge, that no species of fox, no matter how many of us there are, would be able to survive its onslaught if it decided to attack."

"The army has been created for one purpose and one purpose only; to find us and to kill us. They know no fear other than that of the humans who command them. They are bloodthirsty and ruthless, and they find us by following our natural scents," Jinx informed them.

"By tracking," Delfin replied sarcastically, looking straight at Streak. Tali's mouth hung open in shock. A mild wave of hysteria swept throughout the dens. "And you led them here!" All eyes fell upon Streak, who himself was battling with the pressure of an entire community that would see him responsible for their eventual demise.

"Yes," he began quietly, "I escaped in here to save my life -"

"And in the process endangered ours!" Delfin replied.

"I... I... didn't mean to," Streak began. "I just ran, as fast as I could in any direction. I didn't know that you all lived here! Please, just let me leave so that I can lead them far from here, from your community."

"I say let him go!" Delfin agreed. The murmur of Shadow Oak began to subside.

From high above them came a shree so piercing that the skulk of foxes jumped. A huge white mass glided and circled in descent upon the clearing, its body glowing in the shine of the bright moonlight. It landed gracefully in the circular area where the meeting was being held, rearing high on its talons, opening its pale wings to full span, its white aura burning and glowing wildly. Snouts from the dens vanished quickly as their owner's sought the safety from within. The wings came to rest at the creature's side and its aura subsided. Stood proudly in the clearing was Cyrius, the oracle of Averon.

"Cyrius..." Delfin began, but that was all he could muster as the barn owl came to settle. After a moment of respite, the oracle addressed them.

"This stranger is the one being that we will soon need to help us," he said softly. Shadow Oak looked on in awe. "You may be tempted to blame him, to scrutinise and belittle him, but he is not the one who has led the Dark Army to the borders of Averon. They had found you long before Streak had arrived."

"You know my name?" Streak asked. The owl turned its heart-shaped face and looked upon him with deep, dark eyes. His lighter face in contrast made him look even more startling.

"I have foreseen you," Cyrius stated. "You are the one to unite this forest for the impending war that will befall Averon."

"Wait," Kedem began, "A war?"

"Yes," he replied, "A war. And your only chance of standing victorious is if you should all exist as one."

"Wait," Jinx interrupted, "If Streak didn't bring the attention of the Dark Army upon us, who did?"

"Nature did," the owl informed them. "The general of the Dark Army is wise. He has known of your existence for many years. When he is released into the Great Vast Open he wishes to lead his soldiers to Averon. He has caught your scents many times when in the vicinity of our borders, and he awaits the day that the army he leads will disregard their keepers and follow his lead unquestionably, when he can run of his own free will and lead his army to our homeland. That day will dawn upon us very soon."

The foxes listened intently. Tali remembered the fear that surged briefly within her when she laid eyes upon Cyrius earlier that day. She had seen him many times before, but her last encounter had seemed more purposeful, and now she understood what Kedem had said to her.

"Streak has arrived here for a purpose," the owl said seriously to the community leaders. Some of the snouts from the surrounding burrows had returned again, curiosity seemingly victorious over fear.

"What may that be?" Doran asked with sarcasm. He wasn't buying much of this story, least of all that Streak was here for a purpose.

"Doran!" Kedem snapped, embarrassed by his attitude toward Cyrius.

"There may be one day, young dog, when you count on Streak's presence to help you. One day for you in particular, Doran."

Doran looked away in disbelief. As if that day would ever arrive.

"What must we do?" Kedem asked respectfully.

"The rabbits are already aware of the situation," Cyrius began, "and will be sending delegates to assemble the Great Council within the next few days. I would suggest you listen to them. Four in particular have witnessed the Dark Army. They have witnessed how immense their numbers are." Cyrius opened his wings ready to ascend into the darkness above. His plumage began glowing brightly once again. "You will all reach an agreement on what to do next." His last eye contact fell upon Kedem. "Streak is important to Shadow Oak. You must keep him. He is the only one who has beaten the general not once, but twice before," he said sternly before opening his wings. "I will return to you at the council meeting."

"Hey! Hey! What'd you say?" Streak asked, wondering if he'd heard correctly. "Hey!"

Cyrius launched high into the air, his aura leaving a glowing, falling trail before vanishing. Somewhere in the darkness of the sky, they heard him scream.

6

Baal awoke from sleep to the stampede of his army vying for their way out of The Lodge. They barked, yelped and nipped at each other as they all tried in vain to exit the resting quarters at the same time. Baal laid prone, his jaw resting across his left leg. He watched them all frenzy in mild amusement. His coat had become ruffled during the night as he rested, and now the browns and whites of the unbalanced pattern on his back had become covered in straw. Outside he could hear the unrecognisable communication of the humans. There were only a few limited words they spoke which he could understand, words like 'stop,' 'heel,' and his name. As he watched the minor riot of hounds leave The Lodge he rose to his feet and shook his body. One of the hounds heard him and looked over. Baal was slowly making his way to the exit. The hound called for attention and stopped the jostling of the hunters. They froze momentarily and quickly separated to form a path allowing.him to pass. Fear and anticipation crossed many of their faces, mainly on those closest to him as he walked by.

Baal nodded once in recognition of this deed, and found that this generosity had been noted by the entire army, who had all stopped pushing and allowed him to pass. They separated instantly, allowing him to enter the pen without having to brush a single hair of any other hunter. After he had passed, the jostling began once again for each canine to be the first hound to the food.

The humans had been placing the fresh food and water in bowls, and now each one of the chrome utensils seemed to have at least ten warriors muzzling inside it to feast on, eating and drinking as much as they could before they were barged off and replaced by another. One of the humans noticed Baal and walked across to him. Baal assumed this human was male. He communicated in his foreign language in a voice that was deep and authoritative. The human reached down and placed an appendage between his ears and stroked his head moderately. It spoke gently to him, believing maybe that Baal fully understood every word that was being said. In fact, Baal only picked out a few words: 'good', 'well', 'get', 'now', and 'eat.'

Humans were strange-looking creatures. For one, they stood on their hind legs, making them bigger than they actually were. If they travelled on all fours like everything else they would probably be no bigger than most of the hunters in The Lodge. Their heads seemed strange too. There was no mistaking their eyes; they seemed similar to every other living creature Baal had encountered. The one thing that seemed so very odd to the hound was the noticeable size of a human's nose, or what he believed was its nose. It grew down instead of out, only protruding slightly at its base with its nostrils underneath rather than facing outwards. The strangest thing of all though was the fact that they had fur growing from their heads, and not all over. The coats on their bodies seemed to change every day, but their fur stayed exactly where it was. On some occasions the fur would be gone, and sometimes it appeared much less on some humans than it had the day before. But, at the moment, Baal was happy to let them believe they controlled his will and desire. He believed that the human who had ruffled his head had been showing praise, and Baal played along.

When the human left, Baal scoured the concrete flooring for his bowl. It rested over by the perimeter fence. As big as the rest of the bowls out there, it lay full of food and untouched. His army knew better than to leave their general without a source of food and water. Many seasons ago, a rookie hunter had been introduced to the ranks, and had seen Baal as nothing more than an average hound, despite the warning from his new colleagues. He had decided to gain some credibility and recognition by challenging Baal for dominance, by eating the general's food and making sure he knew about it. Baal had been furious when Cameo reported it back to him, and leapt from The Lodge completely enraged and clouded with anger. Outside he had launched at the rookie, who was still eating, and been merciless in his onslaught. The rookie sustained enormous gashes from shoulder to pelvis where Baal had lacerated the skin with his claws and dragged them deep down his croup. He had pounced upon the rookie's head, sinking his teeth into his nostrils, tasting the blood as it spilled into his mouth. Clenching his jaw shut, violently shaking his head from side to side, Baal bit deeper into the rookie's nose and tore his mouth free, removing the flesh and nose, exposing the turbinate bones of the challenger. The rest of the soldiers had been cheering and barking, a chorus that had alerted the humans, who had come running. Suffice to say that they separated Baal and the young hunter, dragging the severely injured hound out of the pen and subsequently into Baal's legend. None of them ever saw him again. There were rumours that the attack had been so vicious that the rookie had been killed; some said that he had been injured so badly he was now unable to smell a fox, even if it walked up behind him and urinated on his hind legs. From that day on, at every meal the humans served, Baal had been left his own, and would only share it by offer of invitation.

Baal made his way across the pen, through the mass of feeding bodies, all howling, barking and some fighting with one another. He looked up once more to the distant borders of Averon. The sun had broken through the clouds that had lingered during dawn's first light, and now began to vanquish the coldness that hung damply in the morning air. It was one of those mornings where a chill hung thickly across the Great Vast Open, but he knew that it would soon clear and the sun would sear down with its full heat, turning the day into another summer scorcher.

Baal began eating intently. He was thinking through an idea he had formulated last night when he was at the stage between laying awake and falling asleep. The food was cold but welcoming, whatever it was he was eating.

Baal took a mouthful and looked up across the pen. He scoured the hunters with his good eye whilst chewing his food, and found who he was looking for. He swallowed, licked his lips and shouted "Cameo!"

Across the mass of bodies, Cameo raised his head. He had been feeding in a group, but held enough respect within the battalion for the hunters to allow him to take as much as he wanted. "Join me."

Cameo trotted between the excited hunters with more difficulty than Baal had done, and joined his general as he was instructed. He bore a huge, black, misshapen diamond that wove throughout the fur upon his croup. It tailed away thinly toward his withers and vanished beneath various shades of brown. Baal gestured with his nose to the food bowl, and after a moment they both began eating once again.

"How's the young rookie Rainan coming along?" Baal asked between mouthfuls. Cameo finished his and replied.

"Very well, so far," he began.

Rainan was a young hunter with an extraordinary talent for tracking, surpassed only by Cameo and Baal himself.

"I have a task for him," Baal replied. "How long will it take to burrow underneath our quarters and outside this perimeter?"

Cameo shrugged and shook his head. "I have no idea. Maybe a few hours, maybe a day, I don't know for sure."

"Who would know?" Baal asked, his eye-contact concentrating on the bowl beneath him.

"Kaskar, I assume. He's the smartest tracker in the ranks - aside from yourself, of course."

Baal paid no notice to his praise. "Fetch him," he replied.

Cameo left his general to his meal whilst he searched the feeding ground for Kaskar. Baal had progressed through half of the food by the time Cameo returned, a nervous soldier tailing not far in his wake. Baal looked up, lapped his tongue around his mouth, and looked at the soldier.

"This him?" Baal asked.

"It is," Cameo replied.

Baal wandered over to Kaskar and looked him over. He could see the fear emerging from him, and almost smell it too. Baal enjoyed it when he had established dominance through fear within his ranks. It gave him an authority that no-one would challenge.

"Cameo tells me you're the best, most intelligent hunter in this army. Is that so?"

Kaskar looked across to Cameo, as if for confirmation, and then looked back. "Yes," he replied, and nodded slightly.

"Good," Baal stated, and began walking towards the corner of the pen that he had occupied last night, the corner where he had been gazing from a distance upon Averon. Kaskar looked at Cameo, who flicked his muzzle upwards gesturing for him to follow. Kaskar trotted with him in silence until they reached the farthest end of the perimeter.

"How long would it take to burrow underneath The Lodge, in your opinion? I need to send a tracker into the Great Vast Open without the humans noticing."

Kaskar sighed. "If you get a pack of diligent workers, maybe a morning? It could possibly be less if they hit it hard. That includes breaking through the flimsy wood around the bottom - but only wide enough to allow one through at a time, though."

"That's all I need," Baal confirmed. He fixed his gaze once again upon the distant border of Averon. *He's in there... Somewhere...*

"Sir?"

Baal snapped from his temporary absence, and instantly beckoned Cameo over. "Organise a team of hunters to dig underneath the boards and out of the perimeter boarding when the humans leave us, and set a guard to watch their movements. I want to know exactly what they're up to, when they leave, when they return, and I want to know how many. I want to know everything that they do, you understand?" Cameo nodded. "Kaskar, you will oversee the operation. You will be held in my highest regard should this go according to plan, but if it should encounter any complications..."

Baal left it there. Such was his reputation that Kaskar knew if he failed he'd be history.

"You have work to do," Cameo informed him as Baal entered another trance, no doubt beginning an obsession with the one fox that got away. Kaskar left and finished whatever food he could find before he began preparations for the task. "Do you think this is going to work?"

Baal roared and leapt from his position, swiping Cameo across the snout with his claws. Cameo yelped and fell backwards, instantly feeling the warm trickle of blood emerging from the stinging wounds. The rest of the army froze and gazed upon the conflict.

"Don't you ever question me again!" Baal screamed in a low, demonic voice. His lips pursed into a growl. His brows frowned and his chest rumbled. "Never!"

Cameo's wild, frightened eyes fixed upon his general. "No sir. No -"

"Carry out the order I gave you or I swear the hunters will be feeding on your carcass this evening!"

"Yes -"

"GO!"

Cameo leapt to his feet and sped away across the pen. The rest of the army watched on in silence as Baal looked them over from right to left, turned, sat down, gazing once more across the Great Vast Open and up toward Averon. Baal already knew who would undertake this task, and when; it was just a matter of waiting.

7

Twilight emerged upon the Great Vast Open, bathing the sky orange and providing a comfortable warm breeze for the fine summer evening.

As the stars began to emerge in the skyline, Wickett was leading a final reconnaissance sweep along the southwestern borders of Averon. Coinin had been selected as lead guard and lookout for the party, and was patrolling a small burrow entrance beside a fallen oak. It was an entrance to the western border that did not link well with the rest of the rabbit burrows, but it was safe and secure, even if it did take a vast amount of time to navigate through to the main chamber and General Lupus. Lupus had sent messengers to Rebus, the leader of the badger sett and joint head of the Great Council, detailing exactly what Wickett and his team had previously seen out in the Great Vast Open. He had also issued the order to increase patrols after Sergeant Castor had informed him of the oncoming army, and as it had been Wickett and his team who had initially seen them advancing, the responsibility had been thrust upon his guard to patrol. Coinin had been sent as an overseer. In fact, it was Coinin who had been placed in charge, as Wickett had been deemed too inexperienced to lead this kind of expedition by himself. The southwestern entrance had been ideal for this situation as it allowed Coinin to perch his spotted white underside high upon the fallen, moss-covered tree trunk, and watch the party from further afield, whilst still allowing Wickett the sense of leadership he needed to carry out his task.

Wickett and the three other members of the party had been sent to look for something in particular; any signs that the border had been breached from the outside.

"We'll need to split up and scour the area. That way we'll be able to cover more ground and do it quicker," he said once they emerged on the border.

"How far afield do we go? We could easily follow our noses and end up towards the South if we're not careful," Digby asked.

"Keep an eye on Coinin. If you can see him, you're fine, but don't stray anywhere that will hide you from his view. He's the one you need to run towards if there's any trouble."

The four rabbits chatted a little longer, then separated, all following different directions looking for any signs of unrecognised footprints, severely broken twigs, or events of that nature.

Coinin kept a watchful eye, from Digby to Apollo, Wickett to Blits. Soon enough though they began moving further away, following their noses as Digby had described it, searching for the sign of any breaches that may have occurred into their homeland. They scoured the area intently from good light until dark descended, looking for any sign, no matter how small, for a breach in Averon.

Blits scoured the ground in front of him, the diminishing light having no effect upon his eyes. He was about to finish his task, when he noticed something a little unusual. In the soft ground ahead a paw-print appeared in the mud. Blits' fur was a little darker than that of his grey counterparts, a fact that often caused him to merge with the darkness whenever they patrolled at night time. Looking over and seeing he was still fairly close to Wickett, he strayed from his designated position and hopped over to examine it with a twitching nose. He picked up a scent he didn't recognise. It was fresh and prominent, the mud still soft and damp to touch. The scent lingered, giving him the impression that whatever made it hadn't long passed through this part of the forest. He was puzzled. After a moment of deliberation he looked back toward Wickett. Through the long grass and buttercups he saw Wickett's tail turning from grey to white as he moved around. "Wickett!" he shouted. Wickett turned and stood on his hind legs. "Over here."

Wickett made his way across to Blits. "What is it?" he asked when in earshot of the fellow guard.

"Look."

Wickett followed Blits' eyes down and looked upon the print. The scent hit him immediately, and like Blits he could not place what creature it belonged to.

"This is fresh," Wickett stated, curling his nose in disgust at the foreign smell.

Blits nodded. "This print hasn't been made long. Not long at all."

"Is there any more?" Wickett asked as he investigated the woodland area for himself.

"Not that I can see. This is the only part of the ground that's soft enough to make a print," Blits said, pushing his paw down into the soft mud to confirm his theory. "You think it's a fox?" he asked.

Wickett wondered momentarily, then shook his head. "It looks too big," he replied.

"What've you found?" came Apollo's voice.

Wickett looked up at the approaching Forest Guard. "Take a look for yourself."

All three rabbits crowded the print in the ever diminishing light. The stars were brighter now, and the sky began darkening to blue instead of the orange it had previously been.

From the farthest reaches of the forest, a horrendous scream pierced the tranquil setting. Coinin jumped up immediately and scoured his surroundings. The three rabbits shot to their hind legs.

Wickett turned around. "Digby..." he began.

"Digby!" Blits shouted.

"Oh no..." Apollo trailed off.

The three of them exploded from the grass at full speed in the direction of the scream. Wickett took an easy advantage at the head of the pack, his mind racing into overdrive. They bounded over branches and through grass.

"Where is he?" Blits cried.

"I don't know! Keep your eyes open!" Wickett screamed.

Coinin caught side of the group. "Hey! Hey!" he began, but could not be heard by the sprinting rabbits.

They tore through the roughage and shrubbery until they emerged on a trail. The grass here was shorter and the ground a little more even. They stood in its middle looking around rapidly, panting for breath, their hearts pounding. The trail was silent. There was no movement anywhere.

"Digby!" Blits shouted. No reply.

"Look," Apollo said, and nodded away up the opening. They could see the tell-tale sign of a grey mass on the edge of the grass. The three ran up to it and slowed as they approached.

"Digby?" came Apollo's concerned voice. Laying on his left side - half in the trail, half in the wild grass - lay Digby. His right eye was wild and glassy, and fear was scrawled prominently across his face. He didn't move. Underneath his jaw they could see blood seeping across some fallen leaves. The three rabbits stood looking at him, their eyes wide and their ears flat.

A low rumble emerged behind them, a rumble that turned to a growl. It echoed, deep and menacing. They turned. On the trail behind them stood a monstrous hunter, huge, dark and intimidating. His mouth was pulled back into a snarl, his teeth sharp and exposed. His eyes almost bore red in the diminishing darkness.

Coinin stood watching from the log. His heart sank. "Run!" he shouted. "RUN!"

"GO!" Wickett screamed, and the three guards shot into the grass. The hound exploded from his base and charged after them, their scent fresh and easy to follow. The rabbits pounded the ground as fast as they could, looking for Coinin and their sanctuary. Coinin ran the length of the log to indicate the warren's entrance. The hound leapt a huge fallen branch, and looked upon Apollo in the distance. Apollo dashed through the grass, keeping a fix on Wickett's tail. Blits ran beside him.

"COME ON!" Coinin screamed.

Behind them they could hear the panting of the hunter.

Coinin looked on. They're not going to make it! he thought wildly to himself. They're not going to make it!

From the sky above, a bright light fell like a teardrop from the heavens. It shrieked with wild intimidation and anger. As it fell it twisted, spun, and took flight. Coinin looked up. It glided over his head without making a sound and headed towards the fleeing pack.

"Cyrius?"

Wickett sensed momentary hope as he watched Cyrius emerge from the aura of light and pass rapidly overhead. Cyrius altered his course and descended upon the hunter, his talons open and ready for battle. The hunter saw the ghost approaching and instantly halted in his tracks. Cyrius screamed and sank his claws deep into the hound's croup as he flashed past. The hound yelped and began jumping wildly, trying to shake the phantom from its clutch. Cyrius released his grasp and swiftly climbed into the air. The hound gazed upon him, barking viciously. Cyrius circled and descended again. The hound snapped at him with his razor teeth, chomping nothing but air. This time a claw sliced his head and pierced his ear. The hound yelped back and turned away.

The rabbits emerged into an opening not far from the fallen tree, and could see the entrance ahead. His job done, Coinin jumped down into the burrow and descended deep enough inside, allowing plenty of room for the three rabbits to explode in through. He looked up into the gloomy opening from the safety of the tunnel. Come on...

Wickett crashed through the entrance, knocking Coinin from his feet. He turned. Blits leapt through the hole and smashed into them violently. They gained their bearings and realised that one was missing.

"Apollo..." came an incoherent voice.

Apollo exploded through the entrance, slamming into the group of rabbits. He hit them with such ferocity that they all crashed into the tunnel wall, and tumbled down into the darkness.

The hound began its retreat out through the tree-line and into the Great Vast Open. As he thundered through the trail, the ensuing white aura descended upon him once more. Dismissing retaliation, the hound now concentrated on his escape. This time the perceived ghost did not attack. It tracked above him, screaming terribly as it did so, fear already established as its most potent weapon. The hound burst from Averon, not slowing as it did so, not thinking it was safe, and rapidly headed towards the sanctuary of The Lodge.

When Coinin poked his head out of the tunnel one last time to see what had happened, it had all but ended.

8

"Get up! Come on! Wake up!" came a distant voice.
Streak opened his eyes and saw Doran looking down at
him. He had been nudged with a dark paw, waking him
quicker than usual. "Kedem has asked that we join him.
We need to leave."

Doran left the den, leaving Streak momentarily
alone. He looked around for a moment, yawned, then
shook his head, waking himself up a little more. He
rose to his feet and looked outside. It was a bright day
once again in Averon.

Streak left the den and joined Doran, who was stood
by a clearing that exited Shadow Oak. "Where are we
going?" Streak asked casually.

"Just follow me. Not far."

The two foxes left the community and wondered
away down a well-hidden trail leading through bushes
and between trees. Doran was very abrupt and to-the-
point with Streak, generating a feeling of dislike
between the two. He did indeed feel contempt towards
the visiting fox after the danger he had brought with
him to Averon. Doran was temperamental at times, and
often let his feelings rule his decisions. He would
always do what he thought was the right thing, whether
it was the correct thing to do or not. To him, Streak's
presence at Shadow Oak was a great mistake, and if
he'd had his way, Streak would leave Averon
immediately. However, he did feel some sympathy for
the visiting dog. Doran had secretly rebelled against the
rules implemented by Kedem and himself ventured into
the Great Vast Open, his curiosity getting the better of

him. He was an explorer and adventurer at heart, and believed that the more life experience he gained the greater his chance at becoming an advisor to Shadow Oak.

"There's a small clearing ahead," Doran said as they approached their destination. "We are to wait for his signal."

"What?" Streak asked, a little confused.

"Just shut up, you'll find out in a moment," Doran snapped.

The clearing appeared, as Doran had said it would, towards the end of their journey, and within it held a most amazing spectacle.

"Over here," Doran gestured, and both foxes sat behind a hefty fallen branch.

Streak followed and sat down next to him. "What is this?" he asked, almost in amazement.They had come to rest at the entrance to a small peninsula which stretched out to the Great Lake, as it was known. In its clearing a large number of stones had been arranged into a misshapen circle. At the head of the circle sat Kedem. To his right stood two muntjac, both of them taller than the foxes and animals already gathered there. To his left, two badgers sat upon a set of flattened stones. Next to them Delfin sat alone as representative of Shadow Oak. A group of rabbits sat perched on a bigger rock beside the lone fox, and a group of pheasants perched themselves comfortably next to the deer.

"It's the Great Council," Doran stated. "Whenever anything of great importance or danger threatens Averon, the animals hold a council together to discuss a course of action."

"This is amazing," Streak began, leaning further forward. "I had no idea that such an alliance would exist. Anywhere."

"This is Averon," Doran began, "and it's a very different life to that which exists in the Great Vast Open, or wherever it is you come from."

Streak detected a slight hint of sarcasm in Doran's voice but ignored it, concentrating instead on the sight in front of him, too amazing to be believed.

"We are lucky that Kedem holds the head of the council, joint with Rebus, chief of the badger setts."

"A joint leadership?"

Doran nodded. "In these situations two heads are better than one."

"What about disagreements? Surely all animals don't see things in the same way?"

"That's why there are two heads to this council. Both Kedem and Rebus were voted in by the rest of the woodland dwellers due to their knowledge and respect. They have yet to fail any living creature in this forest."

Tali had followed both foxes out of Shadow Oak. She now rested not far away, hiding her distinctive red fur behind a vast tree root and mound of earth. She too was watching this gathering of woodland creatures from afar, keeping her spying eyes away from the council. She noticed the dogs as they stood away from her at the base of a tree Kedem had designated to Doran. Doran had noticed her too, and cursed her for being too inquisitive.

Streak caught a slight movement from the corner of his eye, and turned to see Tali nestling in her hiding space. She looked over at him, and in what seemed like momentary embarrassment looked at the ground, over her shoulder, and then back to the council. Streak kept a fix on the colourful vixen as she pretended not to notice. A shove on his shoulder rocked him sideways and brought him back to his senses.

He looked over at Doran, who shot him a harsh glare. "Don't even think about it," Doran said in his best 'protector' voice.

"What?" Streak asked, pretending not to know why.

"Just concentrate on the meeting."

They sat there a while longer while the council held what appeared to be silent conversations in the clearing ahead. After a while Kedem looked upon the foxes, and beckoned to Doran.

"Here we go," he said as he sprang to his feet and made his way through the clearing. Streak followed not far behind.

As Streak made his way through the grass and bracken, he felt the animals looking him over. He felt once more as if he were being judged by them all, as if he was being blamed for the misfortune of Averon.

Doran stood in the middle of the stones, the council unevenly spread around him. His reddish fur was vast becoming blotched with patches of grey. It was a distinctive look that gave him a strong sense of individuality.

"Sit down," Kedem asked in a non-threatening tone. The foxes did so.

"So, you are the one?" Rebus asked, as his dark eyes looked upon Streak.

Kedem answered on his behalf. "Yes, this is he."

Rebus looked him over. "Interesting. Very interesting."

"You have been summoned here for a reason," Kedem began. "This is our council, the protectors of Averon, and it is very rare that an outsider such as yourself will ever be involved in such matters here."

Streak looked from the pheasants to the muntjac, the rabbits to the badgers, and back to Kedem. "We are not all here, as you can probably tell," Rebus answered, noticing Streak was looking over the council.

"This is an emergency meeting," one of the muntjac replied. "We have more members, but they cannot be here so soon." Garla was the head doe of the muntjac deer population, sworn in when her predecessor retired from leadership the previous cold season. She was a striking creature with a strange dark marking that engulfed her head and tapered away to the top of both her ears. Her body was various shades of grey, the one colour that themed all creatures living in Averon.

"As Rebus and I are joint leaders of this council, we have authority to sanction any action we deem necessary to keep the peace within our borders," Kedem explained.

"You mean the Dark Army," Doran stated.

Rebus nodded. "Indeed. The Dark Army advances upon us."

There was silence within the council. The breeze blew a little cooler than previous days; it was still warm, but Streak noticed it.

"We have to discuss how to halt it," the second muntjac said, this time a buck. The solid antlers emerging from his head gave it away. A rabbit shook its head and hopped from its perch on the rock.

"There's no way we can halt an army of such vast numbers," he said. This was the chief of rabbits that Wickett had reported to, General Lupus. Lupus had been accompanied on this meeting by Sergeant Castor, Coinin, Wickett, Blits and Apollo. "And such ferocity. They are killing machines, each and every one of them." General Lupus looked over at Streak. "One of my guards was murdered yesterday evening, by one of their legions."

"What?" Doran asked, looking at the shaded rabbit.

"A hunter. Inside our borders. We sent our Western reconnaissance team out to monitor the Great Vast Open. One of our guards, one of our best, was murdered by a lone hunter who had breached the tree-line."

"No? It can't be? They've never crossed into the trees before," Doran replied.

"They've never had a reason, until now," General Lupus replied. He shot Streak a cold glare. Streak felt ashamed.

"Cyrius told me that they picked up our scent long before Streak arrived," Kedem said, defending Streak. This agitated Doran somewhat.

"Ha! Cyrius!" one of the pheasant's exclaimed. The brightly coloured bird was Arley, the head of the pheasant contingency. He was a proud creature who always voiced his opinion when needed. "He's a world of knowledge when he wants to be, but where is he to offer his pearls of wisdom when we need it the most?"

"Now let's just settle down, all of us," Rebus ordered, rather than asked, in a calm manner. "What is a major factor in this situation - and I'm sorry to say it - is you, Streak. I'm a believer in many things, and I, along with Kedem and Cyrius, believe you were sent here for a reason." Doran rolled his eyes. The sooner everyone saw that Streak was nothing more than a troublemaker, the better.

"Now, we have to decide on a course of action to stop this advance from the Dark Army, and we need all the help we can receive," Kedem stated, issuing an invitation to an open floor.

"Relocation deeper into Averon?" Selwyn, second order of the pheasants asked.

Rebus thought about it for a moment and shook his head. "Too difficult. The army will only follow us deeper inside."

"Can we not cover his scent?" Apollo asked, still sitting on the rock.

Again, Rebus shook his head. "They're bred to hunt and to destroy. We would have to cover his scent with other scents and they would leave their own trail. They'd catch up sooner or later."

"How about the kestrels? They are a noble species who venture the entire Great Vast Open. Surely they would know about the threat the Dark Army brings to our forest and provide some assistance to our cause?" General Lupus asked hopefully. The kestrels were fierce warriors when called upon in battle, but were very elusive to every other creature in Averon. In fact, they were so elusive that most animals believed them to be merely a myth, a bedtime story for the younglings and pups to help them sleep whenever fear may creep over them as the darkness descended for yet another night. Neither Kedem nor Rebus had ever witnessed the birds of prey before, or even heard stories of animals witnessing them within Averon. They too also believed them as only a fairytale.

"The kestrels are only a story," Arley began, confirming their personal theories, "to offer false reassurance to the younglings within the forest. I mean, really? A band of warriors residing in Averon without any other creature laying eyes upon them? Impossible."

"How do you know they don't exist, Arley? This forest is huge. We don't even see our own brethren from the deepest and most remote parts of Averon. Does that mean they don't exist either?"

Arley thought about the rabbit's answer, but struggled for a reply.

A familiar chirp echoed through the council. From across the Great Lake they saw Cyrius descending silently to join their meeting. In a matter of moments he had reached the council and came to rest gently next to

Kedem, without disturbing a single leaf or blade of grass in the process. "The kestrels do not dwell within our trees," he hooted confidently as he settled. "They pass through on their journeys across the Great Vast Open and stay no longer than they need to. They have only recently passed over our trees, and I do not believe they will return to us for some time."

"That's that, then," Kedem sighed quietly underneath his breath. He and Rebus looked at each other. What were they going to do?

The antlered muntjac stepped forward. "There is one thing we could do," he stated.

Kedem looked upon him. "The floor is yours, Flicar."

The buck stepped into the clearing. "We could seek the advice of Seerles."

"Preposterous!" Arley shouted.

"Seerles? He's as insane as he is wise," General Lupus reiterated.

"Yes, but wise nonetheless," Flicar replied. Rebus considered the possibility. So did Kedem.

"Who's Seerles?" Streak asked.

Doran looked as confused as the stranger accompanying him. "Seerles?" he said and looked to Kedem.

"Seerles is the most dangerous creature in Averon." Kedem informed them. "So dangerous, in fact, that he has been known to kill humans with one bite."

"One bite?" Wickett asked in amazement.

Kedem looked over and nodded. "Yes. But he is as intelligent as he is dangerous. Some say the most intelligent creature in all of Averon."

"No way!" Doran mused.

"I'm afraid it's true," Rebus confirmed.

"He's unstable, and might choose to give us advice he knows will lead us to fail, or even to our death," General Lupus added.

"I don't know," Delfin began. "Speaking to him could be too risky. He may attempt to kill anyone who treads near his lair, or he may welcome them and give them what they desire."

"He knows the scent of every creature in this forest," Kedem began.

Rebus' dark eyes looked away. He was thinking. "That's it!" he remarked. The council looked towards him. "I have an idea."

Rebus stepped off the rock and walked across the debris-filled floor to Streak. "He knows every scent in Averon, but not yours," he said. "That may play in our favour."

"Yes," Kedem began, quickly following Rebus' pattern of thinking. "If he doesn't recognise you, his curiosity will get the better of him."

"That's every living creature's weakness. Curiosity." Rebus retorted. "He will at least lay eyes upon you."

"If you can engage him, he may listen," Flicar added.

"But he may attack," Delfin replied.

"Indeed he may," Rebus began, "but I believe you are here for a reason."

Streak felt uneasy about meeting a hostile creature who could kill a human with one bite. "I'm not totally sure I'm as important as you believe," he said to the onlooking animals.

"Neither am I. I'll go instead," Doran interrupted.

"This is not your responsibility, Doran," Kedem ordered. Doran looked at him angrily, rejected.

"Wait. You have all forgotten where he resides," General Lupus added. "No matter where you go you will have to cross the Trail of Fallen Stars."

Rebus sighed and nodded. "Ah yes, the trail," he said.

"Send us," Wickett said, leaping from their rock. "We have a burrow underneath the trail. Our warren doesn't stretch far enough to reach it, so our ancestors burrowed underneath it at its edge. The monsters can't leave the trail and so can't get to us."

"He's right," General Lupus agreed. "We can pass through easily and descend upon the Black Lands with minimal risk."

"Until you get to Seerles," Flicar informed. "I'm sorry, but he'd kill you for inconveniencing him. Rabbits hold little threat to one such as he."

Silence once again bestowed the council, until an idea flashed through Kedem's mind. He called Rebus over, and with Garla, Arley and Cyrius they had a conversation. The rest of the animals looked to one another in silence as the minutes passed. Finally, Kedem walked into the circle.

"Doran, you are right. You will take this expedition to the Black Lands," he informed them. "You will lead Streak there, who will speak to Seerles, if he can. The Forest Guards will lead you to their burrow underneath the Trail of Fallen Stars. There you must cross, though. The rabbits can pass underneath, but you must cross the trail. The muntjac are the animals who cross the trail the most, and who know the behaviour of the monsters that guard it, therefore Flicar will accompany you on your quest."

"I have decided to send Brock with you to represent the badger sett," Rebus stated, gesturing towards the badger who had sat beside him. "Also, the bigger the group that accompanies Streak, the less likely Seerles is to attack."

"Then it is decided," Kedem stated. There was an air of anxious excitement and nervousness within the council. And of course there was Streak, who was just left wondering what he'd got himself into.

"If I may suggest," Flicar began, "it may be a good idea to leave at first light. Seerles will be more respondent at dawn - it's in his nature. It will also help to cross the trail. The monsters seem to be less in numbers so early in the day."

"Their eyes still shine brightly at dawn," General Lupus added. "You will have morning's first light and their glowing eyes to inform you of their presence."

"Yes. We will be able to see them clearer."

"It won't help on the return trip, though," Delfin replied. "Their eyes will stop glowing by the time you are heading back."

"No, full light will not help us on the way back unless the day is dark, but it's still a better chance than crossing twice during full daylight. Besides, the monsters make such a horrendous roar and scream when they close in; as long as we keep our wits about us we should be fine," Flicar explained to them.

"What happens if they leave the trail?" Streak asked, his first real contribution to the meeting.

"Only one has ever done so," Rebus began, "and it lost its life."

"It wiped out much of the surrounding area with fire," Kedem replied. "They know better than to leave the trail. They know the consequences."

Doran looked on as the council came to a close. Representatives from the other creatures - such as the squirrels, otters, wood pigeons, and the secondary fox community from The North - were all absent. "What about the other members?" Doran asked for the council's final question.

General Lupus explained his actions. "I have sent my messengers through our maze of tunnels to seek their company as soon as possible."

"I believe that they will be here upon your return," Rebus replied. "Seeking the advice of Seerles does not need a full vote, not in this case."

They sat in momentary silence, before Kedem concluded the council. "I ask that you all stay with us at Shadow Oak until the full council is in session," he asked, an offer that was graciously accepted. Cyrius, however, had other plans. General Lupus had given him an idea that might just work if he began preparations immediately. He vanished silently into the sky, leaving the disbanded council to prepare their representatives for the journey into the Black Lands. He glided effortlessly above the dense treetops as he hit patches of thermal air, thrusting upwards from the trees and pushing him onwards towards his destination. He would have to leave Averon for the time being, which was a risk he seldom chose; but under the circumstances a justifiable one, to say the least. Its reward, if his plan was successful, would be a major step toward repelling the Dark Army back across the Great Vast Open. That's if, of course, he succeeded.

9

Rainan had reported back to The Lodge during the night. None of the humans had noticed he'd gone, and he'd arrived back licking his wounds. He'd delivered the information to Baal, who seemed uncharacteristically concerned about his state, but was happy with the information that he had delivered.

As he suspected, the fox had entered Averon and ventured deep within the trees, probably to hide his trail. Rainan had picked up his musky scent easily, which meant he was still lingering inside there somewhere. Baal was troubled, though. He knew that any of his army would do anything for him, to present themselves capable in order to earn his respect, so his concern at Rainan's injuries would hold credence to his report that he was attacked by the phantom most of the hounds had claimed to see on the day they were at the borders.

Rainan was tending his wounds, but news had spread quickly amongst the ranks that the spirit of Averon had attacked. Fear began to creep into the army. Baal knew that they would follow him on his venture, but only because they feared him more than anything, even ghosts. He knew that if this situation was not addressed he'd lose this personal battle with the fox that had slipped his grasp and gotten away. However, there were the select few who feared nothing. These were the ones he'd take with him when he breached the trees. The rest would serve their purpose, of course, but his plan was formulating nicely inside his mind. When the food stopped being delivered by the humans he would know that the hunt was not far away. When the food stopped being delivered he would address the army of his plan. They would play their part in giving him enough time to escape the control of the humans. Of course, he would return to The Lodge eventually - probably worry the humans enough to look for him while he was gone, too. He knew that his power over the Dark Army was unparalleled whilst there, and that the hunters would follow him to their death if needed, and he liked the power he held. If he left to live in the wild, he knew it would only be a matter of time before hunger and fear descended the ranks of those brave enough to follow. Hunger and fear are the worst feelings to deal with. They make a hound think and act incoherently. He didn't know how much control he'd have over them if they challenged him under these influences.

Yes, The Lodge was his sanctuary. He had all the power and fear he needed here, and The Lodge is where he would return to.

After, of course, he'd slaughtered the fox.

10

Twilight was bestowed on Shadow Oak once more. The guests had been assigned to comfortable dens, and were discussing various topics important to them. In the dying light Doran spied Tali entering her lodgings, probably to settle down for the night. He wandered over and stuck his nose into the entrance. "Can I come in?" he asked, somewhat sheepishly. She looked over and nodded. Doran entered the bracken-littered quarters and plodded around a little.

"Did you want something?" she asked after a while.

Doran had a thought that had been troubling him throughout the day. He saw what had passed between Tali and Streak at the council meeting. He knew it was only a second, but he had seen something spark between the pair, and didn't like it. Not one bit.

"I saw what happened at the council meeting," he began.

"What?"

"You."

"Me?"

"Yes, you. And Streak."

Tali looked puzzled. "You saw what?"

"I saw," Doran began, but stopped momentarily.

"You saw what?" Tali asked again, slightly irritated. Doran sighed and blurted it out.

"The way you looked at him."

"The way I looked..." and then Tali rolled her eyes in realisation. "Doran!"

"I saw it, Tali!" Doran shouted back. "He's nothing more than a troublemaker! He entered Averon to save himself, without consideration of any creature living here!"

"He was going to be killed! Would you have done anything differently if it was you that had been chased?"

"I wouldn't have gotten into that situation in the first place!"

"Maybe it wasn't his fault!"

"Whose fault was it, then?"

"You heard, Cyrius! He said that the Dark Army had picked up our trail long before Streak arrived here!"

"Cyrius!" Doran began, as if dismissing the owl already. "What does he know about our situation? He can fly away whenever he wishes, to the far-off lands of wherever. He doesn't care about our situation!"

"Yes he does! He's helping us! If you remember when he arrived here, he told you that you may need Streak one day!"

"And what for? What could I possibly need a filthy drifter for? I can look after myself."

Tali dropped her head, and sighed. Her brother was exhausting her. Obviously he hadn't thought of the bigger picture. "Did it ever occur to you that maybe you don't need him to save you? Maybe you need him to achieve something else."

"What?"

Tali shook her head and laughed softly. "Think about it," she replied.

Doran was tired of arguing. He imagined that maybe the whole of Shadow Oak could hear their sibling differences. With important guests staying within the community, he could see Kedem bursting into the den any moment now and publicly crucifying the both of them. "I just," he began quietly, "just..."

"Doran?" Tali asked.

"Pups..."

"Pups?" Tali asked in disbelief. "Doran, would it even matter if -"

"Yes, it would," Doran whispered and moved closer to her. "You're my sibling."

Tali was genuinely touched by this affection. She thought that deep down Doran was jealous of Streak, of the attention that he was getting from the council. She looked up and softly rubbed his muzzle with hers. "You have nothing to worry about," she said.

The anger and frustration seemed to vanish from within him instantly. Nothing to worry about, she had said.

Nothing to worry about; at least, not yet, he thought.

Part 2

The Formation of the Warriors

1

Dawn emerged across Averon. Its grey, dull, light emerged from far across the Great Vast Open. A patch of sky was clear above Shadow Oak, leaving a few stars twinkling here and there, before they would soon diminish. The party chosen for the excursion to the Black Lands was rallying together, preparing themselves for the journey ahead. The trip to the Trail of Fallen Stars would be fine. Successfully crossing the trail would be the first real test, the second being the unpredictability of the Black Lands itself.

Flicar brought experience to the expedition. He had often ventured many miles out into the Great Vast Open, and had crossed the legendary trail many times before. Brock, representative of the badger sett, would be accompanying him to offer wisdom and clear thinking.

Not far from the two animals, General Lupus was rallying his guards for their journey. Coinin, Wickett, Apollo and Blits were the first rabbits to ever join a fellowship involving other animals, and he was giving his best do-your-species-proud speech before they ventured out by themselves, representing the rabbit population. The group were joined by Selwyn, chosen by Arley as the representative from the pheasants. He was pompous at times, but his eyes were sharper than a hound's tooth, a talent that would undoubtedly be called into use on this adventure. Then, of course, there was Doran and Streak. Doran had been chosen to lead the expedition to the Black Lands, his task to deliver

Streak as the messenger to the dark entity dwelling in the bleakness ahead.

Kedem and Tali both joined Streak to say their goodbyes. Doran looked on, disapproving.

"You must show no fear when in his presence," Kedem advised Streak as they stood in the unpleasant chill of the breaking dawn. "If he senses fear, he may use it to his advantage."

"What should I say to him?" Streak asked, worrying already about how to handle the situation.

"You will say what you feel is right when you converse with him," Kedem replied.

"If I converse with him."

"You will, my friend. The fact that you are new to Averon will almost certainly tempt him out. His curiosity for seeing a new face, and what it wants, will be too great a temptation for him to resist."

"But be careful, though," Tali interrupted. "His dark mind may tell him to attack."

"I will," Streak replied. He looked over towards Doran. Kedem saw the look of discontent in his eyes.

"Doran is a very proud dog," he stated, gaining Streak's attention once again, "but his feelings often cloud his judgement. Inexperience is his biggest flaw, and eventually he will realise that the right decision in a situation like this comes from a clear mind unmotivated by emotion. By giving him leadership of this task I'm hoping he will realise that being a leader is about making the right decisions for the greater good, whether you personally agree with them or not." Kedem looked from Doran and back to Streak. "But there is one thing I trust with you now to be kept absolutely secret. You must give me your word that you will not repeat what I am about to say?"

Streak nodded. "I give you my word."

"Doran is not the leader of this expedition. That job has been entrusted to Flicar. Doran is aware of this decision, but it is his lead that you will all be following to the Black Lands. This is a test for him to see if he has potential to become one of my advisors. He will not get in the way of your task at hand, as he knows it will cost him too much if he fails. Flicar will be keeping a watchful eye over proceedings, allowing you to converse with Seerles."

"But please, don't aggravate him. If he feels undermined he will lash out, and it will cost him the position he has longed for since he was a pup," Tali added. She so desperately wanted to see her sibling succeed.

"I only have to look his way and he becomes agitated," Streak replied, implying the friction between them both.

"Please. This is important. For both of us."

Streak thought things over for a moment. If he told them that altercations with Doran on this journey hadn't been playing on his mind, he'd be lying. How would he diffuse a situation if Doran instigated it? How would he explain that to Shadow Oak? Why had he run into this godforsaken forest in the first place? Maybe he should have just let the hunters catch him. They probably would have killed him one way or another, if the humans turned a blind eye, which he believed they might. It would have been a lot less painful than the situation he'd rooted himself into now.

"I'll keep out of his nose," he finally replied.

"Thank you," Tali said.

"Come on, Streak!" came the distinct voice of Doran. His voice of authority seemed to be telling, not asking.

Here we go, Streak thought.

"Remember, Streak, no fear," Kedem replied.

Streak nodded as he walked away. "Yes. No fear. Sure. Got it."

He looked up to see Doran pounce immediately in front of him. "Make sure you have," he stated. "The lives of my family and our community, as well as every other creature in Averon, are hinged firmly upon your shoulders."

For the first time since his arrival, Streak looked upon Doran with a genuine feeling of anger. He did not rise to the comment, and slowly walked past him. A vengeful leader? A trail full of monsters? Convincing an evil entity to help? It was going to be one long, long day. Flicar and Brock were waiting ahead. Flicar shot a questioning look to Kedem. Kedem nodded slightly, enforcing Flicar's position as expedition leader. Selwyn joined Brock and the party began to leave, under the watchful eyes of Shadow Oak and its guests.

Rebus made his way to Kedem and Tali as they watched the animals leaving on their quest. "A lot of fire in that one," he said quietly, referring to Doran and his personality.

Kedem nodded. "He needs to learn from this, or he'll never have the attitude to decide for our community."

"Experience is the best form of education," Rebus replied. "Have faith in him."

The four rabbits lagged behind the group and passed a great verge on their right. From its peak both General Lupus and Sergeant Castor were stood on their hinds, saluting the adventurers as they ambled by. "Remember, boys, this one's for the fluffy tails!" Lupus ordered sternly.

"Yes sir!" the rabbits shouted as they passed, trying to hop and salute at the same time.

The unlikely party of woodland animals left Shadow Oak with a task at hand. Could they co-exist long enough to complete the journey without arguing? Would they succeed in convincing Seerles to help? Would they cross the Trail of Fallen Stars without alerting the monsters?

Only time would tell.

2

After an uneventful hour of walking underneath trees, through grass and across bracken, the group had disbanded a little. Doran, Brock and Coinin led the way, followed by Selwyn, Blits and Apollo. Behind them Flicar, Streak and Wickett followed their lead.

"You've seen these monsters before, haven't you?" Streak asked Flicar.

"Yes," he replied bluntly.

"What are they like?" asked Wickett. Flicar saw them in his mind's eye. The many he had seen during his eventful lifetime remained vividly within him.

"They," he began, and stopped. They continued in silence for a moment or so. "They are huge," he finally said as they travelled onward. "Even the smallest of them is vast, and bigger than anything residing in Averon." Streak's heart fell a little, although he wasn't expecting to hear anything different. "And they run fast. Very, very fast."

"But we will hear them before we see them, right?" Wickett asked hopefully.

Flicar nodded. "Yes, you will. It's the only chance you will have should you be spotted on the trail. Although in poor light you will be able to see their eyes from a way in the distance. They glow brilliantly when the conditions are right."

"Don't forget their skin," came a voice from ahead. Selwyn had dropped back a little when he had heard the subject of the conversation. The darkly dotted pheasant had seen the monsters also, and felt he should share his experiences with them.

"Why, what about their skin?" Streak asked him.

Selwyn gently flapped his reddish wings, making himself more comfortable. "It shines in the light."

"Yes, it does," Flicar confirmed, as if Selwyn had triggered some forgotten memory deep inside his mind. "And they are many different colours too." Streak snapped a twig on the floor as they walked. "Sometimes they are bright and vivid, sometimes they are camouflaged darker colours to blend against the forest itself. I've heard stories of them blending almost invisibly with both the trees and the darkness of the nightfall, and only being seen seconds before they scream and strike out."

This unnerved Wickett a little. "But you still hear them from a way away?"

Flicar smiled. "Yes. You can."

"Why do they scream before they attack?" Streak asked once more.

Flicar and Selwyn looked at each other. "We don't know for sure," Flicar began. "A war-cry, maybe?"

Selwyn shrugged his wings. "Maybe. I believe, though, it's to invoke fear before they attack."

Flicar nodded slowly. "Yes, it may well be," he said softly.

Streak and Wickett looked at each other. Change the subject, maybe?

"Are there really fallen stars on the trail?" Wickett asked, trying to sound a little more upbeat.

"Ah, the trail," Flicar replied, and himself sounded happier to change the topic. "There are definitely fallen stars on the trail, although they are not found in Averon. They are found out in the Great Vast Open, dotted in certain places along both sides of the trail as it passes throughout the vastness."

"So we won't see them, then?" Wickett asked disappointedly.

79

"No, I'm afraid we won't," Flicar said to him. "The trail runs right the way through Averon and out past the farthest borders of the Great Vast Open. It is there that you will see the stars, but only at night."

"What do they look like?" Wickett continued.

"Very bright. Their light illuminates the trail greatly. Anything crossing underneath them will do so in relative safety."

"They're also very low," Selwyn began, "and sit on top of dark, solid trunks. They are very beautiful if you ever see them."

"I bet," Wickett replied in a dejected tone.

Further ahead Doran asked Coinin about the burrow the rabbits had created underneath the trail.

"On this side, the entrance is close to the trail. It delves deep underneath and emerges a safe distance on the other side."

"Have you ever ventured past the trail yourself?" Doran asked.

"No. I have been to the burrow, but that's the furthest I've travelled. What about you? Have you been to there?"

"Yes," Doran replied, "but not here. I stumbled upon it while exploring the forest with Jinx, one of our advisors. He told me all about it, and how dangerous it is. I've never been back since."

"Then you are wise," came a distinct voice. It belonged to Brock, who had been walking slightly behind them. "The trail is indeed dangerous, but once we cross we must then focus our attention to the Black Lands. We must be cautious of the ground we walk on. Those lands will become deadly, maybe more so than the trail itself." Doran and Coinin took notice of the wise badger. "The creatures living there are ruthless savages, forced into that existence by the conditions of the land. They have little food to forage for, and more often than not they must fend off other scavengers to protect their meal."

"That's terrible," Coinin said, disbelieving that anywhere in Averon could be so harsh.

"Yes, it is," Brock replied.

"Why do they live there if conditions are so bad?" asked Doran.

"Because there is nowhere else for them to go!" the badger snapped. He felt sorry for the creatures living across the trail; always had. "If a rugged, darkened vixen or dog entered Shadow Oak requesting to live amongst you, would you allow it?"

Doran turned away. He knew that if that decision was thrust upon him he'd reject it immediately. He'd learnt his lesson with Streak.

"Thought not," Brock answered in disgust.

"Then is this why Seerles is unpredictable?" Coinin asked him.

"No," he replied. Doran and Coinin became more interested. "Seerles chooses to reside there because of the chaos. Because of the conditions. He revels in torment and dysfunction. He was born of the dark side of nature in Averon. He is the most ultimate evil in these trees. He is nature's way of balancing both evil and good."

"With so much good in the forest, he must be the epitome of darkness?" Coinin said quietly.

Brock turned away and looked ahead at their path. "He is."

The trek had become somewhat repetitive for Streak. They walked, they talked, they walked past a tree or a rock, an opening or a hill, and then the process started again. He felt like they had been walking forever without even a sign of the trail, let alone the Black Lands.

"What's it like out in the Great Vast Open?" Wickett asked him. Wickett and the rest of the rabbits had been slightly unnerved at the beginning of the expedition, mainly due to their small stature compared to the other members of the party. However, as the journey wore on they were becoming more comfortable with their comrades, and with it becoming more confident within themselves. Apollo and Blits had dropped back with Selwyn to join Streak's little group.

"Simple," Streak replied. There was no pressure out there in the Great Vast Open. He relied solely on himself, and had no other dependents to provide for. He had survived under the most extreme of conditions. The few times when the wind had frozen other animals completely and the sky had fallen, covering the Great Vast Open with its cold white clouds, he'd found adequate shelter and food to see him through. He'd enjoyed the challenge of jumping wire borders and catching feathered prey, then running from the humans and their weapons under the cover of darkness. He was a warrior, born of necessity rather than choice, although he was kind-hearted and would assist with anything in times of need. Like now. Kedem had seen this within him. Streak's short stay at Shadow Oak had been horrendous, thanks mainly to Doran, but still he stayed calm and settled, and allowed a clear mind to make his answers, not exaggerated emotions.

Doran had been like many other dogs he'd met on his vast travels; all of them vying for leadership status within their skulks, or in this case their community. He knew that when Doran and Tali stumbled across him in the clearing there had been mistrust between the both of them from the start. Doran had helped, but Streak thought maybe this had only been proof for the leadership test he seemed to be taking. It seemed as though he'd delivered Streak to Shadow Oak to say

Here! There you are! Proof that I can be caring when I need to and be a great leader!

At the time Streak was grateful for the help, but now he wished that they'd left him to tend his own wounds and be on his way. One thought crossed his mind, though. If that had happened, would he have left Shadow Oak and the creatures of Averon to face the Dark Army without him, or would the army have tracked him and left Averon alone? He had certainly believed the latter to begin with, but the barn owl had said the army was ready to advance upon Averon even without Streak's presence. In fact, had Streak been left in the clearing by Doran and Tali he may have brought Averon some time, but after they had either caught Streak or been unable to catch him, their next descent would almost certainly fall upon Averon and Shadow Oak.

The council had also opened his eyes to the power of belief. Kedem, Rebus, and most of the other councillors believed strongly in fate, and saw him as some kind of saviour for the forest. This in turn had ignited Doran's hatred for him, as he now felt challenged for dominancy by an outsider he had brought to Shadow Oak. It seemed clear now. Kedem was testing both Doran and Streak. If Streak succeeded, like Doran he'd be offered an advisory role at Shadow Oak. It wouldn't happen straight away, of course. There'd be years of tutorship with the advisors and a promise of a higher role when he was ready. Streak, of course, had no intention of taking this role. He deeply believed that Doran would be by far the better leader, and also the recent events of hostility proved in Streak's mind exactly why he went it alone in the Great Vast Open in the first place. Sure, he'd been offered to join various skulks, but he'd preferred to be on his own for these reasons exactly. However, if he was successful and opted to stay, there was always the lure of Tali. If he was to ever settle down, he was sure she'd be the one that would tame his wild side.

"Streak?" Wickett asked.

Streak roused himself from his thoughts. "What?" he asked.

"I asked how simple it was?"

Streak had been so deep in thought he hadn't even heard the question. "Simpler than trekking through a forest to cross a trail full of monsters, that's for sure."

"Do you have anyone out there to worry about you - you know, family? Just in case we don't make it?"

"We'll make it," Streak assured him, "you have my word. But no, I don't have anyone else out there. I prefer to be on my own."

"What happened to them?" Apollo asked. "You must have had family at some time?"

An image of Streak's mother being shredded flashed into his mind. He saw red and pink within her body, torn with ferocity and thrown into a pack of hunters scrambling at the entrance to their den. They barged and fought to get their scraps of flesh, howling their war cries that pierced Streak's ears.

"She was killed when I was very young," he said solemnly. Apollo went to ask another question, but saw Selwyn shaking his head.

They walked on, the leaves rustling in the wind the only noise that seemed to be accompanying them. Doran, Brock and Coinin were still leading the way. Somewhere in the trees above them, a deep hooting noise emerged.

"A wood pigeon," Selwyn stated, his sharp eyes peering from their red markings and up into the treetops. No-one took him up on the change in subject, so he plodded along, looking up at the emerging grey daybreak and noticing the drop in temperature in Averon. It had fallen significantly from the days previous.

"But you weren't. Did you escape?" Apollo asked, turning the subject back to Streak. Wickett glared at him with widened eyes. What?' Apollo mouthed silently to him.

"Yes." Streak replayed the event in his mind and described what he saw. "The Dark Army was to blame, only back then it wasn't as vast as it is now. One of them tracked my mother as she ran back to our den. She got halfway inside it before she yelped. She stared at me, her final look, before she was thrust from the entrance and shredded." The adventurers listened with full remorse. Apollo now realised what he had done. "While they were killing her, another hunter attempted to enter the den. I just remember lashing out wildly with my claws. I felt myself cut into him. I heard him yelp and momentarily fall back. I knew that if I'd stayed any longer I too would be dead, so I ran out while they were distracted and never turned back. That distraction was the last thing my mother was ever able to do for me."

The story was shocking. The rabbits had never heard such a terrible account of the Dark Army. There was much sadness felt for him, but Streak felt none. He continued walking as if nothing had bothered him. He was also the first to notice that Doran, Brock and Coinin had stopped by a burrow up ahead and were waiting for them. He was the first to notice a dark trail looming, running horizontally beyond the leaders, much darker than the ground they were walking on now.

"We're here," he said quietly.

3

A strange look crossed Flicar's face as Streak joined the leading pack.

"What is it?" Streak asked him.

"Look," the buck replied, and nodded his small antlers towards the trail. There upon its hard surface lay the lifeless body of a red fox. Streak's stomach fell.

"We should go and see," Brock suggested.

Doran looked at Streak with concern. "Come on," he said. "Selwyn, stand at the side of the trail and keep your eyes peeled," he ordered.

Selwyn left the rabbits and stood beside a huge fir overhanging the trail. He could see the trail was relatively straight as it passed through this stretch of Averon, and could see very far indeed down both sides. With his eyes, they would be long gone across it before the monsters even knew they had been there. "Coinin, take your guards underneath the burrow to the other side. Establish perimeter guard," he stated. "If something moves, I want to know about it."

"Immediately," Coinin replied.

The rabbits hadn't actually established a hierarchy for this adventure yet, but all of them respected Coinin enough to follow his lead. They followed him and vanished into the unused tunnel as it bore deep underneath the trail.

"Clear," Selwyn said pompously once all posts had been established. He enjoyed being the creature with the most responsibility for this task.

Doran, Streak, Flicar and Brock wandered onto the trail. There were indeed no fallen stars, a fact that had upset Wickett somewhat, but the trail did boast some very strange markings. The greying, smooth surface was solid underneath Streak's paws, but more noticeable were the long dashes of white through the middle of the trail.

The body of the fox was laying on its right side. Its fur was matted and only looked red in places, now being more of a brown hue than anything else. Its legs spread out at full stretch, almost making it look as though it should have been standing. There was no blood, no innards anywhere, and Streak thought it must have died on an impact, or even maybe naturally.

"Look," Brock said, pointing his nose to a set of black wavy marks swerving across the trail. "It left prints."

The fox lay exactly between these prints on the surface. "Definitely an attack," Flicar began, "but no blood. Monsters nearly always draw blood at the very least when they attack."

"Maybe it was weakened?" Doran asked.

Flicar nodded. "Maybe. I've know creatures survive attacks before now. Maybe it didn't have the strength to destroy the fox completely."

Selwyn scoured the trail left then right, left then right again. All clear. The guards detected no movement in the trees on the dark side of the trail. All clear.

Slowly, Doran and Streak moved closer to the body for investigation. Its eyes were glazed, its jaw open. Its tongue lay motionless on the trail floor.

"A vixen," Streak stated, telling immediately by her eye shape.

"Yes," Doran said quietly.

"One of yours?"

Doran took a moment investigating, and slowly shook his head. "No," he began softly. "There are many random skulks living in Averon - maybe she belonged to one of them."

"What about the party to The North?" Flicar asked.

Again, Doran shook his head. "I don't think so. I don't think any of their skulks would venture this far south and west."

"Maybe she was coming to Shadow Oak?" Streak answered.

The very thought of it moved Doran immensely. What if she had been heading to Shadow Oak? Doran shook the thought from his head and ignored the fox. "There's nothing we can do for her now," he replied. "We can't let this affect our task."

Selwyn scoured the trail left, right, left. All clear. The guards detected no movement in the trees. All clear.

"We should get moving," Brock advised. "Selwyn?"

Selwyn left his post and quickly crossed the solid greying surface. They left the vixen where she lay, motionless on top of the trail floor. Streak felt uneasy about leaving her, but there was no other option.

"Forget about it," Doran said to him once they had crossed, almost sensing his despair.

"Fall in!" Coinin ordered, and the rabbits regrouped with their comrades.

"There was nothing that we could do for her," Doran explained.

"I know," Streak replied, but it still fell heavy in his heart.

"I need you to be strong, Streak. We've been chosen to fulfil this task on behalf of the council. We must not fail."

For the first time since they met in the clearing, Doran actually spoke to him civilly. "We won't," Streak replied.

"Okay, listen up," Doran began, addressing the explorers. "We've crossed the trail and we're still together and in one piece. If we continue together as a unit, we will succeed. Things are going to get worse - I'm not going to lie to any of you about that - but remember, we are all in this together. All of us."

They began heading deeper into the trees, following Doran's lead. Suddenly a rush of cold air passed them, ruffling the branches above and throwing the loose leaves into the air. A low groan erupted from far ahead of them, shaking the ground and trembling the trees. The wind blew past them from behind and into the darkness in which they were heading. Blits looked up to see dark clouds racing in the same direction. The rumble then subsided, and the wind settled. The hundreds of loose leaves that had swirled in the air now gently fell to the floor.

"We're close," Flicar said.

4

Their adventure had led them deep into the heart of Averon. They were entering the Black Lands, and the atmosphere had darkened. The shadows seemed alive; creeping out from all crevices, out of trees and from under rocks and bushes. It seemed to swirl and float gently across the woodland floor, and melt away when it came into contact with the moving animals. The trees were the same as anywhere in Averon. The ground was the same. The leaves were the same. It all seemed so much darker, though. Dawn didn't seem to break completely, and they still wandered in a relatively poor light. An occasionally sharp gust of wind would whistle past them and down the dimming trail they were heading on. The land was barren and rough. It truly deserved its foreboding name.

"This is a bad place," Wickett observed to himself.

Flicar offered no answer, just advice. "Remain cautious."

"It almost looks dead," Coinin replied. The tree bark he was looking at was much darker than any he had ever seen before. The leaves looked as though they had been burnt and were soon going to flake away.

"Most of the life here vanished when Seerles descended upon it," Brock informed them as they continued on their journey. "This is the darkness that surrounds him."

"I don't like it," Doran replied. "It doesn't feel right."

"Who are we to decide what is right?" Brock questioned him. "To those who live here, this is their normality."

"Still, it feels wrong."

Blits stopped in front of them and stood on his hind legs. His ears perked up as he caught the sound of something on the wind. The trees ahead rose vastly into the sky, and joined together high above the middle of the trail. It looked like a tunnel leading into a dark, dense coppice that lay ahead. "Do you hear that?" he said quietly, almost in a whisper.

"What?" Streak asked.

"There."

"Where?" Selwyn replied.

"Up ahead. Inside the trees."

Selwyn scoured the entrance with his powerful eyes, back and forth, no wind-flicked leaf or flapping branch unchecked. "I see nothing," he informed them.

"Listen," Blits asked him.

Coinin's ears flapped as he began to hear the sound. Wickett and Apollo also had their ears engaged and were stood on their hinds.

"What do you hear?" Doran whispered.

Coinin's face crumpled in confusion. "Sounds like, like -"

"Laughter," Blits whispered.

"Wait - I hear it too," Streak confirmed. He too had caught the sound away in the distance.

The group looked upon each other. Who was it? Where was it coming from?

The laughter grew louder, and turned into a cackle. An explosion of air erupted from the tunnel ahead, throwing loose debris across the trail. The wind swirled and danced around their feet and bodies, throwing the debris it carried against them rapidly. Their fur and feathers ruffled violently in the attacking element. The

91

cackle grew louder still, seemingly engulfing them from all directions. The trees swayed their branches. The clouds thundered past. The shadows grew stronger and merged with the wind. A low groan boomed from their destination, rumbling underneath their feet and shaking the trees.

"WELCOME..."

"Seerles," Brock said angrily. "Show no fear."

Fear had engulfed the rabbits, though they stood tall. It niggled at Selwyn and Flicar, and passed through Doran and Streak.

"Stand together!" Doran shouted. "We are together!"

"HAHAHA..."

The trees shook violently. Shadows engulfed the entire plain, turning it grey. The ground quaked beneath them.

"We do not fear you!" Doran shouted.

"HAHAHAHAHA..."

"WE DO NOT FEAR YOU!"

Silence. Leaves fell to the floor. No shadows. No wind. Nothing.

Fear had indeed gripped the party, but all had hidden it deeply. Doran took a deep breath. "No turning back now," he said.

His lead inspired the others to follow. Slowly, they trailed behind him as he made his way across the small opening towards a cluster of trees that spread from one end of the forest to the other. The darkening branches loomed closer with every step they took, almost reaching out towards them, beckoning them in.

Apollo laid his ears flat against his head, his eyes opening a little wider. He was beginning to feel afraid. "Apollo," Wickett said. Apollo turned, with a look of fear or sadness on his face. "We will be fine."

Apollo nodded slowly. "Yes," he began. "We are together."

"That's right," Selwyn replied, "and nothing will happen." He hoped, rather than believed.

Flicar was more curious than afraid. He wondered if this was the Haunted Woods the deer had told stories about for many generations. Coinin and Blits were also very curious, but probably more fearful, deep down, than they showed. Brock, however, felt pity and grief, more so for the animals dwelling inside that had no escape from this way of life. He shuddered when he thought about living under the influence of the darkness coursing through these trees.

Doran was leading the party ever closer. A slight feeling of dread crept upon him as they neared the tree's entrance, but being able to face his fears for the sake of the greater good only increased his chances of sitting at Kedem's side. Streak too began to feel frightened. In the many adventures he'd had in the Great Vast Open, he'd never come across anything like this - not anything.

As they drew nearer they heard rustling away to their left, as a set of shadows emerged from the trees. Five of them, all dark and haggard, slowly glided from the dark borders, gracefully descending towards them. One shadow led the group as they approached slowly, taking shape and resembling creatures familiar. Their fur was dark and a mixture of greys, blacks and occasional whites. They walked on all fours like most of the animals in Averon, but the most striking feature was their eyes, burning red, each and every one of them.

"Foxes?" Flicar asked in confusion. He'd never seen such a species before.

"Taken by the darkness," Brock replied.

Streak turned back to the rabbits. "Show no fear, remember?" he whispered. They nodded, although he knew that they must be terrified. Rabbits, being one of the smallest of animals in Averon, tended to burrow to different destinations, relying heavily on the safety of being underground. This must have been terrifying for them. Doran, however, stood there, tall and proud.

"Well, well. What is this we have here, then?" a voice came from atop the lead dog, as he came to rest a few feet ahead of them. The voice was deep and scratchy, and somewhat distressing.

"It must be that group we were told about," replied another fox behind him, this time in a more natural voice.

From the shoulders of the leader, a long black shape dropped down on to the ground. It was a rat. "So it is," he said, standing on his hind legs as he looked the visitors over. His fur was jet-black and spiked up in patches. His eyes were also red, and his teeth and claws yellow and ragged. "What should we do with them?"

"How about you let us pass," Doran replied defiantly. The dark animals murmured a few grunts of laughter.

The rat looked back at them. "We just let them pass?" he asked mockingly. They laughed again. "Or what?" he said more seriously, his beady red eyes fixing firmly upon Doran.

"Or maybe I should shred your gut with my teeth?"

Flicar closed his eyes in despair as the dark animals this time howled with laughter. Their shrieks cut through the adventurers ears, chilling them to the bone.

"All of us?" the rat replied, the humour still imminent in his voice.

"No," Doran began. "Just you."

The smile froze on the rat's face as he stood there. Momentary silence engulfed the opening, as if each party was waiting for the other to reply. Suddenly the rat squealed and shrieked, almost sounding like he was crying, and quickly began laughing loudly once more. From the darkness of the forest a thunderous cry of squeaks and squeals erupted from the trees. The long grass shook and swayed and disappeared as hundreds of rats emerged from the darkness, jostling over one another, around the tree trunks and over mounds. They swarmed around the group in an instant, the grass of the opening being replaced with dark, spiky fur. Each rat was as fearsome as the leader, their eyes red and their teeth sharp.

Selwyn moved behind the rabbits and opened his vast wings to protect them from behind. Flicar fell back to their right and Brock to their left, protecting them from both sides. Streak stood level with Doran at the head of the pack.

The army of rats came to rest, engulfing what remained of the grassy opening. Hundreds, maybe thousands, of them.

"Still want to eat me?" the lead rat asked. Doran ignored him. "I am Rogo, protector of the Black Lands and servant to the darkness," he began, making his way through his fellow rodents who parted for him as he walked. "Let me explain one thing to you all about our home. It is very different from the green lands from whence you came. Here, we live by any means we can. We eat whatever we can. We do it however we can." Many of the rats gave intermittent squeaks as they looked on. Their leader stood only inches away from Doran. "You can count yourself extremely lucky that your arrival was foretold," he whispered, "or you and your friends would be on our menu this evening. Your lack of respect will be your demise one day, my friend."

"I'm not your friend," Doran replied firmly, standing his ground.

The Rogo exhaled through his nose in amusement. "Take my advice. Do what you must, and then leave. Do it quickly. You are protected only on your journey into the darkness. That is all."

"By who?" Doran asked.

"Someone."

The rodent turned slightly and gestured with his nose into the tunnel of darkened trees. "Follow the trail; it will lead you to him. Stay no longer than you need."

The sea of rats parted once again, showing the grass of the opening floor. "Remember, you are only protected on your way there, not your way back, so be civil," Rogo added and laughed, causing the army of rodents to join in. Doran ignored them and, with Streak by his side, made his way to the opening. The others followed close behind.

"Be civil," Rogo advised them as they entered the tree-line. "It may be your only hope for survival."

The adventurers disappeared inside the borders.

5

The darkness swept through them like the chilling breeze that had greeted them as they entered the Black Lands. It chilled their bodies and swirled across their path, and through the middle of the dark and dying trees. Streak looked deeply inside the dark trunks and dead branches. There were squeals and cries from animals he had never heard before. Huge silver cobwebs gently fluttered between branches. Wickett hoped he never met the spider that made them. The trees swirled and creaked above them as a gust of wind emanated from somewhere in the darkness.

As they continued down the trail, swirls of mist began to cover the woodland floor. It swirled upwards as they broke its barrier and walked intently through it. Selwyn continued walking behind the rabbits. The mist was deep in some parts, and he did not want to lose them beneath it.

"This is unlike anything I have ever seen before," Streak whispered, as though he was trying not to disturb anything lurking within the trees.

"It's foreign to Averon," Doran replied.

"Not foreign," Brock began. "Unknown."

"The dark arts are strong here," Flicar said as he looked in wonder around the forest.

They journeyed on through the darkness. Eventually the dull sky emerged from the branches, and they once more entered a small opening. This time it was almost circular, and the ground was shades of grey and black, covered with rotting vegetation, rocks, branches and solid mud. Maybe the sun did shine here at times? The mist that was prominent in the woods was also here in the open, gently gliding above the ground, breaking as it passed woodland objects, and sealing once more as it passed.

"Look," Brock said. In the middle of the opening stood a mound of jagged rocks. "There."

"Is that where we'll find him?" Coinin asked.

Flicar nodded. "That's where he lays."

The adventurers slowly crossed the mist-covered ground.

"Welcome, travellers."

Doran stopped suddenly. He looked around at the group. The voice engulfed them once again.

"I know the scent of every single creature living in Averon, but there is one with you who remains unknown to me."

Streak paid closer attention. "We are representative of the Great Council. We have travelled here to deliver a message from Kedem and Rebus, the council leaders," Doran replied to the emptiness. A laugh engulfed the clearing. Streak knew it was coming from the small opening underneath the rocks ahead.

"The Great Council leaders sent you with an invitation requesting my help or presence at the next meeting, no doubt?"

"Yes," Doran confirmed to the voice.

"Why now, after all this time, does the Great Council need my humble opinion? When has it ever needed my opinion?"

"It needs your opinion now," Flicar interrupted.

"Ah, the buck speaks. Why were you given this task? Why have you joined this party?"

"I'm here representing my species. We were chosen to come here, to request your advice and presence at the next council."

There was silence in the darkened wilderness. Mist floated past.

"I decline your invitation. Leave, now."

Doran looked discouraged. The task had failed, as had he. "You must come with us," he replied.

"Leave. Now."

Streak stepped forward. He walked across the ground until he was a few feet from the opening inside the rocks.

"Streak!" Wickett shouted, his eyes wide with fear for the fox. Streak looked at him and then the group. He'd helped create the situation, and he would do whatever he could to help.

"I call upon you now, creature of darkness, to show yourself and listen to the message we bring." He heard movement from within. It was working. "I request - no, I demand - you face us and listen to our message!"

From the opening, a creature burst from the darkness. Its jaws opened, and it hissed wildly. It arched back on its scaly body and raised its head level height with Streak. Apollo jumped. Doran shuddered and stepped back. Streak stood tall in the face of this nemesis. It had no legs or paws.

Streak knew this creature. He had come across its kind a number of times in the Great Vast Open, but none quite this big. It was an adder. It was a snake.

"Seerles," Brock whispered.

Seerles' body was dark and bore blackened zigzag markings, running over his entire body. His eyes were the most frightening shade of red Streak had ever seen.

"You dare to enter my forest and demand of me? Who are you to make demands?" Seerles hissed, his eyes lighting wild with rage, his fangs ready to strike.

"The impending attack on Averon will affect all creatures living here, including you," Streak replied calmly. "You can take what we say at face value and do nothing, or you can help the council and attend. We must all be united if we are to deal with this threat."

"There is no threat to me, stranger. I know of what you speak. The Dark Army will never venture this deep into Averon."

"But there is threat to the rest of us," Doran began, "and we need your help to ensure that our borders cannot be breached."

Seerles swayed as he looked from Streak to Doran. "And why should I help you?" he hissed. "What has the council done for me?"

"I'm not here to argue any difficulties you may have with the Great Council," Streak began, "but you may ask them yourself should you attend the meeting."

"If the Dark Army breaches Averon, it will affect everything living within the forest. It will first strike at Shadow Oak, where the trail begins. Soon after they will detect the scent of other foxes living here and will hunt every single one down, one at a time, killing everything that stands in their way. Once one fox is destroyed they will move to the next, and the next, until we are all wiped out or sent scurrying into the Great Vast Open. Everything will be at their mercy. Rabbits, badgers, rats, squirrels, all of us - including you," Doran said firmly. "You might be all-powerful and the most dangerous creature that exists in the forest, but when you're overwhelmed with such vast numbers as they tear through your Black Lands killing everything they find, you too will succumb to their numbers, no matter how dangerous you are."

Seerles swayed some more, looking as though he would strike at any moment. He shifted his red eyes over the party, his tiny, slick tongue now darting and flicking from his closed mouth as he listened.

"The army fears what it sees," the snake began. "You must cloud their eyes and make them believe in those fears. I will do this should they advance this deep."

"Please. Help us," came an unnerved voice. It belonged to Wickett, who had now left the others and was making his way to Streak. Wickett! What are you doing?' Coinin thought but dared not stay. "We have travelled a great journey to get here and ask you, and we still have that journey to make to get back."

Seerles dropped his head and eyed Wickett. "If you get back," he replied intently. His long, scaly body moved, and he began circling the rabbit as he stood fearless and defiant. "Usually I would kill one such as you and feed you to the rats," he hissed, "but there's something different about you." He pondered the question a moment as he circled Wickett, his body scraping roughly over the mist-covered ground. He moved his head closer to the Forest Guard, his rostra merely a few inches from Wickett's ear. The grey rabbit could feel the gentle tickle of Seerles' tongue as it darted in and out. "You are brave, and have the heart of a true warrior," he said finally. "You will indeed play a most important part in this adventure. You will be key to your friend's plan when the Dark Army marches forth on these borders."

"Then they will march?" Brock asked.

Seerles turned to him. "Yes. They will march upon this forest very soon."

"Can you see it?" Selwyn asked.

"I see only shadows. Shadows of things that may or may not occur. However, some things are shown clearer than anything else. This rabbit's courage is clear, as is his role in this attack." Seerles looked over the entire party and returned to the entrance of his lair. "You all have a role to play, some more important than others; but should one of you fail, you will all fail."

"Can you see our fate?" Flicar asked.

"I see vaguely what the darkness will show."

"What will happen?"

Seerles turned and made his way toward to his nest. For a moment he slowed, and then turned back to them. "You will fail to keep them out of Averon. All of you will meet your fates in their jaws. I cannot help you."

"Wait! You can't..." Streak replied, but it was too late. Seerles vanished into the darkness.

"Leave..."

."The council!" Doran shouted.

"Any decision you make will not save you. Leave now, before I change my mind. Very few animals leave my dwellings; make sure you are one of them..."

"But..."

"Doran," Flicar interrupted. "Let's go."

"We need him to help!"

"He has decided not to. It's far too dangerous to stand here and argue the point. As a leader, you must take responsibility of those who look to you for guidance."

The group had fallen in. Streak and Wickett had joined the others, safely away from Seerles' lair. "I have failed," Doran said, and hung his head.

"No you have not," Brock began, encouraging the red fox. "Your task was to deliver the message, which you did so successfully. Streak was asked to convince him to help, but we knew it would be more hope than expectancy. These are obstacles all leaders encounter. You are judged upon how you deal with them."

"Your next obstacle is returning the party safely back to Shadow Oak," Flicar said to him gently. "Your work here is done."

Doran took up the helm, with his head still hung in shame. They left the opening and entered into the dark trees, through which they walked along in silence. It didn't seem as dark and foreboding as it had done the first time they passed through. They emerged soon after, the rats and foxes there waiting for them. "What did he say?" sniggered Rogo.

"What happened?" asked the lead fox.

The group carried on in silence as the rats laughed and jeered at them. The dark foxes watched in amusement. Soon the adventurers had left the opening and vanished in the direction of the Trail of Fallen Stars. Rogo scurried over to his fox counterpart and jumped on his back.

"Should we do it now?" the fox asked.

The rodent sniggered. "Not yet. Let them cross the trail first."

6

The adventurers came upon the trail without anyone uttering a single word. All hope seemed to be lost. No matter what they tried they would fail, or at least that's now what they believed. The only thing they could do was to report back to the Great Council and at least try and formulate a plan that would see them through.

The body of the vixen upon the trail loomed in the dim light. Doran snapped back to alertness. Her body had been moved. Blood was now strewn across the hard surface which they would have to cross. "What happened?" Coinin asked, noticing the change as quickly as the fox had.

It suddenly hit Doran. "They've been through. The monsters." Adrenaline burst into Doran as he took charge. "Selwyn, point. Rabbits, under the burrow and stay clear on the other side."

All took up their points. The rabbits vanished into the burrow and emerged safely on the other side. "Clear!" Selwyn chirped.

Brock and Flicar were the first to cross, avoiding the body. Selwyn crossed and took point on the other side. Streak crossed quickly. He heard the low hum of something approaching not far away. A monster had heard them. Doran stepped onto the trail and seemed drawn to the vixen. He stopped in a clear patch of the trail and looked down on the lifeless shell. The fox looked her over, his mind transfixed. It was as if he could hear Seerles' voice ringing in his head.

'This is what will happen when the Dark Army advances...'

He did not hear Selwyn shouting, or the rest for that matter. He did not feel the rumbling of the monster as its growl grew louder and shook the ground. There it was, speeding ferociously at Doran in the middle of the trail; its shiny white skin reflecting the dull forest daylight.

'This is what you are responsible for. All of Shadow Oak will meet their demise...'

Now it looked like the vixen was smiling at him. Was she speaking?

'All of them will die!'

"DORAN!" Brock screamed. He turned to see the monster thundering at him - merely a few feet away, its eyes huge, its body growling viciously. Doran shrank. His ears flattened against his head. The monster screamed thunderously, filling his head with the shrieking, piercing war-cry they roared before they killed.

Doran was hit from his right-hand side and sent tumbling off the track towards the Black Lands. He rolled and rolled and rolled, his head and limbs smacking heavily against the debris-filled floor. Somewhere, the monster was still shrieking. He rolled even more, thrown with such ferocity he thought he'd never stop. He came to rest in the middle of the dark trail he had walked through not minutes before, and lay there panting. The shrieking had subsided.

The rest of the animals had hidden deep in the trees as the white monster rested in the middle of the trail, still growling quietly to itself. It too had left long, dark footprints on the solid floor. Apollo had poked his head out to see what was happening. Coinin quickly dragged him back under the bush and slapped his head. "Idiot," he whispered.

After a few moments the monster growled louder and began moving, first slowly, then faster as it moved away. It ran rapidly into the distance, roaring in anger and disappointment.

"It's gone," Selwyn finally informed them from his lookout position, and then ran toward the others. Brock and Flicar emerged from behind dense greenery, and the rabbits burrowed out from their yellowing bush. They all checked they were together.

"Doran!" Wickett cried and dashed towards the trail.

"Wickett! Careful!" Flicar shouted.

Doran lay almost motionless, panting heavily for breath. He was shocked. After a moment or two he took hold of himself. He moved his paws. All working. He bent his legs. All working. The only pain he felt was on his right side where he was struck. He breathed in then out, then in again. It didn't hurt when he inhaled, or when he exhaled. It just hurt constantly. He coughed a little and dragged himself slowly to his feet. He shook his head wildly, removing the fuzziness from inside. In front of him, Flicar and Wickett approached.

"Amazing," Flicar said in awe. "Looks like you have a guardian angel."

Doran saw he was being looked past. He turned slowly to see Streak standing up from the damp floor. Had the monster caught him too? He saw a few leaves plastered to his red fur, then shook his own, just in case. Doran stopped. Realisation set in. It wasn't the monster that had struck him. He looked back at Streak.

"You..." he began, more angry than appreciative.

"He saved your life," Wickett informed him.

Doran ignored the rabbit. "You?"

He lunged at Streak, and they once again fell to the ground. This time Doran snarled and swiped his claws toward the fox that had saved his life. His jaws clamped the air as he tried to bite him. Streak yelped. "You!" was all Doran could shout. "YOU!"

Doran felt a claw swipe at his muzzle, and suddenly flew back with force. Streak had kicked him away.

"Is this the thanks I get?" Streak snarled, panting heavily.

Doran rose to his feet, but this time didn't attack. "You stay away from me!" he snarled angrily. "I can look after myself!"

Flicar and Wickett stepped to the side as Doran raced passed them, across the trail and deep into the forest.

"Doran!" Brock shouted after him, but gained no response.

Wickett looked puzzled. "You saved him," he said, unable to understand Doran's hostility.

"Come on," Flicar suggested, trying not to dwell on the situation, and they left quickly. Once they had crossed the trail they joined with the others.

"Doran's gone," Brock informed them when they regrouped.

Flicar shook his head. "He'll have to fend for himself. We have to get back to Shadow Oak as soon as we can."

Selwyn nodded. "You did what you could, Streak. You should be pleased with what you've achieved." Streak said nothing.

Brock offered encouragement to the fox. "We all saw what happened, you did everything -"

"This is all my fault," Streak replied.

Selwyn looked puzzled. "You saved -"

"It shouldn't have come to this. I should have never entered Averon."

Flicar gestured for the rest of the group to begin walking ahead. Brock nodded in agreement and took charge. "Let's get going," he said. Wickett took one last look at Streak before turning and heading away.

"Talk with me," Flicar said, as the group advanced ahead of them. Both he and Streak walked slowly, ensuring they were beyond earshot of the other animals. "Why do you think Doran is acting in this way?" he asked.

Streak shook his head. "I have no idea."

"Think about it."

Streak thought. He knew Doran hated him for leading the Dark Army to Averon. He knew Doran disapproved of the relationship that he seemed to be forming with Tali. He also thought Doran may regard him as a better leader for Shadow Oak. These things Streak told Flicar - except, of course, his relationship with Tali.

"They both play a part," Flicar began when he'd finished, "but the main concern is how the army tracked you to Averon."

"They followed me here," Streak replied.

"Ah, but did they?"

Streak stopped and looked at Flicar. "What?"

"What if the Dark Army tracked you, but previously knew of the existence of foxes in the forest? What if another fox's scent had lead them to Averon?"

"But it was me. They were tracking me across the Great Vast Open. I led them here."

"What if a curious dog had left Averon and ventured into the Great Vast Open previous to your arrival? On many occasions one has done this, since before you appeared. He believed he was scouting for danger. Of course, you did play your part, but the army knew of foxes' existence in Averon long before you entered."

"Doran..." Streak whispered.

Flicar agreed. "Yes, Doran. He knows he should not have ventured outside the forest, but he did. He knows it was his scent that was originally tracked here, and he feels guilt and shame. You just confirmed that foxes were in existence within these trees."

"It's still enough," Streak said, not feeling any better.

"Yes, it is. But you still have a role to play. Fate sent you here, remember?"

"So you keep reminding me."

"And so we will until you believe."

They walked on, heading back toward Shadow Oak. Maybe they'd catch up with Doran. Maybe he'd wait for them. Maybe he'd attack Streak again. Maybe he wouldn't. Averon was filled with ifs, buts and maybes as they drew closer to Shadow Oak and the Great Council. What would happen now after they reported Seerles' vision of utter failure and imminent death of all dwelling within Averon? That they did not know; just like they did not know that they had been followed.

7

There were breaks of sunshine casting through the dull sky every now and again as the adventurers made their way back to Shadow Oak. Was it becoming brighter the further they ventured from the Black Lands, or was it just Mother Nature throwing them a mixed day? Streak was the only one who wondered this as they travelled. Doran had been gone for a while now, after his mad dash escape into the trees. The rabbits speculated about where he had gone, what he had done, but Streak kept his muzzle out and said nothing. His rage had been suppressed with every footstep away from the Trail of Fallen Stars, and his chat with Flicar had helped settle him a little bit more.

Blits raised an ear once again, as he had done when they first crossed the trail.

"What is it?" Streak asked, taking notice.

"I don't know," Blits replied. "It sounds like..."

From behind them the ground came alive and darted in different directions. It looked like a wave of dark water crashing through the trees, devouring the ground as it hurtled towards them. Within the wave, five large shadows emerged.

"Rats!" Blits shouted.

"RUN!" Streak screamed.

The adventurers began sprinting through the trees, the wave of rats closing down upon them rapidly. The rabbits sped away into the distance, Wickett the fastest of the group. The squeaks and squeals drew louder. Streak looked over his shoulder and saw that the foxes were chasing too.

"We're not going to make it!" he shouted to Selwyn. The rats began snapping at Streak's paws as he ran.

Selwyn opened his wings and flapped them down with powerful force. He glided quickly up into the air. A rat lunged through the air, snapping at his talons. Streak knew he'd be overrun within a matter of seconds, and chose the only other option he knew. Suddenly, he stopped, allowing the rats to speed past him. The lead fox from the Black Lands didn't see him in time, nor did Rogo, who clung to the fur on his back. As he rapidly descended upon the red fox Streak spread his paw, maximising his claws to full effect, and swiped viciously.

The fox tumbled and yelped as he flew past, throwing the rat from his back. Another fox had pounced on Streak already, snapping his jaws as Streak held him away. The fox suddenly jolted as Flicar kicked him with his hinds, sending him crashing into the wave of darkness.

The rabbits had assembled a defence formation. They stood in a close circle, their hind legs and tails all facing outwards. They thrust their legs out relentlessly, powerfully knocking all rats that attacked them back from where they came. Brock stood above the moving darkness and swiped ravenously, as wave upon wave attacked him and were knocked back.

Streak felt a breeze of air pass above him. Selwyn descended onto the battle, his sharp eye focusing on the one he wanted. Rogo was still recovering from the fall he'd taken. He stood no chance. Selwyn clenched him in his talons and rose above the darkness, avoiding the jaws of the rats and foxes. He gained a credible height for all to see and then hovered, hanging in the air as his wings kept thrusting. Many of the rats looked at him and saw the rat in his claws. The rat was squirming and squealing, trying to break free. Selwyn clenched his claws, rupturing the rat's body and spilling dark blood upon his soldiers. He swooped down, releasing the body from his claws, sending it thudding to the feet of the lead fox. Rogo coughed and spluttered as he hit the ground and then attempted to gain his footing. He had been greatly injured by the pheasant hovering above.

The army stopped. It was as Selwyn thought. The rat was their leader, protected by the foxes, and now he had been injured they had no direction and no leadership.

From ahead of the battle, a red fox charged toward them. "Doran!" Coinin shouted.

Doran charged into battle, but he was not alone. From behind his lead a pack of foxes ran beside him, crashing into the rats, ripping, shredding and attacking without consequence. The adventurers attacked once more, finding the nearest rat and attacking it as hard as they could.

Streak watched as the dark foxes began their retreat, followed swiftly by the rats. The wave subsided as they ran back to the Black Lands and the safety of its borders. Their squeals disappeared until all that was left was the panting of the adventurers and their new allies, drawing deeply to catch their breath. Selwyn disturbed the peace as he landed close by, brushing through the branches as he found an appropriate area to land.

"You came back," Apollo said to Doran when his breath would allow him.

"Yes," he replied, "and I found some friends. This is Lyro, a warrior of the tribe to The North, and these are their best warriors."

Lyro nodded in greeting and acknowledgement. "We'll accompany you back to Shadow Oak," he said.

"Thank you," Brock replied, his claws glistening with rat blood.

"We're not far away now," Doran told them. "Let's make sure we get back in one piece."

The adventurers arrived back during the early dusk. Their trip had taken almost a day, and in Doran's eyes had been a complete failure. Seerles had refused to attend the council meeting or even offer advice, and his spat with Streak had culminated with a brief fight and subsequent exit. His conscience told him that had he not dashed away into the forest, he'd not have stumbled across the fox tribe from The North heading to Shadow Oak. The leader inside him had explained to their tribal chief Akando what had happened on his journey, and he had released Lyro and some of his accompanying soldiers to find the group and safely accompany them home. However, he knew that the way in which he left the group and his behaviour towards Streak in particular would almost seal his fate when delivering his report to the Great Council.

8

Shadow Oak had been full of different animals when they had returned, amazing Streak in particular. He had never known an alliance such as this had existed in the hidden world of Averon. Usually he'd be hunting and eating rabbits and pheasants in the Great Vast Open, but here he was working with them to try and restore order to their homeland. As he walked through Shadow Oak towards Tali he noticed more badgers, pheasants, muntjac, foxes, squirrels, otters, birds, and other animals he'd never seen before. Some of the animals were in the process of making their way to the council entrance, and would definitely have been the representatives of their species.

"No time to talk," Tali said as Streak reached her. "You must attend the meeting."

"Streak!" Flicar called over the murmuring of the animals.

Streak nodded and turned back to Tali. "Got to run," he said. Tali nodded and gestured him away. He smiled back at her, and joined Flicar.

This time the stone seating had been filled of every species' representative needed for a full council. Kedem and Rebus sat at the head, chairing the meeting with their elected authority. General Lupus and Sergeant Castor sat atop a fairly empty rock as Coinin and his fellow rabbits accompanied Flicar, Brock, Doran, Selwyn and Streak in addressing them. Some other lower-ranked representatives had been posted guard around the outside of the clearing, ensuring that this time no prying ears could listen in and begin rumours before the council adjourned.

Kedem eventually brought order to the Great Council and asked Doran, as leader of the expedition, to relay the facts of their trip to the higher powers. Each animal listened intently as Doran described the body on the Trail of Fallen Stars, the darkness that had engulfed them, their encounters with the dark animals and with Seerles himself. He also explained his altercation with Streak and departure from the group. He'd though it best to be honest, as no doubt Flicar and Brock would tell the truth anyway. The council remained silent as he relayed the story, helped in part by Wickett and Flicar.

When the tale had been told, Kedem and Rebus thanked him, and asked them to join their counterparts by their designated stones. Streak looked momentarily confused until Kedem subtly gestured with his eyes over to Jinx and Delfin, the direction Doran was heading. Streak did so, and officially sat in on his first meeting.

"The future seems, then, to be a bleak one," Kedem said as he began the discussion. "With Seerles' vision predicting the end of Averon, we must discuss a way forward for our survival."

"Seerles' predictions are often misinterpreted and clouded by the darkness he lives in," Akando explained. He was an intelligent fox, but held a vast disliking and grudge towards Kedem after he had been rejected to lead the council in Kedem's favour. "I wish to know how you both had authority to seek Seerles' advice without consultation with all parties of the Great Council?"

A murmur from the council confirmed that some of the members either agreed or disagreed with the leader from The North, and so began the first political attack of the meeting.

"In extreme circumstances we have authority to act rapidly and in any action we deem necessary," Rebus replied. "That is why our communities are close together, so that in times of crisis we can meet quickly and make these decisions if needed."

"A meeting with Seerles is extremely dangerous. I don't see how any respectful leaders can place the lives of his own clan, let alone those from others, in certain danger without the agreement of a full council." More murmurs emerged.

"Akando, this is a full council meeting to discuss the very real threat to Averon and to our lives," Garla, lead doe of the muntjac, replied. "Not an opportunity to use this as a potential vying tool for political gain."

"And, of course, you would know all about vying for political gain."

There had been rumours that Garla had ousted the former head of the muntjac by leading a hate campaign to her followers whilst out foraging in the Great Vast Open. This was, of course, just a rumour. Garla had been selected by her former leader to take leadership of the deer as he grew older and felt unable to continue his post.

"Settle down!" Brock snapped, forcing a glare from Akando. "If you cannot contribute effectively to this meeting you will be removed forthwith."

"On whose authority?" he asked slyly.

"All of ours," General Lupus replied.

Every single animal in the meeting stood to show their unification. Akando looked away in disgust, shaking his head. The wind rustled the leaves and branches of the trees shading the meeting.

"This is the biggest threat to our existence," Kedem began solemnly as they returned to their seats. "We cannot sit idly by and hope that it passes over us like we have done before. Now, the Dark Army will descend down upon us in a very short time, and unless we have a plan or an idea, we will be killed. It won't just be the skulks of foxes; it will be the badgers, the squirrels, the pheasants, the otters, all of us. A member of their army has already entered Averon and killed one of our friends. A rabbit, who ran with Wickett and his scout team, has already been murdered." Wickett nodded slowly in remembrance of his old friend. "Unless we act now, more of us will succumb to the army, and Forest Guard Digby would have died in vain."

"We must do something," Wickett replied. "Anything. No matter how impossible it seems. Digby was headstrong, and although most of you look down upon us as 'only' rabbits - slight in stature compared to the rest of you - if it came down to a fight or a battle, he would have charged forward into war having no care for how big, how many, or how vicious his opponents were. We are the rabbits, and we are the runners, the fastest animals in Averon."

He looked over at General Lupus, who now looked upon his guard with a sense of pride. Rebus smiled. Kedem nodded slowly.

"Maybe it's time we didn't run. Maybe we shouldn't run. Maybe we should stand and fight for our forest. Maybe we should fight for our families and our species. Maybe we should all form an alliance, or an army. Look at all of you here. You represent your kind. There are many more of you back at your setts, your families, your clans and your communities. If we all aligned together right here, right now, between all the animals in Averon, we could amass a great army, a huge army that would outnumber the evil one that knocks on the door to our borders. We could be so vast and huge that nothing would penetrate our defence. Not the army, not the humans nor the monsters. We could protect Averon and all that dwell inside, and we could continue to do so for many years to come. We could be warriors. The Warriors of Averon. I do not fear them. I will stand. Stand and fight, on my own if need be."

"You will not stand on your own, my friend," Flicar said as he wandered into the middle of the circle. "Seerles was indeed correct. You are brave, and somewhat motivating. I assure you that no-one at the council looks down upon you as 'only' a rabbit. You are now a warrior, and have conducted yourself in that way since you ventured to the Black Lands and overcame your fear." Flicar looked at the host of animals circling the woodland opening, and for the first time caught the scent of pine on the breeze. "I will stand with you," he said, looking toward Akando.

"As will I," came a familiar voice. They turned to see Streak join them. "I played a huge role in bringing them here, and for that I apologise, to all of you." The once depressed-looking dog now held his head high. "I will serve the council in any way that I can, and help you wherever possible." Wickett looked at Streak. Streak winked back.

Arley, the head of the pheasants, rose from his flattened rock. "Based on the pure fact that you all ventured into the Black Lands and came back together, I offer the council the full support of the pheasants, and at his own wish, release Selwyn from his role with us to join you as a warrior."

Selwyn wandered towards his friends, who graciously received him. "I can't fight for anything, but if my eyes can assist you, I will use them."

"Tell that to the rats," Streak replied humorously.

"We will stand with you," said Glif, leader of the squirrels, "although we can only battle alongside you in mass. We will be unable to release a single squirrel to join your order, but when needed we will empty the trees and fight for your cause."

"And it will be gratefully accepted," Kedem stated.

Coinin looked over at General Lupus and Sergeant Castor, along with Blits and Apollo. "Wait for us!" Blits shouted as the three white-tails burst into the opening.

"We couldn't let you have all of the fun," Apollo said as he joined the adventurers.

Brock ventured over to them and looked at Rebus. "With your permission?" he asked.

"Granted, my friend. And I hereby announce that the badgers will join you in your hour of need."

Doran sheepishly wandered into the circle. "I need to make amends, for my behaviour towards you all during our journey. I will fight alongside you, if you will let me?"

Kedem smiled. The fox knew the error of his ways. He admitted to it, and was strong enough to accept that he'd been wrong. A learning curve, yes, and proof beyond a doubt that Doran was a natural leader.

"You are always welcome," Flicar said, completing the party that had originally ventured out on the route to the Black Lands. The rest of the council animals volunteered their services to fight when the time arrived; all but one.

Akando and his pack rose from their place. "We will not help, or assist the council or its new-found guardianship," he snarled disgustedly.

"Akando," Rebus began solemnly.

"We will not help! When has anyone entered The North to assist us when we have needed it? Not one of you has ventured into our lands to show unity within our species!"

"That is a lie!" Kedem shouted. "I worked tirelessly to form bonds with your tribe and establish good relations! Had you accepted my request, great leader, you would have had the full support of Shadow Oak when you needed it, no matter how great the issue that troubled you!"

"I will never accept help from you or your council!" Akando snapped. "Each of you is as corrupt as the other!"

"Corrupt because we did not vote you to be our joint leader?" Glif snapped. The grey squirrel seemed pushed to the limit by the argumentative fox chief. "The behaviour you're displaying now is exactly why you didn't gain a single vote in the ballot!"

Akando rose from his place. Anger snarled across his eyes and muzzle. How dare they insult a great leader like him! How dare they! They would pay the price for this outrage!

On his order, the pack turned and slowly left the council in stunned silence. Akando turned back to them. "Have your war," he said bluntly, "but do not crawl to our clan when it has finished. If you survive, that is."

He turned and left, walking slowly behind Lyro and the rest of the foxes who had accompanied him, his bushy sweep gently swaying.

"Akando!" Rebus shouted. He ignored them stubbornly.

Flicar had been proud of the animal's achievements, with Akando's exception, and did not want the mood to dampen after the emotional speech that Wickett had given.

"Let it be known that on this day, Wickett of the rabbits united the council, and founded the forest's greatest line of defence; the Warriors of Averon."

Suddenly a cold wind blustered through the opening, rattling the branches and stirring the grass.

"How very rousing."

From inside a swirl of darkness Seerles emerged, his head rowing from left to right as he slithered into the opening. The guardians stood in disbelief for a moment or so, unable to comprehend that the serpent had indeed listened to their plea when they ventured across to his lair, deep within Averon. They moved back, allowing his long, coiling body room in front of the council.

Seerles raised his head and addressed Kedem at eye level. "Although maybe it's a little late," he replied.

"What are you doing here?" Kedem asked.

"I'm sorry, didn't you send your representatives to invite me to this meeting?" he replied sarcastically.

"What do you really want?" Rebus asked.

Seerles flicked his tongue at them. "I am intrigued by the situation you have become involved in," he replied. "I am intrigued as to how you are going to deal with this threat from the Dark Army."

"We are about to discuss this situation," Kedem informed him.

"Well then, don't let me stop you," Seerles said, and spun round to look at the council. "Does anyone have an idea? Anyone?"

The council had fallen silent. Whether it was due to a lack of ideas or just the fact the Seerles had arrived, Kedem didn't know.

Seerles gave a wry, evil smile, and turned back to Kedem. "The very fate of Averon swings in the balance. You have to fight, but have no plan."

"And I suppose you do?" Doran asked, stepping forward.

"Ah, the incomparable leader. How did it feel to turn your back on your companions?"

Doran snarled, and lunged at the snake. Seerles hissed and opened his jaw, revealing his deadly fangs. Streak rapidly trod down on Doran's tail, halting him in full flow. Seerles bobbed his head back, expecting an attack.

"It's not worth it," Streak said to Doran as he turned around. For a moment Streak thought he saw the look of intent in Doran's eyes that he'd seen before they fought back at the Trail of Fallen Stars, but it quickly diminished. Doran sighed and nodded. Seerles smiled in victory.

"I say he's just trying to kill us," Doran informed the council after a moment or so. "I wouldn't trust him."

"Like the party you were leading trusted you?"

Doran again made an attempt to get to Seerles, but was this time was thwarted by both Streak and Flicar. Seerles looked on, highly enjoying the show.

A scream bellowed from deep inside the forest, making some of the animals jump. Between the trees, Streak saw a white bird flying towards them. It descended rapidly and came to rest outside the circle of animals.

"Cyrius," Seerles hissed with a hint of animosity.

Cyrius hopped into the council meeting and stood beside Rebus. "The time is upon us," he said, addressing the council. "Decisions must be made. The Dark Army will make its move very soon. You must act now in formulating a plan."

"That's just it, though. We don't know how to engage an army of hunters," Streak said.

"You must think logically," Seerles replied.

"Can we even trust you?" Flicar asked.

"You can," Cyrius hooted. "If Averon is destroyed, his legacy and grip on the forest dies within it. The fear he strikes within the animals will be forgotten, and without fear he becomes just another animal living amongst us. His legacy will have to begin once more, and will take even longer to establish. He has more to lose than most."

"You are so wise and intelligent," Seerles said, again with sarcasm. "You now have a decision to make. Trust me, or not."

A low murmur emerged across the Great Council as the leaders began asking each other if they could, if they should, or if they should just ignore.

Rebus hushed the mumblings. "We all need to make that decision, and make it quick. If anyone here disagrees with using Seerles, speak now." A short breeze of chilled wind cut through the council, making the leaves and grass rustle once more. That was the only noise that emerged.

"Then it is settled," Kedem decided. "What is your plan?"

Seerles, once again, smiled in victory. "An army is led by leaders. Generals, captains, sergeants - just like your army will be, once assembled. What would happen if these leaders became separated from their soldiers?"

"Chaos," Streak replied. "With no-one to make decisions they would have no guidance in what to do."

"Exactly," Seerles hissed in agreement. "You must separate the leaders from the pack to begin with."

"And how will we do that?" Brock asked.

Seerles coiled a little as he turned to face the warriors. "I have a plan, although it may involve an element of danger."

"It can't be as dangerous as entering your domain," Doran stated.

"It is nothing like entering my domain. I control everything."

"My point exactly."

"Alright, that's enough," Kedem ordered. "What's your plan, Seerles?"

"Out beyond the western borders, in the Great Vast Open, lie the dwellings of the Dark Army. They are kept behind barriers by the humans, released only to hunt. The first thing you must do is re-establish the reason they are hunting you all."

"What?!" Doran asked, astounded. Flicar settled him.

Seerles turned to Streak. "You are the main reason they are invading Averon. To fight them, you must lead them into certain areas of the forest. What you must do is fill their noses with your scent once more. Remind them that it is you they are looking for."

"And how do I do that?" Streak asked, believing this may be a potential death trap.

"You must venture down to the barriers they live behind. Walk up and down, back and forth, send them into frenzy. Fill their noses so much that they will still smell you when they are released. Their leaders will see you, smell you, and know exactly who to look for when they are released."

"But if Streak were to do this, how would it separate them from the rest of the army?" asked Kedem.

"You must leave that to me," Seerles replied, "but you must place them on your trail. If their leader decides to chase another, your plan will fail."

"What plan?" Wickett asked.

"You will know in time."

"So if we get their leader to track Streak, our plan will work?" asked Selwyn.

"Not necessarily," Seerles began. "My visions are not always clear. You stand a better chance following this line of thinking than any other way." He looked at Streak with his evil red eyes. "You must go there. You must anger them. Their leader is named Baal. He is the one hunting you."

"Baal..." Streak said as he tailed away in thought.

"Infuriate him. Anger him so that he wishes to kill you even more than he does now, all the while filling the air with your scent. Be warned, though. When the Dark Army is released, make sure you do not fail, or you will be the first one to meet death by his jaws."

Streak looked at him with an air of suspicion. It was the only idea they had, and the only one that seemed to make sense. If the Dark Army picked up his trail quickly he could lead them anywhere he wanted. He could lead them into...

"I understand!" Streak cried emphatically.

"Understand what?" Kedem asked.

Streak explained the plan he'd created with Seerles help, informing all council members of their roles. It was dangerous, and carried a risk of failure, but it was the best they had. All of them would somehow be involved in danger, but it was a price they had to pay. After finally explaining what they should do the day had entered its twilight, with all guests being invited to stay at Shadow Oak; and both Cyrius and Seerles all but disappeared, as mysteriously as they both had entered.

Part 3

The Dark Army Advances

1

As night fell across Averon, the cloud cover lifted and revealed bright stars burning in the darkened sky. The Lodge had come to rest somewhat easily this evening, and a few hounds loitered around the pen outside. Inside, they rested peacefully. Some slept, some talked, and some just laid and did nothing.

Cameo had been taken outside the pen by the humans and had his wounds tended. The liquid they used to clean his injury had stung intensely, and now as he rested it smarted painfully from time to time. He noticed it even more when a rogue breeze crossed him from the flap leading outside. That evening he'd been given the task of guarding the boards that Rainan had escaped underneath.

Baal had spoken to him since his return, and acted as though nothing had happened. Cameo too could be ruthless when needed, but chose to be a little more relaxed than his senior. He was the go-between that conveyed messages from the warriors to Baal, and vice versa. Occasionally, Baal would address them if he wished to, all of them hanging on his every word. Usually this was done before each hunt. He'd rally them and fill their minds full of hate and malice.

Baal rested in his corner, and although awake, appeared calm. That soon changed when a hunter came bounding into The Lodge, causing more hounds to jump out of his way.

"General! General! You need to see this!" a black-furred hunter shouted. Baal raised his head from the ground and looked at him in confusion. "Sir."

"What is it?" Baal asked quietly.

The hound paused a moment. "It's him."

"Who?"

"Him. The fox."

Baal's nostrils flared and his good eye dilated. He rose to his feet. "Cameo," he ordered.

Cameo rose to his paws in anticipation, and as Baal exited The Lodge he quickly caught up. The rest of the army looked upon him in wonder. "Everyone stay here," the second-in-command ordered, before he too slipped outside.

Baal was growling in the darkness. It was the low, rumbling growl Cameo had become accustomed to when they were in the open, hunting prey. It was the rumbling growl he knew too well as the sound of anger and frustration. Baal was in a bad place, and having seen the fox sat opposite him on the other side of the fence, he knew his mood would undoubtedly sink to its worst form.

"You!" Baal growled, his nose full of the pungent smell of his new nemesis. "What is your business here?"

"So, you're the one who's hunting me. You're the one determined to rip me to shreds," Streak asked, as he sat defiantly beyond his reach.

"Should I send someone to catch him?" Cameo asked, remembering the escape route from their home.

"Don't you think I've already thought of that?" Baal snapped immediately. "What is the point of a kill if you cannot promote fear in your prey beforehand?"

"So that's what you're going to do? Make me fear you?"

Baal growled. "You will fear me."

"I've run from you, and why? I look upon you now, and I wonder."

Baal approached the fence carefully until he could get no closer. "I could kill you in an instant," he said angrily.

"Then why don't you?"

"Because I'm going to wait. Wait, and when I catch you, kill you slowly. I'm going to make you feel every flap of skin and organ I tear, and I'm going to eat them while you watch."

Streak, now unsettled, rose from his seated position and, fantastically hiding his fear, walked slowly along the side of the fence, prompting Baal to accompany him.

"We'll enter your forest, and we'll slaughter everything that gets between us and you."

"I hear you sent one of your warriors in already, killing a rabbit just inside the border?"

Baal grunted in amusement. "A rabbit? A useless creature that doesn't deserve its place in the animal kingdom."

Streak smarted at the comment. He knew how much Digby had meant to Wickett and the rest of the rabbits now in the guardianship. "The rest of the animals saw you for what you were, then and there. A coward who sends others to do his business for him."

Baal smiled. This fox knew nothing of the tortures he was doomed towards. The air hung thick with the scent of their tormentor, reminding both Baal and Cameo of their previous expedition.

Streak stopped. "I'll leave you to your army, General," he said eventually, "but know this. No living animal in Averon fears you."

"Then there will be no living animal left after we have been through there."

Streak darted away into the darkness, leaving his scent hanging in the air. He'd done his job. He'd also told Baal that he was indeed hiding in Averon, making no doubt that the forest would now be the first place they headed for.

Streak ran across the inclining grassy meadow towards Averon's western border, the one he'd entered what now felt like many seasons ago. Kedem, Selwyn, Flicar and Wickett waited for his return just beyond the trees. Soon enough they caught glimpse of his eyes as he glided through the darkness.

"How did it go?" Kedem asked once Streak had settled.

"He seriously wants to kill me," he replied.

"It couldn't have gone better!" Wickett said, smiling.

2

In a thicket not far from Shadow Oak, Akando emerged into the open, stretching his body and shaking his fur. Lyro emerged not far behind and followed him to the edge of the Great Lake. The council peninsula was now across the water, and Akando gave it a quick glimpse before taking in his morning drink.

"You think it will work?" Lyro asked him.

Akando lifted his muzzle from the water, causing drops of water to fall from his chin. "Absolutely. He's an outcast. They won't give him what he needs in Shadow Oak. We'll offer him everything he wants, and give it to him within our clan, and then he'll see our way of life and exactly what it is Kedem is doing to our kind. What we have to do first, though, is make sure he'll listen."

Lyro nodded. "His loyalty to them is not at its peak, and if we can convince him before they do, we stand a greater chance of tempting him to The North."

"Yes. He will have spent enough time with them by now to know their weaknesses. Using his knowledge correctly will give us the advantage we need."

"And then we can advance."

Akando smiled grimly. "And then we can advance," he repeated.

3

The animals began work on their plan. All species worked tirelessly to uphold their end of the commitment. Squirrels overran Shadow Oak under the watchful eye of Glif as they set up in the trees surrounding the huge den. The circular clearing of the dens would serve well for their role.

The rabbits began burrowing brand-new tunnels from the western borders, zigzagging across Averon, past Shadow Oak, and deep into the forest. Sergeant Castor worked closely with Coinin, Wickett and the group to formulate how they would get this to work. Selwyn and the pheasants worked intently with them, explaining to the Forest Guards exactly how their own plan was going to proceed.

Kedem, Delfin and Jinx hosted Rebus, Brock and Flicar as they planned the best approach to the impending advancement from the Dark Army, and how Doran and Streak should lead them.

Across the Great Vast Open, and down to The Lodge, the Dark Army frenzied. At first Baal didn't know what had caused his legions to become agitated so severely, and then he noticed. A feeling of contentment crossed him. Today, no food had been served.

Streak had been out for a walk around the Great Lake. He'd walked it almost completely whilst in deep thought, not noticing the beauty on show within Averon. Butterflies floated past with no interest. Shafts of sunlight broke through the trees as fluff from dandelions floated past. Patches of daisies lined his trail at the vegetation's edge, but he knew nothing of it. His thought lay within the coming hours, after daybreak tomorrow.

The sun began hiding behind dark, swirling clouds, playing hide-and-seek with him as he walked. The temperature had dropped quite considerably in the last day or so, and Streak always noticed this as a sign that the hot weather was coming to an end, and the cold season would soon be arriving.

He exited the area for the Great Council and was about to head through the shrubbery to Shadow Oak when he saw Doran at the water's edge not far away, taking in a drink.

"Was wondering where you'd got to?" Doran said, lifting his muzzle as Streak approached him.

"Just out for a walk. Clearing my head before tomorrow."

Doran nodded. "Tomorrow for sure," he replied.

"Is everyone ready for it?"

"Yes. The squirrels have finished at Shadow Oak. Coinin and the rabbits have finished their burrowing and have helped find somewhere for the pheasants. We just need to wait and do the final preparations at dawn. Those who cannot fight are going deep into Averon to Bluebell Clearing."

"What's that?" Streak asked.

"It's the biggest open area in the forest, deep inside the trees. It's the safest place for those who cannot fight to go to."

"If we can keep the army from getting there," Streak thought aloud.

"If," Doran replied.

"What are you two up to?" came a voice behind them. They turned to see Tali approaching them from a small clearing shaded by small trees and bushes. "You both can't be speaking to each other? And amicably too?"

Doran shook his head and dropped his eyes when Streak looked at him. "My darling sibling. I was wondering when you'd appear to ruin things."

"Can't disappear too long. Isn't it the job of every sibling to annoy her counterpart?" she said smugly.

Doran looked back at the water and noticed something strange on a bank not far away. "What the..." he began.

Streak frowned. "What?"

Doran gestured with his muzzle across the water. "There, is that -"

"Akando," Tali replied intensely. "What's he doing here?"

"I thought they left yesterday?" Streak asked, confused.

Akando looked over at them and vanished underneath some reddening bushes. Doran headed in that direction.

"Doran! What are you doing?" Tali asked.

"Wait here a minute, I'm going to go and see what he's up to."

"Doran," Streak began, "do you think that's a good idea?"

"I'm just going to ask, that's all. I'll be fine." Streak began walking with him. "No, wait here. He may run if we all approach him."

"Doran!"

"Tali!" Doran snapped. "By the time we'd get back and report this to Kedem he'd be long gone. I'm just going to see what he's doing and if he needs help - that is all."

Doran began a steady canter around the lake, leaving Streak and Tali behind at the water's edge.

Streak began to run, but was stopped when Tali called his name.

"Streak, it's not worth it. That dog is too headstrong."

Streak stopped and nodded. "Don't I know it."

They looked on as Doran arrived at the spot Akando had been standing at, and watched him vanish into the bushes.

For a while there was almost an awkward silence between the two foxes as they waited for Doran. Streak eventually broke it when he commented on the cold weather moving in. Tali agreed, and informed him that Shadow Oak was so dense inside Averon that usually it didn't get as cold as it did elsewhere, and Kedem often made sure that all foxes were well cared for during the cold months.

From seemingly nowhere, Wickett appeared beside them. "What are you doing?" he asked inquisitively. Streak explained what had happened and why they were there. "That's not good. Should we go and see if he's okay?"

Just as Streak was considering this, Doran emerged from across the water and began walking back towards them. Tali sighed and closed her eyes. Being the sibling of a fox who wanted to be a leader was a seriously hard job.

"What happened?" Streak asked as Doran came into hearing distance.

Doran looked somewhat angry. "Nothing," he replied.

"Nothing?"

"No. Make sure you stay away from them, Streak - way away. He's not good company. If he gets in your ear, there's no saying what you will do."

Doran walked past and headed to Shadow Oak. "What are you doing now?" Tali asked him.

"Reporting it," he shouted back.

Doran slinked away without saying anything else, leaving Streak, Tali and Wickett in the woodland silence.

"What are you doing here, anyway?" Streak asked Wickett. "Aren't you supposed to be doing other things?"

"I already know what we're doing. I'm the fastest runner in Averon, and I already know what to do."

"The fastest?" Streak said, the white dash across his eye rising with his brow.

Wickett knew when a situation called for a demonstration instead of an explanation. "Race you to Shadow Oak?"

"Alright," Streak said, accepting the challenge. "Tali, count down from three."

"I don't believe you two," she replied. They both stood together and looked at her. She sighed and laughed simultaneously. "All right. Three... two... one... GO!"

Wickett tore away like a rocket, leaving only his tail for Streak to follow.

"Hey! That's not fair!" he shouted. "You went before she finished!"

4

The Dark Army had gathered outside in the pen. They formed rank and held discipline whilst waiting for Baal to address them. Cameo was already standing out front, joined by Kaskar, his successful performance in organising the breach from The Lodge earning him a promotion. Rainan also stood ahead of the army, his dependability and skill finally pushing him to the forefront of the army's hierarchy.

The temperature had dropped to a comfortable coolness, a sign that the cold season had emerged in its infancy. The clouds above them appeared dark and flat, and the swirling bases brought the promise of rain to the Great Vast Open.

The Dark Army stood in silence as Baal made his entrance from The Lodge. He had an aura about him that dropped the mood in his followers and incited fear, but also respect. The hounds at the back of the ranks didn't even have to see him to know he was there.

Baal trotted slowly across the concrete, past Cameo and Kaskar, until his dark fur rested at the head of his army. "Tomorrow we leave The Lodge in search of our target."

The hounds howled in unison, creating a deafening war-cry.

"We will leave here to pick up the trail of our nemesis, the one stupid enough to visit us at our gates. He is the one we will be hunting at daybreak, regardless of what the humans think. We will serve as our own masters tomorrow, no longer controlled by the bugle that leads us in battle." Some of the hounds looked at each other. "You will all follow me, or you will perish. I will make sure of it. The humans will not kill you, but I will. Tomorrow we run across the Great Vast Open and deep into the forest of Averon. There, we will track and kill our target."

Baal began wandering back and forth along the first line of rank. "For years, we have been unable to do this. For years we have tracked our prey only to see it released by the humans, killing only by accident. Tomorrow we will break their rules by implementing our own, and we will tear him apart. Dining on his flesh will be our deserved reward for mutinying against the humans!"

The army roared with agreement.

"For too long we have been caged and domesticated; only releasing part of our potential and being suppressed from what we were born to do. Tomorrow we will invade Averon in search of our target, and we will kill him. We will ignore the humans until we have completed our quest, and we will slaughter every animal in the forest that stands in our way! All of them!" The army chanted its war-cry once again. "Tomorrow we revoke the years of misery we have been forced to endure. Tomorrow we leave this cage to commit our own goal and purpose. Tomorrow we will turn the ground we run on red with blood. We will evoke fear in our enemies. They will all once again cower in terror at the very thought of the Dark Army!"

5

"Okay, you have to make sure you hold on tight," Streak explained to the rabbit perched upon his back. They were about to leave Shadow Oak on a test run, and the fox was issuing last-minute orders.

"Doesn't it hurt if I pull your fur tightly?"

"No Wickett, it doesn't. You have to make sure you have a firm grasp or you'll come flying off. If you do that tomorrow, you're on your own."

Both animals were about to head across a small open meadow known as Meadoway, and to the peak of Berry Hill, the highest point in Averon.

"I think the question is, do you even know where you're going?" Doran asked in a humorous tone.

Wickett looked a little anxious. "I was going to guide him, but I've never given directions from the back of a fox before."

Doran trotted around, and smiled. "Tell you what, Streak. I'll run with you and lead you to Berry Hill - if you can keep up, that is?" Both foxes looked upon each other for the first time as equals.

Wickett whistled. "Sounds like a challenge to me!" he said to Streak.

"It does, doesn't it?" he replied. He turned to Doran. "Okay, you're on."

Tali trotted into the clearing underneath the great oak, emerging from the trail the two foxes were about to sprint through. "Count us down!" Doran shouted to her, as rays of sunlight broke through from the clouds above them.

"Again? You're racing again?" she asked Streak as the two dogs took their positions.

"This time it's to test our plan," he began, "and Doran's leading me to Berry Hill. I don't know where it is?"

Tali looked up at Wickett. "I'm just along for the ride," he said, and smiled. Tali sighed. Boys will be boys.

"Okay, but you be careful. Flicar is running with Brock out in Meadoway. I'm assuming he's trying the same techniques as you," she said to Wickett and Streak, "only being a little more mature about it."

The clearing had now gathered many animals, who were taking an interest in what was about to happen. Garla, Glif and Arley looked on as Kedem and Rebus emerged from their dens to join them. Glif explained what was going to happen to the council leaders. Rebus clapped his paws together, and laughed. "That's what I like to see!" he bellowed to the duelling foxes. "Nothing like a bit of friendly competition to get the old blood pumping, eh?"

"I don't think we should be encouraging them," Kedem whispered quietly to the badger.

"Nonsense! Go for it, boys! Let us see who will be the victor!"

"Three... two... one..."

Wickett gulped.

"GO!"

The foxes dashed across the opening to the cheers of the surrounding animals, throwing leaves and mud into the air as they sprinted across the twigs and out onto the trail. Kedem smiled. Doran was back.

"WOAH! WOAH!" Wickett screamed as he clung to the fur on Streak's back. "WOAH!"

The two foxes tore rapidly between the trail, neck-and-neck as they thundered past the shrubbery and into the clearing of Meadoway. Selwyn and the rabbits of the guardianship were stood by the trail's exit, watching Flicar coaching Brock on how to keep his balance as the buck ran across the vivid grassland. Apollo heard the sound of sprinting paws rushing towards them. He saw the foxes running directly towards him.

"INCOMING!" he screamed, and dived from the path of the sprinting warriors. Selwyn and the rest of the rabbits instinctively dived from their path as they exploded into the clearing and out into the grass. Blits jumped to his feet and shouted at the others.

"Come on! Something's going on!" he told them, and dashed after the racing foxes. Coinin and Apollo swiftly followed. Wickett gained his composure and looked back at his counterparts, rapidly catching up. Selwyn took flight, and thrust his wings rapidly to catch his comrades.

Flicar stopped as he saw the commotion in the tall grass. "What are they doing?" Brock asked as he clung comfortably around the grey fur of Flicar's neck.

"I don't know," the muntjac replied. They watched the racers enter the middle of the meadow and alter their course towards the steep incline of Berry Hill. "Hold on," Flicar ordered the badger, and he too joined the chase.

The grass in this part of the meadow was longer than anywhere else, and began obscuring Streak's view as it brushed into his eyes and muzzle. "Keep going!" Wickett shouted as he clung dearly to the dog. Doran had moved slightly away to Streak's left, and now took a minor advantage.

"Look," Brock said as he clung to the sprinting buck. "The rest are following them."

The rabbits had utilised their strength and put their speed to use. They ran in line behind the battling foxes.

Flicar merged with them from their right, and ran alongside his comrades.

The sun broke from the dense clouds and rapidly vanished as they glided quickly through the sky, illuminating and shading the meadow as the animals sped across its openness, trampling the grass and leaving tracks in their wake. Selwyn soared from the back of the sprinting pack and passed low overhead, taking point at the head of the warriors. Wickett looked up and cheered as the pheasant soared past.

The first order of Averon warriors joined as one across the open meadow and ascended the steep verge of Berry Hill, tiring as they darted through the berry bushes and plants that gave the great hill its name.

"Don't give up!" Wickett shouted, as they neared the peak of the hill. Doran was still ahead slightly and the hill was now running out. Streak lowered his ears and pushed himself one final time. Doran began drifting closer to him as they amassed the final part of the hill. He drifted closer and closer until Streak had his muzzle inched out for the lead. Doran pushed himself harder still and regained a slight advantage over his opponent. The hill was ending. They sprinted harder. The incline stopped. One final push...

"YES!" Doran screamed and stopped rapidly, panting for breath. Streak also came to a rapid halt. They both looked at each other for a moment, and burst out laughing. The rest of the warriors joined them as Wickett hopped down from Streak's back and looked out across Averon. He stood in awe as he gazed across the dense forestry of his homeland. The trees were various shades of greens, yellows and an occasional red. They filled his entire eye-line and left no room for the Great Vast Open. Away in the distance he could see the hint of the darkened trees they had passed inside the

Black Lands. He could see the sunlight rippling and reflecting from the Great Lake near Shadow Oak.

"Amazing," he said softly to himself.

"Yes, it is," Doran agreed. "This is what we're fighting to save, Wickett. This is our forest, and our home. If the Dark Army succeeds in eliminating us there will be no creature in Averon left to enjoy it."

"We will succeed," Brock replied, still atop Flicar's back. "I have no doubt."

"We will," Streak said as he joined Wickett. "You have my word."

6

The morning arrived, as all mornings do. The daylight emerged slowly across the trees, and gently began illuminating the darkness. Fog loitered, slowly passing throughout the dense forest. Shadow Oak was busy. Those who could not fight were leaving the den and heading towards Bluebell Clearing.

Rebus, Arley, Garla, Jinx and Delfin led the mass exodus of creatures unable to fight for the cause. They would soon be joined by Tali, who at the moment was arguing with Kedem. She wanted to stay with them and fight the Dark Army, but the wise old red would not allow it.

"I mean you no disrespect, Tali, but you are not going to compete with the hounds in this battle."

"Just because I'm a vixen doesn't mean I can't fight!" she argued. The mass exodus of animals was in full operation. They passed the confrontational foxes in the dim daylight.

"It's not that at all -"

"Then what is it?"

Kedem sighed. "Firstly, I need someone I can count on with Jinx and Delfin to lead our community through Averon and to the clearing -"

"Don't give me that!" she snapped.

"Secondly," he began, in a calmer temperament than the vixen, "I need someone that if, if..." He stumbled momentarily. "If I don't make it out of this battle, I need someone I can trust to assist Jinx and Delfin as an advisor to Shadow Oak."

Tali was stunned. The reality of the situation finally hit her. "Don't talk like that," she insisted as they stood in the cold morning air.

"Tali, it's a possibility that may happen."

"Don't -"

"Tali..." Kedem wandered closer to her and offered her comfort. "I have to be sure that the foxes of Shadow Oak can be safe in my absence. That responsibility lies with you."

A lone tear fell from her left eye as she nodded. "Okay," she began, "but you're coming back. All of you."

Kedem flashed her a smile that settled her emotions a little. "Speak to your sibling before you leave." Tali agreed, and left her leader to gather his thoughts.

"Tali! You should be gone by now!" Doran shouted, as he watched the various animals leaving the clearing.

"I came to wish you luck," she replied, still a little dejected that she could not stand on the front line beside him. "And love."

Doran walked over to her. "Just promise me you'll do what's right for everyone leaving. Remember, for the greater good, okay?"

"For the greater good." Tali smiled, and both foxes brushed muzzles. "Be careful," she replied.

Through the vixens and pups leaving the den, Tali noticed Streak standing beside Wickett. They were looking on as the steady flow of walking animals passed in front of them and out of the community. Tali slowly wandered over to them, both appearing as shadows in the patchy fog.

"Shouldn't you be on your way?" Streak asked as she approached him. Wickett thought for a moment that the fox had been speaking to him. He looked up, about to answer, and saw that the statement was intended for Tali.

"I came to wish you both luck today."

"Thank you," Wickett replied. Streak didn't answer. He looked at Tali as if this may be the last time his eyes would ever set upon her. It was an uncomfortable silence.

"Well, then, I'll leave you -"

"Wait!" Streak snapped as she began to leave. They stood in a stare, their eyes firmly focused upon each other. Streak sighed. "Now or never," he said. Wickett looked on in confusion. "If I get back -"

"When," Tali corrected, as she stood in the cold cloud.

"When I get back," Streak rephrased, "how would you like to walk with me sometime?" Tali laughed. Wickett shook his head.

"Is that the best you can offer?" she asked him playfully. Streak shrugged and smiled, with a nervous disposition.

"Well, maybe if you can tempt me with something better, I may consider spending time with you."

"Like what?"

Tali thought for a moment. "I always enjoy watching the moon rise on Berry Hill."

"That'll be fine - Streak will be happy to walk you there," Wickett joked.

Streak kicked the rabbit with his front paw. "Hey!" Wickett snapped.

"That sounds great," Streak said sheepishly.

"Okay. We'll discuss it when you return," Tali replied. "Good luck."

Jinx and Delfin had been waiting for her to say her goodbyes. She turned and made her way to the advisors, looking back one final time over her shoulder.

"Walking," Wickett said, as they watched her join the other foxes leaving the community. "All the things you can tempt her with, and you choose the one thing she does every day." After a few moments, she disappeared beyond the mist and out of harm's way.

"You will see her again," came Doran's voice. Doran joined his comrades as the exodus continued. Streak seemed a little shocked at his forceful statement.

"I know, I know," Doran began as they looked at each other. "This adventure that we've been on has made me think. Maybe you're not that bad after all."

Streak disbelieved his ears. Was this the same Doran of previous days?

"After all we've been through, and all that we're about to go through, you're not that bad. You stood beside our community in the face of danger when you could have run. You could have disappeared and left us to fight this battle on our own, but you didn't. You stayed with the community, and you helped us. That goes a long way in my estimation."

Streak was at a loss for words. Wickett looked at him from the corner of his eyes, and raised his brows.

"If my sister was to settle down soon, I guess I'd want it to be with you." Streak began to say something, but Doran hushed him. "Just let's make sure we come back to her." Streak nodded, and said nothing more.

From the mist, the ground began moving. Darkness bobbed and weaved unpredictably. It emerged from the fog and crashed around tree trunks and rocks. Within the darkness, five larger shadows emerged. Doran and Streak had seen this sight before. They adopted an attacking stance, and snarled as hundreds of black rats engulfed Shadow Oak and surrounded the trio within the fog, squeaking and squealing as they descended.

"On my back, Wickett." Streak ordered.

"I can fight -"

"On my back! You're too important to the plan!"

Streak lowered himself, allowing Wickett to clamber between his shoulders. The rats parted, as a fox emerged from the ensuing darkness. From his back, their leader Rogo dropped once again to the floor and scurried over toward them.

"How can it be? You were greatly injured!" Wickett cried in disbelief, as the rat they saw maimed by Selwyn unnaturally stood before them. He grinned his toothy, dark grin.

"Anything is possible when you're governed by the dark arts," he replied. "Never underestimate the power of the darkness. It is stronger than you can most possibly imagine."

The trio prepared for attack as Kedem, Flicar, Brock and Rebus made their way through the sea of rodents.

"What brings you here?" Rebus asked angrily, smashing a rat from his path as he did so.

The leader's smile diminished, and he became serious. "Seerles sent us," he began. "He has released us to fight under your order for one time only."

Kedem looked upon him with a suspicious eye. "Why?" he asked sternly. He had never trusted Seerles or the darkness he worshipped until only a day or so ago, and still had doubts as to his motivation in this time of need.

"He sent us to assist you so that Averon can remain as it stands now, but also to inform you that whatever the outcome, no alliance between us will ever exist after the battle is over."

"And why should we trust you?" Doran asked, in the disapproving tone that Streak had come to know so well.

"You have no choice," the rat informed him. "Take our assistance, and more bodies fight for your cause. Reject it, and your odds of survival decrease greatly."

Doran looked to Kedem. Kedem stood firm and offered nothing in return. Doran realised what was happening. Judgement was still being passed on his leadership skills, even in their final hour. The decision was his to make. Should he take the offer? He looked at the animals leaving, just visible to his eyes as they traipsed shadily inside fog. He looked at his comrades. They returned the look. "Will you follow my orders?" he asked the ragged rodent.

"To the end," the dark rat replied.

"Well, Rogo, you and your army have given me an idea."

Baal rallied the troops into the pen. They snarled and barked. Saliva frothed at their mouths. They clawed at the concrete in anticipation. They howled in the early daylight of dawn. The fog was lifting in the Great Vast Open. Rain had started to fall lightly. Their frenzy was about to be unleashed.

The humans were coming to release them.

7

Doran rallied the warriors at the western border. The fog was lifting rapidly as the falling rain penetrated its density and cleared the air. Joining him were Streak, Kedem, Wickett and Brock. Thunder rumbled to itself away in the distance. A line of foxes and muntjac stretched away from them in both directions, forming a tight row of animals willing to fight against the advancing evil of the Dark Army. The rain hissed loudly as it penetrated the leaves above them, and fell heavily upon the woodland floor. Flicar trotted slowly over to his comrades. "They are on their way," he said solemnly.

Doran turned to him, the grey fur on his face harbouring small dew-drops from the increasing rain. "Then it begins."

The sound of wings beating the cool air signalled the arrival of Selwyn, who couldn't help but smash branches and leaves from his course as he descended into the tight grass they were waiting inside.

"The army is rapidly making its way here. Their numbers are huge," he said as he landed.

"We knew the risk of the situation," Kedem informed him, "but we have courage. We can win this battle."

Wickett raised his ears. Across the Great Vast Open he heard the war-cry of the Dark Army as it advanced quickly across the meadow. "I can hear them," he whispered. "They're upon us."

Through the rain, a gust of wind rippled the trees. The breeze it brought cut through the animals with a freezing, jagged edge, making the animals shiver as it passed by. Streak looked down to see darkness gliding from the shadows, and bleeding out in ripples across the floor. "Look," Selwyn said as the darkness crept over them. The animals looked on as the shadows continued to dance around their paws and cover the bracken and debris.

"Wickett," Streak said calmly, and gestured to his back. He lowered his shoulders, allowing Wickett to clamber on top.

"Fall back into the forest. Your warriors need to initiate their plans. I will separate the generals from the army..."

"It's Seerles!" Doran cried, recognising the voice of the darkened adder. "Do as he says! Fall back! FALL BACK!" he shouted to the line of guards stretching the border. The animals complied with his order, and ventured deeper back inside the forest. The battle would now begin inside the border of their home.

A shadow of doubt crept over Streak. Was Seerles really trying to help? Doran believed him, though if the serpent was indeed manipulating the situation he would undoubtedly have given the hound's free passage into Averon, destroying their carefully initiated plans, and giving the animals less chance of survival than they held already. It was a huge risk that had been taken by their leader on the front line. The first move had been completed by the alliance as they raced through the rain and further inside the forest. The next move would be taken by the Dark Army.

Battle was indeed upon them.

8

The Dark Army marched slowly across the grassy meadow they had tracked Streak across many days previously. They marched in rank, keeping strict discipline as they moved closer to Averon and towards battle. The rain fell heavily now, and served only to infuriate the hounds even more as it battered them from the thunder-clouds above. They marched under the lashing rain and over the inclining grassland until they were almost upon the darkened forest itself. Baal barked an order and halted the army. They stood in rank as he and his leaders emerged from their mass of darkness and formed a line in front of them. The humans were screaming in anger. The horn was bugling loudly, but no hound paid attention. They stood there motionless as the rain soaked them through and dripped from the edge of their noses.

"Hunters! You know what to do next! On my order, attack!" He waited a moment. The humans were livid. Baal smiled in their defiance. "ATTACK!"

The first wave of hounds leapt into action and thundered past them into the trees of Averon. The hounds behind them turned, focusing on their human masters. The humans looked on in bemusement. They had stopped shouting. The bugle no longer controlled their canines, and now they slowly wandered towards their masters, growling and snarling as they crossed the dampening grass. The humans became unnerved and began to back-track as their army closed down on them, surrounding them from most sides.

The frenzied hounds launched into an attack with no remorse. They clawed and bit at the humans wherever they could find flesh to grab. A horse reared up on its hinds, throwing the human from its back and to the sodden ground. Another became frightened of the attacking hunters and galloped away from them, regardless of its human rider. Chaos ensued across the Great Vast Open. Baal laughed wickedly. His plan had worked.

The first wave of hounds broke through the tree-line of western Averon. The smell of the foxes was pungent, even with the suppression of the falling rain. They had all traced the scent of Streak when he visited The Lodge, and had now been ordered by Baal to follow his trail as their prime target. As they had now rebelled against the humans, Baal encouraged them to annihilate any living creature that ventured between them and the fox they were hunting. Anything...

They passed deeper into the greenery. The forest became darker with every step. The darkness began swirling intently about them. It amassed and rose into the dank air. It covered the floor they were standing on, and engulfed the entire western border. No light penetrated its thick mass. They hounds had become lost and disorientated, swallowed whole by the dense shadows. They began to panic. Not even the rain was strong enough to penetrate the darkness.

The hounds were terrified.

"Welcome to my home..."

Each hound was hit with a vision of Seerles. He coiled and hissed as he drew his scaled body back and lashed out upon them.

The hunters sprinted away in fear, whimpering and yelping as they ran blindly inside the darkness. An opening of low light emerged in the shadows and

155

presented them with an exit out to the Great Vast Open. Each hound exploded from their torment and out into the meadow, rapidly. Baal angered as he saw his legions approaching, and swiped one across the snout as he dashed past.

The humans had been scared by the army enough to retreat back across the meadow and away from their charge. The remaining hounds gave chase, keeping their captors at bay, whilst Baal and his leaders entered Averon. He was joined by Cameo, Kaskar and Rainan, all looking to him for the next order. The darkness had all but vanished, allowing the next stage of the plan to commence for Doran and his warriors.

"We split up. We kill everything in our path. Leave no fox alive. If you find my target, wound him and bring him to me. No-One is to kill him. No-one," Baal stressed.

The four hounds walked side by side in the rain until they had passed the border. The smells of the many foxes confused Rainan and Kaskar. "You two. That way," Baal ordered, gesturing his nose towards the northwest area of the forest. "Kill everything. Cameo, with me."

The hounds split into twos, and began their advance upon the foxes.

"They're coming!" Selwyn cried from a perch high above in a fir tree.

"This is it!" Doran shouted. "Those involved in a plan, take your position. The rest of you, follow Selwyn!"

The forest came alive with the sound of animals scurrying quickly away from their base. Selwyn vanished from the treetops with his followers in tow.

Baal heard the stampede, and growled. "This way!" he barked.

Wickett clung tightly to Streak's back. "Ready?" the fox asked.

"Go!" Wickett shouted.

Streak sped away through the wet shrubbery with the rabbit clinging tightly to his fur. Baal caught his scent, and began tracking him over the distance. He sped rapidly over the fallen leaves and sodden ground, and glided effortlessly above the first few puddles that had began to form from the heavy rainfall.

Streak sped out onto a small trail. His vision was slightly impaired by the rain, but he kept his composure. Wickett was atop his back, his grey fur absorbing the scent from Streak's body.

"No wonder they tracked you! You stink!" he said, as Streak dashed down the trail. A flimsy branch hung at just the right height, its brown leaves drenched with rainwater. He darted underneath it, allowing the branch to slap Wickett fully round the head. "Guess I asked for that," Wickett mumbled as he shook the water from his fur. Streak just kept on running.

Baal and Cameo had Streak's scent fully traced. They ignored the vast amount of other foxes they were picking out and focused solely on the one who had escaped their grasp once before. They dashed through the rain, and emerged on the trail Streak had taken. Their feet pounded the floor harshly as they pushed their bodies to the limit in order to catch him. Mud splashed back from the ground as they ran deeper.

Ahead of Streak, a fork emerged in the trail. "Ready?" Streak shouted.

"Ready!" Wickett replied.

"GO!"

Wickett leapt from the fox's back and glided quickly through the air. His lightning-fast paws hit the cold bracken, and he was gone in a flash. They both veered away in different directions - Wickett taking the left path, Streak taking the right.

Baal burst through the branch that had not long ago attacked Wickett. The scent became stronger. They were closing in. A fork emerged in the trail ahead. They ran faster forward, their hearts pounding in their chests. They came upon the fork. Baal stopped rapidly and went skidding into some bushes off the trail. Cameo halted instantly and slid across a patch of browning leaves. Baal screamed in anger.

"Two?" he snarled, his patience completely destroyed. "How can there be two trails for one fox?" He roared loudly and swiped the bark of a nearby tree in frustration. He paced around momentarily. "Okay," he whispered to himself as he emerged back on the trail and gained composure. His mind leapt into action quickly, and he issued Cameo a new order. "You take that side, I'll continue on this one."

"Yes sir," Cameo replied.

"If you find him, bring him to me."

"Sir," Cameo said, as he began his sprint away down the trail. Baal growled once more in agitation and took up the scent once again. Cameo vanished left, Baal headed right.

9

Rainan was wandering alone through a dense part of the forest. The scent of a fox grew ever stronger to him, but he was sure that this was not the animal Baal was intent on destroying. He slowed to walking pace and scoured the trees, when he noticed a fox ahead in the distance. It wasn't the one who was primarily being tracked, but it was a fox nonetheless. His esteem would be praised by Baal and Cameo if he killed one, regardless of who it was. They hadn't hunted to kill for many years, since before his own birth even, but he knew killing this fox would hold him in the highest regard and keep his place in the hierarchy of hounds. He turned and ventured into the darkened area where the fox waited.

Through the rain, Kedem saw a hound approaching. He was stood in a tiny clearing surrounded by dense ferns. It was so dense in this part of Averon that darkness occupied the immediate greenery situated behind him. Daylight simply couldn't breach the density of the leaves and bushes surrounding the fox, and he hoped that the element would play greatly to his advantage.

The hound emerged cautiously in front of him. The rain had drenched both creatures from its relentless downpour and darkened their furs even more. The hound walked across the grass and sat ominously in front of the fox.

"Why aren't you running?" Rainan asked the courageous dog. Lightning flickered through the tree-tops, and a clap of thunder rumbled above them.

"I have no need."

A rumble echoed deep inside Rainan's chest as the fox began to anger him. Kedem slowly headed backward and disappeared into the ferns and darkness behind. Rainan rose to his paws and followed him in.

The darkness engulfed the hound as he explored the open area. Only a dim shaft of dull, grey light penetrated the clearing from a small gap in the greenery above. The fox's trail was strong, and Rainan didn't have to see him to know where he was. He caught a thousand different smells in the opening. All belonged to animals who had passed through here at one stage or another. Ahead of him, Rainan saw the white glow of two eyes in the darkness.

"I see you," he said playfully, setting himself up to lunge upon the fox. For a moment, he though he heard a squeak. He shook his head. Then he heard it again. Squeaks and squeals. Around the eyes of the fox, he saw another set of eyes emerge. Then another. And another. Suddenly eyes were emerging rapidly throughout the darkness, hundreds of them staring at him as the rain rattled heavily on the shrubbery outside. Lightning and thunder collided at the same time, illuminating the darkness for a split second. In that split second, Rainan yelped at the amount of rats he saw engulfing him from the darkness.

Kaskar trotted through an opening as the rain fell heavily upon him. His paws began to sink into the earth as it softened and gave way under his weight. He followed his nose over a sodden hill and emerged in a clearing surrounded by flowers and shrubs. It was the Western Clearing, the same one Doran and Tali had discovered Streak unconscious within many days ago.

Kaskar wandered into the grass, his nose following the various trails he'd discovered. He placed his snout to the ground in order to gauge a stronger smell.

From nowhere he felt a claw swipe the left side of his body, stinging as it scratched through his brown fur. Kaskar yelped and span around, finding Brock in his eye-line. "Where did you emerge from?" Kaskar growled, angry with himself that a badger - of all creatures - had managed to attack him without his awareness. The badger stood his ground, curling his lips back into a snarl.

"You are very brave for one so slight," Kaskar informed him as he settled to face his adversary.

"And you are very stupid for one so fearful," Brock replied. Kaskar frowned.

From the depths of the forest an army of muntjac and foxes emerged, their plethora of reds and greys surrounding the clearing and sealing it from escape. The dark foxes from the Black Lands looked more menacing than any other he had seen before in his life, their red eyes glowing as they bore upon him. Kaskar back-tracked and looked for an escape route. He had no such luck. The distressed hound was now trapped. Brock made his way to Flicar's side. Flicar lowered himself down, allowing Brock to climb upon his back. Kaskar began barking and growling in an attempt to unnerve his captors. Thunder and lightning clattered the opening. Kaskar turned this way and that, expecting the animals to attack. They stood silently still, watching the hound work itself into a state of anxiety.

"ATTACK!" came a distinctive cry from beyond the captors. Between the animals an army of pheasants emerged, running through the legs of the muntjac and into the clearing. The brown speckled bodies followed Selwyn as he launched at Kaskar, as aggressive and brave as any warrior in Averon. Kaskar snapped at his attackers as they descended upon him, nipping feathers and wings of his tormentors. Beaks and claws began jabbing and catching his body, opening wounds on the hunter's torso. Kaskar swiped and shredded relentlessly under a mass of multi-coloured bodies, all of them tearing his body in a calculated attack. Feathers seared into the air as Kaskar blindly lashed out at an enemy he could not see.

Flicar looked down at the mass of bodies engulfing the hound. "It is time!" he cried. "Now we march upon the Great Vast Open! Now we take the battle to the enemy!"

A cheer rallied from the muntjac and foxes as they followed both Flicar and Brock around the attacking pheasants, and darted towards the border of Averon.

They thundered through the forest as the rain crashed upon them, darting between trees and bushes. They pushed forward through branches and shrubs, and trampled flowers and grass as they rapidly ascended upon the Great Vast Open. They emerged on the western border and saw their exit through the swaying leaves and branches ahead of them. The Great Vast Open loomed rapidly, as the makeshift army followed Flicar through the rainfall and closer to the edge of the forest.

Flicar cried as they approached. Brock screamed in unison. From behind them a war-cry thundered throughout the army, all animals screaming as they emerged upon the front line. They drew closer and screamed louder. In the meadow beyond the trees, the Dark Army turned its attention to the strange noise emerging from the forest. Many of the hounds looked on in confusion.

"THIS IS OUR FOREST!" Flicar screamed at the top of his voice. "WE WILL NOT LET THEM TAKE IT!"

The army cheered.

From the border of Averon, an army of bucks and foxes exploded from the trees, each animal bellowing its own war-cry. They thundered across the meadow and headed towards the stunned army. The hounds saw them and stumbled momentarily. An army of forest animals rapidly approached them through the rainfall. One hound barked and snarled. "For Baal!" he shouted, and ran headfirst towards the oncoming mass of warriors.

"For Baal!" shouted another, and gave chase. The hounds re-established their motivation, and for the praises of their general all gave chase and ran towards the oncoming animals.

Flicar still screamed as the wave of darkened bodies rushed to greet them. Lightning illuminated the battlefield, and thunder embellished it as the two armies showed no intent of surrendering.

"Show no fear!" Flicar cried as the hounds approached across the meadow. "SHOW NO FEAR!"

A shree bellowed from the sky above. Joining the deer to lead the warriors descended Cyrius, his white plumage glowing brightly.

Flicar smiled and adrenaline coursed throughout his body. "To war!" he shouted.

"TO WAR!" his warriors cried.

Flicar focused on a hound rushing towards him. The hound focused back upon him. Flicar screamed. The hound snarled. Brock launched from his back.

The armies clattered together violently underneath the rainfall, as the first battle in Averon's history viciously began.

10

Doran sat inside a deserted Shadow Oak in front of the great tree, as they had planned. The trail which lead to the community had two more oak trees on both its sides, and it was beside these trees that two fresh rabbit tunnels had been burrowed. Doran was drenched with rain, cold, and now beginning to worry. Wickett had not passed through yet. He knew the conditions would make things worse, but surely the rabbit should have passed through by now? He felt the ground rumble as thunder clapped above the forest, adding to the fox's tension. Where is he? Suddenly Doran noticed a sodden grey animal rapidly approaching the clearing. He gave a small sigh of relief. Wickett sped towards him, down the trail and towards Shadow Oak. Doran rose to his feet and prepared for his role.

Behind the rabbit a dark shadow emerged, giving chase. Wickett had done his job. The generals were separated. As Wickett passed between the two trees he shouted "NOW!" and darted toward his comrade. Coinin and Sergeant Castor raised one end of a hefty stick at the left side of the trail; Apollo and Blits raised the other on the right-hand side. They pushed the stick toward the tree trunks so they wouldn't take the weight of the charging hound. Cameo didn't see the branch being raised, and violently tumbled over it as his paws were taken from beneath him. His impact snapped the branch, sending the rabbits tumbling onto the trail. Wickett veered away and avoided the rolling hound, quickly turning back to the trail and to his comrades. The rabbits rose quickly from the ground and disappeared into the safety of the newly-formed tunnels.

Cameo lay for a moment, wondering exactly what had happened, then jumped swiftly to his paws when he remembered what he was doing. The air was full of the musty scent of a fox, but not the one he'd been tracking moments before. Under the rain, a dog stood defiantly in front of him. Cameo looked at him, somewhat confused.

"What's the matter?" Doran asked sternly. "Were you expecting someone else?"

Cameo growled. "You're not the one I tracked."

"No. No, I'm not. I'm merely one fox you will hunt down and kill, unless we put a stop to you."

"Oh, and how do you intend to do that?"

"Remove the fear that you incite within our kind."

Cameo grinned. "You will always fear us. As long as you exist, we will hunt you. Now we are not bound by the rules implemented by the humans, we will kill you too."

"Can you really kill an animal that does not fear you? How will your reputation stand if I laugh and turn my back? Our kind has spent so long running from your armies, and all it would take is a show of unison to throw you into chaos and challenge your dominance."

"And you are brave enough to turn your back on me?"

"I do not fear you. I do not fear your kind. My mind is sharp. I have no need to run from you here." Doran turned his back on Cameo, showing him his greying, red sweep. Doran gave one final inviting glance over his shoulder, and vanished into the den underneath the great oak.

Cameo snarled at the embarrassment the fox had welled inside of him. He walked to the middle of the clearing.

"NOW!" Coinin shouted. Cameo span round rapidly and focused on the rabbit. He was ready to pounce, when he noticed movement in the branches up above.

The trees came to life, with a mass of grey squirrels all lining the intermittent branches and trunks. In their paws they clutched stones, small rocks, pine-cones and acorns. From the branches above heavy objects began raining down on Cameo, battering his lean body. Wave after wave of woodland debris crashed down upon him, opening wounds that began to bleed instantly. The army of squirrels pelted him from the safety of the leaves, relentless and unforgiving.

Cameo considered hiding in the den that the fox had entered, but knew now that he was in no condition to fight. He continued to be flogged, as the debris showed no sign of diminishing. More and more objects battered his now-injured body, slicing cuts and forming grazes as the hound darted around the clearing, trying to avoid the pummelling objects bestowed upon him from above. Fearing for his safety, Cameo turned and ran blindly out of Shadow Oak. The squirrels cheered as Cameo vanished into the forest, broken and humiliated. Doran emerged from the den as the rabbits joined him in the clearing. The chorus of cheers made Doran smile. He hoped that the rest of the animals had also been successful. Streak had been right. Ambushing the generals would be the greatest way to defeat the army.

"It worked! It worked!" Apollo shouted, leaping around the dens, boxing and jabbing his paws against an imaginary opponent.

"Not yet, we have to see if we can help the others," Wickett replied.

"No," Doran said seriously, "you have done your part. I'll go and check. Wait here until we return."

"But -"

"No, Wickett. You must stay here. There's no way of knowing what has happened out there."

Wickett nodded regretfully. "Streak was being tracked by the other hunter. They headed towards Treetop Hillstretch."

"That's not far away. Wait here, I'll see if I can help him."

Doran ran from Shadow Oak and headed in the direction Wickett had told him.

Baal walked through the trees. He didn't need to run anymore; the fox's scent lingered heavily in the air, which meant his foe was close. The rain pelted him tirelessly, and water dropped slightly from the edge of his ears and snout. He wandered into a small, grassy area surrounded by mounds that housed trees and bushes on top of them. The grass he passed over was cold and slippery in places, causing him to tread carefully as he followed his nose.

Streak appeared at the top of a small hill, looking down at the hound who had successfully tracked him. There was no more running. If Streak didn't put an end to this now, the hound would track him forever. Baal looked up and noticed the fox peering down upon him. They stood there a moment, glaring intently at one another. Baal expected to give chase once again, but to his surprise Streak carefully descended the hill and came to rest on the grass in front of him. The rain rattled the leaves and branches as the two enemies faced each other in the downpour.

"I've hunted many of your kind," Baal began. "Dogs, vixens - and you know what? Only one had ever escaped me before you did. I argue that, had I not been bound by the humans, I would have ventured into this forest and found you, caught you, and killed you. But, I had no way of convincing my army to follow me at such short notice." The two animals continued to stare at each another through the rainfall.

"This time is different. This time we have ignored the humans. This time the army follows my orders, and mine only. And it's this time that I now stand before you, having successfully hunted you into this fine forest."

Streak noticed Baal's milky eye glaring blindly upon him. For the first time, he noticed a familiarity with him. A picture of his mother flashed through his mind. He saw her being yanked from the den, but another image rapidly replaced it. He saw his paws relentlessly swiping as a hound pummelled his way through the entrance. He saw the canine shriek away in pain as he sliced his claws across its face. His claws snatched at the hound's eye, the same one that was now dysfunctional for the general ahead of him.

Baal had tried to kill him when he was a pup.

Baal was there when his mother was slaughtered.

Baal was blind in that lifeless organ because of him. Streak remembered what Cyrius had said at the council meeting. "He is the only one who has beaten the general not once, but twice before."

"You," Streak began, full of bitter rage. "You killed my mother. You yanked her from our den and threw her to the army." Baal looked momentarily confused as he tried to remember. "I attacked you as you attempted to get at me. I swiped you across your face!"

Baal remembered. His tongue licked the dark scar that curled away from his top lip. "You did this to me," he began softly, "and you escaped. That means you are the only fox that has ever escaped me."

"You killed my mother!"

"You escaped me!"

"YOU KILLED MY MOTHER!"

The two animals roared and charged at each other. Streak launched through the air and swiped once again at Baal's eye.

The battle raged on in the Great Vast Open. The muntjac kicked out viciously as the Dark Army bit and clawed their way through the animals. The foxes darted in different directions, confusing the hounds and disorientating them. The foxes swiped violently at their enemies whilst trying to avoid their jaws. Cyrius dive-bombed the hounds from above, injuring them with his talons and beak. Blood was spilling onto the meadow grass. Many animals were injured. The battle continued through the thunderstorm. Brock was stood on his hinds, swiping the hunters as they approached. He cheered and jeered them on. Flicar kicked a hound powerfully and sent him crashing into a group of hunters tackling a fox. The hounds swiped at their opponents. They clamped their jaws on the bucks, and savaged the foxes with their claws. Flicar began to lose hope as wave after wave of hounds descended upon them from the Great Vast Open. The hounds began working together and surrounding lone foxes and muntjac. They savaged them intently, their numbers giving them a huge advantage. Cyrius took flight and left the battle.

"NO!" Flicar screamed as the white barn owl vanished from the Great Vast Open. Brock stood tall, enjoying the challenge that the Dark Army thrust upon him.

Flicar became dejected in the battle field. They were outnumbered. The hounds were relentless in their slaughtering. Flicar's hope had vanished with Cyrius, but still he battled on, kicking and maiming the enemy with his hinds and antlers. He would have one last stand before the inevitable took hold.

Streak tumbled over Baal, who grabbed him viciously and thrust him to the ground. His teeth snapped at Streak's neck but were halted by a swift paw to his face. Baal lurched back, allowing Streak to jump to his feet and swipe him yet again. Baal launched at the fox, grabbing his midriff and sinking his claws into the muddy red fur. Streak yelped and bit at Baal's ear, tearing a small gash in the flapping skin. Baal shook free and swiped Streak across his shoulder, drawing blood. Both animals growled and pounced at each other yet again.

The Great Vast Open was engulfed in an intimidating thunderstorm. Many of the woodland animals were tiring and now battling injured, as the hounds took a great advantage. Flicar and Brock stood tall, knowing that soon they would be bestowed by the Dark Army and the battle lost. They found each other on the field and stood together in one final stand.

"If we're going to go, let's take as many as these evil creatures with us as we can!" Brock shouted.

Flicar simply smiled to himself, before they charged headfirst into the hounds for one, final battle. They kicked and swiped, bit and clawed the sea of darkness. The bodies of the hounds descended rapidly on top of them, wrestling them to the floor to take the final advantage. Flicar looked towards the sky one final time, before his vision was blocked and darkness took him...

Suddenly, over the thunder they heard a chorus of screams. They heard Cyrius hoot. The Dark Army halted. The woodland animals halted. From the treetops of Averon a huge fluttering cloud emerged, following the bright aura of Cyrius. It descended rapidly across the Great Vast Open. Flicar looked up from the parting hounds in amazement. It wasn't a cloud - it was kestrels! They weren't just a story! Cyrius had formed the legendary warriors, and was now leading them on to the battlefield!

From the border of Averon, a wave of colour exploded from the trees. It was Selwyn! He had led the pheasants out of the forest, and now they flew across the ground and into battle!

For the first time during a hunt, the hounds became scared. They watched in horror as the mass of birds left the trees and rapidly crossed the meadow. Flicar roared. The woodland animals cheered. The battle ignited once more; this time the hounds were bombed from above by the birds of prey, ruthless in their attack. They tore flesh from the hounds and sank their claws deep beneath their skin. The pheasants joined the foxes and muntjac, and engulfed the Dark Army with their vast numbers.

"Fall back! Fall back!" a hound ordered erratically. He turned and began sprinting across the meadow and back towards The Lodge. More followed.

Soon the entire Dark Army turned about and ran the great distance across the meadow, given one final chase by Flicar, Brock and Selwyn. The animals cheered as the army sped across the Great Vast Open and away from Averon. Rainan and Kaskar flew past the battlefield so quickly that none of the animals would have caught them if they had tried. The warriors looked on as the Dark Army fled the battlefield in defeat.

Streak and Baal suffered many lacerations. Baal had never fought a fox as strong and agile as Streak. Streak had never battled a creature as intense as Baal. They lashed out aimlessly, hoping to land a blow and injure one another. As they fought, Streak was kicked to the floor. The wind had been knocked from him. He lay there panting for breath, trying to subside the pain in his midriff.

"Streak?" came a concerned voice within the grass. He rolled over and saw the face of Tali looking back towards him.

"Tali?" he said in shock and anger. "Run! RUN!" The stubborn vixen had yet again ignored her peers, and this time placed her life in severe danger. Baal smiled as he saw the vixen freeze to her spot.

Easy.

He lunged through the rain, his jaws wide open. Tali turned away and closed her eyes. The general grasped fur within his teeth and shredded a huge wound from a moving body.

Baal thudded into the grass, knocked senseless and off-course. In front of him lay Doran, fatally injured. Doran panted rapidly as the huge wound in his side gaped open and allowed the rain to pour inside. Baal spat the furry flesh from his mouth and focused on Tali.

"DORAN!" she screamed as she ran over to him. "Doran! Doran!"

"He will die soon," Baal said in a soft and calm voice. "The injury he has is too great to recover from."

Streak rose to his paws slowly and looked upon Tali and his injured guardian comrade. "NO!" he screamed.

Streak launched at Baal, and relentlessly swiped the hound with his paws. He swiped, bit and shredded the hound, who could offer nothing in the way of retaliation. Blood seared from the hound as Streak relentlessly attacked his nemesis, wounding him deeply.

"Streak!" he heard Tali shout from his consciousness. "STREAK!"

A loud explosion echoed through the forest. Streak leapt back from Baal, and noticed he'd greatly injured the hound. Emerging from a thicket not far away emerged a human, his weapon poised and pointing at the foxes. The weapon appeared to be two bonded metallic pipes that could destroy them with a single explosion. The two barrels on the end were smoking slightly in the cold, damp air. The human slowly emerged into the area, the long grass hiding its feet. It looked down at Baal.

"Major," it said, and gestured away from the skulk. Baal turned and glared at Streak. Major was the name the humans used when they addressed him.

"If he doesn't kill you, I will," he croaked. "If you do not die now, I will lead my army upon your forest once again." He limped away behind the human, bleeding and broken. Cameo joined Baal in the greenery and together they vanished, two war-torn hunters whose battle was over. For now.

The human stepped closer, clad in its red fur and dark footing. Its weapon was raised and now pointed directly toward Streak. Streak had seen these weapons before. They fired something at their target with a loud bang, exploding body parts and ending lives. The human raised the weapon so that it was at eye level. The last thing Streak focused on was the rainfall between the human and himself. This was it. This was the end...

Seerles launched from the long grass and sank his fangs deep inside the human's right leg, causing him to scream out in agony. The human fell and dropped its weapon in the soaking grass beside him. Seerles released venom into the bite, causing the appendage to go numb almost instantly. He released his grasp and coiled on top of the weapon as the human writhed in agony, covering himself in mud and leaves. Seerles adopted an 'S' shaped attacking pose as the human reached for the weapon, and hissed. Struggling to its feet, the human backed away from the adder, limping heavily as he did so. The human knew that its life now depended on how quickly he could leave the forest and gain attention to the deadly wound. The conditions of the ground caused it to slip as it stumbled away, leaving its weapon and forgetting entirely the skulk of foxes it had been about to destroy.

The rain fell heavy on Doran as he was surrounded by the unlikely allies. Tali looked down upon him in despair. Streak looked on in disbelief. The patch of flesh that Baal had removed was big, and left a huge hole in the warrior's side. He panted uncontrollably as he lay there, waiting to die.

"This can't be happening!" Tali sobbed as her sibling lay helpless on the grass. "There must be something!"

Seerles moved closer to the fallen dog and raised his head to converse with the foxes. "There is one thing that can be done," he told her, his black tongue flickering from his mouth.

"What?" she asked despondently through streams of tears.

"I can help him. I can fulfil his health, but it will be at a cost."

"Do it!" Tali snapped immediately, unconcerned by the consequences.

"Tali," Streak began in warning.

"I don't care! Do it! What sibling would I be if I didn't offer my brother a chance at life! Do it!"

Streak looked at Seerles. "Stand back," the adder informed as he nestled beside the quaking body of Doran. The foxes did as they were told, their furs soaked and clinging firmly to their body as they moved.

"This is my fault," Tali began as Seerles prepared himself. "I should never have come back." Streak offered no reply. Knowing what to say was the hardest thing to do in this situation.

Seerles coiled and raised his thin dark body over Doran. He whispered something the foxes couldn't hear. His eyes began illuminating and growing brighter.

A moan echoed through the trees. The wind blew in gales. The rain crashed all around them. Lightning flashed. Thunder exploded. Darkness seeped from all corners, circling and waving its way to the fallen fox. Incantations emerged, and grew louder. Seerles swayed his dark body as if in a trance, still chanting underneath his breath. The darkness glided underneath the foxes as it drew upon Doran from all directions. Slowly it engulfed him, smothering him in darkness until he looked like a hound from the Dark Army, unrecognisable to his skulk. The darkness swirled on top of him and began disappearing inside his wound. It absorbed the darkness, his body drawing on it from the injury he had sustained. Doran emerged from the cloud as he had entered it, only now he seemed to be in a content sleep. The darkness poured deep inside his body, and as the final swirls glided softly over his fur, they bound the wound and vanished inside. The rain subsided. The moan vanished. Lightning flashed one last time. Seerles' eyes returned to normal. He lowered his body and curved himself down to look upon the face of the newly emerged fox. His eyes flickered underneath their lids as he slept.

Seerles turned to the foxes. "He's alive," he informed them. Tali ran over to her sibling. She looked down to see he wasn't panting anymore.

"Heed my advice, young vixen. The fox you once knew may not necessarily be the one you have saved. He is at the will of the darkness now. If he is not strong enough it will overpower him, and turn him toward the Black Lands."

"I don't believe it! You did this on purpose!" Streak shouted in disgust. Doran stirred. His head rose slowly and he rolled to his underside, shaking his head and opening his eyes.

"Tali? Streak?" he asked once he noticed the foxes beside him. For a moment, Streak forgot about Seerles. He thought back to the day when Doran and Tali had discovered him in the clearing. What goes around comes around,' he thought.

Tali smiled and muzzled his neck. "You're alive!" she shouted. "You're alive."

Doran looked at Streak with sheepish eyes. "What happened?" he asked quietly.

"We won," he replied to his guardian comrade. "We won."

Streak studied the area for Seerles. Not for the first time, the snake had vanished without a single trace.

Part 4

A New Threat

1

Bluebell Clearing was full to bursting with almost every single animal that dwelled within Averon. Only Akando and Seerles were absent in the mass celebration that was about to take place. In the middle of the vast field a huge log rose triumphantly from the dandelions and daisies. On top of the natural landmark, Kedem was joined by the warriors. The autumn day was warm and pleasant, and excitement rippled through the crowd of animals as they stood there waiting for Kedem to begin proceedings.

"My friends!" he shouted, subsiding the murmurs as the animals focused upon him. "My friends! Today is truly a most historic day in the history of Averon!" The animals hushed as Kedem launched into his victory speech.

"The Dark Army advanced upon us! It entered our borders and brought war to our homeland! With an almost impossible task of repelling an army so huge, we believed our fate fell within the hounds who hunted us!" Kedem looked down the line at the warriors. Tali looked up at them from her front row place on the grass below. "But a handful of animals believed otherwise! They believed they could fight for our freedom and repel the evil that darkened our forest! Those animals stand before you now upon this landmark! Those animals have led our numbers successfully in battle! No longer shall we fear for our existence to any impending fate which may try to bestow itself upon us! Let it be known, from this day forth, that an order of protectors has saved the forest and those who live within it! May this group be known as the forest's protectors in its hour of need! Whenever the need arises, our interests will be protected by this brave band of animals - the Warriors of Averon!"

A huge cheer erupted throughout the clearing as each animal showed its appreciation to the warriors. From the smallest mouse to the largest buck they cheered, admiring the bravery and fortitude shown by this handful of Averon dwellers. The warriors basked in the praise, Doran a little embarrassed, and looked out upon the sea of creatures they had sworn to protect. Selwyn puffed out his chest with pride. Brock looked down upon the entire badger sett, who were being led in their applause by Rebus. Flicar stood beside the log and felt the excitement pass through his body as the crowd cheered. Garla and the rest of the muntjac applauded the fact that he had unified a battalion of bucks and foxes and lead them into battle. General Lupus and Sergeant Castor stood upright and sternly saluted their Forest Guards on top of the log. The rabbits stood and smiled at the animals - all except Apollo, of course, who was bounding up and down with his paws in the air. He misjudged his placement on the dry bark, and after a moment of flapping about attempting to gain his balance fell backwards from his perch, thudding to the grass below. Tali laughed as he vanished from sight.

"Stupid boy!" General Lupus muttered to himself. The Forest Guards laughed and looked down upon Apollo from the horizontal log above. He lay laughing in the bluebells, and shrugged at them. Streak looked out in utter awe. This way of life had amazed him no end since he passed into Averon many days ago. For the first time in his life he felt accepted, a part of something that mattered, and knew from that moment on that Averon and Shadow Oak would play a huge role in his imminent future.

The moment belonged to those brave individuals that stood together through their adventure and emerged in victory.

"To the Warriors!" Kedem shouted.

"TO THE WARRIORS!" the crowd bellowed back.

And with that cheer, their adventures began.

2

Berry Hill truly was a majestic place by night. The trees below spread from horizon to horizon, and dipped unevenly as the contours of the land spread across the forest. The moon sat full and high in the chilly night, glowing brightly down upon Streak and Tali as they sat gazing upon it.

"This place is amazing," Streak said, smitten by the moon.

Tali smiled. "Better than walking?" she asked in amusement. Streak looked at her from the corner of his eye, and gave a wry smile.

"Hey! Streak! Tali!" came a familiar voice. Wickett bounded up the moonlit hill, followed closely by Kedem and his advisors.

"What are you doing here?" Streak gasped, trying to gesture that he was here with Tali. Wickett took no notice. "We've got great news!" he said enthusiastically.

"What's that?" Tali asked as she wandered over and sat next to Streak.

"Streak," Kedem began in a solemn voice, "we have been discussing your role at Shadow Oak. We know you have no family in the Great Vast Open, and after your help in defending our community, we would be honoured if you would become a part of ours?"

It had seemed the only way that Shadow Oak could show its appreciation. Streak had done what Kedem had failed to do. He had awakened belief within Doran that the greater good stretched far beyond the reaches of his own community, and now he was realising a whole world may be affected by a simple decision that he may inadvertently make. The smallest of decisions could have huge consequences within Averon, and now Doran understood. Doran had finally succeeded in all the tests Shadow Oak threw at him, and had now become a natural replacement to Kedem when he stepped down. Doran had emerged on the battlefield with a purpose that day, and stood defiantly in the face of the Dark Army. He had led the animals from the western border and successfully organised the ambushes Streak had imagined.

They had also asked Streak to stay in recognition for all he had done for Shadow Oak. He had done more since his arrival in the forest than any other animal in Averon. He had fought for their cause without question, and cemented his nobility without even noticing.

A wave of emotion swept through the lone fox. Finally, he would have his own place in the world, a place that now resided within the borders of Averon. He looked at Tali, who subtly nodded. He looked at Wickett, who was doing the same.

"I appreciate your offer," he began, "and I accept. Thank you, Kedem."

"Warriors," a familiar voice hooted from the darkness. The glowing aura of Cyrius fell from the stars and landed on the hill not far from Tali. He flapped his wings and rested them comfortably at his side.

"Cyrius, old friend. What can I do for you?" Kedem asked as his glow subsided.

"I am the bearer of bad news," he replied solemnly as he addressed the troupe.

"What might that be?" Streak asked in a calm but worried tone.

"There is unrest in The North," Cyrius began, "great unrest. Akando is rallying his soldiers to march upon the warriors and all who follow them. He intends to invoke fear within the fox communities of our forest."

"No," Kedem whispered, disheartened. A new foe now emerging from within?

"However, this is not the least of our problems. A huge, powerful beast has emerged from the Great Vast Open, and is now taking residence within our borders."

"A beast? Wickett asked with concern.

"Yes. A powerful black feline, larger and stronger than any creature you can ever imagine. It is a beast so vicious and immense that nothing thus far has been able to challenge it. You must be aware. The Great Council must be aware. If this beast decides to launch an attack upon the dwellers of the forest, it will be like battling the entire Dark Army in one nemesis."

"Can we stop it?" Streak asked, his eyes glowing in the moonlight.

Cyrius sighed. "As of yet, I fail to see a way to do so."

"And what of the Dark Army?" Kedem asked the glowing owl.

"They are broken, but one day they will return. They will come back for Streak."

Streak though as much. When you defeat your biggest nemesis in battle there will always be another day when you meet again. Always.

"Be warned, warriors. You're greatest test is yet to come. The first signs are emerging of the Great War, a war foretold by my ancestors over the ages. If the signs continue the war looks likely to emerge during our time, and will affect all the animals living within our forest. We must remain vigilant."

Cyrius left them and ascended quietly into the moonlit sky. His bright wings stretched out in a vast span and carried him far from Berry Hill and out of sight. Streak looked down to Wickett.

"It would seem our adventures are only just beginning," he said to the rabbit, his fur glowing in the moon's aura.

"Looks like the Warriors of Averon will form again," he replied.

The Beast

Part 1

Disbanded

1

Darkness covered the Great Forest as it rested silently in the midnight starlight. The clouds had vanished leaving a clear, still night that allowed the stars to twinkle brightly at anything that might have laid eyes upon them. The cold season had engulfed the lands and brought with it a vast mixture of weather and elements that should now have passed, allowing for the big thaw to set in.

However, this cold season had been unusually long, and as the animals that awoke from a long slumber of hibernation emerged, they were greeted with the unusual presence of the snowfall that had fallen relentlessly that very day. It rested undisturbed between the trees and on top of the woodland floor. It had fallen so heavily that even the densest part of the forest had at least seen a flurry and dusting as it fell throughout the Great Vast Open and beyond. Averon had felt the full brunt of the natural element, and now the forest rested gently in the darkness, save for the noise of a muntjac foraging between the trees for some food of his own. He had wandered away from his contingency in an attempt to find something to eat, but the berries and vegetation he had come accustomed to during the summer months had now dwindled and almost vanished, forcing the deer to be less choosy about his meal.

He wandered slowly between the trees in the darkness. The moonlight reflected the snow's white shade, allowing it to glow almost unnaturally, and offer more light than usual at any other time in the forest. He heard his hooves crunch loudly as they broke down into

189

the fresh, undisturbed snow, and saw his own breath leave his mouth every time he exhaled. The buck trotted on a little further and foraged a bush. Nothing.

As he turned, he felt a strange sensation he'd only felt a few times previously in his life. He froze momentarily and scoured his surroundings. The phosphorescent floor offered nothing in return. He opened his eyes wider and held his breath. He noticed his heart thumping in his chest.

He was being watched. He felt it.

The deer slowly breathed out, and once again watched his smoky breath swirl out into the freezing air. He heard nothing and could see nothing, but still he could feel it. He could feel eyes boring deep into his mind, cutting effortlessly through the flesh and bone to get there. The muntjac turned slightly around and darted his eyes over the mounds of snow and between the trees. Still nothing, but he most definitely could feel it. Something was watching him. Something was there.

He turned once more, his ears engaged and his eyes concentrating, searching the woodland for any reason of his nervousness. Still there was no movement, no noises, not even a gust of wind large enough to disturb the woodland's branches and leaves that surrounded him.

The moonlight glared down upon him, and he noticed to himself that the track that headed home to the contingency seemed brighter than any other path at that moment. There would be food if he desperately needed it, but his appetite had suddenly been suppressed and his instinct was telling him to leave. He turned around one last time and scoured the area. There was nothing out of place. There was no sign of disturbances, and no signs of life. The muntjac turned and began a slow trot back home. He picked up and followed his own hoof-prints along the path he had created on his journey this deep into the wilderness. He brushed tightly through a small coppice of ferns and back out to where the trail widened. The trees in this part of the forest became much further spaced apart, and easier to navigate in the cold night's darkness. The deer noticed the snow glowing wildly from the light above and also how brightly it had illuminated his path, bathing the forest in a dull orange and red glow.

He stopped rapidly. As he looked down into the snow, he noticed his own hoof-prints. Next to them lay a huge set of paw-prints indented into the tell-tale snow. His heart sank. What creature could make prints this big? Fear overcame the buck and he rapidly began sprinting away, his hooves thundering across the snow-covered ground. He darted through the forest, his breath held as his legs pounded through the cold air. A thunderous roar boomed through the trees behind the fleeing buck. He pushed himself faster as terror gripped him. A snarl from behind drew closer towards the terrified deer as he darted along the track. A final, terrifying roar engulfed the buck, and instantly his view changed to the full moon and the stars above.

The buck's body smashed into the cold floor as he was tackled from behind by an unseen enemy. His breath exhaled violently as he attempted to stand, but was again dragged down, thudding heavily into the snow and sending chunks of the element flying into the air. He felt his flesh tear and sting as sharp objects slashed down both sides of his back. A huge weight pounced upon him, and suddenly his throat was clamped shut by a powerful jaw. The muntjac squirmed in an attempt to break free and kicked out his legs rapidly, but the clamp remained firmly around his throat. He fought fearfully as he attempted to gain breath, gasping nothing but whispers of air as his struggle continued. Slowly, he began to feel sleepy. As the fight began to leave him and his struggle subsided, the weight shifted from his back but remained firmly clasped around his throat. It clamped down one last time, leaving the muntjac with a final image of the phosphorescent snow glowing around him. Once the deer had died the clamp was removed, and within seconds his blood had been shed and his innards strewn across the freezing snow.

A terrible fate had emerged within Averon, just as Cyrius, the guardian of the Great Forest, had warned. The terrible beast he had seen prowling within the Great Vast Open had now discovered his homeland, and with it the animals who dwelled there.

2

The snow had fallen vastly during the cold season and now had gripped and engulfed Averon with a firm, cold grasp. It fell harsh at times, light at others, but remained a constant reminder of just how cruel Mother Nature could be during this period.

The western border was no exception. In fact, it saw a great deal of the downpour as the eastern winds guided it from the Great Vast Open and into the trees. At times the snow was so deep that most animals dared not venture out for threat of losing their bearings and becoming lost.

Today was slightly different, though. The sky was clear blue without even a hint of a cloud in the fresh, crisp morning. The snow had begun to disappear, and General Lupus had deemed it safe to send his reconnaissance teams, or Forest Guards as they were more commonly known, to each of the borders of Averon on foot patrol. The security of his rabbits was of utmost importance to him, and he didn't believe in slacking from his duty if there was no good reason to do so.

Apollo and Blits had been sat on a rock for most of the morning, at the furthest reaches of the border. They sat looking out into the Great Vast Open at the fallen snow and noticed how it blanketed the fields and meadows in one simple shade of white. They noticed drops of water dripping away from the branches of the trees and bushes as the snow slowly began to melt away. Apollo had spent most of the morning digging around in the element, looking for a long blade of grass to chew upon instead of keeping a lookout for anything suspicious. He had finally found one he deemed suitable, and now that blade of grass dangled from the corner of his mouth and rotated quickly as he chewed on it.

"You think this is it? The last time the snow will fall before the warm season gets here?" he asked methodically.

"I don't know," Blits replied. "Maybe? We seem to have been in this season for longer than usual."

Apollo nodded. "Yep. I hope so. I don't know how much more of this chill my hide can take," he said, taking a quick look over his right side and ruffling his tail to remove the rogue snow that had inconspicuously nestled there.

"What are you talking about?" Blits said in a confused voice. "You're a rabbit. You're supposed to be enduring the cold season with ease. You're supposed to laugh in the face of anything that it can throw at you."

Apollo continued chewing his blade of grass. "Not me," he said, straight and to the point. "Give me a warm chamber and fresh berries over patrolling these trees at this precise point in time."

Blits shook his head and returned his attention to the Great Vast Open. He could only see the occasional break of darkened bushes or trees out there; the West was otherwise completely hidden under a blanket of white.

"You don't see old Lupus or Castor patrolling much these days, do you?" Apollo said with the grass churning in his mouth.

"I'd be careful how you address them. If word gets back that you didn't call them by their rank, you'd be strung up by your tail. Besides, they've done it all before. They've patrolled these trees long before we even existed."

"Exactly. Do you think that maybe they are getting too old? They seem to be full of grey hares!"

"What do you mean, grey -" And then it struck him. Apollo was a fine Forest Guard beyond question, but joke teller? There was no-one worse in the entire warren or Averon, Blits thought silently to himself. Apollo began laughing uncontrollably.

"Terrible. That was terrible. You get worse, you know," Blits said shaking his head and rolling his eyes. Apollo stopped laughing, and then started again. Then stopped. Then sniggered. "How did you end up being a Forest Guard?" Blits asked with intrigue.

"Oh, I don't know," Apollo began, still amused with himself. "Last I heard, Sergeant Castor took me in after finding me under a fern."

Apollo was struck by a huge mound of snow and sent toppling backwards off the rock. He let out a groan as the snow smashed him and sent him thudding to the freezing ground. Blits turned to see Wickett and Coinin hopping over the snowfall towards them.

"What are you two doing?" Wickett asked as they made their way over. Apollo jumped up and began brushing away the snow that clung to his fur. "You've got a job to do. If Sergeant Castor caught you sitting down on the job, he'd string us up -"

"By our tails," Apollo said, repeating Blits' words from only a moment earlier.

"Right," Wickett said, looking at his friend. "I need you both pulling together for our team. We'll get split if anyone finds out about this and I will get diced if they find out I let you carry on like this."

Apollo brushed his right foot down. When he finished, he pointed it at Wickett and shook it gently. "Don't worry. We have our lucky charms."

"Apollo, this is serious," Coinin began. His fuse was a lot shorter than Wickett's. "We're a team. We've been through a lot together, and I don't want us split up because of your tomfoolery."

Apollo placed his foot back in the snow and sighed. "We were just setting up to look out into the Great Vast Open," he said, this time seriously, the grass now missing from his mouth. "We patrolled all the way to the tip of the southern border, like you said, and we were setting up here to wait for you both."

Wickett sighed. "Okay, that's all I needed to know," he said softly. Coinin cast more of a doubt on his story than Wickett did, but although he would never admit it, he liked working in this group and didn't like the thought of being re-stationed to another border patrol. "Come on - let's go check the Great Vast Open, and then we're done."

The rabbits followed Wickett's lead until they left the trees and stood a foot or two inside the meadow that signified the beginning of the Great Vast Open.

Blits could feel the bright sun attempting to warm him through the bitter cold air as they stood, scouring their surroundings. They darted their eyes left and right and engaged their ears to pick up any sounds unfamiliar to the area.

"Look," Apollo said, and gestured along the right-hand side of the forest. Walking along its border was a human, clad in a thick coat of seemingly black fur. It kicked up the snow erratically as it trudged unknowingly towards them. In its hand a red line extended downwards. On the end of the line walked a creature very familiar to the Forest Guard. It was a hound.

"It's a hound!" Blits shouted, stating the obvious.

"Wait," Coinin said calmly, settling Blits. He looked on intently as the pair slowly made their way towards them. "It is a hound, but it's not from the ranks of the Dark Army. It's too light."

The hound was almost the same shade as the snow it ploughed through, except for a patch of black across its head, its side and on its back. The canine wandered closely to its master's legs, its tongue swaying from its jaw as it trotted. The dog looked up into the chilly air ahead as it followed the track with no conscious thought of navigation. Its breath plumed out in front of its muzzle as it wandered beside its owner, panting in the cold air as it took the light exercise of a walk. As the hound wandered it began aimlessly looking around, catching many scents and smells that stimulated its nostrils and forced it to take notice. It picked up a scent unfamiliar but not too far away in the distance, and then spotted them. Its gaze fixed firmly upon the Forest Guard as he moved closer, his jaw now shut and his ears engaged, the human none the wiser.

"Um, I think maybe we should leave now," Blits said, turning to head back inside the forest, noticing that they'd been spotted. The human had now stopped and was kneeling beside the canine that still firmly eyeballed the Forest Guards.

"No, don't worry," Apollo said as he looked on intently. "It's restrained by the line. The human's tightening it up now."

"I don't think he's tightening it!" Wickett shouted. The hound exploded from its position and thundered across the snow towards the rabbits.

"RUN!" Coinin screamed. The rabbits shot away into the forest and ploughed through the snow as rapidly as it would allow them. They heard the human shouting at the top of its voice somewhere in the distance. The hound kicked up plumes of snow as it tore across the element and rapidly descended upon the rabbits.

Wickett took the lead as they entered the dense shrubs between the trees. His vision blurred slightly as he bounded up and down through the depths of the freezing snow. "COME ON!" he shouted behind him.

The Forest Guards followed closely but were hampered by the vast amount of snow engulfing the forest. It struck Apollo head-on as Coinin's feet thrust it backwards, but still he ran. The hound pounced into the entrance they had taken and quickly saw them in the distance disappearing into the trees. It gave chase rapidly and began hunting them down. The rabbits bounded over rocks, logs and hidden bracken as they followed Wickett's wake. He was leading them to their closest tunnel, which was found in the Western Clearing. The hound leapt the low branches and ploughed through the shrubbery as though it didn't exist. The snow exploded from the leaves as it pushed through, gaining on the guards.

"STICK WITH ME!" Wickett ordered. The rabbits ran tightly as he led them through the trees, over roots and small mounds. Apollo could now hear the panting as the hound drew closer. The clearing drew closer. The trees seemed to shrink and narrow their escape route. The panting grew louder. The clearing closer. Louder. Closer. Louder...

They shot into the open and continued their sprint. Blits looked back. The hound was upon Apollo! Apollo glared at his friend. "APOLLO!"

The hound lurched violently and veered rapidly away to its left, tumbling and cracking the snow as it rolled relentlessly through the cold opening. It jumped to his feet and adopted an attacking stance. It growled intently as it stood looking firmly upon a defiant fox. The fox looked bright against the bland background of the clearing, his dark paws rooted firmly inside the snow. He snarled at the canine, proving to his opponent that he was not intimidated. His vibrant eyes glared from his red face, the white dash of fur through his left eye creasing in rage. "That's the last mistake you will ever make!" the hound snapped at the defiant fox.

The fox simply raised his brows in return and looked beyond his enemy. The hound turned and noticed another fox stood behind him, his grey fur showing the remnants of un-cleared snow between its strands. The hound looked back and forth between them. It growled. The foxes stood firm. They began circling, expecting a fight to ensue at any moment. They stalked almost in unison as the hound flicked its eyes between the both of them. Its chest rumbled as its agitation grew and it surveyed the situation.

"Today's your lucky day!" the hound replied, before finally dashing away in defeat from the dogs, leaving the clearing rapidly and momentarily silent for those who now stood there.

"Streak! Doran!" came a jubilant voice moments later. They looked over to see Wickett leading the rabbits to their warrior comrades.

Streak smiled. "Wickett. Coinin. Apollo. Blits," he said, acknowledging them all individually. "How are you all? It's been a while."

"Oh, thank you. Thank you, thank you, thank you, thank you..." Apollo trailed off.

"Still getting yourself into scrapes, I see?" Doran asked him humorously.

"Comes with the territory," Apollo replied in a tough-for-show voice.

Streak laughed at him. "Let's head back out to the border," he began. "We'll check and make sure the hound is gone for sure."

The small reunion of warriors headed in unison towards the border under the tight grip of the cold season.

199

Everywhere was covered with snow, from the tops of the trees to the rogue flakes that had miraculously drifted into the tunnels and warrens of the Great Forest. Every gust of wind, no matter how small or how immense, seemed to blow with a thousand icicles cutting sharply away at anything that stood defiantly in its path.

"You need to inform General Lupus that a Great Council meeting is to be held very soon," Doran informed the rabbits as they made their way through the cold snow and back out towards the border.

"Why? What's happening?" Wickett asked as he ambled alongside Streak.

"You haven't heard?" Streak asked.

"No. Nothing," Coinin replied.

"A creature has been attacking the muntjac and larger animals here in the forest," Doran began as he relayed events to the rabbits. "But it's no ordinary creature. It's very elusive and hard to track. Garla has lost many of her contingency to the beast, and now Flicar is calling a council to discuss how to deal with it."

"That's bad..." Wickett trailed off.

"What type of creature is it?" Blits asked as he hopped into a patch of undisturbed snow.

"We don't know," Doran replied hastily. "We think it has to be a creature from outside the forest to be able to bring down a fully-grown muntjac by itself and shred it beyond recognition. No animal born of these trees has the power or the ability to do such a thing."

Wickett looked up at Streak. "Do you think it's the creature that Cyrius warned us about?" he asked.

"Yes," he said as he slowly nodded. "I think it is."

"That's why the meeting has been called. Cyrius has some information to share with us, although not much it has to be said," Doran informed them.

"Like what?" Apollo asked.

Doran smiled at him. "It is not my position to say. Just make sure you're all at the meeting, and you will find out."

The warriors emerged once more upon the border and returned the rabbits to the position they had been in when scouting the Great Vast Open. They all looked across the meadow and away into the distance.

Streak noticed something unusual in the vastness out there. "Do you have scouts out there already?" he asked Wickett as they stood in the chilly open.

"No, we -"

Just then, he saw it too. Three sets of ears emerged from the snow away in the distance, and vanished once again. Then another set further over to the right. They looked like rabbit ears...

"That's exactly what we're scouting for!" Wickett informed them with authority.

"What?" Doran asked.

"Hares," Coinin whispered as he focused on the emergence of yet more ears.

"What are they doing?" Streak asked, almost in the same whisper.

"The same as us. They're scouting," Wickett replied.

"Scouting for entrances to our warren," Blits added.

"Why do they need to know that?" Doran asked.

"Every so often the hares mount a charge on our dwellings," Coinin informed the dog. "They invade our warren and stay there until they have depleted our food and supplies. During their first attack on us many seasons ago they burrowed our tunnels and chambers, making them large enough for the hares to move through. They know it's a place they can shelter inside easily; that's why they return. Many great battles have been held here as we've attempted to repel their armies. Sometimes we win, sometimes we lose, but the earlier we spot their threat the better prepared for them we will be."

"That's what we patrol for," Wickett added.

Streak looked on as the hares regrouped out in the snow and dashed away into the open. "We have another invasion to report," Apollo said quietly.

3

The Black Lands sat undisturbed under a sheet of even, crisp snow. The dark trees protruded gently from their dusting, making the woodland seem even more barren and desolate. Even the white cloud that had covered the forest did not seem to spark any signs of life within the limbs and leaves of the stretching branches and leaves. The open area once trodden by the warriors now lay motionless in the chilly air. It lay undisturbed for a moment more until a set of dark paws finally crunched through its fresh layer and brought a welcome sign of sound to the barren landscape. Akando stood in front of the haunted forest as Streak and Doran had done merely a few seasons ago, and he too had brought his own party of followers to help assist him in his quest. Lyro undoubtedly stood by his side, a dog who had sworn to follow his leader until the bitter end. Six other foxes also joined their band as they bore upon the darkened forest that lurked eerily upon them.

"He will answer, or he will die," Akando said in his low voice to Lyro. Lyro's vibrancy stood out boldly against the colourless snow. His red fur was one complete shade and bore no signs of greying anywhere through his coat.

"Will he entertain us?" the colourful fox asked.

"Yes, he will. He knows we're coming, and he knows what we are capable of." Akando smiled at Lyro. "He knows what we will do."

The skulk of warrior foxes showed no fear as they entered the trail that led through the darkened trees. They wandered through, alert and aware of every single cry and shree that engulfed their ears over the sound of their paws treading the untouched snow. The cobwebs between the trees still hung defiantly in the face of the cold season, and twinkled with the remnants of condensation hanging from their strands. The gnarly bark and twisted branches of the trees reached out and upwards, beckoning at them to continue their journey. Lyro noticed dark swirls of mist emanating from the trees either side of the trail. It glided swiftly above the dusting of snow and then down to engulf the trail rapidly. It plumed away as the band of foxes moved purposefully through the decaying landscape. Some of the foxes in Akando's wake became unnerved as they continued on. "He knows we are here," Akando began, as if sensing their concern. "Stay focused." The dogs continued wandering the decaying trees and toward an opening ahead of them. As they approached the clearing they noticed eyes popping open from within the woodland, their red tint glinting brightly in the right light.

"Rats..." Lyro said as the woods came to life with an army of thousands of eyes, all watching with interest as another band of animals once again breached their homeland. The eyes lined on either side of the trail, watching the warriors continue with their journey. The foxes showed no cause for concern as they passed through the infested trees. One rat stood taller than the others and grinned as they passed. Akando threw him a harsh look before returning his gaze to the path ahead, ignoring the darkened rodent as he strolled defiantly past.

They exited the tree-line and went out into a circular clearing. Ahead of them lay a mound of jagged rocks, slightly dusted with snow where it was able to settle. Akando stopped and gestured to his followers to do the same. Lyro nodded and held the warriors back, allowing his leader to continue forward alone. As Akando moved slowly into the desolate opening, he noticed bones and fur from animals long destroyed secretly protruding from the snow upon the ground. He took care with his steps and slowly came to rest in front of the rocks.

'I've been expecting you.'

"Then you know why I have journeyed here," Akando replied to the elusive creature.

'You've come to ask why I did it.'

"Yes, I have. Why would you meddle in my affairs when you knew what I was planning?"

'I knew nothing.'

"Don't give me that!" Akando snapped. "You know everything that happens in these trees!"

From the entrance between the rocks the serpentine body of Seerles emerged, his head rowing gently as he propelled himself forward. The dark markings that resided upon his scaly back looked even more dramatic in comparison with the white glare of the colourless snow. Seerles was one of the creatures within the forest that slept for the duration of the cold season in hibernation. During this time his lair was protected by Rogo, the scrawny rat who led his armies of both rats and foxes taken by the darkness that dwelled within the Black Lands.

"I know only what the darkness will show," the adder said as he glided into the snow and in front of the visiting dog. His head rose on his limbless body to look at Akando directly.

"You knew my plan, and you interfered. You, of all creatures," Akando replied, fused with anger.

"Settle down; this may play in your favour."

Akando snarled and swiped the serpent with his claw, knocking Seerles to the snow. The stunned adder did not have time to react as the fox placed a heavy paw on his scaly body behind his head, keeping the snake's head sideways up and immobile. Seerles' rage grew and his eyes burned red. His fangs quickly exposed and began trickling venom as his body squirmed and coiled around the fox's paw and leg.

"You know what I always wondered?" Akando asked in a harsh, deep voice. "I wonder what will happen if the lord of the darkness himself is killed, and there's no other creature in the entire forest that can control it enough to bring him back?"

Seerles hissed and then muttered an eccentric laugh. "Why don't you try it and see for yourself?"

Akando snarled and pushed down harder, causing the serpent to open his jaws wider and gasp out. "Maybe I will."

"Or you can listen to the plan I have for Doran and Shadow Oak that involves you," Seerles hissed.

Akando slightly relaxed his grip on the serpent. "What plan?" he asked inquisitively but sternly.

"Release your paw and I will tell you," the reptile replied.

Akando hesitated for a moment, thinking things through in his mind. "If you try anything, Seerles, I will slaughter you immediately."

He pushed down on the snake harshly, causing Seerles to gasp one last time, and then released his paw, allowing the coiled, darkened body to release from his leg and drop to the snow. Lyro and the warriors looked on from a safe distance. Seerles gained his composure and coiled his body upright to Akando's eye level once again.

"You can have the fox you so desperately desire," Seerles hissed. His eyes had returned to their normal shade, but it was clear that anger was still prominent within them.

"How? He is now under your control."

"Not quite," the adder replied, "but soon he will be. He is fighting the darkness that now resides firmly within his mind, but slowly it takes him, and soon enough he will be under my command. His will is strong - stronger than any animal I have ever cursed before - but his demise has begun, and it will only be a matter of time before he returns here to the Black Lands."

"And how does that help me?" Akando asked, his patience wearing thin.

"Think about this; what would you do with an army of foxes all under your control?"

Akando didn't answer. He simply looked upon his adversary with studious eyes. Seerles began slithering around his rock patch.

"The answer is anything," he said looking back at Akando as he moved. "With an army of foxes that would eclipse the warrior numbers from Shadow Oak, you could take from them whatever you wanted."

"How am I going to convince more foxes to follow me? No other seems to see the damage that Kedem and the Great Council is inflicting upon this forest. I am seen as the enemy to them, and will not convince any free-thinking fox anywhere in Averon to follow me."

Seerles stopped and looked upon him. "I don't recall mentioning anything about 'free-thinking' foxes?"

Akando realised exactly what Seerles was proposing. His eyes narrowed and he gave the sign of a smile. A look of confusion then crossed his face. "How do I know I can trust you? And what do you want in return?"

Seerles flicked his tongue rapidly and slithered back toward Akando. "You can take whatever you want from within this forest," he began, "and in doing so sweep fear completely throughout its trees. I thrive on fear and chaos -"

"And with it you will become the greatest fear to all who dwell within the forest of Averon."

Seerles nodded. "Yes," he hissed, "and our alliance will answer to no-one."

Akando smiled at his new ally. "What shall I do?" he asked.

"Round up as many as you can. Bring them here. I will do the rest. But do not attract the attention of the Great Council. They will attempt to stop us if they find out what we are doing. The more we can do silently, the greater our achievement will be."

Akando nodded. "I know what to do, but it must start immediately. You must do what you need with them as quickly as you can. I will release my warriors to begin capturing the foxes and delivering them to you."

"And I will order Rogo and his army to assist your warriors with this task," Seerles replied. Akando turned to see the dark rat in question emerge into the opening. "When you send word from your council," Seerles began in a malicious, evil tone, "your very own army will advance, and your grip over the forest will tighten."

Akando grinned evilly. "Then our war can commence," he replied.

4

Shadow Oak was virtually empty during the cold season. The snow usually sent its inhabitants deep into their dens to avoid the chills and freezes it brought with it, and only the strongest dogs were called upon to gather food for the community. The great oak that housed the community's main den underneath its roots had glistened brightly during the cloudless day, allowing the sun to warm the snow. Slowly it had melted and fell slightly to ground, but now the rolling snow clouds had passed overhead-once again, and a light flurry of snow had begun to flutter down from the high clouds above. Only the strongest representatives of the Great Council had journeyed under these conditions; to represent their species, but also to represent themselves.

The council peninsula hosted the mass of woodland animals that made the Great Council, with the lake behind them frozen solid at its edges. The middle of the lake seemed to be as usual, with the gentle lap of water faintly carried towards them on the cold wind. Most animals were represented and present, including General Lupus and Sergeant Castor, who sat atop their large rock with the rabbits of the Forest Guard. Arley and Selwyn faithfully journeyed through the elements to represent the pheasants, and Glif had been accompanied by two squirrels to ensure her safe passage to the great meeting after their emergence from hibernation. Danjo and Pea-pod were the two squirrels in the drey she presided over that she trusted the most. Shadow Oak was represented by Doran, Streak, Jinx and Delfin, with their leader Kedem hosting the meeting once again. The badger sett was represented by Rebus, the joint head of the Great Council, and by Brock within the misshapen circle of animals. He was joined also by Linus, another warrior from their sett.

Also making the cold journey was Dallie, the leader of the otter contingency within Averon. She had been joined by two companions Chance and Checkers, also accompanying her to see safe passage to and from Shadow Oak. The tribal leader Akando and his foxes from The North were this time missing, no doubt due to his outburst and denial of assistance at the previous meeting. The final animals that made the meeting in these harsh conditions were Garla and Flicar, the muntjac who had initially requested to hold the council session. The animals had heard stories of a new threat prowling the trees during the cold season, and believed that now was the time it would be clarified one way or the other. As usual, a sentry of trusted animals kept guard outside the peninsula to keep away any prying ears that could leak information to the rest of the woodland before the council could address them. Shadow Oak served as a resting place for any animals who had undertaken the journey but who were not involved directly with the meeting, but on occasion some who stayed there had attempted to sneak closer to the council meeting and see if they could find out anything of interest. There were groups of foxes, badgers, squirrels, otters and rabbits who loitered within its frozen clearing, but far fewer compared to the last meeting that had been held when the sun was high during the warm season.

"This meeting has been called on behalf of Garla and Flicar, as a threat has arisen that may affect all of our clans, tribes and communities," Kedem began as he opened the session. Streak looked on as his words brought silence over the chatter amongst the settling representatives. The animals turned their focus on to the council leaders as they began to pay attention. Streak felt the sharp gust of cold wind that had begun to cut deeply at his fur. Although the animals were used to living in such harsh conditions in the forest, sometimes the elements did throw an occasional gust of wind or temperature drop that quickly attacked their bodies and made them shiver. Streak felt this one fairly harshly, and thought if it got much colder or sharper it may slice the trees in half.

"Akando?" Wickett asked, remembering the conversation he held on top of Berry Hill during the remnants of the warm season. Some of the animals looked upon the open, vacant rock that had been Akando's place within the council.

"No," Kedem replied. "The threat is focused firmly upon the muntjac, but will most definitely affect our own kinds as well."

Rebus looked over to Garla. "Please," he asked in his authoritative voice.

Garla trotted slowly but gracefully to the centre of the circle to address the Great Council. The light flurry of snow had begun to fall a little heavier now, but still it remained fluttery and eccentric as it flickered to the floor. Garla looked at the ground momentarily, as if struggling with what she would have to say. The strange, dark marking on her face and muzzle stood out tremendously against the falling snow. The council representatives finally fell completely silent as she started to speak.

"A new threat has invaded our trees," she began in a solemn tone. "This cold season we have lost nearly twenty of our kind to an invisible predator strong enough to destroy a muntjac on its own."

A sigh of concern swept throughout the listening animals. Rebus leaned forward, paying close attention to the doe. Doran and Streak looked at one another. Doran raised his brow slightly.

"Please continue, Garla," Rebus stated as he hushed the council once more.

"We have a creature amongst us that can shred the largest animal in this forest within seconds. The bodies of our communities have all been..." Garla stopped as emotion overcame her. The community she had sworn to protect was now at the mercy of a killer who had yet to show itself or any signs of weakness. She sighed and looked at the snow-plastered ground once again.

"They've all been torn to pieces, some so severe that we don't even know or recognise our own deer," Flicar interrupted. He made his way to the centre of the circle, and after a moment or so agreed with Garla to continue on in her place. The doe returned to her stone and gave the council permission for Flicar to speak on her behalf. "Nearly twenty of our kind, eighteen to be correct, have fallen by this beast. Eighteen. And we don't even know what it looks like."

"Is it maybe a pack of beasts instead of one solitary creature?" Dallie asked. Her smooth, shiny fur rested immaculately against her skin. Having spent most of their time in freezing waters within the forest, the three otters did not feel the least bit cold in the deteriorating conditions.

"I do not believe so," Flicar began. "There would surely be more signs of their presence if there was a group of them within these borders."

"And I believe you would have seen them by now," Rebus stated. "We are coming to the end of the cold season. Our friends are now awake once again," he said in recognition to all those who hibernated during the cold months, "and if these attacks have been ongoing since it started, by now all of us would have found more evidence of a pack rather than a lone hunter, even those who slept most of the season."

The snow continued on its flurrying fall to the ground. A lone flake came to rest upon Apollo's nose. He flapped it away rapidly. "We stand before the Great Council to ask for your help and assistance in vanquishing this creature before it can kill anymore of our kind, but also before it begins attacking the rest of the animals that dwell here. Please?" Flicar asked, being blunt.

"Flicar, Garla. You will have full support of the council, no matter how great the task at hand," Kedem replied, without a moment's hesitation. "We will help you, but our first task is to find out how to defeat this immense beast you speak of."

A shree bellowed from the sky above. It pierced the winds that gusted around the council and engulfed the entire peninsula. From above the lake a star fell gracefully and floated above the frozen waters. Brightly it drew closer, its aura engulfing the trees and snow-covered elements. Many of the animals turned their eyes or shaded them as the star landed inside the council next to Flicar. As the glow subsided a proud barn owl emerged, brilliant and white.

"Cyrius," Doran said as the glow gently vanished, leaving the animals with the grey daylight and clear snowfall once more.

"The creature that is destroying your communities has simply become known as 'the beast' amongst all who dwell within the Great Vast Open, not just yourselves," he hooted as he came to rest.

"What is the beast?" Glif asked the owl, having heard stories of such a creature over the many seasons.

"It is a huge, feline animal that has travelled from beyond the Great Vast Open. It is a vicious and lethal warrior that hunts for food tirelessly, and has found everything it needs within our Great Forest."

"If it has found its way across the Great Vast Open, where did it come from?" Kedem enquired.

Cyrius flapped his wings gently and turned to Kedem. "No creature knows for sure where it originates from. Some say it once belonged to a human and escaped its enclosure, where others suggest it has been here all along," he began informatively. "The beast has lived outside our trees for many seasons, and has sparked a great interest within the humans, as it should not exist in these lands. There have been many stories told of humans who hunt the creature, and some who even question its existence. It has remained one step ahead of its hunters and survived many human attacks, and done so for many, many seasons. It has also been nomadic in its territories, as nowhere has been able to accommodate its needs."

"Until now," Flicar stated quietly.

Cyrius turned to him. "Until now," he repeated. "Within Averon it has found everything it needs; shelter from the elements, fresh water, and food."

"With everything it needs in one place, chances are it's not going to go away," General Lupus replied.

"Indeed," Cyrius began. "It is here to stay." Flicar looked away in disbelief. Rebus sat back and sighed.

"There must be a way?" Flicar asked in a dejected voice. "There has to be?"

"How about Seerles?" Doran asked the council. "He helped me when I needed it. Why wouldn't he do it again? His bite has been known to kill humans. Why wouldn't it work on this beast?"

"Seerles is too complicated to involve," Cyrius replied to the warrior fox. "Yes, he did help us defeat the Dark Army and heal your wounds, but he has existed in the darkness for as long as I have brought light to the forest. I would not trust him on an occasion such as this. This time he has nothing to lose with the beast entering our border. Involving him may be even more dangerous than you may think."

"Then what?" Rebus asked, and raised his paws upwards. "We cannot fight it as it's too strong. We cannot negotiate with it. We cannot enlist the help of Seerles or any other creature within Averon as no animal, or group of animals, can match the beast for its strength. Where do we turn?"

A twinkle glittered in Cyrius' eyes. "There is one possibility," he said, with a sparkle of hope in his voice.

"What is it?" Brock asked, the striped boar hearing the change within Cyrius' words.

"Across the Trail Of Fallen Stars, deep within the Haunted Woods, lies an element unlike any other within the forest," the wise oracle began. "It is an oak tree, stood solitary on a small island within a huge lake." The animals looked on as Cyrius explained his theory. "It is said that the tree is a living creature, just like us. Legend has it that it is indeed the very heart of Averon, the one tree that will always keep our forest alive as long as it stands and is kept safe from any threat."

"How will a tree assist us?" Kedem asked, remembering the stories he'd heard of this tree from a distant past.

"Not the tree, Kedem - the one who protects it."

"A protector?" Rebus asked.

"Indeed," the wise owl began. "Someone much like Seerles; only this creature is bound to use his knowledge and power to protect the forest and ensure the safety of the oak by living within its branches. He is a powerful force within his forest, and he will know what we must do to outsmart the beast and force it from our homeland."

Kedem looked to Garla. "If it's true, he can show us how to deal with the threat of the beast lurking within our trees," he answered, following the barn owl's line of thought.

"If ," Garla added sceptically.

"How do we know he will help?" came Doran's voice from the listening circle of animals. "The warriors undertook a similar journey to seek the advice of Seerles, only to be turned away. We crossed the Trail of Fallen Stars and engaged in a battle with his minions, placing our lives in serious danger. Is it worthwhile endangering our lives yet again?"

"He will help," Cyrius replied confidently. "He has the most important duty within the whole of Averon. He protects its life-force, ensuring that no matter what, our forest will always live."

"And where might we find him?" Dallie asked, her sleek fur beginning to miss the lake from whence she came.

"There is only one way to get to the lake and to the oak tree he guards. You must journey through the Forest of the Damned."

"The forest!" Rebus exclaimed with surprise.

Cyrius nodded slowly. "Yes. The only way in and out is along a single, solitary track that leads through the heart of the Damned."

"The Forest of the Damned? It exists?" Doran asked with an element of confusion lingering from his voice. "I thought it was just an old ghost story, told to us when we were young?"

"No, brave dog," Cyrius began in a threatening, warning, voice. "The stories you hear are very much true. The forest does indeed exist."

The council again rallied into a subtle chorus of conversation and concern, forcing Kedem to restore order.

"What is this forest you speak of?" Streak asked as the hush began to subside. Not being born within the trees of Averon, he knew nothing of its legends and lore.

"It's a forest of damnation," Cyrius replied sternly. "It is stuck between the realm of the living and the realm of the dead. It does not exist in either plains, but it does exist." Streak was still as confused as when he asked the question.

"Legend has it that when an animal dies within these woods and has done so before the realm of the dead is ready to take them, they become banafrits, lost souls, and are forced to wander the forest until the time comes that they can pass over," General Lupus informed him.

"They are Damned," Doran stated in agreement. "They can go nowhere until the time is right. Doomed to wander the trees and woodland for however long it takes."

"Because the forest exists between two realms, it stands in its own existence. This means that great perils and dangers are imminent for all who attempt to wander its track," Rebus began. "It is the most dangerous and hostile area within the entire Great Forest of Averon. Countless expeditions have entered there over the seasons, and none have ever returned."

"Then this is a journey from which we hold no hope of returning," Doran added. For the briefest of moments the council was engulfed in silence as the reality of the situation settled in. The animals watched on under the snowfall and could see Rebus deciding upon his next move.

"Why can't you just fly over to him, Cyrius, and say, 'Hey, erm, protector. Can you tell me how to save the forest from the beast, please?'" Apollo asked. He thought it sounded quite a plausible request as he sat upon the rabbit's rock.

"Idiot," Coinin whispered underneath his breath.

"If I were able to, I would be making that very journey," Cyrius replied to the Forest Guard, "but I'm afraid I'm of no use to you on this occasion. The trail that leads through the forest is the only path that will lead you to the oak tree, and to the one you must seek. You must complete the trials. You must navigate the forest, and only then can you find the lake in which the island resides."

"But how will the protector help us?" Flicar asked Cyrius. "What can he do to stop the beast attacking my kind?"

"He lives within the realm of the dead," the owl began, "and he knows everything about the strange and ghostly entities that prowl throughout both realms. He is a master of the occult. He uses strange and powerful beliefs and magic to protect our forest from the safety of his own realm."

"Well he's not doing a very good job, is he? What with the Dark Army first, and now this beast waltzing through Averon," Apollo replied.

"Shut up, boy!" General Lupus snapped back at him. "This is serious!"

Apollo waited until General Lupus turned back to the council and then stuck out his tongue at his leader. Blits nudged him and prompted his friend to pay attention.

"He will help," Cyrius confirmed to the entire council. "Of that you have my word."

After a moment of deliberation, Kedem finally offered his own thoughts. "It's the only thing we have," he said eventually. "There is no other way we can deal with this. I agree with Cyrius. I vote we send the warriors on a quest to discover the oak tree and the protector who guards it."

An air of expectancy had engulfed the warriors who had undertaken the first trip across the Trail of Fallen Stars and into The Black Lands. Each one had known that this was the only outcome the council could reach, and that this decision was the only way they could help preserve the forest's way of life from the invading beast, even if it cost them their own.

"Wait, wait, wait," came the voice of General Lupus. "I cannot release the rabbits from my warren to assist with this adventure."

"What!" Wickett said abruptly, turning his leader's head. Although daunted by the task, he had been looking forward to another adventure with the warriors. "Wickett, council members," General Lupus said, addressing the entire council, "we have our own threat to deal with."

"The hares," Doran said softly as he remembered the chance encounter he and Streak had shared with the Forest Guards. Streak heard and nodded subtly.

"We are expecting an imminent attack from the mass of hares who are scouting the borders," General Lupus explained.

"Why did you not inform us of this sooner?" Rebus asked gently.

"Because we are used to dealing with this ourselves."

"What threat do they bring?" Kedem inquired. General Lupus hopped down from his rock and into the crunching snow.

"The hares relentlessly attack our warren, but there is never any sign of how or when they will strike. Sometimes it may be season after season, sometimes we do not see them for many cycles. This is what we patrol the borders for." The animals listened as General

Lupus explained the situation. A sharp gust of cold wind rattled the branches around them and chilled Streak once more to the bone.

"They attack us mainly to pillage our food and to take shelter during the main seasons, whether it be warm or cold. Our warren has been invaded so many times in our history that it is big enough to allow access to any hare strong enough to enter. Mainly they remain in open areas, but when conditions become too harsh, say too hot or too cold, we expect an attack. If they overrun us we have to concede defeat and allow them to take whatever they want. Usually it ends in the rabbits seeking shelter in a disused warren near Bluebell Clearing that can only manage to hold part of our community. The Forest Guards and stronger members of the warren have no shelter when this occurs. We then have to wait until the season passes and until the hares leave. Only then do we prompt our community to begin a mass clean-up operation within our chambers that the hares have destroyed. Should we defeat them, however, they simply move along until they find another warren to attack."

"Hares are often bigger than rabbits, though. How do you repel them?" Brock asked.

"The only way we can," General Lupus replied. "We have to outsmart them. We attempt to create plans which will repel the hares without fighting them. They are too strong for us to simply head straight into battle with. Sometimes, though, fights and battles do emerge during this time." He sighed and looked around at his fellow council leaders. "Now you understand why I can't release Wickett and the team for this adventure. I need my best warriors with me to protect our home."

Kedem and Rebus agreed. To expect the rabbits to release their greatest warriors under these circumstances would be detrimental and unnecessary.

They were needed elsewhere, and with their warren they would stay.

"I cannot join you on this quest either, my friends," came the distinguished voice of Flicar. He stepped towards the council leaders. "I cannot leave my community in the midst of these attacks. I am sorry," he said quietly.

"And no-one would expect you to," Kedem replied. "Or the rabbits," he said looking towards General Lupus and the rock that housed their representatives. Wickett looked dejected, as did they all, but they knew deep down they were needed this time to protect their own. "In light of the task at hand, as leader of Shadow Oak I release Doran and Streak to form the warriors once again, and to undertake this task with the utmost importance." Doran and Streak both rose from their seated position.

"As you wish," Doran confirmed.

"I release Selwyn, once again, to join the band that saved our forest before. If any animals within these trees can complete this journey, it will be they," Arley said. Selwyn looked across to the foxes he had come to know so well.

"And once more I will release Brock to take his rightful place in the warriors, and represent the badger sett on this quest." Brock looked momentarily stunned at this decision. He shifted his multi-shaded face to look at Rebus. "They need you more than we at this precise moment."

"I will not fail you," he simply said, and accepted his role. Once again, the warriors had been called to action in the wake of a new threat. The makeshift group waited under the snowfall for their next orders.

Cyrius looked across the band, much smaller than the one they had celebrated in Bluebell Clearing, what now seemed like an age ago. "Such a small group for such a big task," he hooted.

"Then maybe that is where I can help you," came a distant voice. The council looked towards Shadow Oak, where they saw a group of foxes approaching through the heavier snow.

"Akando!" Rebus snapped. "What are you doing here? How did you get past our sentries?"

"You are not welcome!" General Lupus argued.

"Hold on," Kedem ordered the rabbit, as the foxes approached. Akando came into clear view in the middle of the council. The animals who had been stood there returned to their stones, allowing the skulk of foxes room to stand and be heard.

"Kedem, Rebus, I have attended many council meetings here before with the both of you," the tribal leader began, "and none disappoint me more than the one we held previously." The animals sat in silence as Akando began his explanation. The wind had picked up a little and made the tree branches roar slightly as it gusted between their naked limbs, swaying them steadily to an oblivious audience.

"I am disappointed with myself and my behaviour towards you. Towards all of you," he said, turning his damp, greying fur to address the council. "This long, cold season I have thought greatly about the error of my ways and concluded that you all were indeed right, and I was wrong." The council looked at each other, Streak to Wickett, Flicar to Brock and Arley to Delfin.

"I ask only that you allow me to sit once again as a council member, as a friend, and help the animals of this forest in their hour of need."

"It is your trust that we call to question, Akando," Rebus stated. "How can we trust you after what you did to us? You left us to fend for ourselves against the Dark Army, and sealed your own fate in the process."

Akando looked toward the warriors that stood in league behind him. "I understand your concern," he began, "and the only way I can show you that I can once more become involved is to make up your numbers on the journey I overheard that you are about to take."

Three dogs moved forward into the eye-line of the leaders. Doran and Streak both recognised one as Lyro; the fox that had helped them repel the attack of rats and dark foxes from their journey across the Trail Of Fallen Stars. "I release Lyro, Makoto and Pairo, three of my greatest fighters, to accompany your warriors on their adventure."

The council began mumbling in shock and disbelief. Rebus sat back and turned his attention to Kedem. Kedem returned his look.

"Do your dogs know exactly what is needed from them if they join the warriors?" Cyrius asked in an aggressive tone. "I believe fully in Doran, Streak, Selwyn, and Brock, as I do in Flicar, Wickett, Coinin, Apollo and Blits. Their hearts and bravery are second to no creature within this forest, and that is exactly what is expected of any animal joining the warriors for any period of time, or task."

"We are trustworthy and brave. We need the chance to prove ourselves to you and to the council," Lyro added in a youthful, vibrant voice. "Please, give us the chance."

"And do you know exactly what this journey will need from you, or what the warriors will need from you? This journey is unlike any undertaken in this forest. The oak tree you must reach is protected by many traps and pitfalls that you must navigate to be successful. All creatures who have set out on this quest previously have never returned. The dangers are unlike any ever experienced by any of you before. There is a high risk that some of you may not even make it back. Is that the risk you are willing to take, Lyro? The risk that for your master's error you may never return?"

"I fear nothing. We fear nothing. If we can assist the warriors in any way, we will."

Cyrius turned to Kedem and Rebus. The look on his heart-shaped face told them all they needed to know.

"Wait," came the gentler voice of Dallie. She had been listening intently with her fellow otters Chance and Checkers. "You said that the tree was situated on an island within a lake?"

"That is correct," Cyrius replied.

"It's protected," came the voice of Danjo, one of the grey squirrels chosen to accompany Glif through the elements. " Only one creature in Averon knows the entrance to the forest in which it stands."

"How did you find this out?" Rebus asked him with intrigue.

"I was exploring the woods across the Trail Of Fallen Stars during the warm season. I ventured south from the rabbit's tunnel underneath the trail and stumbled across an old hermit living near the entrance to the forest. He spoke about a secret gateway that leads to the forest where the tree stands. He also said he was the only one who knew how to find it. If you let me join the warriors, I can lead them there."

"He is right," Cyrius added. "The only entrance into the Forest of the Damned is through a gateway that connects our realm with theirs. You must seek the Twins of Despair. By passing between those two trees you will find the forest which you must navigate. Finding the twins will be the first task of your adventure."

The snow had slowly begun to subside and fell lighter and lighter, until eventually it had stopped completely. Only Wickett had consciously noticed.

Kedem and Rebus discussed proceedings with Cyrius privately, leaving the rest of the council in silence as they muttered and whispered to themselves.

"I remember your visit to Berry Hill last season, Cyrius. You informed us that Akando was planning to unrest our communities and attack the warriors. Why now do you appear to entertain the idea that three of his clan may accompany the warriors on this quest?" Kedem asked quietly to the barn owl underneath the cold trees.

"You are indeed correct," Cyrius stated in an equally low voice, "Akando is one who we cannot trust, but his warriors are different."

"How different?" Rebus asked.

"Different in the fact that they are not yet completely corrupted by his influence; at least, not all of them."

"The ones he has offered to help?" Kedem asked.

Cyrius waited a moment, as though he was collecting a deep thought hidden within the depths of his gizzard. His head moved gently as if he were navigating his wise mind to the exact point where the memory rested. "There will be a confrontation on their journey," he relayed to the council leaders without looking upon them. "I cannot see how or why, but there will be a cause for concern."

"But you cannot see what happens?" Kedem asked the trance-like owl.

"No. No, I cannot. There will be death, that much I can see - but who, I do not know," he said coldly. The council leaders looked at each other. "But the warriors will return, one way or another."

"Will they obtain the knowledge we seek?" Rebus asked intently. Cyrius' eyes were now closed, and his head bobbed gently to one side.

"I cannot see," he whispered in his conscious slumber. "It's as though I'm being blocked."

Silence, save for wind, engulfed Council Peninsula as Cyrius slowly woke and opened his eyes. He looked upon the leaders with the now-familiar eyes they had always been accustomed to. "I cannot see whether this task will be a success or a failure," he said in an unsettled voice that Kedem and Rebus had never heard from the owl before. "All I see is that the warriors will find the gateway that will lead them to the Forest of the Damned, and that there will be a confrontation somewhere along their journey. But if you do not send the warrior clan from The North, our Warriors of Averon will return in fewer numbers than without them." The wise old oracle sighed. "The journey must take place, and Lyro and his warriors must go with our own. If we do nothing, the beast will destroy the muntjac population, and then seek out whatever food it can find afterwards."

"Us," Rebus whispered as realisation set in.

"Our warriors will return, maybe less than those who set out, but they will return," the owl informed them.

"And when they do, they may have the knowledge we need to repel this beast," Kedem theorised.

The silence still engulfed the peninsula, and Kedem wondered if any of the council may have overheard the conversation over the gusting wind.

"What do we do?" Rebus asked, for the first time not knowing or even having an idea of what may be best. Kedem subtly looked towards Garla. She was still visibly upset at the events of the cold season, and could see that her contingency looked to her for leadership and a stop to their slaughter. The council had been formed in a time long ago by their ancestors, for times such as these. Whenever a threat to Averon emerged within the Great Forest, it was the council's responsibility to create an answer, no matter what the risk may be. The warriors had been sworn into protect their homeland no matter what, and an old saying of Kedem's swirled within his mind, a saying that had become Shadow Oak's way of life: For the greater good.

He looked towards Doran and Streak. There were no better dogs anywhere in Averon, both with a warrior's spirit and will to succeed. There was only one outcome. No matter what happened, the warriors must take this journey, and do what they were sworn to do. Under the leadership of Doran and with the will of Streak, their chances stood as good as any.

"We do what we have to," Kedem replied to Rebus, softly.

Streak looked over and nodded to Wickett and the rabbits, who returned him the gesture. Doran whispered a comment about the cold, and Akando and his warriors remained inside the opening while the events of the meeting had been discussed. Eventually, the leaders turned their attention back to the council and addressed them.

"We have decided to accept your request of help, Akando," Kedem said in a hopeful voice, still having a seed of doubt in the back of his mind. "We have also agreed to accept the help of the squirrels to join our warriors, and we also request the help of Dallie and the otters. As we believe the tree is surrounded by a lake, we must ask your assistance in helping our warriors to cross the water, should it be unthawed."

"We will accept your request," Dallie confirmed. "And I release Chance and Checkers to assist the warriors."

"Then we are in agreement," Cyrius stated. All members, including Akando, agreed. "Warriors, there is something you must know," he informed them sternly. "There may be a chance that not all of you will return to us from this journey." A whisper of concern passed through the council yet again, all except those who had been chosen for the journey. "This is the most dangerous task the Great Council has ever asked of any animal dwelling within these trees. You will all be tested, and at times darkness may seem more viable than the light." A flutter of nerves swept quickly through Doran. Was that aimed at him?

"But you must resist. Remember, you are a band of animals chosen to seek the knowledge we need to defeat this new nemesis, and should remain together, even when times may seem harsh." Cyrius opened his mighty wingspan. "I wish you all the greatest of luck. I will return to you when I am needed once again, but I must warn you that the dangers you face are of utmost peril. Remain calm, alert, and together. That is all I ask of you. The one you seek is named Stryder. He is an owl like myself, and he can be found within the branches of the oak tree which he must protect. Approach him carefully and respectfully, or he may deem you a threat."

The great owl's plumage once again began to glow, and within seconds he had vanished into the sky, leaving nothing more than a rogue feather and glowing trail to signify that he had been in attendance at the Great Council once again.

Kedem stepped forward. "With the task at hand, we have decided not to force any of you into taking this quest. If you do not wish to participate with this journey, and with the perils that lie ahead, we will not expect you to."

"We ask only for volunteers to take this adventure," Rebus added. "We will not think any less of any animal who wishes to stay behind."

Doran stepped forward. "As leader of our warriors, I will go," he informed them.

"As will I," Streak said as he trotted to Doran's side.

"It sounds like you will need great warriors for this adventure. I will go with you," Brock said as he joined the band. Rebus beamed with pride.

"I'm too involved to back out now," Selwyn said as he joined his warrior comrades. "If worst comes to the worst, I can fly away."

"And you would do that, would you?" Streak asked humorously, knowing that Selwyn wouldn't leave any of them behind, not even in the face of death.

"You will need someone to lead you there," Danjo informed them as he bounded gracefully over the snow.

"And you're not going to get anywhere if the lake you need to cross is unfrozen," Checkers said as he and Chance joined Danjo.

Lyro looked over at Akando, who gestured towards the new band of warriors. "We will offer you the support and assistance you need," he said, stating his intent as his sweep brushed softly over the snow.

"Then it is decided," Rebus acknowledged. "You will leave at dawn."

The council adjourned under a fresh layer of snowfall. Those who could be of no further assistance to the council left the peninsula and headed towards their own lands. Glif remained at Shadow Oak to offer support to Danjo, as did Dallie and Rebus. Akando also stayed with his once-enemies. In a private conversation later that day, Kedem and Rebus had decided it was for the best. If he was at Shadow Oak they could keep a vigorous eye upon him, rather than leaving him time to plot with his own clan away across the forest in his homeland to the north. Keep your friends close, but your enemies closer, Rebus had said during that conversation, and Kedem could not agree more.

As the council disbanded Flicar made his way to Doran, Streak and Selwyn, who had remained together as the animals vanished from the meeting. "I am so sorry not to be accompanying you on this quest," he said with the deepest of regret, that was easily heard within his voice.

"You must leave, Flicar. Your contingency needs you," Doran informed him.

"A warrior such as yourself will be needed more with your contingency than with us," Selwyn confirmed.

"You are right," Streak added. "You must stay with them, they look up to you. If there is any way of defeating the beast, we will find it; you have my word." The rest of the remaining warriors agreed.

"Thank you. Your bravery will be remembered amongst our kind." Doran nodded in acknowledgement. "Good luck to you all."

Flicar turned, and joined by Garla, trotted out of the meeting area and out of the peninsula.

"I hope we find what we're looking for," Selwyn said as they watched the muntjac vanish through the whitened trees.

"So do I," Doran added in a less-than-convincing voice.

"You there!" came the distinct voice of General Lupus, who was tentatively hopping through the snow, trying not to get much of the sky fall on his fur. Streak smiled and acknowledged him. "You have my word that should we repel the hares sooner than expected I will send these fine Forest Guards to Shadow Oak, where they may be of some use to you." Wickett's eyes lighted as his general informed the warriors of his intent. "Until then, though, they must stay with the warren."

The warriors agreed with the decision as the council had, and informed General Lupus that their help would be much appreciated.

Streak shot Wickett one last glance as the rabbits left the peninsula and headed to their warren.

"Wow. What a journey they've got," Apollo added as they crossed the snowfall towards their nearest tunnel. They had excavated a new entrance directly opposite the great oak within the foxes' community that then joined onto another tunnel deep under the woodland earth. It had been decided by General Lupus and Kedem that this would be a great idea, in case the rabbits needed assistance immediately or had information that needed bringing to his attention urgently.

Wickett sighed. "There's always next time," he said.

"Are you kidding?" Apollo asked as they headed down a snow-filled trail. "A venture i to the Haunted Woods and then into a forest of damnation? Imminent danger and probable death?"

"What an adventure!" Blits added to the conversation. "Can you imagine our legacy if we had been involved with that?"

"A legacy!" Apollo shouted. "I am already making my legacy! I have braved certain death in the face of the Dark Army for the return of legendary status. 'Apollo the Mighty' I will be remembered as."

Wickett looked at Coinin, who rolled his eyes. "Stupid boy," General Lupus whispered to Sergeant Castor.

"The slayer of hounds," Apollo continued, "the fearless and loyal member of the Forest Guard. The rabbit of rabbits."

"Where does he get this?" Blits asked the rest of them.

Apollo was too far into his own praise now to be listening. "The loyal and great warrior who would have faced death head-on..."

"Offering his droppings as a gift, I imagine," Coinin added.

Apollo looked at him with a grin on his face. "All I can say is, I'm so glad we didn't go!"

Part 2

One Dark Night

1

As the night fell a large coppice within the Great Vast Open came to life. It was large enough to hold the mass of brown hares that sheltered within comfortably, and dense enough to offer a great amount of protection from the snowfall that fell earlier that day. The largest of the hares sat looking out upon the snow. He scoured the entire blanket of whiteness from between branches and twigs of an almost frozen birch, decorated indulgently with the fall of the sky. He looked towards one of his allies. "Tolka," he ordered. A small hare, no bigger than the rabbits, made his way through the mass of bodies to his leader.

"Yes Lisket?" he asked politely.

"Tolka, I need you to gather some information on that warren in there," he said gesturing in the distance towards Averon. Tolka was the smallest hare in the ranks and was often used as an intelligence gatherer. He had proved himself more than capable in situations far more dangerous than this. He was nimble and almost silent, which made him one of the greatest assets to his leader Lisket. "This is not a suicide mission," he informed the hare, "I just need you to breach the forest at the western point to see if the rabbits still use the tunnel that was there the last time we invaded."

"I remember. The one near the fallen log?"

"Exactly," Lisket confirmed. "You're a great fighter, Tolka, for your size. I want to utilise you with this mission for two reasons. Firstly, you're less noticeable than the larger hares that battle beside us, and secondly, at a distance, if you were to be spotted you would most certainly be passed as a rabbit."

The plan made sense to Tolka. The entrance had not been that far inside the forest. He could dash into see if it was still there then dash out again without even being noticed. "Use your warpaint, warrior, our battle begins with your invasion," Lisket ordered the stealth. Lisket had always enjoyed the battles he'd been involved in. As they mostly fought rabbits, the odds had always been in their favour, giving Lisket a sense of invulnerability during his battles. Lisket nodded at Tolka informing him that his mission had already begun. Tolka found a patch of wet mud that had remained damp within the dense coppice. He rolled around in the uncomfortable coldness and dabbed his face and ears in the mud. When he rose to his hinds he looked more menacing, his hair ruffled and the mud contorting his head unnaturally.

"Go," Lisket ordered as the rest of the hares looked on. "Bring me that information."

Tolka nodded and vanished underneath a bush. Lisket turned his attention back to the Great Vast Open where he saw his stealth bounding over the snow and towards the trees of Averon.

2

Doran's promotion had earned him a sense of respect throughout Shadow Oak. He had been given an advisory role to the community which he now served, and his new den now nestled next to the huge oak where Kedem resided as the community leader. Inside he had welcomed Streak and Tali, and was discussing his plan of action with them for the journey at dawn. Tali looked out upon the circular opening, checking that no prying ears were within the vicinity.

"I don't think so," Streak had begun in an answer to Doran. "It just doesn't seem right."

"We have to," Doran replied, "we can't go against the Great Council's wishes. Cyrius believes in them, and so must we."

Streak shook his head. "I'm not convinced. Why help us now?"

Doran gave the foxes a gesture of a shrug. "Maybe he feels that the biggest danger has passed with the Dark Army. Maybe he doesn't see this as that much of a threat."

"I agree with Streak," Tali began, turning away from the opening. Doran's eyes quickly swirled with a passing dark fog.

"You would, wouldn't you!" he snapped angrily. Streak took notice and stepped back slightly. "You always know better than me, don't you?"

"Doran," Streak began in a soft voice. The rage built within the dog as he slowly moved towards them. His eyes swirled with an inky mass, looking like a storm was passing menacingly throughout the both of them. Doran pulled his lips into a snarl and began growling. Tali shrank back in terror and surprise, her eyes wide and fearful.

"Tali, out," Streak informed her softly, keeping his gaze on the enraged Doran.

"No!" Doran screamed in reply, "you don't listen to him! He's the one who started all our problems!"

"Tali," Streak again said softly, ordering rather than asking. He too was now moving backwards. Doran was moving slow and methodically, swaying his head gently in a menacing manner, almost like a snake...

Tali leapt out of the den and into the snow.

"Why do you always contradict me, Streak? Why, after all I have done for you?"

"Doran, you asked my opinion -"

"And you prompted my sister, my own sister, to speak against me! Soon, all of the foxes in Shadow Oak will do the same, leaving me on my own, and it will all be of your doing!"

Streak backed up as the delusional dog advanced towards him, anger seething from his eyes and jaws. Streak jumped out of the den into the snow where Tali stood, still frozen with fear.

"Tali!" he insisted, almost angry that she hadn't run away. Doran leapt with an air of grace from the den and into the cold air outside. His breath flowed out into clouds as the snarl continued and the growl echoed.

"I intend to finish what I started back at the Trail of Fallen Stars. Do you remember, Streak?" Streak did, of course, and resigned himself to the fact that he would have to fight Doran once more. The clouded dog lowered himself down.

"Tali, get out of here!" Streak informed her. "Get out!"

"DORAN!" boomed the voice of the incomparable Kedem, who dashed from underneath the towering oak with Rebus and Akando. Doran jolted as if being woken and looked around in seeming confusion as to how he got outside.

"Tali?" he asked softly to his sibling. She offered no reply. "Streak?" he asked to his friend and fellow warrior. Then he remembered his actions, as if they had been a faraway dream. Kedem, Rebus and Akando all glared at him without offering a reply. He looked around, almost looking for forgiveness. "I'm sorry," he began with sincerity, "I'm so sorry. I was aware of what I was doing, but I couldn't control myself. I'm so sorry."

"Doran, you must remain strong and not allow your feelings to govern your actions," Rebus began in his distinct tone. "That's how the darkness thrives. It feeds on the anger, hate and malice you carry within you. You must control your emotions, and if you can do this then the darkness will soon fade. You must ignore these feelings and focus only on what is good. If you feel anger beginning to surge within you, turn your attention to happier thoughts and times, and fight it."

Doran nodded slowly, almost looking exhausted, as if all along he had been battling with the darkness as it took hold of him. "Remember your responsibility," Kedem ordered.

"I will," he replied, then looked towards Tali. "I'm sorry, Tali, Streak," he said acknowledging them both. Tali simply nodded, looked at him for a moment, and then disappeared into the den she dwelled within.

"You're a fighter, Doran, don't give up," Streak said as he vanished from the clearing and into his own sleeping place.

The animals turned and left Doran on his own in the crisp clearing of Shadow Oak; all except for Akando, who nodded once before turning and entering the den underneath the great oak tree. If Doran had paid closer attention, he would have seen the smile Akando harboured slyly to himself.

3

The muntjac contingency dwelled within the northwestern forests of Averon. It was widely open in this area, allowing the muntjac to roam with relative ease with their larger bodies compared to the closer, tighter areas of the Great Forest where the foxes and badgers dwelled. It was littered with tall elms and occasional birches, but was mostly dominated by the rolling mounds and open areas which spread throughout the landscape, except for one circular opening that was encircled with dense oaks. They stood together, allowing gaps and trails to be formed between them; but so hidden was the area beyond them that even during the day the area drew a dark, green haze that engulfed the leaves and branches. As the moon glowed proudly it allowed the unnatural orange glow from the snow to once again emerge from the blanketed ground, giving a brighter light than any creature was used to during the night-time in the forest.

Garla had decided that whilst the muntjac's older and weaker contingency rested, the younger, stronger bucks would defend their realm to the best of their ability during the hours of darkness. Lead by Flicar, they began each night by meeting in the enclosed circular clearing where buck issued orders for the coming hours. The deer rallied together as the preparations for that evening's sentry duty began. As he was speaking, the unnatural crunch of a twig caught his ear, and he stopped. He looked to Favradin, his second-in-command, who nodded in confirmation. Favradin was a brave buck who often ventured deep into the Great Vast Open by himself. A great warrior in battle, he had been summoned to Flicar's side after his performance and bravery during the first battle of Averon against the Dark Army.

Silence then engulfed the herd. No wind blew, no leaves rattled. A few silent moments passed before Flicar noticed he had been holding his breath. He exhaled quietly and saw his breath stream into the unnatural light.

Crack! The noise came again, only this time clearer. Clearer meant closer.

A slight surge of adrenaline quickly engulfed Flicar, who gestured a circular movement with his slight antlers. Understanding what he meant instantly, the muntjac slowly turned into a circular formation within the opening, each buck facing outwards. Their eyes could not pick up any movement in the darkness as they scoured their surroundings and beyond for a reason why the noises had emerged. Flicar squinted slightly into the black shapes which had once been the forest. He caught sound of his allies breathing; some panting, some slow and methodical, as if calming themselves.

"Any signs?" Flicar asked in a low but audible voice.

"None," came Favradin's quiet reply from behind. Even though his nerves were fraying and his heartbeat increased, the second-in-command stood strong and brave against the rogue sounds emanating from the darkness.

There was a long pause of silence within the clearing afterwards that almost confirmed an overreaction in Flicar's mind; but the Favradin had heard it too, and in this situation neither Flicar nor the rest of the contingency could dismiss it as merely forest creatures or noises. A sharp gust of cold wind sliced at Flicar as he stood motionless in the snow.

A thunderous roar exploded from the trees, and then a shriek. Flicar turned around instantly and saw bucks to his left slowly backing further into the opening. One had vanished from the ranks. A wave of hysteria swept through them as Flicar noticed dark watery patches staining the glowing snow.

"Stand together!" Flicar ordered. "Back to your positions!" The brave muntjac slowly made their way to their previous formation and looked out into the darkness. "Stand your ground against this beast!"

From all around them they could now hear the sound of galloping paws churning away the snow as they circled the entire circumference of the opening, hidden by the thick darkness and dense trees. Flicar tried to track them with his eyes but found nothing out there to see. The breathing of the bucks grew louder and more rapid as their nerves increased. Branches broke and twigs snapped as the invisible feet ploughed through their obstacles and continued their journey, rustling the branches they passed through and snapping the brittle ones that had succumbed to the cold season. Suddenly the sound of galloping footfalls stopped. Nothing. Silence.

Flicar slowly moved forward in the direction that the footfalls had vanished. His hooves slowly pressed down into already disturbed snow. His breath fogged his vision momentarily, before returning it to darkness.

Then he heard it; a low, thunderous growl much deeper than any hound of the Dark Army. It was deep and menacing, almost primeval. A cat-like roar engulfed the bucks and Flicar jumped round to see another buck dragged invisibly into the darkness. He kicked and screamed as he was pulled by an unseen entity into the trees, terror engulfing his cries and shrieks. The screaming stopped immediately with the dull sound of a crack within the darkness.

The remaining deer fled in every direction as fear coursed throughout them. Flicar turned and ran, his heart pounding deep within his body. Over the mounds and open areas he dashed with others in his contingency, and underneath the bright aura of the glowing moon above. He sprinted as fast as he had ever done so before, his hooves pounding the frozen bracken away from the clearing, his mind engulfed with fear and self-preservation. Once fatigue set in he slowed down with two others who had raced beside him. Slowly the three bucks came to a standstill, panting heavily as they drew cold air into their bodies. One of the bucks was Favradin, who had purposely followed Flicar in the event that their attacker made an attempt at the lead buck's life.

"Two. It's now taken two more," Favradin stated as he caught his breath.

Flicar dropped his head in disbelief. "And it did so with our entire contingency of bucks there to protect them. An entire battalion of warriors could not see it, or even get close to fighting it. Not one."

The three bucks stood panting under the moonlit sky in a small opening surrounded by beeches.

They had no idea that the beast had picked up their trail, and was slowly stalking them.

4

Tolka silently and unknowingly drew onto the snow-covered track where Forest Guard Digby had lost his life. He remembered vaguely that a fallen log rested beside a tunnel entrance that the rabbits had flooded from when they invaded the warren, many seasons ago. As he continued softly on the trail his eyes darted through the darkness, looking for any sign of the landmark. He continued further along the trail until an unnatural, elongated mound of snow emerged from the trees to his left. He looked upon it a moment and realised it was indeed a log, only obscured this time by the covering of the falling sky. He quickly scouted the area for enemies, then when satisfied he was alone stealthily made his way towards the fallen tree. He weaved effortlessly over the snow-covered bracken that now littered the woodland floor, until he came to rest at the base of the log. There, he re-discovered the entrance to the rabbits warren and smiled to himself. "Gotcha," he whispered quietly.

"Now!" came a piercing scream from the woodland behind. Before he knew it, Tolka was thrust to the floor and smashed into the cold snow. He struggled out of instinct but was piled on by one, maybe two, bodies. Another struggle ensued, and this time a body fell into the snow and damp mud beside him. Rapidly another body took its place and lurched on top of his own, immobilising Tolka completely.

Apollo stood to his feet, shaking his body in an attempt to empty his fur of snow and mud. "Got him!" he shouted in jubilation.

"Who? You did?" asked Coinin, who perched himself uncomfortably on top of the hare with the assistance of Blits.

Wickett ambled slowly towards the downed hare, who began in vain to struggle once more.

"It's useless fighting," the Forest Guard began. "You have two of the best warriors in this forest restraining you." Wickett looked over towards Apollo, who was gesturing an 'and me' sign to his leader. "Two of our best warriors and Apollo," he added afterward. Apollo scrunched his face in disapproval. Sensing defeat, Tolka sighed and ceased his struggle.

"What do we do with him?" Blits asked as he held the invader down.

Wickett thought to himself momentarily. "Take him to the general," he finally replied.

"We'll interrogate this unwelcome guest," Coinin added.

"What are you going to do with me?" asked the unsettled hare.

"That all depends on you," Coinin replied from above him. "Didn't your superiors tell you how vicious the rabbits of Averon are?" The hare struggled slightly, but didn't answer. "We've been known to kill hares, and even other rabbits that get this close to our warren."

Apollo opened his mud-caked eyes and raised his brows. He looked toward Blits, his expression asking if any truth could be found in Coinin's statement. Blits shot him an equally baffled don't-ask-me look.

"No you haven't," Tolka moaned as the weight on top of him showed no sign of easing. "We invaded your warren seasons ago and you ran away. You're not warriors, you're cowards."

"What did you say, Coinin? I couldn't hear you from over there," Apollo said as he too made his way between Coinin and Blits, standing on the intruder and placing more pressure on the felled hare. Tolka gasped out and expelled almost all the air filling his lungs.

"That's enough," Wickett ordered. "Pull him up." Blits and Apollo flanked Tolka as Coinin helped him slowly from the ground, standing solidly behind him. "A lot has changed since you rats invaded our warren," Wickett began. "If you knew even half of what our warren has done in the recent past, you'd steer clear of our forest and run far away." Tolka sniggered in disbelief.

"Should we injure him and leave his wounded body for the foxes to find?" asked Apollo, effortlessly playing along.

"The foxes," Coinin began, "they should be rolling through here pretty soon. We better leave."

"Yes, but first we have to decide if the rat should go for interrogation. I mean, we know the rest of them are out there now, and we know they'll invade any time soon. What else do we need to know? Maybe we don't need him to speak to the general after all?"

"You won't leave me for the foxes," Tolka began defiantly. "They'd feast on your guts if they lived in this forest. Your kind would have been slaughtered many, many seasons ago. You rabbits are small and pathetic. Your cowardice stems from weakness."

A rustle of paws trudging through snow emerged behind them. Wickett gestured for Tolka to turn around. The sly smirk on the hare's face rapidly vanished as he turned and beheld a red fox standing only a few paces from him. The white dash over his eye lifted as he looked the petrified hare over.

"Living in this forest means we only eat berries and vegetation," Streak began as the rest of the rabbits looked on in amusement. "I guess you fellows wouldn't inform anyone if I took, say, an unknown hare out into

247

the Great Vast Open and had myself a sneaky meal, would you?"

Tolka immediately turned to Wickett. "Please!" he gasped. "Please! I'll do whatever you want. Please!"

"We'll take you back to our general," Wickett began slowly, "and you'll talk."

Tolka nodded rapidly. "Yes. Yes!" he began, with an expression of fear passing over his face.

"Because if you don't, our friend here will never be far away," Wickett continued. Streak's expression told the hare that this was true.

"Whatever! I'll tell you everything that you want to know!"

The Forest Guard had been successful in capturing this enemy spy from the Great Vast Open. Wickett stood aside as Coinin entered the tunnel first, quickly followed by Blits. Apollo gently nudged the hare, which prompted him to follow.

"Glad we bumped into you," Wickett said, turning to Streak.

"Pleasure's mine," he said, before turning to leave.

"Streak!" Wickett shouted as the red fox began to wander away. The dog stopped in his tracks and looked questioningly over his shoulder. "Good luck. With the journey and everything."

Streak looked at his warrior comrade. After a moment of silence he offered no reply; just a subtle, solitary nod, before turning away and this time dashing into the night.

Streak vanished into the darkening forest, and the task at hand for the Forest Guards began. Wickett entered the gloomy tunnel behind the hare, and was closely followed by Apollo, who chuckled to himself from the back of his comrades.

"What are you laughing for?" Wickett asked as they passed through the tunnel.

"That will be the first tale of my legacy. The night Apollo the Great felled a hare with his own bare paws."

Wickett laughed. "Apollo, you jumped on his back, fell off, and landed face-first in the mud," he replied, informing his friend of how he had seen the incident. "And besides, I thought it was Apollo the Mighty?"

"It was, it was," Apollo began as though he had though this over many times, "but then I decided that 'Great' sounded far better than Mighty," he added in his best heroic voice. "As generations of rabbits in the far future speak of and remember all of my deeds and heroics, it will now sound as it should. Not the individual might I possess, but the empowerment and hope I brought - not only to the Forest Guards, but to the entire animals of the Great Forest Averon."

"How about Apollo the Dramatic?" came Blits' reply, echoing through the tunnel. Both Coinin and Wickett found this hilarious and began laughing uncontrollably ahead of him.

"One day you'll all be counting on me," began the great and legendary rabbit from the rear of the tunnel, "and it will be down to me to do something so dramatic, so heroic, that you'll have no choice but to lower your heads in disbelief and awe." Apollo threw his nose in the air, signalling the end of his speech.

"If that day ever arrives, I'll undoubtedly address you as the 'Great' or 'Mighty,' whatever you choose," Coinin added, still laughing at Blits' rapid wit.

None of them knew that this day was merely hours away.

5

A small skulk of foxes slept peacefully underneath the trees of Averon. Their den had been created underneath a hefty bush that sheltered the slumbering animals from the elements of the prolonged cold season. The snow had finished falling as dusk fell across the forest, and even the cold it emitted as it lay solidly upon the ground did not penetrate deep enough to disturb the resting skulk. Two dogs, two vixens and three pups formed the small family that resided somewhere deep within the trees of the Great Forest.

One of the dogs drowsily awoke to the noise of what sounded like many footfalls through the crisp snow. He drew a deep breath and batted his eyelids, slowly standing as high as his den would allow him. He stretched his body, ruffling the orange colour of his fur that was lost in the darkness. As he came closer to consciousness he realised that he was indeed hearing a strange noise from the woods outside that sounded like great movement, as though many creatures were passing along the desolate track that existed not far from their den.

"What's that noise, Djekin?" came the dreary voice of a vixen that had also roused from her sleep.

"I have no idea," Djekin replied as his senses came back to him fully. Sensing the movement and noise from outside their home, the second dog also awoke.

"What's going on?" he asked in a deep voice, before yawning his jaws wide and licking his lips.

"I don't know, Nevrin," Djekin replied, "but it doesn't sound natural."

Nevrin looked at his counterpart and noticed a small, hunched shadow at the entrance of their den. The shadow slowly took form, with red eyes glowing in the darkness. The woken vixen saw it, and gasped.

"Look!" she shouted. Both dogs saw the completed shadow of a rat sat firmly within the entrance to their den. It squeaked loudly, laughed, then quickly vanished from the bush.

"Get it!" Nevrin shouted, and sprang to his paws. Djekin leapt rapidly from the den and out into the darkness.

"What's happening?" came a timid cub's voice as the den awoke. Nevrin scrambled over his family and out into the snow.

"Stay here!" he whispered to her as he too pounced outside to give chase to the intruding rodent.

He landed firmly in the glowing, freezing snow outside the bush. As he did so he noticed Djekin flanked by two shadows, bigger than that of the rat who taunted them. Their eyes also glowed wildly red in the darkness, as if they were consumed by the purest forms of anger and evil. They weren't rats. They were foxes.

The sound that had awoken the sleeping skulk was the sound of what looked like hundreds of red foxes marching one by one along the rarely-used trail that passed by their den. Here and there more dark foxes wandered on either side of their line, as if keeping guard over a line of prisoners. They were joined in mass by the rats they clearly associated with.

Through the night-time gloom, they looked on as a fox walking inside the line attempted to escape. He darted to his right and leapt over the rats wandering there to keep them captive. "Breach!" came an invisible cry from within the darkness.

Within seconds of the fox's attempted escape, three shadows glided rapidly in chase and bore down upon the fox as it sprinted away into the trees. After only seconds of the shadows emerging from nowhere, a terrified yelp echoed through the darkness. Snarls and growls drifted along the breeze to the now-motionless line of foxes and darkened animals, all listening to the demise of the fox who had attempted to escape. The silence revealed more yelps and cries, and now the sound of torn flesh emerged through the darkness. After a final, high-pitched scream, the woods returned to silence, fear now spreading quickly throughout the captives. The three shadows emerged from within the black tree trunks, with only their glowing eyes as any sign of life.

"Get them moving!" came the same voice again, this time issuing a firm order. The dark foxes keeping guard over the long line of captured dogs began nudging their prisoners and kicking them forward. Slowly the line began moving once again, and the three shadows that had slaughtered the escapee formed into foxes. They walked slowly away into the distance as the huge line of captors and captives began to move. They continued past both the bush and the dogs that dwelled there without even looking over to them or acknowledging their presence.

"It's useless resisting," came a haggard voice to Nevrin, the fox attempting to protect his family. A skulk of five dark foxes emerged gracefully from the darkness, surrounding the dogs that only moments ago had been sleeping within their den. "If you try, we'll take your family instead." From its resting place upon the shoulders of a darkened dog a ragged rat stood ominously, sneering down upon the new foxes who had given chase to one of his minions. It was Rogo, the leader of the rat army Seerles commanded. Nevrin growled in anger as he prepared to defend his family.

"Ah, ah, ah," the rat began, goading the fox. "I mean it."

Screams erupted from the den underneath the bush, and the dogs turned to see a dark fox emerge from its entrance, carrying a cub in his mouth by the scruff of her neck. "No!" Djekin shouted. The cub was thrust harshly to the snow-covered floor in front of Rogo and his foxes, who all slowly bore down upon it. "No!" Djekin yelled again. "What do you want?"

The cub quaked as she looked up at the advancing foxes. "Wait," Rogo ordered. The foxes halted. "You two dogs join the line, and don't ask any questions!" the rat squealed through the darkness. The dogs looked at each other. "Now!" Rogo barked, "or my legions will be having a light snack."

The dogs both looked at the quaking, terrified cub, and sighed in defeat. There was no way they would be able to protect their skulk with such a vast amount of enemies ready to pounce upon them if they resisted. The vixens and remaining cubs watched on from their dwelling, in the grip of fear. Djekin lowered his head and slowly turned to make his way towards the line.

"No!" screamed a vixen from the den's entrance. The dark fox that had raided it for the cub turned and growled in reply.

"It's okay," Djekin said as he made his way towards the line. "It's okay." The cub that had been used as a bargaining tool quickly scampered up from the snow and back inside the den. "Look after them," Nevrin informed the vixen, before he too turned and joined the line.

"Would you look at that?" Rogo said to his fox as he marvelled at the amount of red foxes passing along the hidden trail. "What an army we can amass." He turned back one final time to the terrified foxes that had been left behind, and laughed.

6

Cyrius glided silently from Averon, using his wings to propel himself more so now than at any point during the warm season. When the sun was high and the weather was fine, thermal air was more common and allowed him to glide with minimal effort, compared instead to the cold season and big thaw when they were extremely scarce. During the warm, clear nights of the warm season the thermals arose from the treetops of the Great Forest and helped lift him as he flew over and beyond the borders of Averon. This night, though, the remnants of the cold season had brought with them extremely cold air that completely engulfed the land from horizon to horizon, and forced the barn owl to beat his wings much harder in order to fly.

Cyrius passed high above the Great Vast Open, looking down upon the moonlit snow as it glared back upwards toward the soaring owl travelling distantly above. After traversing the empty skies for what seemed like an age, he found the landmark he was looking for, and came to rest on a structure he was certain that the humans had once built. He was well aware of human habits, having studied them for many, many seasons from a distance. He looked towards a dwelling place he had observed humans inside many times before, and noticed that the tree they had placed inside their lodgings at the height of the cold season had now vanished. The tree had been greatly decorated with bright stars that the humans had reached somehow, but now it had vanished completely from within their home. He had noticed that the tree appeared repeatedly at the same time of the cold season, and had often wondered how they had reached the stars in order to decorate it in this way. After observing this particular tradition the humans had held for many cold seasons, he had come to the conclusion that they had some type of celebration for a relatively short time during the long, dark nights.

A low growl emitted from the snow within the enclosure Cyrius was perched upon, and with his piercing eyes he looked down upon a creature glaring back at him.

"What are you doing here?" came a deep voice rumbling from below.

"I came to talk with you," came Cyrius' factual reply.

The creature below snorted in amusement. "And why would you want to speak to me?" the creature asked, its milky eye glowing dimly in the moon-lit darkness.

"I want to warn you about the beast roaming our Great Forest," Cyrius informed him.

"Ah yes, the one now living in your precious Averon," Baal rumbled as he made his way towards the perimeter fence that faced the Great Forest. "You didn't come to warn me," the hound began after a moment treading the enclosure in the snow. "You came to see if I had any information to share with you."

Cyrius bobbed his body up and down and gently flapped his wings a little as he caught his balance and made himself more comfortable. "Yes, there was that as well."

Baal shook his head in disbelief, and smiled to himself. "Why should I help you?" he asked with a twinge of sarcasm. He looked up once again at the bird of prey. "You rallied those animals against my army. You harboured that dirty animal I was set to slay."

"Every creature has a right to life," the owl began. "It is not yours to take whenever you wish."

Baal grunted in laughter, seemingly unaffected by the cold element. "I will find him, sooner or later. And I will kill him; of that I promise."

"Not if the beast gets to him first," Cyrius replied firmly. "Soon all the muntjac the beast is hunting will be no more. What do you think it will prey upon afterwards?" Baal offered no reply. "How long do you think Streak will survive?"

"Ah yes, Streak," Baal began, seeing his nemesis flashing inside his mind's eye. He saw the battle they held in the thunderstorm at the tail end of the warm season and remembered the recovery period he had endured ever since.

"We tracked the beast for a while back at the height of the warm season," Baal began, accessing a recently forgotten memory that had been tucked away at the back of his mind. "We'd never caught a scent like that before. So strong, so different," he said, looking up towards Cyrius. "The stronger the scent became, the more destruction we came across. Slaughtered sheep, slaughtered cows - it's as if nothing is strong enough to compete with its ferocity." Baal sat in the cold snow, now talking to Cyrius as if he were an old friend. "After the carnage we stumbled upon, the humans decided they were on to something bigger than merely foxes. They decided to hunt this beast, but not with us. They took their weapons instead in an attempt to kill it."

"I remember," Cyrius confirmed. He had witnessed this different hunt himself, but never fully understood what was happening.

"They tried, but they never had a trail to follow. Their senses are nothing like ours. Humans are stupid and underdeveloped, even though they think they're smart and clever. Eventually, without a trail to follow, Cameo and I were called upon to lead them. We were summoned to pick up the trail they couldn't find and hunt down this creature that was successfully eluding them." Baal spoke to the oracle without even a hint of aggression or malice within his deep voice. He simply spoke a factual account of what he had done on that hunt long, long ago. "We found nothing, except more carcasses. It left a trail of death and destruction in its powerful wake."

Baal stood again, the cold finally getting to his war-torn body. He shook his fur and looked towards the barn owl perched upon the fence above him, and sighed. "We caught her trail, but never caught up to her. The humans were reluctant to stay out after dark. If they had, we'd have got her," Baal informed him. During that hunt, Baal knew he was close to tracking the beast. If the humans would have allowed him to continue, the beast would be no more, of that he was certain.

"Creatures like her have nothing to fear," Baal began, unknowingly offering Cyrius a small piece of advice. "She hunts from sunrise to dark descending, and during the moonlight hours if she chooses to. The only creatures who may be able to stop her are the humans, and of course those who follow me into battle."

Baal quickly remembered who it was he was talking to after he relayed his account. The anger engulfed him and returned to his good eye. "That's all I know," he replied, the rumble lowly audible within his chest. "All you need worry about is the invasion I will lead upon your forest, sooner or later. I will slaughter Streak - of that you have my word."

"It may very well be your intention to kill our foxes, but you must remember that the beast must be slaughtered first," Cyrius divulged to the hound. It was information that he hoped would dissuade Baal in another raid upon Averon. "There will be a time when your patience wears thin and you will seriously consider invading our forest. If you choose to do so, you will find Streak gone and the beast waiting. You will lose your life hunting for a creature you could simply forget about." Baal remembered his battle with the fox. He remembered Streak being the only creature he had hunted that ever escaped his jaws.

"The decision to continue your pursuit is yours, and yours alone, general," the barn owl hooted against the back drop of a cloud-filled sky, "but you have been warned."

Cyrius glowed as he opened his wingspan. He took flight in an aura of white light, leaving a falling, glowing trail in his wake. Baal stood in the cold night air, watching the owl's bright aura dwindling far away into the distance.

He knew exactly what he was going to do. His decision had already been made.

7

"Well, well, what do we have here? Sent to infiltrate the warren, I take it?" General Lupus asked inside the dense darkness of his main chamber. The Forest Guards had been posted at the four tunnel entrances to the chamber in order to stop the captive hare escaping. Sergeant Castor sat beside the general as they interrogated the intruding soldier, who continued to ignore them.

"He won't talk," Sergeant Castor said, stating the obvious. "He'll have been sworn to secrecy by his superiors."

"We take him back outside," Wickett added. The rabbits looked at him. "He met our friend Streak."

"Did he now?" Sergeant Lupus added. "The fox who roams this area of the forest? I imagine he's quite hungry at this precise moment."

The hare sighed, remembering the fox. "I don't know much," Tolka began, defeat slowly emerging in his tame voice. "All they're doing so far is waiting for my scout report before they take action."

"Gathering intelligence," Sergeant Castor said. "You were right," he informed General Lupus.

"As they always do," the general replied matter-of-factly. "If only there was a way we could feed them false information, get them running in different directions. If they chase their tails they're not chasing us, so to speak."

"As soon as this rat makes it back to wherever he came from he's going to tell them everything,"

Sergeant Castor replied, foreseeing the imminent future.

General Lupus looked over the hare momentarily to Apollo who was stood directly behind him and, as usual, away with the fairies. The day-dreaming rabbit was completely unaware of anything. General Lupus looked to Tolka, then slowly back to Apollo. To Tolka, to Apollo. Tolka, Apollo. The hare was small. In fact, he was about the same size as the Forest Guard stood in partial consciousness behind him. Apollo was smeared with mud that made him look almost exactly identical to Tolka. The size of the rabbit, the markings, the mud - the entire likeness between the two was uncanny. Had Apollo not been stood directly behind the captured hare, General Lupus would have thought them one and the same.

"Well, there's a discovery," the general said with mild amusement. "I think I may just have hatched a cunning plan." He looked at Forest Guard Apollo with a twinkle in his eye.

"What?" Apollo asked, flicking his eyelids as he emerged from his daydream. "You what, sir?"

8

Doran looked to stir uneasily in his slumber. He sighed, stirred again momentarily, then licked his lips, making himself comfortable once again. Streak looked on within the gloom. Kedem rested alongside the fox to keep a watchful eye upon the young warrior for which he had so many hopes. Streak also observed the sleeping dog in silence, his own sleep broken with the onset of dawn. Tali slumbered deeply somewhere within the den, her breathing shallow and almost silent. Doran began stirring yet again, shaking slightly as though he had suddenly fallen into a great chill. He whined slightly as he trembled, causing Streak to engage his ears and raise his head from his paws.

"The darkness," Kedem said in a whisper as he noticed Streak look intently at the distressed fox, trembling uncontrollably. "It's taking him."

Streak watched helplessly as his comrade battled with the entity that dwelled inside of him, even as he slept. "Can't we do anything?" Streak asked quietly.

"We can do nothing," Kedem replied, his voice tainted with gloom. "This is Doran's battle - only he can defeat the darkness within."

Streak sighed. "What about Seerles? If we were to convince him to help, could he do anything?"

Kedem shook his head. "I think that it may be even beyond him to help, if he would."

"But he controls the darkness."

"Yes he does, but he simply cannot withdraw the darkness once it has taken hold of a creature. If Doran succumbs to that entity which is now taking control of him, he will be at the beckoning call of the dark one."

Streak watched as the trembling dog slowly became still once more, and once settled looked to almost sleep peacefully. "Do you think it will take him?" he asked the wise leader of Shadow Oak.

Kedem turned to him, a look of surrender firmly upon his furred face. Streak expected an answer, and in the silence that followed almost prayed for one. Kedem lowered his brows and ears, and turned away.

"He is strong, both in spirit and will. But as strong as he is and as intent as he can be, I fear he will be taken from us."

Streak said nothing in reply. He was hit with guilt as he remembered the scene at Treetop Hillstretch. He knew deep down he should have stopped both Tali and Seerles under the heavy rainfall of that fateful day. Tali had been adamant, though. She deeply loved her sibling and wanted to give him another chance, no matter what the cost. A wave of doubt crossed Streak's mind. Had it all been worth it?

"Are you saying it wasn't?" asked a voice from the darkness. Kedem and Streak jolted from their snooze to find Doran stood opposite, replying it seemed to the question swirling within Streak's mind. "Answer me," demanded the conflicting dog, a tinge of anger within his voice.

"What do you m -"

"He knows!" Doran screamed at Kedem, gesturing to Streak. "Well? Was it worthwhile?" he asked angrily, turning his attention back toward Streak. "Saving my life?"

A wave of unease now swept throughout Streak. Had Doran read his mind? "Of course," Streak replied adamantly.

"Then why do you think otherwise?"

"Doran, why would you say such a thing?" Kedem asked in utter dismay.

Doran loomed slowly from the darkness, his eyes now red and his fur many shades darker than it had been before. "You're the one doing the thinking, Streak," Doran growled as he approached the dog that had given him so many problems since wandering into their community seasons before. "I should have killed you a long time ago," Doran rumbled with discontent.

"Doran," Kedem said sternly.

"Hush your mouth, mighty leader," Doran growled in response, the anger finally engulfing the heroic dog. "For too long I've suffered by your paw. You constantly held me back, willing me to fail -"

"I did no such thing," Kedem replied firmly.

"Yes you did! You chose this filthy drifter over my loyalty!" Doran screamed.

"Doran?"

Doran roared, engaged his claws, and finally lost all control over his actions. He swiped out at the voice in the darkness, hearing a yelp and a squeal.

Tali lurched back as Doran's claw swiped across the left side of her muzzle, drawing blood in one clean cut. She had awoken during the raised voices, and subtly made her way towards the argument in typical Tali inquisitiveness. Streak launched at the angry dog, thrusting him outside the den and into the phosphorescent snow. The ruckus had awoken the guests staying within Shadow Oak. Lyro jumped swiftly into the clearing with Kedem's advisors Jinx and Delfin. Doran lowered his head in an attacking stance until he saw Tali emerge from the den behind Streak, her muzzle covered in her own blood. A shot of recognition flashed through Doran's mind, and he lurched back. The anger vented from his red eyes. He began swirling around in a circle, as though he was chasing his brush, as confusion and chaos engulfed the stricken dog. He screamed out in anger and fear, a blood-curdling howl that engulfed the entire community. Slowly his circles became less rapid and a hint of consciousness and thought passed through his conflicting mind. Finally he stopped and settled down, panting heavily to catch the breath he had exhaled intently during his tirade. The skulk of foxes and remaining animals, disturbed by the chaos, all watched on in dismay as the anger and darkness that had engulfed Doran momentarily subsided. He looked upon all of the animals in apology and disgrace.

"I'm sorry," he whispered, with genuine affection. As the animals at Shadow Oak looked on, he turned in shame and dashed out of the community as fast as his dark paws would take him.

Streak gave chase immediately and caught up to the dog outside the border of Shadow Oak. "Doran!" he shouted, halting the fox who moments ago was ready to kill him.

Doran turned under the first light of dawn. "I'm sorry, Streak, to you and to them. Please tell them for me?" he asked, his face full of sadness and regret.

"What are you doing? Tell them yourself," Streak replied bluntly.

Doran stood silent for a moment as the first birds of the forest began their morning song away in the distance. "I can't," the dog said. "I've done too much already."

Streak shook his head and made his way closer to the trail Doran was stood upon. "You need to stay here. We can help you. We all know what's happened to you."

"But I don't!" Doran snapped back quickly. "Look at me," he said, turning Streak's attention to the black and grey fur that began to appear on his usually red body. "Look at what I'm doing! I hurt my own sister! The entire community is afraid of me!"

"We can help you."

"No you can't," Doran snapped, turning away. He looked at the trees emerging in dawn's first light. "No-one can."

For the first time since his arrival, Streak and Doran shared a bond of understanding. He looked upon the troubled fox and knew immediately his intentions. Deep down, he knew it was for the best; at least in the short term. Doran looked at his comrade and knew that Streak was aware of what he was about to do. He tried to give a smile, but it looked more hopeful than gracious.

"Look after Tali for me," he said, knowing full well that Streak would do everything in his power to keep her safe. Streak offered nothing but a slight nod in return. Doran looked upon him, this time the smile now genuine across his muzzle. He turned away and dashed through the dull light and fallen snow that engulfed the trail.

"Doran!" Tali shouted as she joined Streak, cursing herself for being too late. "We need to -"

"No," Streak snapped back rapidly.

"But -"

"No," Streak reiterated. "He wants to be alone. He believes he should be alone while he deals with this."

"Why does he think that?" Tali replied sorrowfully.

Streak turned and looked at her with genuine affection. "He loves you, Tali. He doesn't want to harm you or place you in any danger."

"Why?" she asked through her blood-drenched muzzle. "I can cope."

"He knows you can cope. He just doesn't want to be here if the darkness takes him completely. He's afraid of what he'll do."

265

Tali watched on as Doran's sweep vanished in the distance. She knew it was for the best, even if she didn't want to admit it.

Doran ran and ran without a single idea of where he was going or what he would do. His thoughts were clouded with decisions and ideas he could not unscramble from his mind. He was afraid that the darkness was only gone temporarily, and that it would return and take him, sooner rather than later.

However, even thought the fox had left Shadow Oak, something told him deep down that he would return. What he didn't know was if he would return as a great protector to the animals that lived there or as their fearsome nemesis, sent to kill them.

9

"There it is," Sergeant Castor said, gesturing far out into the Great Vast Open. Away in the distance stood the coppice that Tolka had informed them of, the one where the hares were plotting their next attack upon General Lupus' warren. He was joined by the ever-faithful Forest Guard, the western team headed by Wickett. There was a silent remorse amongst them as Sergeant Castor relayed the mission to Apollo. For the crime of looking almost identical to the hare that was now a prisoner of war within the warren, he would have to venture into that coppice, pretending to be Tolka in order to relay false information to their leader. Sergeant Castor was lecturing the rabbit as the surprisingly warm air began to thaw the cold snow on the woodland floor. Coinin noticed that its consistency had gone from frozen and cold to cold and dispersing. They listened on as a dejected Apollo received his orders.

"Now listen, boy," the sergeant began very sternly, "the name of their leader is Lisket. He's the one you must relay the message to. Don't get broiled in any other activity. As soon as you've said your piece, get your fluffy rear end out of there, and fast."

Apollo looked with deep, dark eyes towards his friends, his ears flat and his eyes wide. Sergeant Castor noticed, and became almost irritated.

"What are you looking like that for?" the sergeant snapped. "This is what you were selected to do. It is the job of a Forest Guard to protect his home, and that is what you are doing. Snap out of it, and remember the job at hand."

Wickett remembered something as another warm gust of wind passed through the waving trees. "Don't forget, Apollo, this is the second chapter in your legend," he began. Apollo shot him a glare that said he may just be listening. Wickett noticed the sly glance from his comrade and relayed a speech he thought Apollo would want to hear. "Think about it. The rabbit that single-handedly invaded an area full of thousands - " He looked at Blits, who was subtly shaking his head in warning. Wickett knew exactly what he had done and rectified it immediately. "Hundreds, erm, I mean a hundred or so, probably less - I mean much less, maybe..."

"The legend of Apollo infiltrating the hares for the good and safety of his own warren," Coinin began in an attempt to rescue Wickett. "Now who wouldn't want to listen to a story like that?" Wickett sighed, having being successfully rescued.

"The bravery and courage. The drama and adventure. The legend would have it all," Blits added.

Wickett could see they were convincing Apollo, and noticed a change within the Forest Guard. Swept away with the praise, he was probably imagining the legend as if it had already come to pass. "The second legend of Apollo the Great," Wickett confirmed.

"Apollo the Brave," the future legend added after a moment or so. He turned to the rest of the rabbits as they sat at the western border overlooking the Great Vast Open. "The bravery and sacrifice I made taking on this perilous adventure," he added, using his now famous heroic voice.

"Yes, Apollo, you will be known as 'the brave'," Sergeant Castor added.

As dull light quickly emerged from the cloudy sky, Apollo turned to face the Great Vast Open. He had seen the coppice many times on his patrols away in the distance, and now for the first time would be heading out into the unknown by himself. "In and out, how hard can it be?" Apollo asked, to himself more than anyone. It was clear that the rabbit was still afraid, but the promise of legendary status within the warren had seemed to work. He was prepared to defend his home, no matter what the cost. He turned to his comrades. "You'll wait here for me?" he asked, needing to know they would be there if he needed them.

"Won't move until you return," Wickett replied.

"General's orders," Sergeant Castor added.

"Then there's nothing left for me to do."

Apollo turned, and as he laid the first few paws out into his adventure, was stopped suddenly.

"Wait!" Blits shouted. The rabbits turned to him. He sighed. "You know something, Apollo?" he began, taking a few steps closer to his friend. "You were the first rabbit I ever met when I was able to leave the warren by myself." Wickett could see Apollo trying to remember. "We joined the Forest Guard together, we patrolled the same area together, and we even partnered up when our team was , to further our reconnaissance." Apollo nodded subtly.

Blits found a damp area of mud he'd spied as the snow slowly gave away, and without any hesitation threw himself into its chill, rolling comically until his fur was smeared. Coinin knew exactly what he was doing. "Sir," Blits began when his episode had finished, "I'd like to accompany Apollo on this mission, please?" Apollo's eyes lighted as Blits made his intentions clear. "None of us have ever been split before, and I'd hate for that to happen when so much rests upon his shoulders."

"So you want to go as support to your Forest Guard comrade, eh?" Sergeant Castor asked, admiring the bravery of the guard.

"Yes sir."

"Well," Sergeant Castor began, inspecting the rabbit for any flaws. "You're not quite as big as a hare, but you'll pass," he replied informatively. "You must remember to keep a low profile, though. Do not enter the coppice at the same time. Apollo first, Blits second. Keep your head and your wits, boys."

"Yes sir," they both replied in unison.

Having his lifelong friend accompany him seemed to give Apollo a fresh wave of confidence. "Good luck," Wickett finally said as the two Forest Guards lay paws out into the Great Vast Open.

"Son," Apollo began in a stern voice, "you need no luck when accompanying Apollo the Fantastic." He turned to Blits. "To the hares!" he shouted, and both he and Blits dashed out into the melting snow and towards the commandeered coppice across the openness.

"Idiot," Coinin stated as they ran away.

"Yes, but a brave one. Blits too," Sergeant Castor replied, with a very well-hidden sense of pride.

Wickett and Coinin had elected to stay in the western border as lookouts for their comrades. Sergeant Castor had vanished back to the warren to inform General Lupus of proceedings. As the daylight grew and the temperature warmed, Wickett sat in the thawing snow and laughed to himself. Coinin looked at him. "What are you laughing for?" he asked inquisitively.

"Apollo. Will there ever be another like him?"

"Oh, I hope not," Coinin replied.

Wickett looked on at the hazy coppice that his friends were heading to. For the first time in a very long time concern fluttered throughout his small body for his friends, but then he remembered exactly how they both complimented each other in their duties as Forest Guards. Blits was clever and could see things developing before they even took place. He could divert any situation with a well-laid plan even before anyone else would know there was a problem. And he cared, too. He'd never leave a fellow rabbit on his own in a situation like this, and had proved that to the rabbits when he chose to accompany Apollo on this dangerous quest. And Apollo was - well, he was Apollo, and that's what made Wickett laugh. He'd stumbled and fallen magnificently through every single mission he'd ever been given whilst serving the Forest Guard with Wickett. But he was the only rabbit in all Forest Guards across the whole of Averon to actually complete every task he'd undertaken.

A sense of hope engulfed their leader. With Blits' knowledge and heart, and Apollo's stupidity, he was sure they'd scrape through this somehow.

Part 3

Many Enemies, Few Friends

1

The warm dawn greeted the new-formed warriors as they assembled at the borders of Shadow Oak. With Doran gone, Streak had now been given leadership of the animals with the assistance of Brock, the ever wise and faithful badger. It was so unlike their first venture, with both the rabbits' Forest Guard and Flicar of the muntjac absent, replaced by three warrior dogs from Akando's clan, two otters, and also a squirrel. No-one knew where the trail began that would lead them into the Forest of the Damned, but Danjo knew of an old hermit who may point them in the right direction.

With the exception of Garla and Flicar, the remaining great council representatives who had stayed within Shadow Oak assembled with the warriors as their quest began. Akando spoke quietly to his tribe as the rest assembled. "Remember," he ordered sternly to Lyro, Makoto and Pairo. "The rats will follow you to the entrance of the forest. They will be subtle and discreet. Enter the forest; find out what you need to know, and when you emerge -"

"They'll be waiting for us," Makoto added in a sinister voice.

"Yes, they will." Akando notice Lyro looking somewhat troubled. "Lyro!" Akando whispered subtly. Lyro snapped from whatever it was he was thinking.

"Yes," he replied quickly, then added "I will not fail you."

"Good," Akando said in a commanding tone. "You are my greatest warriors, and I don't expect that you will," he added in encouragement.

Pairo looked slyly over his shoulder towards Streak, who seemed to be holding a conversation with Kedem. "What should we do if they begin to suspect us?" he asked, his deep eyes glaring intently upon the warriors.

"They must not suspect a thing, or the plan will fail. Do not fail me," Akando warned them.

After his conversation with Kedem, Streak noticed Tali wander over to him. He smiled reluctantly as the task at hand loomed ominously upon them.

"I came to wish you luck, again," she said in her surprisingly upbeat voice. He knew she was making references to his previous escapades. The injury she had sustained by Doran's paw was still prominent across her muzzle. "And make sure you come back."

Streak saw that the new band of warriors was getting ready to leave. Chance and Checkers were extremely motivated, he thought - especially as they were heading into certain danger, and for the first time too.

"Listen, Tali. Doran -"

"I know what Doran's like," Tali interrupted. Streak simply looked upon her as she continued with her speech. "I've lived with him long enough to know how stubborn that dog is," she said as Shadow Oak came to life with well-wishers for the departing party. "He's gone with the thought that what he is doing will help us all in the end. If he feels that this is the best way forward, and because he believes it, I believe it too."

"Streak!" came Brock's voice as the newly-assembled warriors were preparing to leave.

"Just concentrate on what you have to do, and don't worry about Doran," she then added. Streak turned to her and nodded as he replied with his silent goodbye.

He wandered quickly toward Brock, Selwyn, Danjo, Chance, Checkers, Lyro, Makoto and Pairo to complete the second group of warriors to undertake a great task at the request of the Great Council. Pairo glared at him with malice. Akando watched on with Kedem and Rebus, as the warriors vanished from Shadow Oak and onto their journey.

"Do you think they're capable of venturing through the Damned?" Dallie asked, as she watched two of her contingents slowly depart as warriors.

"They have strong wills and courageous hearts," Kedem replied to her as he watched a band of warriors leaving Shadow Oak for a second time. "Can you ask any more of any creature navigating those forbidden trees?"

"Certainly not," Rebus answered in a prominent voice. "As Cyrius often retorts, there is always hope."

The mention of Cyrius prompted Kedem to remember the conversation both he and Rebus held during the meeting of the Great Council, the one where Cyrius warned them there would be bloodshed and death on this venture for the warriors. Please don't let it be theirs,'he thought silently to himself.

"This is going to be great!" exclaimed Chance as he bounded along next to his new friends.

"This is not a trip," Lyro began in a stern but friendly voice. "You must keep your wits about you; the forest we are heading to is full of danger."

"We can handle danger," Checkers interrupted as he walked beside Chance, both otters excited to be involved in such a venture.

"It's not just danger you'll encounter," Streak began as they completely passed across the boundaries of Shadow Oak, "it's the elements -"

"We're otters, we can survive through almost any element the Great Forest can throw at us," Chance chipped in.

Checkers agreed. "Anything," he replied.

Brock and Selwyn plodded along with a sense of amusement. "It's like having the rabbits with us," the boar stated. The pheasant agreed.

"We're just as brave as they are," Chance replied.

"I don't doubt it for a second," Brock replied to him. Even Makoto and Pairo raised a smile.

"That's what we need. Brave warriors on this quest," Streak said, as the warriors trod an undisturbed trail of diminishing snow. The trees above were leaking dew, and fresh water droplets splashed on to the warriors and into the patchy element as they passed through the dense woodland and out towards the Trail of Fallen Stars. Danjo kept a step ahead in front of them as he led the way towards their destination.

"Warriors who are fearless in the face of danger," Selwyn added as he followed the squirrel.

"That's us!" Chance chirped. They wandered on together, this new band of warriors thrown together at a moment's notice.

"Warriors who are unafraid of any living creature," Brock added in amusement.

"Otters are known for their bravery!" Checkers replied, full of confidence. Still they wandered on together. The otters walked proudly beside Streak and Lyro at the head of the party, flanked by Makoto and Pairo, followed by Brock and Selwyn.

"Warriors who can stand face-to-face with the ghosts who dwell deep within the Haunted Woods and the banafrits who walk vastly through the Forest of the Damned," Pairo added slyly. Streak and Lyro wandered on momentarily until a call from Brock halted them and turned their attention back behind the trail they had just wandered. Stood isolated on their hinds were both Chance and Checkers, frozen solidly in their tracks.

"Banafrits? Ghosts?" Chance asked as he looked at Checkers. "I thought Cyrius was joking? You told me he was joking," he said in a concerned voice as he looked at the other otter.

"I thought he was," Checkers replied.

"Banafrits?" Chance said again. "Ghosts?" Silence engulfed the warriors momentarily as they looked upon the otter. Finally he took a few steps forward, before stopping again. He looked at the bigger creatures ahead of him. "You lot better be the greatest warriors in this forest," he informed them as they began their journey again through the cold air.

"The best," Lyro added, to settle the distressed creature.

"We'll be fine," Checkers said to Chance as the journey began again towards the Haunted Woods. Chance looked away, almost in disgust.

Danjo had been scouting ahead of the pack but had heard the concerns of the otters as they advanced closer toward him on the trail. He stopped his patchy brown and grey body and waited for the animals to reach him.

"How are you?" he asked Chance when they arrived.

"Fine," the silky otter added as his lean body glided over the disappearing snow.

"You know something," Danjo began subtly. Selwyn and Brock watched on from the rear of the pack.

"What?" Chance asked inquisitively.

"You know you can't kill banafrits or ghosts, right?"

"WHAT?" Chance shouted, and froze once more. Selwyn nearly barged into him and only just managed to stop in time. He looked towards Brock and confirmed it.

"Just like having rabbits," he said.

As the animals settled and Shadow Oak cleared of the well-wishers, Akando remained in silence and smiled to himself. Two rats emerged from their hiding place when the entire clearing was empty. Akando said nothing, simply nodded his head towards the wiry, dark furred rodents. They both turned and vanished over the melting snow and into the trees and shrubbery surrounding the vast clearing. One was gathering its followers to track the warriors.

The other gathered its counterparts and ran towards The Black Lands.

2

The beast slumbered within the lower branches of a thick oak tree as the sun rose in the sky and melted the snow from the branches of Averon. She laid prone, her front paws stretching out the length of the wide branch as it reached out in front of her and inclined towards the tops of the trees. Her rear paws tucked up comfortably at the base of the branch as she drifted in and out of consciousness, her black tail hanging limply down from the lofts of the tree.

Humans had discussed and debated her existence for many, many seasons, and still did not know fully whether she existed or was simply just a story they shared with one another. She had been given many names by them in their tales - the black cat, the beast of the moor, to name but a few - but her jet-black fur and striking yellow eyes confirmed the status which many of the humans believed. She was a panther. She had been kept enclosed in a pen by humans long ago, and one night during a huge thunderstorm an immense bolt of lightning had struck the enforced masts that held the pen together, blowing it wide open and allowing her to escape. Since then she had travelled the length and depth of the Great Vast Open and beyond, occasionally being spotted by the humans as she passed through. For a panther to be roaming in the wild within the Great Vast Open was unnatural and often dismissed, and her legend slowly began to creep into lore.

The cold and damp branch the beast rested her darkened body upon went unnoticed as she slumbered. Her body was tired from the attack upon the muntjac the previous night. She rested now whilst her stomach was full and her mind contented.

Somewhere not too far away, the hunted muntjac contingency also rested.

3

Apollo and Blits passed through the Great Vast Open in relative safety. Of course, there were the threatening noises which kept them alert; from birds flying high above them to what sounded like hounds and monsters racing to attack them from all directions. At least, to Apollo, that was what they sounded like. Blits had noticed that the birds watching them were kestrels, and after the part they played during the great battle knew that they were relatively safe from any attack from above.

As they bounded over the depleting snow, they began to feel more worried with every step towards the coppice overrun with the enemy hares. Apollo engaged his ears and kept his eyes wide open. They weren't far away from the coppice now, and had now begun merging and passing through groups of hares scattered in this area of openness. Apollo's first reaction was that every hare he passed would see that he was in fact a rabbit, and would attack him at the first chance they had. He could feel their eyes boring deep into his mind, seeing through his disguise and bounding over to attack him. Hares boxed with their paws and would break all the bones in his body. They'd break his bones first, then they'd stomp on him, then kick him, then -

"Apollo!" Blits snapped in a whisper.

"What?" he replied quickly. They had come to rest not far from the now-huge coppice, and could see that it sank deep into the ground and was surrounded by dense shrubbery. Some hares were looking them over not far away, but not in a threatening manner. They all bore the warpaint that Lisket was favourable to, and the two rabbits blended in perfectly.

"You need to go in," Blits informed his partner.

"Where are you going?" Apollo whispered back.

"Don't be such a fool!" Blits snapped. "They know Tolka left on his own. What do you think they'll say when you turn up with me in tow? I'll be in there soon - I'm going to wait for a moment and find another way in."

"How will I know where you are?"

"If you don't see me, you know this camouflage is working."

"Blits!"

"I will be in there, okay? I'll find a way of grabbing your attention somehow." Both rabbits stood looking at each other one final time. "Go on, Apollo, the great and mighty one," Blits said with a mild hint of sarcasm. Apollo turned and faced the coppice opening from which hares were emerging and descending. He looked back at his comrade.

"Apollo the Unfortunate," he replied unenthusiastically. Blits began making some strange and wonderful noises as frustration set in, and began kicking snow at Apollo to get him moving. "All right, all right," Apollo began, and slowly hopped his mud-covered grey fur towards the coppice. "Just make sure my legend lives on in the heart of all rabbits," he said in one final dramatic voice.

"Idiot," Blits said to himself, as the brave rabbit eventually disappeared into the coppice. He knew he would have to follow soon enough, and began to scout around for a different entry point. He passed hares without even returning a blink from them, and found a smaller entrance on the other side of their hiding place. Come on, he said to himself, grateful that Apollo couldn't hear him. You can do this, Blits. You can do this! And when his confidence had peaked, he too vanished into the middle of the hare's hideout.

Apollo entered the dank hideaway, and almost left pellets when he saw what he had entered. Underneath the shrubbery and trees above he found himself in a crater of earth that seemed to have been scraped out by many paws. The tunnel he had entered from had declined dramatically into the opening, and within the excavated earth now amassed an army of brown hares, all going about their daily duties. The sun streamed in between the branches and leaves above him, but Apollo couldn't tell what type of trees they were. Bracken and dry leaves scattered atop the ground he was stood upon, making for a warmer footing than the remnants of the melting snow outside. Across the coppice the bracken began to incline into a mound, where a number of bushes nestled silently and undisturbed by the hares rushing around them. It was from one bush that Apollo noticed a humongous hare emerging. His heart sank. He knew that this would be Lisket, the leader of the hares he would be forced to speak with.

It has to be, he said to himself as he pondered his own thoughts. It looks like he's on a fresh diet of berries, leaves, and infiltrating rabbits. One hare barged past the disguised Forest Guard, pushing him firmly to one side. Apollo corrected himself and was disgusted that the hare offered no apology. "Morning," Apollo said sarcastically as the ignorant creature passed by. More of the hares ran past and in front of him, leading him to believe that something was going on.

"Tolka!" boomed a voice across the busy coppice. Apollo engaged his ears.

Here goes,'he thought. He looked up towards the mound above and saw Lisket leering down upon him. Apollo did the next thing he thought of, and nodded towards the great hare in acknowledgement. Lisket gestured for Apollo to join him, and with a quivering sigh the brave rabbit mustered all of his courage and made his way through the bustling coppice.

"Status report," Lisket ordered as Apollo crept up the inclining mound. "What did you find?"

Apollo's mind went into overdrive. Would he remember what he was supposed to say? "Erm... yes... sir," Apollo replied less than convincingly. Lisket looked him over with a deducing eye. "The warren, is, well, it's still there," he added, almost sensing that Lisket could feel the fear emerging from his mud-covered fur. Lisket continued to look over him, confused by his stealth warrior's behaviour.

"What's the matter, Tolka?" he asked sternly.

"Nothing," Apollo added, trying rapidly to form an explanation. "Just a tad tired is all. All this exploring is very tiring."

"A tad tired?" Lisket asked in confusion. He had never heard a hare use that expression before.

"Yes, a tad. Er, little, small, you know, erm, a little tired from the expedition." Apollo felt fear engulf him, but at the same time keep it subdued enough to keep a clear head.

"Right," Lisket queried before looking away, then returning his gaze as if knowing that something was not quite right. "Soldiers!" he suddenly boomed at the top of his voice, bringing the entire coppice to an immediate standstill. Blits had managed to infiltrate the hares successfully, but whilst entering during the hustle and bustle had not noticed Apollo stood high on the mound above him. Likewise, Apollo had not noticed Blits, having been too engrossed in the conversation with the giant hare. He would not have recognised Blits anyway; he blended in immaculately with the hares that surrounded him. Thank Averon they used mud as warpaint!

The hares turned their attention to Lisket who towered above them. "Tolka has returned from the forest where the rabbits dwell," Lisket began in his authoritative voice, "and will now explain to all of us what he has found."

Lisket stood back and gestured for Apollo to address the mass. "What?" asked the shocked rabbit.

Lisket closed his eyes in frustration. "Address our soldiers on what you found!" he snapped.

"Erm," Apollo began as what seemed like thousands of eyes fixed firmly upon him. "Okay," he said, slowly shuffling to the edge of the mound. Apollo was done for; at least that's what he thought. This was it. This was the end. Apollo the Amazing would now meet his demise here in the huge coppice, torn to shreds by a battalion of angry hares. Having resigned himself to imminent death, of the worst possible kind, Apollo gave up and did what came naturally to him.

Spoke nonsense.

"My friends!" he began in a loud, jovial voice, throwing his paws into the air. "I return with news from the Great Forest of Aver- whatever you call it!" he changed quickly, knowing that the hares wouldn't know it by its true name.

Here we go!'Blits thought to himself, and shook his head.

"YAAAR!" came the thunderous war-cry from the army of hares. Good. So far, they believed him.

"I return with news that will amaze you! News that will astound you all in your quest to pillage the rabbit's warren!"

"YAAAR!" came the unified response.

Apollo's mind suddenly drew blank. He forgot everything he was supposed to be saying. He looked around in an attempt to think of something to say, anything to keep them on his side and hanging on his words. "Erm," he said loudly, then noticed the sun beaming down between the leaves. "It is indeed fine weather we're having today!" he shouted at the top of his voice.

Silence engulfed the coppice, except for the partial breeze that rustled the leaves high up above them. The hares all glared at him intently. Lisket simply stared at his soldier in bewilderment. You idiot! Blits screamed within his mind. Still the hares said nothing, leaving Apollo stood alone in solitude in front of the ruthless creatures. Apollo's ears drooped as he looked out upon the sea of eyes. Blits did the only thing he could think of to save his friend and hoped for the best. He closed his eyes...

"YAAAR!" he yelled at the top of his voice. After a moment of silence and dread, the hares responded.

"YAAAR!" the coppice erupted, although it did so questioningly.

Both Apollo and Blits sighed secretly under their breath, and once more Apollo addressed his listeners with the facts he had been ordered to deploy now fresh inside his mind once again. "I have discovered that the tunnel we used to raid the rabbits warren seasons ago is still intact and being used." The hares drew silent as Apollo relayed the perfectly created plan out to the masses. "The tunnel has since been modified. Every branching tunnel it sprouted has now been blocked and fallen into disrepair, but the main tunnel itself leads directly to the chamber where General Lup- I mean, their general resides."

Another slip-up quickly corrected was only noted this time by Blits. He sat shoulder to shoulder with the hares and was completely stunned that they believed this eccentric preacher jabbering on above them.

"If we take this tunnel and besiege their chamber, we can ransom their general into leaving, allowing us free reign of their warren until we decide to move on!" A loud cheer erupted from the coppice. Blits was knocked from side to side as the larger hares jumped up in cheer. "So I say we go! We go, and we invade their forest!" Another cheer engulfed the hares as their adrenaline burst into life and the promise of a warm chamber and warren beckoned to them.

Realising what he had just done, Apollo prayed that he could find Blits in the mass of fur and mud, and that the rabbits themselves were now ready for Lisket and his hordes - who would soon be invading.

4

Doran wandered slowly into a woodland enchanted by evergreens. They towered vastly above him and rustled as the warm breeze passed between their limbs and leaves, shaking snow from their branches and clearing their greenery once more. The scent of pine was wonderfully strong in the air as Doran crunched over the final patches of snow still to be melted, and now began to see the dull, brown hue of the woodland floor he had been accustomed to whilst living within the forest. He walked amongst an alley of trees as he pondered his situation and what he was going to do.

With every day that passed he could feel the darkness taking a further grip on him, turning him from the fox he had been into the vicious, angry dog he was becoming. His outbursts at Shadow Oak towards Tali and Streak had proved that to him. He had watched on, almost as a passenger in his own body, as he had confronted the foxes on both occasions; trying in vain to stop, but being unsuccessful in his attempts. The darkness was now beginning to govern him and control his every thought and emotion. Patches of black fur appeared in his greying coat, making the few red patches he had seem scarce and irrelevant. The worst thing for him though was the battle that was raging within his mind. He was fighting this curse with all his might, but it was failing. A lesser dog would have succumbed quickly to the influence of the darkness, but still he fought this exhausting battle, and now it had taken its toll. Doran firmly believed that the darkness would shroud and engulf him completely, and that soon he would just be another minion of the dark arts. This thought terrified him, but he knew this would eventually be the outcome. And when it did happen, when the darkness did eventually take him, he did not want to be at Shadow Oak. He wanted to be remembered as a warrior, as one of the animals who repelled the Dark Army, not as a fox who turned to darkness and savaged his homeland.

From nowhere the sound of running paws jolted him from his wandering day-dream. Doran scouted amongst the trees either side of the trail. Their trunks were spaced loosely apart from one another, giving the fox an eye-line deep into the trees. The green haze of faraway vegetation and trees revealed nothing suspicious. There were no hiding places anywhere between the bark, meaning that whatever made the noise was darting between the trees, and thus small enough to hide behind them. Doran waited a moment longer, just in case it had been his imagination. Sometimes the breeze had ways of sounding different as it glided through the forest. When he was happy the sound had ceased, he continued along the avenue as though nothing had happened. His dark paws found the trail's floor as he passed across the grass and continued his journey to nowhere.

There it was again. Doran stopped and turned once more, this time knowing that the sound of the paws he had just heard was not created from his imagination. A flurry of anger passed through the fox, and a cloud of darkness passed briefly through his eyes.

"Hey!" came a voice, and an animal launched from the trees and into the middle of the trail behind him. Doran turned and focused on the long, slinky body that rested face-down in the diminishing snow. Its head shook, and banished snow from its whiskers and snout.

A stoat? Doran asked himself, as he looked at the creature push itself up from the snow and on to all-fours. The stoat's appearance reminded him of a weasel, long and slender. His eyes and ears were unusually small, his fur a shade of reddish brown, and white on his underside. He also noticed how incredibly short the stoat's legs were.

"You," the stoat began, almost in astonishment, "you have it too?"

"Have what?" the dog asked.

The stoat took a step closer. "The darkness," he replied. Doran almost shrank away in fear or excitement, he couldn't tell which. The stoat knew about the darkness? "It dwells within you," he added, coming ever closer to Doran.

"How do you know about it?" the fox asked ponderously. What would a creature this far into desolation know about it?

"We must be connected," the stoat added, and smiled. From his mouth a plume of dark swirls expelled and danced joyously around his head and neck. Doran watched in amazement as the stoat tracked the swirls with his nose, floating by as if they were choreographed in an exaggerated dance. The swirls disbanded into three more plumes and coasted into the air in different directions. Suddenly they jolted and hovered above the cursed stoat. The breeze that passed along the trail couldn't even dispel them as they began swirling and merging into an outline of a circle, spinning rapidly above the creatures head. The circle exploded into a small puff of dark mass, and then drew back to its residence in long, smoky lines through the stoat's nose and mouth.

"You," began the amazed fox, "you can control it?"

The stoat nodded. "I escaped the Black Lands and came to this remote part of the forest," he explained.

"The very thought of being controlled by darkness and to be used for evil deeds repulsed me. Here, I managed to tame the darkness and bend it to my own will. I am no longer governed by the darkness. It is the darkness that is now governed by me."

A spark of hope ignited within Doran. It was possible to emerge victorious over the evil dwelling from within, just as Cyrius had told him. "Can you -"

"Help you?" the stoat interrupted, as though he had read Doran's mind. Doran looked on momentarily, before nodding his snout. The stoat sighed and looked over the fox as though he was studying him. "I see your battle is great with the darkness. At times it has almost taken you, but, but..."

"What?" Doran asked, as the stoat placed a fresh seed of doubt in the fox's mind.

"You were brought back from imminent death by the darkness. You have so much of it lurking inside you, and yet you have not succumbed to its will," the slender animal replied in amazement. "You were turned directly by Seerles himself, and so harshly, and still it hasn't taken you."

"Not yet, but I can't fight it much longer."

"Do you know what this means?"

Doran looked on in confusion. "What?" he asked.

The stoat became excited. "The power that lies within you is immense," he began as the warm breeze picked up again. "It eclipses anything I have ever found in the Black Lands or otherwise." Doran stood without saying a word. "You are second only to Seerles himself."

"What does that mean?" Doran asked.

The stoat bounded closer to the dog. "It means that if we can teach you to control it, you may very well be the strongest warrior within this Great Forest. You may be the one who can restore order to Averon and repel the darkness and its followers during the Mighty War."

"War!" Doran shouted. "What war?"

"I see only possibilities that the darkness allows," the stoat began sternly, "and I believe there to be an immense war looming between your Warriors of Averon and the darkness from the Black Lands."

"No..." Doran replied, his voice trailing away.

"I'm afraid it is true," the stoat replied. "Not immediately, but a few seasons away at most. Seerles is in league with Akando -"

"Akando!" Doran snapped in anger. His eyes swirled with inky darkness.

"They are gathering warriors together to attack Shadow Oak."

"I have to go back," Doran began, as realisation set in. He had felt it too. He knew that something was bound to happen at Shadow Oak. With every day that passed something inside had told him of bad things looming for the warriors and the foxes of his community, but because his mastery of the darkness was poor, he believed it would be himself who would launch the attack - not Seerles or Akando.

"You must not go back, my friend. Not yet," the stoat replied. "If you return now, you will be merely another fox with warrior skills that will fall to their masses." Doran looked at the stoat, who now rose himself to his hinds. "If you stay here with me, we can attempt to put you in control of the vast darkness that lives inside you - and you can then return, using the darkness for the good of all animals living within the forest, and using it in war to combat the Black Lands."

Doran considered this a moment. "I can't just leave them," he added after a moment's thought.

"You won't be. You will return a greater warrior than you are now, and the difference in battle you will make will be far greater with the darkness as your ally, not as your foe."

Doran sighed, and looked away into the trees. His home would be under attack within the next few seasons - that's if the stoat was right, of course. But if he was right, he had time to attempt the mastery of the darkness with his new friend, a creature who had done so already. It is what Doran had wanted, to control it for himself and not to be controlled. He looked back at the stoat stood in the trail.

"How long will it take?" he asked.

"The fact that you have lasted so long without being taken by the vast darkness within would suggest you're stronger than most who are cursed by its power. I don't know exactly how long, but the sooner we start the quicker we will finish."

Doran looked around at the trees and leaves. The sunshine now broke the clouds completely and shone down in shafts between the branches into the greenery beyond the avenue he was standing in. He noticed again the fresh scent of pine wafting through his nose. If Seerles and Akando overpowered the Great Council and Shadow Oak, the forest of Averon would fall entirely to the Black Lands. Trees would die, leaves shrivel, and fog would descend upon the entire forest.

"Is it worth fighting for?" the stoat asked seriously, as though reading Doran's mind yet again.

"What do I call you?" the dog asked.

Loat, a voice echoed loudly inside his mind.

Doran nodded, and accepted the connection that they shared. "I am Doran of Shadow Oak. I will stay with you and learn your ways in an attempt to assist the Great Council in repelling this threat of which you have foreseen."

"Then there is not a moment to lose. Follow me."

Doran followed as Loat ran from the trail and into the evergreens. Now, he could finally begin his recovery from the darkness.

Far, far away across the forest, Seerles stirred in his lair. He hissed loudly in anger. His eyes burned red and lighted through the darkness of his dwelling. He had witnessed the meeting between Doran and Loat. Since he had saved the injured dog seasons ago he had tried to take him and turn the dog toward the Black Lands. Doran had resisted strongly, and Seerles had respected his fight, almost knowing that one day he would turn and be in league with the darkness. Now his plan was foiled, and he would have to make sure he could keep the upper hand. His scales scratched the floor as he shifted in the gloom. He would have to take something that belonged to Doran or meant something greatly to him to keep an advantage.

Something like a sibling.

5

Coinin had been sat solitary for a while now, looking out into the warm morning that had engulfed the Great Vast Open. The snow had all but vanished, and the warm temperature on the breeze signified that this may indeed finally be the end of the cold season. With the harsh weather dwindling away, the big thaw could begin, and after that the warm season would be upon them. The big thaw was the season that joined the cold and warm together, a time when flowers sprouted, butterflies appeared, and the grass began holding a brilliant green colour within their blades. Coinin however preferred the warm season over any other. The warm nights, the bright days; that was definitely the season he adored the most.

As he sat thinking of warm sunshine and colourful leaves, he was disturbed by the noise of rustling coming from the opening behind him. He turned, and over the damp grass saw Wickett approaching him. "Any sign?" the Forest Guard asked as he settled next to Coinin.

Coinin shook his head. "None," he replied bluntly. Wickett nodded slowly and joined his gaze out into the Great Vast Open. "How are the preparations?" he then asked his comrade.

"Complete," Wickett stated. "The tunnels are blocked and the warren safe."

"All we need now is for Apollo to complete his task."

Wickett offered nothing in reply, just a gaze out towards the coppice in the far distance. Somewhere inside it were Apollo and Blits, either having successfully infiltrated their nemesis, or - well, the latter didn't even bear thinking about.

6

It was early afternoon by the time the warriors had reached the Trail of Fallen Stars, an obstacle that had played such an important role in their last expedition. Danjo had successfully navigated to its easiest crossing point in the forest, and would now have to lead them deep inside the Black Lands to the Haunted Woods. Streak immediately noticed the burrow beneath the trail that had been used by the rabbits. Danjo and the otters would pass safely underneath; it was the rest who must make the treacherous crossing.

The trail itself was also covered by huge puddles of melted snow and was only distinguishable through the patches of grey and black that had appeared where the melting element could not rest. Streak brought the warriors to a stand-still. "Here we are," he said subtly. Lyro looked on with Pairo and Makoto. "The trail." But Streak had noticed something else too, and a glance towards Brock and Selwyn revealed that they had also noticed.

"What in Averon's name has happened here?" Selwyn asked in awe and concern. "Look at this."

The trees and leaves on their side of the trail had become withered, twisted and dark. Piles of shrivelled leaves rested contently at the bases of their twisted trunks. The ground was darker and seemed to be reaching toward the forest behind them, as though the darkness from the Black Lands had crossed the trail and was now reaching out toward the rest of the forest.

"What?" Pairo asked as he frowned with confusion. The animals stood in silence, waiting for a reply.

"The Black Lands," Brock eventually said, looking at the now-darkened forest reaching out toward them. "It's spreading."

"He is becoming stronger," Streak replied as he scoured the dark trees, noticing the greenery of a shaded fern beginning to become infected with various darkened shades.

The animals stood and gazed in the silent forest as the reality of the situation slowly set in. Fear was gripping the animals of Averon and making Seerles stronger with each one that became afraid. As he became stronger his grip over Averon increased, and now the Black Lands was expanding, eating away at the forest and making him more powerful.

"We must continue with our task at hand," Streak finally said, pushing this discovery to the back of his mind. "If we don't succeed, we are adding to his power."

"Shall I look out?" Selwyn asked, ruffling his spotted wings and returning the thoughts of the animals to the reason why they were there.

Streak looked at him and nodded. "Yes. Keep a sharp eye."

Selwyn waddled towards the lookout point he had used during his previous visit. It harboured the best view along both sides of the trail.

"The weather has been known to deter the monsters before now," Brock began as he moved closer forward. "Perhaps we will have a stroke of luck."

"Maybe," Makoto replied.

"Danjo. Otters. Use the burrow and meet us on the other side," Streak ordered. The smaller animals left the group and vanished down into the burrow safely. "Come on," he said to the rest, gesturing that they follow him. "The sooner we cross, the sooner we continue."

With Selwyn on lookout, the warriors crossed with relative ease. There were no monsters this time round to contend with, and not even the hint of one approaching from within the far reaches of the trail.

The animals regrouped once they had safely crossed. The atmosphere had changed almost completely and a gust of wind engulfed them rapidly. It came from the deepest part of the dark trees ahead of them and rustled the branches immensely as the warriors looked on. Four foxes, two otters, a badger, a pheasant and a squirrel stood ominously on the depleted snow, looking towards a hidden destination. "Welcome to the Haunted Woods," Streak informed them.

7

The muntjac rested in communion after the attack from the beast the previous night. In an opening segregated by bushes and shrubbery they rested, with wary buck keeping a stern look out for any signs that the beast was near. History had told them they would rest in relative safety during the day, as the elusive beast had previously attacked during the dark hours during nightfall.

Flicar and Garla were still awake as the warm breezes set in. They were lying in an isolated coppice big enough to hold the both of them, and dry enough for both deer to rest in comfortably.

Flicar raised his antlers as his nose caught a scent of freshness travelling on the breeze. "The big thaw," he said, as he recognised the forest's new scents and smells that signified the changing of the season.

Garla raised her own head and took a deep breath. "Finally," she began, as the breeze engulfed her. "Something to be cheerful for."

"Not long until the warm season is upon us."

"I hope so," Garla agreed, "it shouldn't be long at all. We have had a longer than usual cold season."

"Too long," the buck replied.

"Daisy!" Favradin snapped as he approached a young fawn trotting through some tall trees. Daisy snapped her head and looked upon the buck as he trotted over toward her. "Daisy!" he said once again as he approached her. The small doe looked up with concern. "What have we told you about wandering off

302

on your own? You know the forest can be dangerous for one as inexperienced as yourself."

"I was just exploring," Daisy replied in a slight, timid voice. Daisy was a young fallow deer found wandering alone through the forest at the beginning of the last warm season. She had no trace of any family or fallow deer to look after her, and being so young was extremely vulnerable to the elements and to the threats that could befall her. Garla had taken her in as one of her own, and she had lived with the muntjac ever since.

Favradin sighed. "You know, Garla will discipline me if anything happens to you. You must always tell me where you're going whenever you decide to take up an adventure such as this." Daisy nodded gently, realising she had done wrong. Favradin looked at her, knowing that she had learnt her lesson. The trees they were stood inside were not far away from the rest of the contingency, and Favradin was sure Daisy would be fine as long as she stayed where she was.

"Stay in this wood," he ordered finally, "and if I call you, you come to me immediately, understand?"

"Yes Favradin," the doe replied, seemingly happy she hadn't had the ear-bashing she expected. "I'll stay here."

Flicar lay watching the deer outside as they patrolled the area. Many were trying to rest, having spent a night fleeing en masse from the beast that hunted them. He lay in a state of semi-consciousness, until something caught his attention. The body of a doe darted past the opening. Then another. Flicar frowned. A buck and a doe shot past. Then a buck. Flicar became alarmed and rose to his hooves. He was greeted by the sight of the contingency rapidly vanishing in all different directions and into the trees. He stepped from the coppice and looked out.

"Run!" came an excitable voice.

"Run!" screamed another.

"What's happening?" Garla asked with concern as she emerged from her resting place. She looked out to see her entire contingency fleeing in all different directions. Flicar's eyes scoured the trees. There. He saw it. Slowly stalking its way into the opening emerged a huge, black creature, muscular and powerful.

"No..." Flicar trailed off.

"The beast!" Garla screamed.

"Run!" Flicar ordered his leader, his gaze continually upon the stalking predator. "Run!" he ordered, this time looking directly toward her.

Then it happened.

The beast turned its eyes to Flicar, their deep, yellow colour locking with those of the warrior. They stared at one another momentarily as fleeing bucks and terrified does passed rapidly between them. The beast began advancing and cantered into a slow trot.

"Come on!" Flicar ordered, and rallied Garla to follow. They forced their hooves into the warming ground and both deer broke into an immediate run, tearing across the small opening and into the chaos. Flicar looked to his right to see the beast now in full sprint, hunting them down callously. They darted into a small woodland of tight birches, passing gracefully between the dull trunks as they bounded through at great speed. The leaves high above them merged and blocked much of the sky and its natural light, leaving the muntjac to sprint inside a relatively dark, close, woodland area. They thundered through the gloom and emerged on a small uneven trail that had completely thawed of its frost, leaving a soft, muddy floor for their hooves to sink into. Flicar took an advantage against his leader, who was struggling to keep up with the awkward flooring. Flicar looked over his shoulder to see the huge bulk of the beast closing them down. Run!'his mind screamed. RUN!

Garla screamed as she was pounced upon from behind. The weight of the beast slammed her into the sodden floor harshly. Flicar turned, having heard the commotion behind, and charged without fear to protect his leader. He slammed into the beast with his antlers, thrusting it sideways and from the body of the targeted doe. Garla attempted to stand, but something was wrong. She couldn't. The beast roared thunderously as she leapt to her paws, and swiped at Flicar with vicious claws. The power of the attack sent Flicar tumbling away, her claws penetrating his body so deeply that blood oozed out of his fresh laceration. The injury stung viciously down the buck's entire left side, reeling him into momentary shock. He rolled in pain upon the ground, before hearing a blood-curdling yelp. Rousing from the drowsiness of the heavy attack, he stumbled to his hooves and remembered Garla.

But it was too late.

The beast had taken advantage of the injured doe and clamped its vice-like jaws around her throat, snapping her neck instantly. "NO!" screamed Flicar, as the beast dropped the lifeless deer from her powerful grasp.

Flicar moved tentatively. Every step he took sent pains screaming through his left side. The beast looked upon him with unforgiving eyes, and snarled. The small woodland of birches would be his final memory. He had failed to protect his leader, and would be remembered as the buck that had not repelled the terrible beast of Averon. Once again the beast slowly stalked him as he stumbled clumsily over the treacherous ground. She circled him slowly, her chest thundering as she growled, her yellow eyes dilated and concentrated on her next target. If only there had been more time,Flicar thought as his last memories passed rapidly through his mind. If only there had been more time!

The beast planted her paws into the sodden ground and lurched back. Flicar stood motionless, unable to do anything more. He simply stared at his doom, waiting for his fate to finally be fulfilled.

The beast lurched back further, her jet-black fur glowing shades of grey and white as the branches above them broke and closed with the breeze, adding light to the shaded woodland. Her eyes shrank. The growl turned into a ferocious roar. Her ears flattened and her jaws opened. She pushed with all her might and thrust through the air, her front legs reaching out toward the buck...

The beast was slammed from the air by two bucks using their small antlers to throw her off-course. She crashed into the unforgiving tree trunks of the birches.

"GO!" Favradin shouted, rescuing his second-in-command and attracting the attention of the hunter. "Go! Inform the council!" he ordered. Flicar looked at the beast and noticed it was dazed. "GO!" the buck ordered once again, "or with your injury you'll be next. We'll do all that we can to keep it away from your trail."

"Favradin," Flicar began emotionally.

The beast growled as she gained composure and turned her focus to Favradin and his companion, both stood ready to protect Flicar in any way that they could. "Go!" Favradin ordered one final time.

Flicar looked towards his companions and then to the lifeless body of Garla hunched unnaturally on the floor. "I will tell them," he said forlornly. "I will do what I can."

Flicar darted away as fast as his injury would allow him, hearing the beast roar as she turned her attention to the brave bucks who had rescued him. The events raced through his mind as he sped from the woodland in the direction of Kedem, Brock and the Great Council. He had to get to Shadow Oak and inform them of what had happened. If he didn't, with his injury he would be an easy target for the relentless beast.

Favradin stood tall as the beast lurched to her paws. With his companion they lowered the small antlers that emerged from their skulls and adopted an attacking pose. As they stood, unintimidated, a group of bucks bounded through the trees to assist them. The beast was faced with a group of warriors now prepared to do battle, and to do whatever it took to protect their kind. The beast looked them over, aching from the attack that had jarred her senses. The woods they stood in came to rest, and the rumble in the beast's chest grew louder. She growled as she faced the bucks, preparing for battle. With her body hurting and her head dazed, the beast turned from the confrontation and leapt silently into the trees, darting rapidly into the depths of Averon. Favradin sighed as the panther disappeared from the wood and left the deer standing in the silence. Then a thought struck him. This was the same woods he had left the young fawn Daisy exploring. His heart sank. "What is it?" one of the bucks asked, noticing the change on Favradin's face.

"Oh no," Favradin replied, his body bounding erratically through the trees. "Daisy? Where's Daisy?"

8

Gloom replaced the sunlight as the warriors ventured deeper into the Haunted Woods. They had placed a lot of faith in the small grey squirrel who was acting as their guide within the Black Lands. The trees around them became darker and foreboding, and patches of fog began to scupper the adventure as Danjo vanished further ahead to scout the area.

"Does he even know where he's going?" Pairo eventually whispered to Lyro as the squirrel darted off again in the distance.

Lyro shrugged. "He says so," he replied.

The trees that were so vibrant and colourful far back across the trail had now turned into dark, dead, leafless shells with spindly arms stretched out erratically. The ground underneath, that had once been soft under-paw, had now become solid and firm. Fog seemed to have descended quickly, and as the warriors passed slowly between the trees their branches emerged silently from the fallen clouds. Strange calls and odd noises emanated from deep within the hidden woodland. Chance jumped slightly and turned at every single one that glided towards them from the clouds.

"What is this place?" Makoto asked, in marvel of the trees he had never yet explored, until now.

"This is where it begins," Brock added from a little further behind.

Slowly they emerged into a small opening, hidden in part by the fog. Danjo stood in front of them on the hardened, leaf-littered floor. "We're here," he informed them.

The warriors slowed to a standstill in front of a gnarled, twisted tree with many branches sprouting from its dark trunk. It harboured cobwebs glistening with dew, and droplets from the very tips of its twigs as the fog rested invisibly upon them. After a moment of marvelling at the strange woodland they had ventured into, a strange, scraping noise emerged from the base of an open tree trunk ahead of them. From the hollow within the trunk a small creature emerged on to the woodland ground. A rounded body appeared in front of the warriors, covered emphatically with yellow-tipped spines. The animal harboured a pointed face with a small, stout nose leading the direction it wandered. As he walked, his short legs shuffled loudly over the bracken.

"A hedgehog!" Selwyn exclaimed as the small mammal emerged from his resting hole.

"Indeed I am," the hedgehog replied as he approached the band of warriors. "I am simply known as Prickly, and I live here in the dark side of the forest. Are you the adventurers following Danjo?"

"We are," Streak said, stepping forward from the pack. "There are many animals counting on us succeeding in our quest through the trees."

"So there are," Prickly informed him as he wandered closer to the animals through the misty opening. "I hear that the beast has finally entered our forest, and with it brought death to any creature who should haplessly stumble into its path." Streak looked momentarily shocked at the hedgehog's statement.

"How do you know about the beast?" Brock asked as he stepped out from the group of warriors. He had asked the very question Streak had intended to.

"My friend," Prickly began over-dramatically, as he nestled his round body into a comfortable position, "do not be so naïve to think that animals are the only living

309

creatures within our forest. Look around you," he asked, prompting the boar to squint at the trees not hidden by the fog. "Everything lives within Averon. The grasses you tread, the mounds you shelter in - the very trees themselves are alive, and watch our every move." The warriors looked on, almost mesmerised by this wondrous creature. "If you listen closely and understand, you too will hear the trees talking. Word travels fast in the forest, if you know how to listen."

"Do you know of any way that we can defeat this beast?" Lyro asked the hedgehog, wondering if the small animal was always this dramatic in the presence of others.

"Sadly, no," Prickly replied. "I can offer no assistance to you on a quest as vast as this."

"What about the forest we intend to navigate?" Selwyn chirped from the pack of warriors. "Danjo said you may be able to help us locate the entrance to the Forest of the Damned?"

For a moment, Prickly's dark eyes widened. He looked from Danjo to the warriors. "The forest, you say?" he replied in a quiet, hypnotic voice. "What business do you have that takes you in there?"

"The oak tree," Chance snapped, and was rapidly nudged by Checkers to keep him quiet.

Streak had turned to look at the otter, before addressing the hedgehog stood before them. "Yes, we seek the advice of Stryder, the owl who protects the oak tree hidden within its borders."

Prickly sighed. "I have witnessed countless animals pass through here; some stood exactly where you are now, and who have asked me exactly the same question. I have yet to see any of them return from their quest."

"But -" Chance this time was nudged harder by his counterpart, informing him to shut his snout.

"Is it really worth it, travellers? Is it worth the risk you take entering those heinous trees for a council with Stryder that you may not even make?"

"We knew the risk when we accepted this task," Lyro began. "We were not ordered to come here; we did so of our own free will. We know what to expect."

"No. No you don't," Prickly replied in a sinister tone that unnerved Chance. "I can show you the way," he then added, after a moment of silence, "but you must be aware that the forest you are entering is unlike anything you have ever seen or experienced before." Pairo looked on, his dark mind wondering if Cyrius had said something not too dissimilar at the council meeting. "It is between the realm of the living and the realm of the dead. It is where the lost souls of the forest roam until they are able to set themselves free."

"We know the dangers," Streak began, "and we knowingly accept the consequences of anything that happens inside the forest. We enter of our own free will."

Prickly looked to his left. The warriors noticed and turned to face the direction he was looking. The beginning of a trail had mysteriously appeared from behind the fog.

"Follow the trail," the hedgehog began. "It will lead you to the Twins of Despair, the gateway to the forest. Pass between them, and you are no longer of this world." The fog swirled and pouted from all directions as the trail was revealed, making Selwyn wonder if the hedgehog himself had some control over the element. "At times you will be split from one another, and you may find yourselves back at a point on the trail you have previously passed, as though you have travelled in a huge circle. Should this happen to any of you, turn about and follow the trail back; it will lead you here. It is the natural progression of elimination. If you are returned to a place you have previously passed, do not head deeper back inside the forest. It is the only warning the forest will give you. I fear that many of the animals who passed before you attempted to continue on again, thinking they had made a mistake, and then suffered the consequences. Return back here and you will return to safety."

"We will," Streak added in confirmation, "and thank you."

"Be wary, travellers," Prickly added as he began moving from his resting place on the damp bracken. "If you do indeed make it to the oak tree that you so desire to reach, make sure that Stryder knows of your intentions. If he feels you are a threat upon the life source of our forest, he will attack you without a moment's hesitation. Remember, the Forest of the Damned is a forest not of this world. Stryder is strongly articulated in strange and un-natural events from our realm. If you can successfully navigate the trials in place that protect the trail leading to his tree, he will converse with you and assist in any way that he can, considering that your actions and intentions are pure of heart." Lyro felt the surge of adrenaline rapidly pass through his body. Would the owl know of his intentions? "But," Prickly began once again, "you must pass through the trials that protect the tree from intruders such as yourself. Only then will you reach the tree you so desire."

Prickly silently turned, revealing again the spines upon his circular body, and returned to the hollow from which he emerged.

Streak watched his prickly body vanish back inside the hollow, before turning about to address the warriors. "From now on, we stick together. All of us. If we become lost, separated or return to a previous area from our journey, we head back here, and we wait.

Understand?" All animals nodded, except Pairo. Streak looked at the trail and back to the warriors. "This is it," he began once more, "this is the trail we need to follow to pass through the forest and to the oak tree. Remember what Cyrius said? Stick together, at all costs."

"We are the warriors," Brock began, almost cementing Streak's advice with the newcomers, "and we always stay together."

Streak nodded, and turned towards the trail. The fog was dancing and swirling at its edges, as though the trail itself bore an invisible tunnel that broke the fog. Streak took a deep breath, sighed, and slowly began the journey onto the mysterious trail.

Part 4

Siege at Shadow Oak

1

Tali had taken herself away from Shadow Oak and decided on a slow walk around the Great Lake. She had wandered it many times before, but never with so much on her mind. The red vixen noticed now that the snow had vanished in the warm temperatures during the day, and herself come to the conclusion that the big thaw had finally set in upon them. The woodland around her was abuzz with fresh chirps and song as the cold season drew away and beckoned the warm season to make haste and arrive. She momentarily felt the warm season breaking through, the fresh scent of pine on the breeze, the momentary warmth from the setting sun, the red sky as it vanished to the west. All of these things she usually enjoyed, but not this time around. Her thoughts were with Streak and the warriors, but mostly fell with her brother Doran. She had watched the past seasons pass rapidly, and seen the struggle he'd endured in suppressing the darkness that dwelled deep inside of him. She felt guilt and blame every time his anger flared from within. She had allowed Seerles to save her brother's life, but at what cost? He was trapped. Governed by an entity he could not control. Little by little it consumed him as each day passed, until finally its grip was so overwhelming that he had fled Shadow Oak in fear of what he might turn into. Had she listened to Streak, Doran would have died, of that there was no question, but now she questioned as to whether it would have been easier than to damn her brother to this life he now led. She wandered on in silence as the amazing sunset continued above her, offering it no appreciation whatsoever.

Kedem hosted Rebus, Akando, Glif and Dallie inside the main den at Shadow Oak. They had remained mostly content during the warm day, their thoughts with the warriors. They had spoken about various topics from within the Great Forest, but always in their minds the mission at hand and the faith they placed within the select few adventurers rested soundly.

"Kedem!" a voice bellowed from the open. One of Kedem's advisors, Jinx, entered rapidly from the warm evening. "Come quick!" the ageing dog said, his eyes wide and fearful. Kedem immediately responded to his advisor's concern and leapt from the den. As he stood looking out upon the circular woodland eclipsed by the towering oak tree, he noticed two dark foxes emerge from a trail across from him.

"What are you -" came Rebus' snarled voice from behind, but stopped when he noticed more foxes appearing from the dense forestry to their left. Five, six, seven, eight... more appeared from their right. Akando jumped out beside Jinx. The Shadow Oak community looked towards Kedem, their leader.

"In your dens!" he ordered sternly. They rapidly obliged, as yet more foxes emerged from the forest. Twelve, thirteen, fourteen... Over the growling and snarling of all the dark foxes entering Shadow Oak came the tell-tale squeaks of the rats that had flooded from the Black Lands.

"What is this?" Glif stated as the army of foxes surrounded the community, along with the seeming hundreds of dark, wiry rodents. They engulfed Shadow Oak, keeping its occupant in a forced curfew.

"What is the meaning of this?" Rebus demanded.

"Maybe I can explain," Akando began, and walked out into the opening. He turned to face the council

318

members and grinned evilly. Kedem knew exactly what had happened.

"You -"

Snarling emitted close to the council leader as he moved forward. Kedem was suddenly flanked by two dark foxes growling viciously back at him. "Careful," Akando began in a wary tone, "or my warriors may have to deal with you!"

"This is an outrage!" Rebus boomed, and propelled his dark body forward. He was immediately repelled by a further fox under Akando's control, forcing him to take a step backwards.

"An outrage? An outrage?" Akando screamed back at the boar. "You know nothing of outrage! Outrage is watching two menial animals take charge of this forest! Outrage is bending to their will when they are incapable of what they order!" The dark foxes looked on, their eyes glowing red with the same colour of the sunset in the sky above. "For too long you and your Great Council have controlled the welfare of every animal in this forest, and not always for the best! Look at what you have already done! You have sent a group of animals to certain death just to seek knowledge! Your irresponsibility is far greater than any threat I bring to Averon!"

"It is the only course of action we can take! We need to know how to repel the beast! Simply fighting it will certainly be sending all of our dogs and warriors to death! Not even the muntjac contingency is strong enough to defeat it!" Kedem yelled.

"The muntjac are no warriors! They could not defeat the beast! But foxes? We fight in many battles to hone our skills. We could take it down ourselves," Akando replied.

"The muntjac are warriors!" Rebus shouted. "They played a most important part in defeating the Dark Army."

"And you talk about your warriors?" an infuriated Kedem began. "Where were yours when we took to battle in the Great Vast Open?" Akando looked on defiantly. "They were nowhere. Like you, they cowered in the furthest reaches of the forest."

Akando leapt at the council leader and lashed out with his right paw. His claw gashed the left side of Kedem's snout, causing him to yelp and fall back. Anger engulfed the community leader as he prepared to pounce at his rival. "No!" Glif shouted, bounding her small, grey body towards the dog. "Don't. It's too dangerous."

Kedem looked around at the dark foxes and rats that had descended upon Shadow Oak and engulfed his beloved home. "She's wise," Akando began, the hint of anger still apparent in his voice. "For once in your life, listen."

Kedem looked around some more. "It's not worth losing your life for," Rebus confirmed as he made his way to Kedem's side. He looked towards his friend, the white stripes of fur running along his head seemingly more vibrant than ever before. "It is out of our hands now."

The fox lowered his eyes. He saw the fear etched upon Dallie's face. The foxes that had been banished into their dens now looked out upon the scene with terror and fear. It was no use. If he challenged Akando he would be slaughtered, and nothing would change. He met Rebus' eyes. The boar nodded slowly. Kedem sighed and stepped backwards.

Akando laughed. "Ha," he began, and addressed his army of dark foxes and rats. "Shadow Oak is finally ours!" he bellowed. The dark animals screamed and hollered in unison.

Shadow Oak had finally fallen.

2

In the deepest, farthest woodland from Shadow Oak, Doran jumped from his rest. His mind filled with images of Kedem, Shadow Oak and the Great Council, engulfed by darkness.

"Settle down!" Loat ordered him as he came to his senses.

"Shadow Oak! Kedem!" the dog began rapidly.

Loat nodded. "Yes. I saw it too."

"We must go! We must help!"

"No!" the stoat ordered as Doran turned to leave.

"No? What do you mean, no?" Doran asked. Swirls of darkness engulfed his eyes. Sensing confrontation, Loat engaged his control of the darkness. Doran growled intensely at the stoat as plumes of darkness escaped his mouth and nostrils. The reverberation was so great that the ground started rumbling. The trees surrounding them began to sway their branches in a fresh, rainless storm.

Loat remained defiant. "If you leave, you will almost certainly be slaughtered," he began. "If you're not killed, the darkness will take you and you will be like the foxes that have marched upon your homeland. You will be under Seerles' complete control."

"I have to help them."

"You will be of no help to anyone!" Loat screamed, his eyes now burning red so brightly they looked ready to explode. "Whatever happens there will happen regardless! Your presence will make no difference!"

"I must -"

"You must do nothing! If you remain here with me you will become the greatest warrior in the legend of this forest! You will be able to compete with Seerles and his manipulation of the darkness! You will make a difference! You are not ready!"

"I am ready!" Doran roared.

"You will die!"

"I will not die!"

Loat screamed as he released the energy of the darkness at full force towards Doran. The wave it generated threw the dog tremendously through the trees and into a thick, sturdy trunk behind him. Doran yelped as he connected and fell limply to the soft floor. Doran sprang to his paws, the darkness swirling through his eyes. Slowly, his eyes began emitting a dull, red glow that began to break the patches of darkness passing over the once-colourful pupils.

"Control yourself!" Loat ordered. The stoat could feel Doran losing his mind with rage as the darkness connecting them surged throughout their limbs. Doran snarled and dropped his snout to the floor, his entire body shaking as he battled with the forces within. "Control yourself!" Loat screamed again, the air now reverberating with a strange humming noise not natural for the Great Forest. Doran threw his head back and faced the twilight evening from underneath the trees. His eyes glared open, the darkness inside them completely burnt away as anger swept throughout him. His eyes burned red and glowed eerily as his struggle continued. The branches on the trees swayed vigorously. The leaves severed from their limbs and flew upwards in the air, as though huge gusts of wind were being forced from the ground itself an up into the setting sky. Loat released the darkness fully and planted his paws in the ground, his fur ruffled rapidly as the power emitting from Doran increased and increased.

The dog had now lost complete control. Coaching him further would be futile. As the ground shook and the trees swayed, Loat knew that Doran was now at the point of being engulfed and taken entirely by the darkness. A tree began moving as the power from the fox grew ever stronger. Loat tried with every ounce of might in his body to stay planted, but quickly lost his footing and was blown from his paws by a wave of energy that exploded from Doran. A luminous blue ring shot rapidly through the trees, flinging the stoat effortlessly from his position. A tree began to creak thunderously and tumbled backwards, its roots rising from the earth, soil and debris launching in mass into the air as it crashed to the floor. The crash from the falling trunk reverberated throughout the woods, surrounding them. Doran stood firm, his body contorting in different positions as the energy took control over him. Loat shook himself from his landing place and tried one final time to reach Doran. He closed his eyes.

Doran! the stoat shouted in the dog's mind.

Doran heard him, and heard the familiarity of a voice he knew. Loat could feel Doran struggle to answer, and knew that there was a small amount of the dog still left that he could reach out to. Loat thought a moment, and then opened his mind.

Doran suddenly began seeing images of his home, but not the one that lay siege by Akando. He saw Tali, Kedem, Jinx and Delfin. He saw the great oak tree, the Council Peninsula and Meadoway. He saw Streak and Wickett, and the Forest Guards sat within Shadow Oak. He saw Rebus and Brock sat at a meeting of the Great Council. Slowly, his mind began to settle. Selwyn flew past in his mind, as did Flicar and Garla. The energy pulsing through the trees began to dwindle. He saw himself surrounded by the families within his home community. Finally, he saw Cyrius gliding through a moonlit night and coming to rest upon a branch above him.

Leaves and branches fell from the sky as the energy that had torn them free finally vanished, leaving them free to fall back to the ground. The air was full of clattering as they smashed against tree trunks and branches unaffected by the energy. Leaves fluttered en masse to the floor, looking as though they had been raining from the evening skies high above. As the last branch fell, Loat heard animals and birds calling in the distance, no doubt disturbed by the recent events of his friend.

Doran stood shaking as he drew breath, exhausted by his outburst. "Doran?" Loat asked as he bounded over to him, unable to sense this time whether he was now taken by the darkness. Slowly, Doran lifted his muzzle and looked directly at the stoat. There was no darkness in his eyes. Loat smiled at him. "You did it, Doran. You did it! You can control the darkness!"

"And what a show it was too," came a voice from above them. Perched firmly on a branch sat Cyrius, his eyes gazing down upon the carnage Doran had created.

"Cyrius?" Doran began as he raised his muzzle to the owl. "How did you find me?"

"Take a look around, Doran. Waves of energy? Trees uprooted and branches and leaves flying through the air? You're not a difficult fox to find," he replied. "I am glad I found you. I take it you have seen events at Shadow Oak?" Doran nodded as he panted, unable to speak at that precise moment. "Fortunately for you, the event you saw triggered the darkness and pushed you to its very limit. Had it not been for your friend here, you most certainly would be standing here now under the full control of Seerles," the owl said, gesturing towards Loat. "But as you went to the limit and gained control of the darkness at your most vulnerable, you are now strong enough to use the element to your own desire."

"I can feel it. I can feel the control I now have," Doran replied. He shot two plumes of dark mist from his nostrils. They flew around his muzzle, his head, and then vanished back inside his nose.

"There," Loat began. "It's finally yours to control."

"But there is no time to congratulate yourself on your achievement," Cyrius added, his wings flapping to gain balance on the not so sturdy branch. "The both of you are needed to assist with the plight at Shadow Oak. You must now head back there, both of you. I will find you again when the time is right."

With his final words Cyrius took flight and glided into the twilight, leaving Doran and Loat at the scene of the destruction.

"I wish he would just tell us what was happening instead of being so mysterious about it," Doran said as he watched the glowing trail from Cyrius vanish into the air.

"It seems like you get what you wanted," Loat replied. "We're going to Shadow Oak." Loat felt a sensation pass through him. "There," he began excitedly. "Did you feel that?"

Doran nodded. "What was it?"

"A sign. A definite sign. Maybe something will happen at Shadow Oak that Akando hasn't planned for?" That was the exact feeling that Doran had felt, but didn't understand how he could feel such a thing and tell what it was. Something was indeed afoot that Akando would have no way of knowing. "Yes," Loat said with a twinkle in his eye, "there's definitely a twist to this tale yet."

3

Daisy rested inside a tight circling of trees, hidden by the dense ferns scattered about the area. When the beast had attacked her kind, the young fawn had sprinted away through sheer terror. She had followed the bucks and does as they ran from the trees, whilst Favradin had engaged the panther and given his leader time to escape. She had attempted to run as fast as the muntjac fleeing around her, but her small stature and shorter legs had been unable to keep up with them. She had shouted for help as they darted in every direction around her, but none had heard. When she finally became too exhausted to run any more, she was completely alone and lost in the vastness of the Great Forest. After wandering aimlessly for a long time she finally gave up and decided to rest where she lay now, underneath a blanket of greenery hidden mostly from view. After a period of fright, and the realisation she was now on her own, Daisy's nerves settled and she lay quietly on the damp floor, trying to think of a way back to the muntjac contingency. Thinking quietly to herself had relaxed the fawn, and unknowingly she had drifted into a light sleep.

"The atmosphere of this forest is one of foreboding," a gentle voice drifted by the sleeping fawn. "There is great concern for our distant cousins."

A group of four fallow deer stood scouring the surrounding trees and vegetation, looking up into the highest branches and between the bushes and barks as far as their eyes would allow. The four stood in awe, the broad-bladed antlers emerging from their heads, vast in size compared to the muntjac that dwelled within Averon. Their fur was beginning to show the signs of summer, each with a varied shade of chestnut brown dotted with white spots upon their bodies.

"You are right, Achak. I can feel great disdain within the forest," came a subdued reply.

Achak stood at the front of his herd, looking at the dull sky through the dense leaves. The forest around him was so immensely beautiful, yet felt so very bad. Even through the perfectly placed barks and vegetation the leader of the fallow deer could sense something so very wrong.

"Achak," came a voice, bringing the buck back to his senses. He looked over towards his comrade Katori, who was nodding his antlers towards a dense cluster of ferns. "Here."

Achak trotted slowly over, and as he did so Katori parted the leaves, revealing a terrified fawn sat staring at them with utter fright.

"Hello, youngling," Achak said with suppressed surprise at what Katori had found. The fawn tried to jump to her feet but fear gripped her again, and she flopped back to the ground. Achak could see how frightened the fawn was, and tried his utmost to reassure her. "It's okay," he said softly, not approaching the fawn too fast, "we will not harm you. You are safe."

"Safe?" the fawn asked, switching her gaze from Katori to his leader.

"Of course," Katori added gently. "We are friendly."

"What's your name?" Achak asked, lowering himself down to the damp grass. His eyes were now at the same level as the frightened ones he was attempting to comfort.

"Daisy," the fawn replied, after a moment of hesitation, to the buck that lay in front of her.

"Daisy?" Achak asked quietly. "That's a very strange, but wonderful, name."

"I was found in a patch of daisies in the forest. That's how I got it," Daisy replied, her confidence slowly returning.

"A very poignant name, with such an important meaning to it," Katori added.

"What are your names?" Daisy asked from the cover of the ferns.

"I am Achak," the leader began, returning to his feet, "and this is Katori. We are fallow deer like you from across the Great Vast Open. Those two back there are Ciros and Tienos," Achak replied, gesturing his antlers at the two bucks across the foliage. "But what are you doing here on your own? Where is the rest of your kind?"

"It was the beast," Daisy replied, fear returning to her as she remembered.

"It's okay, you're safe now," Achak began, returning a look of concern from Katori. After a moment of thought, Achak asked Daisy about the beast she spoke of.

"It's black, darker than the darkest night, with burning yellow eyes and huge claws. It roars so loud that the ground shakes."

"The creature that terrorised the Great Vast Open," Katori said, hearing something familiar in the fawn's description.

"I thought it had gone," Achak replied quietly.

"It did. It came here."

Achak lowered his head to Daisy. "Did it come for your kind?" he asked slowly.

Daisy nodded. "It did," she whispered. "It killed many of the bucks in the forest, and when it came for us I ran, just like the rest of them. I ran so far I got lost, and ended up here."

"Then you are very brave, and very lucky," Katori added. "Not many creatures in the Great Vast Open can escape the beast, but you did." Achak sighed and looked towards Katori, who seemed fairly concerned. "What shall we do?" he asked his leader, as a slight breeze rustled the ferns.

Achak looked towards the two bucks and back to Katori. "We can't leave her here; it's not safe for a youngling to be on their own, especially now that the beast has entered these trees."

"Then what?" Katori asked in the quiet wilderness.

"I am aware of a council that presides over the forest of Averon," Achak began as the branches rustled in a breeze. "It has been in order for many, many seasons. If the fawn is aware of the beast, I'm sure by now the council will also know. We should return her there. They will know how to contact the deer she belongs with."

"Do you know where this council will be?" Katori asked, the vastness of Averon his main concern.

"No. We're going to have to locate it by using our heads and following our instincts. I'm sure it can't be far," Katori replied with a simple nod.

"Daisy?" Achak asked, turning his attention to the fawn, "will you come with us? We're going to try and return you to your loved ones. We're going to search the forest until we find them, but we can't do it on our own. Will you come with us?"

"We'll keep you safe," Katori added softly.

Now free from any fear, and feeling immensely lucky that Katori had found her sleeping under the ferns, Daisy rose to her hooves and looked towards Achak. His words now bound her to the small group of fallow deer travelling through Averon. They would have to protect her as promised, and return her to the muntjac.

4

The hares had settled for their final rest before their advancement upon the rabbits. The coppice they now resided in was full of mud-covered animals as they slept, wandered and relaxed before the night-time attack. Lisket had looked upon Apollo with weary eyes. He knew something wasn't quite right with his scout.

Apollo tried to blend in as best as he could. He joined the hares, and gradually, as they began to rest, made his way to a far corner of the coppice that housed no other bodies. Here he rested and anxiously awaited for Blits to somehow find him in the sea of mud and fur, under the swaying trees and within the dense bushes.

"Hey!" came a whispered exclamation from a bush bordered with the Great Vast Open. Apollo felt the flurry of adrenaline quickly pass through his body, as he knew he was being spoken to. He turned to his left and saw a hare plastered in warpaint poke its nose from the bushes. "Apollo!" the hare whispered with intent. Apollo's heart leapt in his chest. He had been discovered.

"Who, me?" he whispered in reply, his voice coolly hiding the fear that had quickly engulfed him.

"No, the other Apollo, over there! Of course you!" the hare snapped.

"Erm," the flustered rabbit began. "I know nothing of this Apollo of whom you speak," he replied boldly.

The hare closed its eyes in despair and shook its head. "It's me, you idiot!" he snapped.

Apollo's eyes widened. "Blits?" he exclaimed in a whisper.

"Who else?" the cunningly disguised rabbit answered.

Apollo's ears engaged, and he made his way towards the bush from where his friend was hiding. "What are you doing in there?" Apollo asked secretively as he approached.

"I've found a way out through here," the rabbit began. "If we do it quickly, we can escape and head back without anyone taking notice. But we have to be quick, they have patrols outside. Come on."

Apollo nodded and scraped his way through the bushes, rustling their wiry twigs and coarse leaves. "How did you find me?" Apollo asked as they passed underneath the dense bush.

"You weren't hard to find after your rousing little speech," Blits began. "I just followed you and hid out of sight. Here we are," he said, as they drew upon an exit from beneath the shrubbery and out into the Great Vast Open. "We have to act calmly when we get outside, but in case we get found, be prepared to run."

"Great. Run. It's all I seem to be doing these days," Apollo said glumly.

Blits shook his head. "Just," he said, laying down the law firmly with the one, solitary word.

"Okay, okay," Apollo trailed off, as he prepared for yet another mad dash. Blits nodded to him, and slowly they emerged into the world outside.

They walked calmly together across the freezing grass under their paws, the melted snow leaving patches of cold water dotted around the Great Vast Open. There were no hare patrols in the area as far as they could see, and if they kept a cool head they were in with a chance.

"Hey, we may just make it," Apollo said softly. He too had noticed the lack of patrols around the coppice. Slowly, the two rabbits began to make their escape.

"Hey!" came a stern voice from behind the duo. Apollo leapt with fright as they turned together. From the coppice emerged a small patrol of three hares. "Where do you two think you're going?" the first mud covered leader asked them.

"Um, just patrolling," Blits added hesitantly.

"On whose authority?" the hare asked.

"On mine," Apollo added quickly. "I am Tolka, and I'm looking for an attack route to the Great Forest."

"All patrols are organised through me," the hare boomed sternly, "no matter who you are or what your business is." Some of the hares had emerged from the coppice at the sound of the ruckus outside, and now the rabbits stood eclipsed in numbers to the gigantic enemies who now confronted them. A dried mud flake detached itself from the warpaint covering the fur underneath Apollo's right eye. Both Apollo and Blits watched it in unison as it fell to the grassy floor. The hare that confronted them looked on in disbelief. His eyes widened from shock to anger.

"Rabbits," he whispered quietly. "You're rabbits?" he screamed at the top of his voice.

"This is not good," Blits said turning to run.

"Impostors!" the hare bellowed as the coppice began its evacuation of mammals.

"Run, run, run, run, run, run, run!" Blits yelled as the army of hares pelted towards them.

Apollo and Blits darted across the cold grass as the hares descended down upon them. "Stop them!" came the recognisable voice of Lisket, who had emerged from his resting place. The one thing that the rabbits had over the hares were smaller and more nimble bodies, making them faster than their enemies. If they could keep the sprint up, they could outrun their stalkers. They looked upon the distant trees of Averon that seemed so far away across the Great Vast Open. One final sprint and the plan would come to life.

Wickett and Coinin had sat for most of the day at the western border of the Great Forest, looking out towards the hazy shadow of the coppice. The red sky of the sinking sun had not made it any clearer, and now with the fading light and impending darkness it would seem Apollo and Blits would be spending the night out there.

"Still no sign," Coinin added as his grey body felt the chill of a short, sharp breeze pass through the forest. "I hope they're okay," he then added.

Usually Wickett was upbeat and looked on the positive side of anything thrown at him. "So do I," was the only thing he could offer in reply to his friend.

"Is the general secure?" Coinin then asked for the umpteenth time. Wickett had not long returned from the warren to make sure everything was in order.

"Yes, the tunnels that lead to the various chambers are sealed. The rest of the rabbits are safely behind the blockade. There's a small chamber at the end of the main tunnel that will hold the four of us. If we get a head start and if Apollo fed them the right information, the hares that give chase should continue down the tunnel and straight past us."

Coinin nodded. "Then we wait."

Wickett sighed next to him. "Yes. We wait."

They sat there in silence staring out into the beautiful sunset that had gripped the entire Great Vast Open, turning the clouds from dashes of white to ominous grey shards pointing precisely in the directions they were drifting.

Coinin noticed something and jerked upwards. His ears engaged and he stood on his hinds.

"What?" Wickett asked, and followed his gaze out into the open.

"What is that?" Coinin asked, gesturing across the countryside. From the distant decreasing meadow both rabbits could see a continuous line of hazy grey, almost like a river of bobbles gently approaching. Wickett could feel a gentle rumble through the ground he was stood upon. "No," he gasped.

"Yes," Coinin corrected as they stood together, watching the river-line slowly approach. Two blobs emerged from the foreground of the approaching mass, and rapidly took the shape of two well-known creatures.

"Run!" came the distinctive voice of Blits.

"GO!" Apollo screamed in confirmation. Behind them the river formed and cleared itself into the shape of an immense army of hares bounding their way towards the forest.

"What have you two done?" Coinin shouted as he turned towards the dense greenery and the tunnel that lead to their chambers.

Apollo and Blits hurtled towards the remaining Forest Guards and entered the tree-line without stopping. The exploded past Wickett and Coinin without muttering a single word. The hares drew closer, merely a matter of seconds before they entered the Great Forest.

"Oh pellets!" Wickett shouted as he and Coinin gave chase to Apollo and Blits.

"Cease them!" came the voice of Lisket as he entered their home. The rabbits bounded over the soft ground beneath their paws and churned the grass and mud as they pushed through the woodland. Apollo headed the pack and raced for the fallen log, the landmark that pointed to the entrance of their tunnel. Blits darted right to avoid a stone. Wickett and Coinin split from each other and pushed through a group of weeds they had no time to identify. Brittle twigs cracked under their paws. Branches swayed above them in the hidden breeze. Lisket targeted Wickett. He bounded closer to the fleeing rabbit. The tunnel loomed from the forest's twilight as Apollo bore down upon it rapidly, closely followed by Blits.

"Keep running!" Blits shouted to him. Apollo leapt and landed gracefully within the confines of the tunnel's entrance, kicking back dry debris from the tunnel floor. Lisket gained quickly on Wickett. Blits bounded through the tunnel and kept racing.

Nearly!'Wickett thought as he followed the tuft of Coinin's tail. He could feel the vibration of Lisket's footfalls from behind. Coinin leapt and entered the tunnel without touching its sides. With a clear route ahead, Wickett frowned with determination and kicked his legs into top speed.

Lisket watched from his distorted view behind as Wickett pulled away easily. "No!" he screamed to himself, and leapt for the Forest Guard…

He crashed head-first into the tunnel, paws stretched out fully in front of him. He had nicked Wickett's tail in the attack, but that was all. He watched as the rabbit vanished from the perimeter of the warren's entrance. Lisket growled in frustration as his larger body became wedged within the tunnel. After a moment's struggle he retreated and freed himself from the rabbits' dark entrance. He looked about as the hares amassed around him under the tree's shadows.

"Infiltration unit!" he barked angrily. A group of hares emerged from the mass. "Enter their chamber! Slaughter their leader and report back to me! Remember Tolka's directions. Follow the tunnel until you reach an opening! There you must cross and enter the main chamber opposite! Find their leader! Destroy him! Go!"

"Yes sir," came a babble of voices as they entered the tunnel one by one. The real Tolka struggled behind a firmly blocked tunnel, wrestling with other members of the Forest Guard as he heard the commotion of his allies fighting to gain entry.

"Settle him down!" Sergeant Castor ordered as the hare began boxing. After a few well-placed jabs to the rabbits confronting him he was piled on from behind, and restrained to the floor.

The Forest Guard reached their hiding place, a burrowed hole that adjoined on the left hand side to the one they were racing through. Remembering their plan, Blits darted quickly inside it, followed by Apollo, then Coinin. Wickett finally joined them as the footfalls of the advancing hares chased them through the tunnel. "Now!" Wickett ordered.

The hares ran quickly inside the darkness, their nocturnal eyes noticing the blocked entrances to various other tunnels as they raced past. The tunnel wound up and down, left and right, round and round, occasionally with another tunnel's adjoining entrance blocked completely. They ran past one final tunnel and headed out into a clearing that they had been misinformed by Apollo housed the rabbit's general. The Forest Guards looked on from behind the safety of their hidden hiding place. The rabbits of the warren had pushed a manageable rock out towards the entrance to Shadow Oak in preparation of this plan, and sealed it out completely. As Wickett had been the last rabbit in, he overshot the chamber slightly, grabbed the rock, and quickly dragged it back with the help of Coinin, sealing the Forest Guards inside their hiding hole and creating the effect of a blocked tunnel.

Wickett watched through the tiny gaps surrounding the rock as the hares dashed past his hiding place. As the last one passed, he smiled to himself. "Like a treat," he whispered softly.

5

The community and council leaders trapped within Shadow Oak stood eclipsed by the dark foxes around the clearing. Their leader, Akando, swayed his sweep as he approached Kedem.

"What do you want?" Kedem finally asked in the decreasing sunset.

"Ha! What do I want?" Akando repeated in a jovial manner. "Hmm, what do I want?" From nowhere a hare bolted into the clearing, followed by another, and another. Akando and the animals turned in confusion to their uninvited guests. After a few seconds of realisation, the hares froze. More kept exploding from the tunnel, smashing into their frozen comrades.

"Back! Fall back!" a mud-covered hare screamed, and attempted to turn about.

"That's what I want," Akando said grimly. "I want lunch."

"Fall back! Fall back!" the hares began, and in unison began clambering towards the tunnel they had just exited from. They jostled and vied themselves in any way they could to re-enter the tunnel quickly. Akando pounced and flattened one of the first hares that had entered. With his jaws he picked it up by the scruff of its furry neck and threw it into a pack of dark foxes. They snorted and roared as they tore the creature limb from limb, spilling its blood and innards to the floor. Rebus and Dallie turned away in disgust and sorrow.

A look of realisation set in on Akando's face. "Wait!" he ordered to his minions. The dark ones turned their attention to their red leader. "There will be more. Head to the border. Catch as many as you can and bring them back here. Now!"

A pack of dark foxes bounded from the clearing and headed into the dense trees. As the last hare vanished back inside the tunnel and the melee had settled, silence returned once again to the community. Kedem sat with his advisors Jinx and Delfin. Rebus accompanied Glif and Dallie. They sat and stood in a line, their tormentor Akando walking backwards and forwards. He had previously banished all foxes residing in Shadow Oak to their dens, and ordered them not to emerge unless summoned. This left only the council representatives and the community advisors in the presence of Akando and his newly acquired army.

"Now, where were we?" Akando asked his audience. He slowly stopped walking and came to rest in front of the greying Kedem. "Oh yes, that was it," he replied, with a maniacal look upon his snout.

Wickett had seen the hares sprinting back through the tunnel, and led the Forest Guards back out to the western border. They made their way quickly through the winding tunnel, and as they approached the opening heard the sounds of snarling, screaming, and violence.

"What's going on out there?" Blits asked from behind his leader.

"I have no idea," Wickett replied. They made their way closer until the tunnel's entrance allowed Wickett to peer outside. "Oh my..." he trailed off, shock and horror knotting in his voice.

"What?" Coinin added, and barged himself narrowly past the rabbit in front of him. He froze when he saw the carnage outside. An army of dark foxes was hunting and slaughtering the hares on the grass the Forest Guards had not long laid paws on. Blood tainted the woodland, and innards nestled almost naturally in clumps between the long and short grasses. Many of the hares had retreated, but there were many carcasses of slaughtered warriors.

Wickett pushed Coinin to one side. "We must help them!" he cried with concern.

"What's all this ruckus!" came a domineering voice from behind them. General Lupus emerged from a tunnel connecting to the main chamber, Tolka in his tow.

"Sir!" Wickett shouted from the front of the Forest Guards, "we have to help them! The hares! They're being slaughtered by foxes!"

"Foxes?" General Lupus boomed, as the war and slaughter waged on outside. Suddenly a hare thudded into the tunnel, blocking out the late evening twilight as he scrambled fearfully to gain an entrance to safety. Wickett jumped back as the larger hare pawed at the tunnel's walls in an attempt to flee the carnage outside. Wickett leapt to the hare's aid and tried with all his might to drag the intruder to safety. They wrestled and contorted, as the sounds of death engulfed the tunnel from the terrible battle.

"What are you doing?" Sergeant Castor snapped from behind the captive Tolka they were preparing to release. "You don't save our enemy!"

Wickett ignored his superior and continued to drag the blood-drenched hare inside, until he finally scrambled to his feet and into the tunnel, out of harm's way. "On your feet," Wickett ordered as the hare pushed himself to his paws.

"Thank you," the shocked hare mustered as he stood tightly in the safety of the rabbit's warren. Wickett turned and saw his Forest Guard companions nestling to the entrance of their tunnel on the left side of the junction, and General Lupus and his cohorts inside the tunnel on his right, leading to the main chamber.

"This is an outrage!" Sergeant Castor boomed from behind his commander. The look on General Lupus' face suggested he agreed with his sergeant.

"Please," Wickett pleaded as the reality of his actions suddenly sunk in. "They are dying out there," he added, as his general bore down upon him intently.

"Sergeant Castor," General Lupus said in a menacing tone.

"Sah!" the sergeant replied.

"Order the tunnels open! We must save who we can!"

"Sir?" Sergeant Castor replied, flabbergasted by his general's order.

General Lupus turned to him. "We are going to do what we can to help them. Open the warren! Help the hares!" he screamed into the darkness of his home.

Open the warren! Help the hares!'a voice repeated somewhere inside the warren, as the order passed from one end to the other.

"You can't be serious!" Sergeant Castor snapped angrily. "They are our enemies!"

"Indeed they are, Sergeant Castor, but even they do not deserve to die like this. Well done, lad," he said turning back to Wickett. "You and your patrol comrades have turned into fine Forest Guards."

Across the entire warren the blocked tunnels were quickly opened. Rabbits emerged closely to the slaughter outside, and bellowed as loud as they could for the hares to seek shelter within their warren. The dark foxes slaughtered and tore their way through many of the creatures fleeing, but a mass of hares small enough began swarming to their nearest escape. Apollo stood at Willow Junction, deep within the warren, directing the saved hares towards the main chamber. Many hares closer to the forest's boundary managed to dash from harm's way and headed back towards the

Great Vast Open. One of these hares was their leader, Lisket. He saw the rabbits emerging and offering sanctuary to those who could reach their tunnels. He issued one last order to fall back, and along with the survivors of the bloodshed within the Western Clearing, escaped out of Averon and deep inside the sanctuary of the Great Vast Open.

As the battle dwindled down and the living hares escaped their jaws, the foxes picked up the bodies of the untainted dead and left clutching them, as a prize for Akando. The first stars emerged within the darkened sky above as the last foxes left, leaving the western border in violent, bloody silence.

"You helped us," Tolka said as the bustling warren came to life with many hares seeking safety inside their tunnels. "You knew our intentions, yet you still placed your lives in danger to help us," he said to Wickett between the mass of moving animals.

"Of course he did," came an unexpected reply from General Lupus sitting not too far away across the chamber. "He's a Forest Guard, and a fine one at that," he added.

"Thank you," Tolka finally replied, to both the Forest Guard and his general.

Wickett shrugged. "Part of the job," he replied. Emerging into the chamber came his remaining comrades.

"...and then I laughed at them and said 'you are no match for me, Apollo the Destroyer,'" came the tall voice of Apollo, explaining the events of his task to Coinin, or at least the events as he remembered them. He carried on his mumblings as the three of them moved slowly through the mass of bodies, Apollo leaping around in the tight space he occupied, gesturing his paws into punches as he relayed his fantastic story.

"Blammo! Blits and Apollo, protectors of the warren! Saviours of the rabbits! We then made our escape after defeating half the army that attacked us in the coppice!"

"Having fun?" Wickett jested to Coinin, acknowledging the look of utter disdain across his face.

"No!" Coinin snapped harshly. Apollo continued his babbling, blissfully unaware that Coinin was not in the slightest bit interested in what he was saying. Blits simply shook his head at the exaggerated tale Apollo was reciting.

"It was his greatest achievement," Wickett said happily to Coinin. "Just humour him."

Coinin sighed a long, harsh sigh and turned to face Apollo. "…and if it hadn't been for me, Coinin, you'd be laying on the battlefield out there, a fallen warrior in the history of Averon."

"That's it!" Coinin shouted as his tether finally snapped. "That does it! I can take this abuse no more!" Apollo suddenly stopped his tale and looked confused. "All I hear is 'Apollo this' and 'Apollo that,' 'Apollo the Greatest' and 'Apollo the Destroyer!' I can't live like this anymore!" He turned to leave the main chamber. "I am going to sacrifice myself to those foxes in an attempt to get some peace!"

"Don't be so hasty," Wickett replied, attempting to convince his friend otherwise.

"No, no, hold on," came General Lupus as he made his way towards the Forest Guards.

"What?" Coinin shouted to his leader. "You want me to go and meet death at their jaws?!"

"Don't be so foolish, Coinin, of course not!" the general snapped back. "But what I do want is for you to find out where those foxes came from and what they're doing so close to Shadow Oak."

"Sir?" Blits questioned, as the ageing general finally reached them. "I informed the Great Council and the warriors heading to the Forest of the Damned that if I could release you to assist them I would, and now that time has come." Wickett's eyes widened. Another adventure!

"Go to Shadow Oak and see exactly what is happening. I have a feeling all is not well, and your assistance may be urgently required." The Forest Guards assembled as General Lupus issued his orders. "Do whatever is necessary to assist the council and the warriors, but do so wisely. Be stealth's out there whilst this army is invading, and do whatever it is you must to restore order to our homeland."

"We will do as you ask," Wickett replied, suppressing his excitement and fear.

"Go then, warriors, and assist with bringing peace to our forest."

6

The fog thickened as the band of warriors ventured closer to the forest. The trail became lost in the denseness creeping in from both sides, and almost engulfed the animals as they tentatively made their way onwards, lead by Streak and Lyro. Pairo and Makoto fell to the back of the band as they ventured along the trail, allowing Selwyn and Brock to accompany Chance, Checkers and Danjo in the middle. The fog brought with it a chill that Selwyn felt harshly, causing him to ruffle his feathers to feel warmer. Brock looked over to him.

"We are almost there," he implied, as though the cold shiver passing through the pheasant was a warning sign. Selwyn simply nodded his multi-coloured head in agreement and said nothing. Silence had engulfed the intrepid adventurers as they journeyed on towards the unknown. Silence, except for their paw and footfalls on the solid surface.

"The ground is solid," Danjo informed them as they wandered on. Through the cloudy fog he noticed patches of frost decorating the grass of the ground he could see.

Pairo looked down, having been unaware of his surroundings. "The grounds have been saturated and drenched with the melting snow," he began, relaying the prolonged season's last offering. "It shouldn't be frozen solid like this."

The warriors took notice as they moved onwards. "Look," Checkers said, gesturing towards the cold, visible air escaping his body. Streak snorted and watched his own breath spiral from his snout.

"This is it," Makoto began. "We must almost be there."

"Ahead," Selwyn replied, his amazing eyes turning their attention to the trail looming mysteriously from the fog. From its dense swirls, two huge trees loomed from either side of the trail. The warriors stopped. Brock could not tell what type of trees they were. They were simply huge, much the same as the great tree towering above Shadow Oak. Their barks were knotted and twisted, as though an immense creature had twisted them from their tops, their branches huge and spanning vast distances. Twigs on all of their arms appeared foreboding and sharp, but thankfully reached upwards and out, too high to cause any danger to the passing animals. As the trees vanished into the fog they curved over the trail, creating what looked like a gateway. The most bizarre part of the trees was their symmetry. One tree on the left, one on the right, the branches reaching outwards at the same places, barks twisted and knotted exactly. The two trees mirrored each other perfectly.

"The Twins of Despair," Lyro stated quietly to the warriors, his gaze still fixed on the monuments towering above him.

"Indeed," the striped badger replied from behind the foxes. "The gateway to the Forest of the Damned."

"What's that?" Checkers asked, noticing an object on the trail in front of the gateway. The animals wandered slowly closer.

"It looks like a human's foot," Danjo replied, looking over the strange object sat motionlessly in front of them. It was a shade of dark brown, and had small, dark string weaving through holes that lead through the centre up towards the opening at its top.

"Certainly," Brock began as he studied the strange appendage in front of him. "I'm sure I've seen humans wearing items such as this as they have wandered through our forest. But what is it doing this deep in the wilderness? Surely no human would venture this far into Averon?"

"Unless they were lost?" Danjo replied.

"But why would they leave this here?"

"Maybe the forest got them?" Chance suggested. The animals fell silent.

"Maybe..." Brock repeated, looking up at the towering trees.

"The fog," Makoto replied from behind, breaking the badger's trail of thought. Streak took a quick glance behind at his new ally, then looked in the direction Makoto had gestured. Inside the gateway, the fog moved mysteriously. Emerging from a huge plume came the distinct shapes of four foxes, gently drifting upwards as though they were running. The shape of a pheasant in flight emerged from their right and glided by gracefully above them.

"What is this?" Danjo asked in astonishment.

The shape of two otters emerged from the fog towards the right of the trail. They split apart, one up and one down, as the drifting vision of a badger moved quickly between them. As the badger vanished across the trail, a squirrel emerged swirling from the element and glided upwards, until it too blended with the prominent fog and vanished.

"It knows we're coming," Streak informed them as the shapes finally vanished and the fog returned to its usual, cloudy self. They stood a moment longer before their leader turned and addressed them.

"This is it," Streak began, "there's no turning back now. We have to carry on for the fate of our forest. Every living creature that dwells here is counting on us to get through to Stryder and find a way to stop the beast. If we don't, our forest, our families, will be slaughtered, and there will be nothing left. Nothing."

Streak's speech roused Lyro and sent an unfamiliar wave of emotion through him, an emotion he'd never felt before. He looked at the rag-tag band of warriors formed. Four foxes, two otters, a squirrel, a badger and a pheasant. Was he now beginning to feel compassion for them? Pairo noticed Lyro looking around. Somehow, he knew inside what Lyro was feeling.

"We will do what we always do," Selwyn began confidently. "We will continue onward, until the trail runs out if needed."

"Remember. If you return to a place you've already visited, turn around and head back. It will lead you here. To safety." Streak turned and faced the gateway to the forest. Without fear, the brave dog slowly moved closer to the gateway. The warriors watched on as Streak wandered into the fog between the twins. His fur turned from red to grey as the fog engulfed him. The fox turned into a shadow as he ventured between the trees, then vanished as the fog engulfed his path and sealed his entry into the Forest of the Damned. Brock and Selwyn followed bravely with Danjo, the experienced warriors accompanying the nervous addition to their party. They too merged into the grey cloud between the trees, and vanished from sight as they entered the foreboding forest. Lyro was left with his clan and the two otters. Checkers looked towards him. He gestured his snout towards the rolling fog and the intimidating path their comrades had already walked.

"We won't be far behind," he informed them. The otters heeded his advice and tentatively made their way to the gateway. As the otters vanished into the unknown to join those who had gone before them, Pairo wandered toward Lyro and barged him violently.

"Keep focused!" he snapped at his leader.

Lyro growled. "Stand down, Pairo," he ordered. "I have not forgotten our orders."

"Really?" Pairo asked sarcastically. "It didn't look that way just now."

"When?"

"Pairo," came a calm voice from behind them. Makoto joined the argument. "We wait until we return here," he reiterated, "that's what Akando ordered. The rats and the dark foxes will be waiting."

The pointed snout of Pairo turned back to Lyro. "Maybe. But what if they don't make it this far back? What if we destroyed them before we re-emerge? Well, the insignificant ones anyway. The squirrel, the otters."

"You even think of compromising our mission by attacking those creatures, and I'll shred you myself," Lyro growled.

Pairo grinned maliciously. "What happens when the time comes, though? What then, Lyro?"

Lyro paused momentarily as he battled a conflict deep inside his vibrant body. He turned back to his comrades with a look of disgust across his muzzle. "Then... then, we do what we were ordered."

"Don't ever forget that," Pairo said, now beginning his walk towards the gateway and past Lyro. He left the two dogs together as he vanished inside the fog. Makoto looked towards his leader with questioning eyes. Lyro looked at him, looked away, and then looked back. Makoto simply nodded and wandered past the fox. Lyro sighed. Something was conflicting his emotions. Without wasting more time to dwell upon it he too began his journey, vanishing between the Twins of Despair and into the Forest of the Damned.

7

As the darkness of the night crept quickly over Shadow Oak, Akando reiterated the curfew he had placed upon the community of foxes that dwelled there. His army of dark foxes and rats engulfed the perimeter of the circular clearing, leaving the open space for Akando to continue his prowl and dominance of the newly acquired territory. Rogo sat atop his fox along the perimeter, keeping guard for any intruders or escapees. Kedem and Rebus remained seated in front of Akando, and were now joined by Jinx and Delfin, the two other advisors to Shadow Oak who had been summoned from their dens. Glif was also present, her grey body merging dramatically with the darkness, and Dallie lay prone next to her, praying to Averon for an end to the ordeal. With only the stars this evening to bear any light on the Great Forest, Akando prowled mercilessly around his new territory, his temper wearing thin.

"I see this is going to need an example of my intent," he muttered as he paced around slowly. "Bring him here," he ordered, to no creature in particular. Two foxes from his army emerged and from behind pushed Kedem further into the clearing. He leapt to his feet to keep his balance, and looked over his shoulders at the foxes that nudged him harshly. As he turned back, a rapid claw slashed his muzzle from left to right and sent his head jarring to the side.

"What are you -" came the voice of a furious Rebus. "Stop this at once!"

Akando ignored the badger as he turned his attention to his nemesis. His right paw had attacked the dog, and the result had been harsh. Kedem's muzzle had been sliced open from the attack, and though it stung intently and caused Kedem much discomfort, he turned back to Akando slowly, showing nothing but a strong, proud dog.

"Every time you give me the answer I do not want, you will suffer the consequences," Akando explained.

"You are insane!" boomed Rebus as he stood haplessly behind a line of foxes restraining him from assistance.

"Silence!" Akando yelled back with stern authority. "You will obey my command and surrender the authority of the Great Council to me! All of you!"

"I will never release my authority to you," a defiant Kedem said forcefully. "Never."

"Fool!" Akando screamed, and swiped again at the dog. Kedem yelped and lost his balance, tumbling onto his side and down onto the cold woodland floor. "Give it to me!"

"Stop this at once!" Rebus yelled, now trying in vain to push through the fox's barrier between him and his friend.

"Give it to me!" Akando ordered at the fallen fox.

"Never..." Kedem whispered defiantly, his will still unbroken. More dark foxes engulfed the clearing, keeping Jinx and Delfin at bay.

"Give it to him!" Delfin yelled with remorse, a minor scuffle beginning as the occupants of Shadow Oak attempted to barge through their barriers.

Akando raised his right paw high above his head and smashed his claws down into Kedem's exposed midriff. This time Kedem yelped with such agony that a tear welled in Glif's eye. "I want control!" Akando screamed through the trees.

"This is madness!" Jinx shouted.

"Stop it, Akando! Stop it!" Rebus bellowed.

"No…" Kedem whispered, his body panting rapidly. A hint of a wheeze erupted from his snout.

Hidden out of sight from underneath a dense bush Tali looked on, her face saturated with tears. She kept silent as they trickled from her eyes, her presence there remaining secret.

Akando raised his paws yet again, this time battering down violently on top of Kedem's head, causing the fox to groan and cough. Tali drew back with sadness as she watched the scene. She watched on as the vengeful fox relentlessly attacked her leader, screaming and shouting as he did so. A huge struggle began as Delfin and Jinx began fighting their way through the barriers. Rebus began swiping at the dark foxes in an attempt to rescue Kedem. A fight erupted as the animals began pawing and attacking one another. Tali looked away, unable to watch any more of the violence. As she did, she noticed four grey shapes watching the battle from the darkness. "Wickett?" she asked in a quiet whisper.

Wickett turned and looked at her quickly, his ears down and his eyes wide. "Tali?" he asked back in a subdued voice. He was joined silently by the rest of the Forest Guard. "What do we do?" he asked the vixen.

She shook her head and began crying. "I don't… I don't know," she said through the tears. In the trees not far away, a dark fox turned as though he heard something unusual.

Akando was relentless in his beating of Kedem. Every time he raised his paws, splatters of blood flew into the night air.

"Kedem," Blits whispered in a distressed tone. Tali looked towards the violence engulfing Shadow Oak and noticed the dark fox lazily heading in their direction. Panic struck the vixen, and she turned to Wickett.

"Go!" she ordered them. "All of you!"

The dog began running over, clearly having heard her voice. Rogo turned from the battle, having noticed his soldier investigating the trees across from his position. Panic set in as Tali issued her orders to the Forest Guard. "Head across the trail! Find the entrance to the Forest of the Damned and warn Streak and the warriors about what's happening."

Without even second-guessing himself, Wickett suddenly realised exactly what was going on. "Lyro," he added as realisation set in.

The fox drew closer as he sprinted towards them. "Oh no," Tali added as she too finally realised what was happening. "Go!" she shouted. "Find them! Warn them!" Wickett stood and nodded with emergency. "Go!" she said one last time, as she left the bush and headed towards the dark fox.

"Tali!" Apollo yelled after the vixen. The fox pounced and landed harshly on top of her, knocking her violently to the ground. She gave them one last look before being dragged by her scruff towards the now-settling Shadow Oak.

"We've got to go!" Wickett ordered his Forest Guards.

"Intruders!" the dark fox bellowed as he lost hold of Tali's scruff. He had seen the rabbits. Rogo kicked his fox into life and began to give chase. A skulk of foxes bolted from between the trees and headed in their direction.

"Cease them!" came the disembodied voice of Seerles through the darkness.

"Now would be a good time to run," Apollo added quickly.

"Follow me!" Wickett ordered.

The Forest Guards sprinted into action. Their paws pounded the littered floor and their nocturnal eyes navigated the darkness. They tore over the grass and

354

between the trees, relentlessly pursued by Akando's foxes. They broke onto a thin weaving trail that wound through vast oaks. Their paws pounded the wet grass as their legs seared them along the trail. They bounded together, Wickett leading the pack. He had no idea where he was heading, the adrenaline flush in his body taking control. Apollo flew behind at the rear of the pack. He took a quick look behind, and saw the foxes skid out on to the trail. A huge cloud of darkness emerged from the depths of the forest and rolled rapidly behind the chasing foxes. They charged rapidly towards their targets, their eyes burning furious red as their intent increased. They snarled and growled as they drew cold air into their bodies. The skulk of five opened their strides fully and began closing the gap.

Suddenly the floor became littered with branches and bracken falling heavily from the trees. They crashed around the fleeing rabbits, slowing them down as they bounded over and around the debris.

"Not good!" Blits shouted as the raining foliage crashed from the sky.

"The darkness! Seerles is doing this!" Wickett shouted back. Ahead in the far distance the trees broke and Meadoway emerged. "Keep going!" Wickett shouted as he bounded over a huge branch. "If we get out, we can out-sprint them!"

Branches crashed to the floor as the chasing foxes slowly gained upon them, the air full of the thunderous roar of falling debris attacking the rabbits. The grass began clutching at the Forest Guards, rapidly slowing their escape. Coinin ducked a branch swinging out to attack him. Apollo leapt it as it flew over Coinin's head and attempted to slow him down at the rear. The rabbits could not utilise their speed. Shrubs, branches and grasses grabbed out at them as they ran, forcing them to divert to different directions. The rabbits could not find space to sprint without being halted.

The darkness ploughed through the trees, the dark mist taking the shape of a huge, cloud-like serpent emerging at its forefront. It engulfed the trees as it passed swiftly through the wood, the skulk of foxes at its base, gaining rapidly on the running Forest Guards. The rabbits darted in all directions, avoiding the obstacles, kicking back foliage as they did so. Rogo's eyes burned red as his fox dropped his head and flattened his ears. His lean body lowered, and his speed increased. He began leaving his skulk and rapidly closed down on the escaping rabbits. The familiar sound of chasing footfalls emerged quickly upon Apollo, who knew without looking that the foxes were catching. Meadoway drew closer through the falling debris, only metres away, but the rabbits couldn't make their escape. The darkness thundered towards them. It gained on them. Apollo drew closer. A fox opened its jaws to strike...

"Full speed!" Wickett shouted, and exploded into Meadoway. The remaining rabbits dashed from the trees and opened into a full sprint. They pulled quickly away across its open meadow as Rogo and the foxes emerged from the woods.

"Woo-hoo!" Apollo yelled from the back of the rabbits, having taken a glance over his shoulder at the tormentors behind. The darkness exploded from the trees and dispersed as it entered the open meadow and floated silently into the night sky.

The chasing foxes slowed as they emerged in Meadoway. The rabbits had already built an unassailable lead, and had all but vanished into the star-lit night. Rogo snarled as his fox came to rest. "I'll hunt you down," he warned the rabbits as they vanished across the distance. "To the deepest, darkest parts of Averon, if I have to."

Cyrius followed the rabbits silently in the sky as they sprinted across Meadoway and out of harm's reach. They slowed down and came to rest in an area of long grass far away from the woods they almost didn't escape. Cyrius hooted, drawing their attention, and fell gracefully to the grass beside the Forest Guards.

"You took your time," Apollo said as the owl settled beside him.

"You had everything under control," Cyrius began as the rabbits caught their breath.

"What's going on?" Blits asked immediately. "What's happening at Shadow Oak?"

"I'm afraid the news is not good," Cyrius replied glumly.

"Kedem," Wickett said, as he remembered Akando's actions.

"It would seem Akando has amassed an army of followers with the help of Seerles," the owl began, "and the war which I have foreseen for so long seems to be on the verge of beginning."

"A war?" Coinin asked.

"Yes. I have never been able to foresee when it would emerge, but now our forest is in its darkest time, and the alliance between Seerles and Akando grows stronger by the second."

"Kedem fell by Akando's paw at Shadow Oak," Wickett began quietly.

"An event that will most definitely signal the beginning of this battle," the owl replied.

"We must find a way to stop them," Apollo added between his breaths.

"But what can we do - about the war and the siege at Shadow Oak?" Blits asked as his breath slowly came back to him. "We can't fight this alliance on our own."

"And you will not need to, Blits," Cyrius replied. "You will find help in your venture into the Forest of the Damned."

Apollo scrunched his nose. "How'd you know about that?" he asked, his voice emitting his clear disbelief.

Cyrius smiled to himself in the darkness. "How is of no importance at this time. What is important is that you cross the Trail of Fallen Stars, where you went on your first quest to the Black Lands. There, you must head south, and your noses will lead you to a small clearing. You will know it when you arrive, and there you must wait. I will send a warrior of immense strength to assist you, as your quest is not only to find Streak and the warriors."

"What is our quest, then?" Apollo asked in confusion.

"I will send message with the warrior who will join you at the clearing. I must be certain first of the events at Shadow Oak, but in the clearing you must wait. Do not venture to the gateway without him, or you will be placing yourself in great danger."

"Great, more danger," Apollo replied sarcastically.

"But how will we know who the warrior is?" Coinin asked the barn owl sat in front of him.

"You will know him, you have my word."

The rabbits acknowledged their understanding. "What of Lyro?" Wickett asked, concerned for his friends already heading to the forest.

Cyrius' expression changed into a frown of thought. "Akando's tribe have pledged loyalty to him. I foresaw his treachery, but not to the extent it has reached. His tribe will follow him to the ends of the Great Vast Open; they are loyal to his cause. But Lyro? I see

358

something within him that no other of Akando's dogs possesses."

"What's that, then?" Apollo asked comically. Blits drooped his ears and shook his head at the rabbit.

"Hope," Cyrius replied, himself speaking with a hopeful voice. "Remember, Forest Guards, do not venture to the gateway by yourselves. Wait for the warrior in the clearing. And don't forget; there is always hope."

Cyrius opened his wings and gently glided away into the night sky. A glowing gold aura trailed behind him and fell slowly through the darkness.

"No, I'll tell you what there is," Apollo began reluctantly. "Something. There's always something."

"What are you talking about?" Coinin asked with annoyance.

"Well, look at what's happened since dawn. I've ventured across the Great Vast Open. I've infiltrated an army of hares. I placed my life on the line today - and not once, I might add, but twice, having delivered the directions to those wretches and then fleeing from them. Do you know how much a sprint across the Great Vast Open takes out of you? Do you?" The rabbits looked at one another, either in disbelief or entertainment. "No, you don't!" the angry rabbit stated. "And then, and then," he began, as though he had just remembered something else to whinge about, "you leave me at the back of this sprint to get my tail gnawed off by those foxes! Is it really too much to ask to spend the night in a warm, dry warren with a fresh clump of grass and fresh bunch of daisies, eh? Is it really too much to ask?" Apollo turned his back on his comrades and threw his nose in the air, forcing his statement. "When rabbits speak of my legend, I'll be remembered as 'Apollo the Feeble,' or something like that."

"If you carry on with this little speech so close to Shadow Oak, you'll probably be remembered as 'Apollo the Dead,'" Coinin replied bluntly.

Apollo sighed, dropped his ears and turned back to them. "Alright," he said after a moment or so, "but I need to rest."

"It's a deal," Wickett agreed. "Right now, we have a quest to take. Let's find somewhere and rest up; we have a long day ahead of us. I have no doubt that Akando will send out a search party to hunt us down, and The Forest of the Damned doesn't sound like an easy place to navigate."

"It doesn't sound like a place for rabbits, either!" Apollo added.

"No," Wickett began slowly, "but it's something we have to do. We must wait for the warrior and head inside the forest. That's the task of the Forest Guard in the first days of this war."

The rabbits agreed with Wickett's line of thinking. They began slowly heading through Meadoway in the direction of the Trail of Fallen Stars. They would find somewhere safe to rest for the remainder of the night, and would once more be called to enter the Black Lands.

8

"Well, well, what do we have here?" Akando asked as his minions dragged Tali into the opening of Shadow Oak. She resisted, flailing her hinds out in an attempt to escape. The dog thrust her forward and let go of her scruff, sending her tumbling towards the tyrant. As she fell she noticed the immobile body of Kedem resting motionlessly on the foliage.

"Kedem!" she screamed and ran to his side. Fresh tears welled in her eyes as she saw the true extent of the beating he had suffered at the paws of his nemesis.

"Dead," Akando informed her calmly. The tears of sadness suddenly turned to tears of rage. She snarled her lips together and turned to face Akando.

"Tali, no!" Delfin ordered to her.

"No!" Rebus confirmed from behind a line of restraining dogs.

"If you do," Akando began, slowly walking closer to her, "you will meet the same fate as your beloved leader."

The confrontation was broken by the emergence of an animal slowly plodding its way into Shadow Oak. The guarding foxes allowed it to pass, as it posed no threat. Slowly, it entered the clearing and slumped from its hooves to the forest floor.

"Flicar!" Rebus shouted, and barged through his captors. He was joined by Glif, Delfin and Jinx. "Flicar?" Rebus asked as he joined the council member. Flicar was greatly hurt and seemingly short on life. He had sustained huge lacerations along his side, and had amazed the animals who now comforted him as to how he managed to make it all the way back to Shadow Oak.

Akando looked on with an inquisitive eye. "We need to take him to shelter. He is greatly wounded," Jinx informed him.

"The beast..." Flicar whispered through exhaustion.

The friends that surrounded him moved their heads back and looked at each other. "What did he say?" Akando asked, now moving closer to them through curiosity.

"He said 'the beast'," Delfin replied softly. Akando's army began to look around. The foxes and rats scoured their eyes questioningly upon one another and into the eclipsing trees they now lorded.

"He's been attacked," Rebus confirmed, "and judging by the extent of his injuries, I would not be surprised if it was the beast that inflicted damage to this extent."

"We need to take him to shelter," Delfin said to his captor.

After a moment's deliberation, Akando agreed. "Take him where you see fit," he replied swiftly, "but within these borders."

The dark foxes helped Flicar regain his footing. "Through here, to the dense trees," Rebus ordered.

Akando stood in the badger's way. "Try anything, council leader, and you will be next."

"The health and safety of my council friend is my only concern," Rebus replied harshly.

"Make sure it stays that way," Akando added, and stepped from his path. Rebus looked down at the motionless body of Kedem as he passed.

"Kedem..." Flicar mustered with a small ounce of depleted energy.

"Not now," Jinx began as he flanked the muntjac, "let's get you taken care of first."

"Take him away too. Throw him in the den," Akando ordered his followers. Another skulk of foxes began dragging Kedem's body out of the clearing and into the huge den underneath the towering oak.

As they were followed by a skulk of dark dogs, Rebus noticed a bird perched in the branches of a low-laying oak they intended to rest Flicar beneath. The bird was familiar to all those who attended the Great Council. Cyrius offered one final nod to the badger before taking flight and disappearing from Shadow Oak, rattling the branches high above them.

"What was that?" one of the dark foxes asked in a gruff voice, following the injured buck.

"Nothing. Just a bird or something," another replied as they moved closer to the tree.

Rebus looked towards Delfin, who had also seen the barn owl. "Something's happening," he said softly. Rebus nodded in agreement.

Something was indeed afoot.

9

Akando prowled Shadow Oak in the darkness. From the border of the trees the skulk of foxes who had given chase to the rabbits returned, unsuccessful in their quest.

"The rabbits?" their leader asked, approaching Rogo who sat atop his tiring dog.

Rogo shook his snout in disgust. "They reached the Meadow before we could catch them. They were too fast over the open ground."

Akando growled gently in the cold air. "Then you leave now, and search for them." Rogo looked at his leader without replying. "You take your skulk and find them! Kill them, and bring them back here!"

Rogo kicked his fox into gear. "We will, that I promise!" he replied, turning the dog out towards the trees. The chasing foxes joined Rogo and they thundered from Shadow Oak, their sole objective to find Wickett and his team. Tali sat in the clearing and harboured a hopeful smile to herself. The rabbits had escaped. There was still hope.

The sound of a squealing fox jolted her from her thoughts. Somewhere inside the border of Shadow Oak, a dog sounded like it had been greatly injured. Akando lifted his snout and turned in the direction it came from. A gentle breeze rustled the blossoming leaves of the oak trees surrounding the clearing, but nothing else could be heard. Every creature in Shadow Oak remained still, from the dark foxes to the rats, to sense if anything was worthy of their attention. A branch broke somewhere in the darkness.

Akando squinted his eyes as he scoured the depths of his surroundings. Nothing. A few calls from disturbed birds echoed in the branches above. The sound of rustling emerged as the breeze passed through the surrounding foliage. Tali looked to Akando, almost for comfort, as a strange atmosphere loomed over Shadow Oak. Akando returned her gaze then moved only his eyes, as he looked into the higher branches at the disturbance that had happened there. Another branch snapped somewhere. Tali slowly stood to her paws. The dark foxes posted guard around Shadow Oak remained firm. One saw something strange between the trees. He turned his head sideways as he noticed two reflecting orbs of light flicker once and disappear. He began to backtrack slowly. Those weren't lights...

He screamed as he was charged into and thrust to the floor of the clearing. His neck was broken in one mighty swipe of a claw, and tossed away with ease. Tali screamed and jumped back. Akando stood frozen with shock and fear. "The beast!" came the terrified cries from the dark animals. "The beast!"

Full-blown panic erupted through Shadow Oak as the huge panther stood roaring in the darkness. She roared and lashed out at the chaos around her as the foxes and rats darted in all directions for safety. She pounced upon one dog and viciously tore out his throat and neck with her deadly teeth.

"Retreat!" Akando shouted at the top of his voice. "Back to The North!" The beast relentlessly attacked the scurrying animals around her, smashing the rats from her path and maiming the foxes. Tali stood terrified as the beast wandered past her, showing no interest except to the dogs. "The vixen!" Akando screamed. "Get her!"

Tali looked around in confusion as she was engulfed by a skulk of fleeing foxes, surrounding her and pushing her along their path. "Hey!" she shouted as the foxes barged her along. "Let me go!"

Rebus and Delfin arrived to see the carnage of the fleeing animals. "Good Averon!" Rebus stated as the beast rampaged against the dark animals.

"Tali!" Delfin shouted as he saw her being jostled out of Shadow Oak by the skulk surrounding her.

Tali heard him shout. "Delfin! Rebus!" she screamed in return, before vanishing into the trees. Rebus caught sight of Akando's fleeing sweep disappear into the darkness as he made his getaway. The panther slowly turned and noticed the council leader stood on the small trail with the red fox. She growled and flattened her ears, her nose creasing as she opened her jaws. She turned towards them and slowly began stalking.

"If we run, we'll lead her to Flicar and the rest of the council," Delfin said as his mind tried to find a way out of the situation.

"We can't run, we'll endanger all of their lives," Rebus confirmed. Slowly the beast plodded closer, her gaze fixed firmly upon the badger and the fox.

"Then what?" Delfin exclaimed in a whisper.

The beast planted her paws into the sodden ground before roaring one last time. "Then this is it," Rebus stated, as realisation set in...

A grey shadow jumped in front of the boar, and faced the beast head-on. It screamed with such a high pitch that the birds in the trees flooded in mass from their branches and the beast jolted backwards. The ground rumbled as a powerful, invisible force struck the beast head-on. Her paws remained firmly rooted into the woodland floor but skidded across the clearing, leaving the trails of her claws in the damp ground. A flash of light engulfed Shadow Oak and from the sky above fell Cyrius, flashing between the battling animals. The grey shadow leapt at the beast through the glowing trail left by the barn owl. The beast leapt at the shadow. A thunderous smash engulfed the clearing, and the beast fell to the floor. Rebus noticed swirls of dark mist rolling around the body and paws of the shadow. "Doran!" he said excitedly to himself.

Doran and the beast glared at one another from across the clearing. The beast towered over the dog even at a distance, and yet it remained defiant in her awe. She roared once more and threw her jaws back toward the sky. Doran screamed yet again, his eyes burning red and the ground trembling once more. They stared at each other through glaring eyes. The beast looked down upon the fox, his eyes glowing red and swirls of dark mist racing around his body. He was strong, stronger than any creature she had ever encountered before. The beast was still suffering from the attack on the muntjac, but her power remained. She could stand now and attack the , or she could heal in time and return at full strength. With the power and force that the fox possessed, she knew her wounds would hamper her should she stay and fight now.

The beast turned from her challenger and leapt gracefully out into the darkness, her battle conceded on the grounds of Shadow Oak. As she vanished, the fox felt something within the darkness that told him she would be back. She would return stronger; and with his musky scent filling her nose, she would be able to find him easily, no matter where he headed in the Great Forest.

Slowly the darkness returned to the dog that had saved the council, and Doran took on the form he was most accustomed to.

"Doran!" Rebus shouted as he made his way into the blood-drenched clearing, the remains of the dark animals scattered across its grounds. Doran turned and acknowledged Rebus with a wry smile.

"Rebus," he simply said in greeting.

"You came back," Delfin added as he joined the badger.

Doran simply nodded, and looked around for his new friend. "And I brought someone who can help us."

Loat jumped from the hiding place he had found amongst some long grass, and drew the darkness back inside his muzzle as he made his way towards the trio of animals. "Greetings," he simply said as he joined Doran.

"You can control the darkness too?" Delfin asked the stoat as he came to rest.

"Yes," Doran answered on his behalf, "and if it wasn't for him I'd have been taken by the force before now. He is a friend, and an ally in the war that has emerged."

"And a valuable one during our hour of need," came the voice of Cyrius as his wings beat the air about them on his descent to the animals.

"Where's Tali?" Doran asked, his attention taken to the trees.

"Gone," Rebus stated with remorse. "Akando took her. I heard him shout that he was returning to The North." Doran's eyes flickered with rage. "You must keep focused, Doran. We will endeavour to return her here where she belongs. Of that you have my word."

"Kedem?" Doran asked quietly, turning his attention to Rebus and struggling to control the anger he felt at his sister's kidnapping. Rebus simply closed his eyes and shook his snout slowly. Doran turned away, noticing that the dens around the circular clearing hiding the foxes of the community were now filled with their curious faces.

"Can I see him?" he asked quietly, his voice now thick with the signs of sadness.

"He was taken to his den," Delfin replied, gesturing towards the huge oak tree he lived underneath.

Rebus, Delfin and Cyrius began making their way towards the den. "Come on," Doran said to Loat as they stood under the watchful eyes of the community.

They made their way to the tree, and deep inside the den presided over by Kedem during his life. They emerged in a chamber underneath the woodland ground. There, lying on his left side, rested Kedem, motionless and unaware. Slowly, the animals made their way to him; Cyrius hopping steadily through the large chamber, his talons unused to being inside a fox's den. They stood in silence for a long time as Doran looked over his fallen leader, and the seriousness of the situation dawned upon them all.

"I am sorry," Doran whispered to the body of the dog lying in front of him. Loat looked up at his friend and felt great sadness. He was sure that the darkness that connected them was sharing the fox's feeling with him.

"Wait," Rebus said, noticing something unfamiliar. "Look," he said, gesturing towards a small leaf in front of Kedem's nose. Faintly, so very faintly, it quivered at intervals, suggesting that a small breeze was passing gently over the loose foliage. Doran lowered an ear to the trunk of Kedem's body, and very, very gently, he heard the low drum of a slow heartbeat.

"He's alive. He's alive!" Doran shouted with excitement.

"But how?" Delfin asked with excitement and confusion. "He took a very serious beating. How can anything survive such an attack?"

"The forest!" the owl stated with certainty, realising what would have to be done.

Rebus turned to him. "The forest?" he asked, repeating his statement.

"Kedem is not dead! He was taken from us before he was intended to! His spirit roams the Forest of the Damned!"

"Of course!" Rebus confirmed with much excitement.

Hope had once again surfaced amongst the animals of Shadow Oak. "Doran, you must head to the Forest of the Damned -"

"No," Doran interrupted the barn owl as he formulated a plan. "I'm going to The North to get Tali back."

"Doran we need you to enter the forest-"

"No!" Doran snapped, his eyes turning red with rage. "Tali is my sibling! I'm going to bring her back to Shadow Oak!"

"Doran!" Cyrius shouted in reply, stopping the dog's rant. "Wickett and the Forest Guards are going to be waiting for you in a clearing before the forest! They will be entering to help you find Kedem and bring him back to help us! But not only must you find him, you must rescue the warriors from Akando's dogs! As we speak, a skulk of foxes lies in wait for them to emerge from the gateway. When they do, they will be engulfed by enemies and slaughtered, with the help of Lyro and his followers!"

"What?" Doran whispered with concern.

"We were tricked, Doran. We didn't know about the alliance Akando had formed with Seerles until long after the warriors had departed. They are in great danger. But we need you to rescue Kedem. We need his leadership in the Mighty War that looms upon us."

"Doran, I will go to The North," Loat began, turning the attention of his friend. The rest of the animals watched on as the stoat, new to Shadow Oak and to the plight of their cause, volunteered to help in their quest and enter imminent danger of his own choosing. "Trust in me, as I did you," he added, prompting Doran to remember the sacrifice he had made and the danger the stoat had placed himself in when the darkness had verged on taking him over.

"Rebus! Delfin! Quick!" came a voice from the opening behind them. The animals turned to see Jinx bounding into the den.

"What is it?" Rebus asked, sensing the concern in the fox's voice.

"Flicar, but not just Flicar. He's on his feet, he's here. But, animals..." he trailed off. Rebus and Doran looked at each other. "Just, quickly," he began, gesturing with his head out to the clearing of Shadow Oak.

With concern at the unclear report relayed to them by Delfin, the animals inside the den followed the excitable dog out of the chamber. They were greeted with a sight unlike anything they ever expected to see. "Good Averon," Cyrius whispered to himself as the sight he beheld overwhelmed him.

From the trees surrounding Shadow Oak emerged a mass of animals walking through the darkness. Muntjac, foxes, badgers, rabbits and hares, as well as a small herd of fallow deer, loomed in from the darkness. Flicar, greatly wounded but strong enough to stand, looked out to the muntjac and saw Favradin accompanying Daisy as they entered the clearing. General Lupus ambled side by side with Lisket and Tolka, and an army of rabbits and hares standing together in peace followed closely behind them.

"What in the good forest's name?" Doran whispered in awe.

Dallie and Glif emerged from the small trail leading to Flicar's previous resting place. The branches came to life as countless squirrels bounded across their reaching limbs, encompassing Shadow Oak from their perches above. Arley emerged from between the shrubbery with some chosen warriors from the pheasant contingency. Shadow Oak was overwhelmed with the mass of animals emerging into its clearing.

"It is true," Favradin began as he trotted slowly towards Flicar. "You did survive the attack from the beast."

"Flicar!" Daisy shouted, and bounded over towards him in the night-time gloom. He smiled down upon the doe as best he could, his injuries still painful and fresh. Daisy noticed and looked up to him, her eyes scouring the fresh injuries he sustained at the hands of the beast. "You look terrible," she added, her voice firmly stating the obvious. Flicar offered a short gasp of laughter at the fawn.

"This one is very lucky," Favradin stated as he looked upon the doe. "Had it not been for a passing herd of fallow deer, I fear she would have remained lost within our Great Forest."

Flicar shifted his gaze from the youngest muntjac in the contingency to Achak and his herd, stood across the clearing. He closed his eyes and gently nodded his head in thanks. Achak smiled and returned the gesture as floods of animals passed between them. Achak had been surprised when they encountered Favradin in the forest. Daisy had run to him instantly, and he was shocked that a herd of muntjac would take a fallow deer as their own. His shock had turned to happiness, and he felt his herd should assist the muntjac as a debt of gratitude.

Slowly the animals came to rest, and in their darkest hour looked towards the remaining council members for guidance in the first day of the Mighty War. The fate of so many animals and lives within Averon rested upon decisions made that very night. Never had such a sense of loss and dependence fallen upon the shoulders of Rebus. He knew as he stood there in the gloom, with so many creatures looking to him, that their very fate would fall upon his paws. With the pressure and fate of the Great Forest firmly dependent upon the sole leader of the Great Council, Rebus knew he must now decide the next action to take.

"My friends," he began solemnly as he made his way into the clearing. "This night is indeed a very dark night upon our Great Forest." The animals stood in unison, as silent as the darkness itself that had engulfed Shadow Oak.

"Akando's intentions are now clear. With the support of Seerles and his fresh army of dogs and other creatures turned by the darkness, I fear that the war Cyrius has warned us of for so long is now finally upon us." The animals were enraptured by Rebus' speech as they stood and sat in the clearing and surrounding trees. Each paid full attention to the wise boar addressing them. "And now we stand together, here in Shadow Oak. I see rabbits and hares existing side by side," he added, gesturing towards General Lupus and Lisket.

"General Lupus and his Forest Guards saved most of my warriors from death at the jaws of those foxes, even as we attempted to raid his warren. I owe him, and your forest, a huge debt in what you have done for us."

"And your help will be greatly received," Rebus replied. "But I have to stand before you now, as leader of the Great Council of Averon, with an immense decision to make. Should we simply allow this deadly alliance to take our home and our freedom - or do we stand and fight, declaring war on all those who threaten our existence as Cyrius has foretold?"

"We fight!" shouted Doran as he leapt into the clearing. "For too long we have existed in fear of

Seerles and the power he possesses. Well, now we have nothing to fear. I have tamed the very darkness he tainted me with when he saved my life those long seasons ago. I can control the darkness and bend it to my will, but I do so to fight against him, and to restore peace to our forest!" Shadow Oak erupted into cheers as the animals aligned themselves to the plight of the Great Council.

"If they want war, I say we give it to them!" he continued as the cheering subsided. "I say we take the battle to them, and we show that no longer will we fear the Black Lands and those who amass there! We show them that we stand united, and no matter what happens - even if the skies fall and our forest ends - that we will stand as we did in the face of the Dark Army, and we will fight! Fight, until the end!"

Shadow Oak exploded with a thousand cheers, shaking the ground and echoing throughout the forest. Doran looked out upon the animals he had motivated. He smiled. Now they stood a chance. With all the animals dedicated to the plight of the Great Council, now they stood a chance.

Akando turned from the skulk he was leading along an isolated trail. All the foxes under his command turned and followed his gaze back through the trees towards the direction of the dull cheering they could hear across the miles. "It starts," he whispered quietly.

Tali looked on from within her guarding captors. "They're coming for me," she said hopefully.

The roars continued to overpower Shadow Oak. General Lupus hopped towards the remaining council members with Lisket in tow. "My boys?" he asked, noticing that Wickett and his team were nowhere to be found.

"Do not worry, they are safe," Cyrius hooted. "They have a most important role to play within this war."

"Of course they do, they are the Forest Guard," General Lupus replied proudly.

"I will go to them, and venture to the Forest of the Damned to bring Kedem and the warriors back," Doran said to Rebus over the cheering.

"Then haste not, Doran. Kedem needs you as quickly as you can before he becomes lost forever," the badger replied. "You are our only hope of bringing him back."

"I will not fail him, not this time," Doran stated as he turned to Loat. "Please. Promise me you'll do everything in your power to bring Tali back?"

The stoat looked upon him with honest eyes. "You have my word. I'll do everything that I can."

"And you won't be alone," came a voice from across the clearing. "We will stand with you on your quest to rescue the vixen, as long as the council allows?" Rebus looked towards Favradin and a herd of bucks approaching them. "Achak, the leader of the fallow deer has agreed to stay and protect Shadow Oak, allowing us to join the stoat on his journey to rescue Tali."

"With the beast still at large, we pledge to do whatever we can to protect your council during the Mighty War," Achak added as he followed the muntjac.

"Then it begins," Cyrius informed them.

"I will return!" Doran shouted, and without a moment's hesitation dashed from his home in the direction of the Trail of Fallen Stars.

As Doran vanished into dawn's early hours, a sense of hope engulfed the animals within Shadow Oak. Hope that now they could stand tall to the threat declared upon them from the Black Lands.

And, as Cyrius had often retorted, there was always hope.

The Forest of the Damned

Part 1

Dawn of the Great War

1

Through the thick swirling fog a pack of five foxes sprinted blindly into its depths, following the faint scent of their hunted targets. The air was chilly and damp, soaking their dark fur to the flesh as they thundered deeper and deeper into the Haunted Woods. The early dawn's light became darker, and between the patches of fallen cloud lifeless bare tree branches loomed eerily, pointing out in all directions in as they attempted to break free of the element that had descended down upon them.

The foxes' eyes burned red with hate and malice, melting through the fog as they thundered along an uneven, leaf-littered trail towards a mysterious gateway. The fox sprinting at the head of the skulk bore a jaded rat atop its back. The rat's red eyes pierced the fog brightly, and his senses determined the presence of their targets in the near distance. The rat sneered to himself as the thrill of the chase engulfed him. He was Rogo, the leader of the armies from the Black Lands, and he was about to capture the four rabbits he had been sent to apprehend.

"Faster!" he yelled, and with his jagged claws yanked the damp fur that rested upon his transporters neck. The dog became angry, and through its aching paws sprinted harder at his master's request. "I have you now..." Rogo whispered to himself.

The skulk of foxes exploded from the fog into a clearer, circular opening. A tree with a small opening in the base of its trunk stood partially hidden by the fog on his left, and the faint signs of similar trees drifted in and out of focus around them as the fog swirled lazily past. Ahead of them stood another skulk of dark foxes from Rogo's army, easily distinguished by the glowing red eyes that his soldiers now bore. They turned in the broken silence and watched as Rogo and his foxes slowed to a canter and glided through fallen clouds towards them.

Rogo hopped down from his ride and bounded across the dank ground, his long tail whipping up and down as he quickly scampered across to his soldiers. His fur was wiry and damp, appearing to the foxes as though spikes protruded from his body.

"Rogo!" one of the foxes snapped as he noticed his general heading towards them.

Rogo looked over the skulk of foxes without even a greeting. He loomed through the fog like a gliding shadow, his eyes bright and red. "Four rabbits from the ranks of General Lupus' Forest Guard. We tracked them this way. Have you seen them?" he asked authoritatively.

"No sir," a fox from the skulk answered. "We've seen no-one since we were deployed here to kill the animals emerging from the Twins of Despair."

"Then they are close," Rogo answered, turning his head to the side as he scoured the shady trees emerging and hiding from the fog as it floated by. "The Forest Guards must be slaughtered before they can enter the Forest of the Damned."

The small general turned back towards the skulk of foxes he had journeyed with on his mission to the clearing. "They are in this immediate area," he began, standing on his hind legs to see them clearer. "Scour the trees! Find them!"

The foxes scattered in various directions and vanished into the fog, not once questioning their evil leader. Rogo returned his gaze to the foxes posting guard on the small trail leading to the Twins of Despair.

"Stay here. If the Forest Guards should emerge, kill them," he ordered grimly.

Rogo leapt from his position and bounded into the tree-line hidden by the fog. He wandered slowly between the exposed tree roots that had twisted themselves from the soil, between vast fallen branches from the trunks around him and scattered mounds of uneven earth as he followed closely the trail of the rabbits he was relentlessly hunting. Their strange scent hung within his nostrils, but the elements of the fog and damp air that surrounded him made the scents harder to follow. They were indeed close - that much he knew - but where exactly, he could not pinpoint.

As he wandered through the fog, following his nose, a strange noise like a fluttering bird skimmed low over his head, forcing him to duck. It vanished into the distance as quickly as it had emerged, and slowly the rat rose to his feet, forgetting the rabbits for a moment and wondering what had just passed overhead. There were no signs of a disturbance within the forest and branches surrounding him; they rested quietly, swayed only by a faint breeze softly assisting the fog pass by on its journey. Rogo stood for a moment longer and wondered if it was something he imagined. It had happened so quickly that now he doubted whether it was something his mind had run away with momentarily, or just a natural element from within the forest. As Rogo began focusing his attention back toward the rabbits he was hunting the sound echoed above him again, this time followed by the sound of a yelp. With a sudden flutter of adrenaline, Rogo leapt into a sprint and headed back towards the clearing. As he emerged from the trees he saw the skulk of guarding foxes in disarray, spooked by something that was happening in the depths of the fog.

"What's going on?" Rogo demanded from them as he quickly approached.

Another yelp emerged from the thick fog, and again the forest fell eerily silent. The foxes formed a circle of defence and looked out into the clearing. Rogo stood at the head of the skulk and looked out in the direction of the trail from which he had travelled. The gentle breeze passing through the forest caused the hidden trees to creak in the silence as their branches swayed beyond the dark rodent's eyesight. Rogo sensed something was wrong in the eerily quiet forest that surrounded them. The trees continued to moan as the breeze took hold of their branches and passed gracefully between them. The debris on the woodland floor rustled in the same cold gusts. Rogo looked skyward out of the corner of his eyes, and tilted his small head as he listened intensely for anything strange within the forest. Silence.

"Do you think -"

"Shut up!" Rogo barked, silencing a fox stood behind him. "Something's wrong."

A body crashed to the ground next to the rat, causing him to leap from its path. From the fog a flurry of bodies launched through the air and crashed to the ground, causing the skulk of foxes to scatter. Bracken launched high into the air as the missiles smashed to the floor and scattered the loose debris in every direction. They thudded limply to the cold ground, one after another, until the carnage came to a sudden halt and the eerie silence of the forest returned.

Rogo slowly approached one of the bodies, realising it was one of the skulk he had sent to find the rabbits. "Is he dead?" came a shaken voice from behind the rodent. He turned and noticed he had been joined by one of the foxes guarding the trail. Rogo returned his gaze to the body lying upon the cold debris, and slowly made his way towards it. He saw the telltale sign of shallow breaths being drawn by the unconscious, dark-furred fox.

"No, he's just injured," Rogo replied, hiding his anxiety behind a strong will.

From the fog ahead, a huge plume of swirling darkness snaked through the air. It drifted gracefully on the wind and dispersed itself into many swirling rivers as it passed through the air and above the onlooking animals. It passed above Rogo and quickly returned into one drifting line. Suddenly it lunged down, attacking the fox behind him. It grasped and lifted the fox from the ground, causing him to roll and contort as he struggled in the open air. Rogo watched helplessly as the darkness engulfed the fox above him, swaying him rapidly in every direction. The fox yelped as he was viciously shaken from side to side, his limbs unable to struggle in the open air. They swung lifelessly as the darkness threw the fox from side to side, like a savage hound feasting upon the carcass of a hunted prey. The dog fell limp and unconscious within the grasp of the tormenting darkness, which quickly released the body to fall harshly to the floor. Four other plumes exploded from the smoky darkness and disappeared into the fog. Rogo heard the remaining foxes yelp as they were hunted by the swirling element. He knew that they would befall a similar fate as the one that he had witnessed, and waited again for the forest to fall silent.

Slowly, the plumes of darkness withdrew through the air, snaking their way erratically back the way they came. Rogo watched as they passed slowly above him once more and back towards they fog in which they emanated. With fear surging rapidly through his wiry body, Rogo turned and vanished quickly from the carnage. He darted quickly along the trail he had followed, this time without the protection of his soldiers. As he bounded along the trail, he noticed something drifting from the fog ahead of him.

There, in the middle of the trail, he saw the shadow of an animal loom slowly from its depths, its eyes burning red through the dense fog.

2

"What is going on out there?" Coinin muttered as he heard the commotion outside. Within a vast hollow tree-trunk, the four Forest Guards had been hidden safely away from their hunters, thanks to a small hedgehog who had agreed to help them.

"I don't know, Coinin," Apollo replied as he struggled to move in the tight space. "Why don't you go and have a look?"

"You're closest!" Coinin snapped back.

"Yes, but I don't want to die!" Apollo said bluntly.

"You're 'Apollo the Brave!' You laugh in the face of death, remember?"

"And you say you're the best Forest Guards in the whole of Averon?" Prickly, the small hedgehog, replied from the depths of the gloomy hollow.

Wickett sighed and closed his eyes. "Apollo," he said in a quiet voice.

"What?" the disgruntled Forest Guard replied.

"Can you sneak outside and see what's going on?"

"Why me?"

"Apollo!" Wickett snapped, "you're a Forest Guard. You have a proven record of infiltrating enemy ranks. You proved that when you infiltrated the hares."

Apollo looked towards his leader. "But Blits was there too. What about him?"

"I knew it!" Blits snapped harshly from the recesses of the trunk. "I knew you'd bring me into this!"

"But it's true!"

"Apollo! Blits!" Wickett snapped, silencing his guards. "All of us are in this position because we are

387

the best in the forest at what we do. That includes what we bring to this team individually as well as together. Apollo, this is a direct order. Sneak outside and gather intelligence so we may plan our next move. Go!"

Apollo muttered under his breath, and exited the hollow cautiously. Wickett looked on as his friend vanished from sight. He was a brave rabbit, and sometimes he felt he added more pressure on Apollo than the others - but he knew that Apollo would get the job done, one way or another.

Apollo glided silently through the long grass at the edge of the clearing. Stealth had become one of his strengths just recently, and putting it to use in such a volatile situation would require all his skill and know-how.

The fog cooled his body rapidly. After being cooped up with three other rabbits and a hedgehog in the large hollow of a tree, he welcomed the cold and acclimatised quickly to the weather outside. Lying prone, he slowly poked his nose from the grass to see what had happened out in the clearing.

Many bodies of unconscious foxes lay randomly upon the damp ground. They were all dark foxes, that much he recognised instantly, and would undoubtedly serve from the ranks of the evil Seerles, the most powerful creature in the forest of Averon. All of the foxes were part of the same army, and without the sign of any other creature in the area, Apollo could not decide if they fought within themselves or if something else had happened. After a moment or so of lying in the grass and surveying his surroundings, Apollo felt safe enough to slowly hop across to the unconscious bodies and investigate further.

He gently made his way across the clearing, through the fog, until he came to the body of the first fallen fox. He looked over the darkened fur and saw no lacerations or blood, no matted fur and no immediate sign of any broken limbs. He hopped over to the next fallen body and scanned it for injuries. Again, nothing unusual was noted by the Forest guard as he carried out his investigation. He did however notice a stick lying next to the unconscious dog, and decided to take his investigation to the next level. Clasping the manageable stick between his teeth, he gently lifted it from the damp ground and moved towards the head of the unconscious fox. Gently, he slapped the stick across its snout to see if any plumes of the darkness vacated his nostril. All foxes corrupted by the darkness had a small amount of the element within them that allowed Seerles to govern their thoughts and actions. If they were alive, he guessed that it would still be resting inside the fallen bodies of these foxes. On occasion, an unconscious animal taken by the darkness may exhale the element as they breathed. As he suspected, a small puff of black smoke left the fox's nostrils when he hit the stick across its unconscious snout. If all of these foxes were under the control of the darkness, they would not have attacked each other, proving to the intrepid investigator that this was the handy work of another creature lurking within the trees. He continued slapping the stick across the fox's snout whilst deep in thought. Was it the beast terrorising Averon? Maybe, but usually when the beast attacked its victims were killed, and there were always immense injuries that the animals would suffer. He continued tormenting the unconscious fox, while his mind tried frantically to find a solution to the mystery. What had done this?

"Apollo, what have you done?" came the familiar voice of his friend Blits. Jolting from his thoughts, he looked across the clearing to see the three Forest Guards and the hedgehog emerge from the tree hollow he had also been hiding inside not long ago.

"I haven't done..." Apollo said, before realising what Blits was referring to. He looked at the unconscious foxes on the ground, and realised how it may look being caught hitting one fairly harshly across the snout with a stick.

"Ha, ha!" Prickly laughed intently. "You are indeed the best Forest Guards, by jove! What did you do, eh? I bet you came out here and gave them all the old one-two! Absolutely splendid, young fellow-me-lad!"

"Apollo?" Wickett asked, somewhat confused.

Apollo looked at the fallen foxes and back towards his comrades. He could not resist it.

"There they were!" he began, his voice full of the usual drama they had come to expect. "I was surrounded on all sides by all these foxes, all of them intent on destroying 'Apollo the Merciless!'"

"Merciless?" Blits asked Coinin as the dramatic hero continued his speech.

"Idiot, more like," was Coinin's less-than-favourable reply.

As the Forest Guards and the hedgehog looked on, mesmerised by the tall tale Apollo was spinning, Wickett noticed a shade of grey behind him drift through the fog and take the shape of a fox. Wickett's eyes widened as the shade drew closer and began approaching Apollo from behind.

"Blammo! One fox fell to my right! I span, disorientated by the vast number of these terrible creatures," the great warrior continued, unaware that a powerful animal was approaching him.

"Apollo," Wickett said in a wary tone. The shade drew closer and stood only a few feet from the tale-telling Forest Guard.

"Apollo!" Blits snapped, halting the rabbit mid speech.

"What?" Apollo snapped back, clearly frustrated that his story was being interrupted.

"To have achieved all that you have, Forest Guard, takes much skill. To fell an entire skulk of warrior foxes single-handedly, as you have told, is surely the work of an amazing warrior. With the power you possess, you will have no hesitation in duelling with me for bragging rights of these fallen foxes."

Apollo turned to see the silhouette of a fox shrouded in swirling darkness standing over him, its bright eyes burning red. His ears dropped immediately and he shrank back through fear of the creature facing him. He offered nothing in reply, just a terrified glare back towards his tormentor. The remaining Forest Guards froze as one of the foxes from the Black Lands prepared to launch its attack.

"There is nothing else left for me to do. The last thing I have left to say to you, mighty Forest Guard, is..."

Apollo shrank back, his doom imminent. Wickett, Coinin and Blits were powerless to help him. They watched on as the fox spoke the final words Apollo would ever hear.

"Is... it is so good to see my old friends once again!"

Apollo tensed, expecting a scathing claw to come slashing down upon him, tearing him in half with one, clean swipe. Then his mind processed what had been said, and looked upon his would-be attacker.

"Huh?" he grunted softly.

The dark mist clouding the fox began to rescind, drawing backwards around the fox's head and pulling the element from its body. Dull red fur emerged where swirling darkness once rested. Dark paws merged with red legs as the darkness drew further into the open muzzle and snout of the fox. A greying white underside now became visible. Finally the darkness vanished, and a proud, familiar fox stood before him.

"Doran!" Blits shouted, subsiding the rabbits' fears.

Doran, the warrior fox of Shadow Oak, had finally found the comrades he had been sent to protect. He smiled as his friends hopped over the damp ground to greet him.

"I didn't think we would see you again," Wickett added as he joined Apollo.

"It is good to see you, my friends," the fox replied as they gathered in front of him.

"How are you? We heard that you had encountered a problem in Shadow Oak?" Coinin asked. Doran's smile subsided and a look of seriousness crossed his muzzle.

"I did," he began, explaining what had happened whilst they protected their warren and investigated the hare invasion in the Great Vast Open. "I battled the darkness inside me, almost to death." The rabbits listened as Doran explained his eventful story.

"It became so strong and overpowering that I left my home of Shadow Oak in the fear that I would lose control of my will and seriously injure anything that got in my way. I ran deep into Averon and encountered Loat, a stoat who had at one time been in league with Seerles and who mastered the art of controlling the darkness. During a battle I had where the darkness overwhelmed me, he reached through my anger and helped me overcome the great force that was draining my mind. Together we brought the darkness under my control, and now it is I who bends it to my own will."

As Doran spoke these last words, his eyes flashed red and once more his smile returned.

"Wow! So you did all this?" Apollo asked, looking at the unconscious foxes littering the floor. Doran nodded gently.

"I believe then that you are to accompany us inside the Forest of the Damned to find Streak and the rest of the warriors, the one Cyrius spoke of?"

"I am," Doran added, "but our priorities have changed. Finding Streak is not the initial reason we are heading there."

"Why not? Streak and the warriors are at great threat, with Lyro and his skulk pretending they will help," Wickett argued.

"They are a threat to our warriors, I will not lie to you about that. But there is something even greater that we need to concern ourselves with first."

"What is it?" Coinin asked.

"Kedem," Doran replied slowly.

"Kedem?" Blits began. "But he was murdered. We saw Akando beat him to death."

"You saw him beaten, but he is not dead."

"You mean, he's alive?" Apollo asked hopefully.

"He is alive, but barely," Doran explained as the excited rabbits listened closely. "He was beaten almost to death, but his body did not die. I saw him with my own eyes in Shadow Oak. His body has almost given out. He is between life and death as we speak."

"And that can mean only one thing," Wickett mused to himself.

"Yes. His banafrit is lurking within the Forest of the Damned, ready to pass into the spirit world."

"But what can we do?" Blits asked, torn between emotions for his friends and the leader of the Great Council. "Even if we do find Kedem's banafrit in the forest, how do we return him to his body?"

"I don't know," Doran said honestly, "but Cyrius was intent that I should find you all and that we should enter the forest to find him. I believe Kedem has an important part to play in the Great War that has now dawned upon us."

"It's begun?" Coinin asked, noticing the cold air glide around them.

"Yes," Doran said slowly, switching his gaze from one rabbit to the other. "Rebus and the Great Council decided to take the battle to Seerles and Akando. We have made many new friends who will now assist us in protecting our forest, and Shadow Oak is now preparing for the battles that will soon begin. My friend Loat is leading the muntjac to Akando's dwellings in The North. He kidnapped Tali, and they have gone to rescue her."

"Oh no," Blits sighed. None of the rabbits had known that Doran's sibling had been taken as the enemies fled from Shadow Oak. The last image they had was of her self-sacrifice that allowed them all time to escape. If she had not distracted Akando and his patrolling soldiers on the outskirts of Shadow Oak, they most certainly would have been captured and killed.

"Poor Tali," Apollo added softly.

A brief surge of emotion swept through Doran as he spared a thought for his sister being held hostage in the furthest reaches of the Great Forest.

"Well then, there's no time for us to lose," Wickett said breaking the silence.

"None whatsoever," Doran replied. "Are you ready to do this?" he asked the four Forest Guards.

"Doran, we were born to do this," Apollo replied seriously.

Coinin sighed and shook his head. "No, Apollo, you were born to do this. I was born to patrol borders and guard tunnels. I was born to eat daisies and bathe in the sunshine during the warm season. How did I ever get involved in all this?"

"Because you're the best at what you do, Coinin," Wickett added quickly.

"Well, when you put it like that," he replied smugly.

The small band of warriors had finally reunited for their quest to the Forest of the Damned to rescue Kedem.

"My friends!" came a shout from behind them as they made their way towards the Twins of Despair. They turned to see Prickly scurry into the clearing between the unconscious foxes. "I will send word to Shadow Oak that you have reunited and entered the forest. Good luck to you! And remember, if you return to a place you have already passed, turn around and head back. But, with your new friend there, I imagine you'll be able to travel anywhere you want to! Good luck! I'll be waiting here for you and your friends to return!"

"If they return before us, inform Streak of Lyro's treachery," Doran asked.

"Consider it done," Prickly replied.

Doran and the Forest Guards began their journey once again, and soon vanished beyond the thick fog.

"Good luck," Prickly said once more to the invisible warriors. "I do so hope that you and your friends will be the first ones to return from that forest. All of Averon now depends on it."

3

The silent warriors slowly emerged from the thick fog that had befallen the Forest of the Damned. Streak, their leader and red fox representative from Shadow Oak, headed the rag-tag animals sent by the Great Council to seek Stryder, the owl who presided over this heinous forest, and who knew everything occult in both the realm of the living and the realm of the dead. The answer to defeating the beast lay within his mind, and if the warriors could reach them - if - they may find a way to rid the forest of the immense creature and return their forest to a degree of safety.

Followed close behind Streak loomed Lyro, another red fox, representative from The North on behalf of Akando's clan. He had been charged by the treacherous Akando to slaughter the warriors he had infiltrated with the two foxes that followed him, Pairo and Makoto. From behind the skulk of foxes Chance and Checkers, two otters new to the warriors, followed slinkily behind.

Streak stopped at the base of a huge fallen tree. It had fallen on its side, and gigantic roots and debris emerged from its base, wildly outreaching in all directions, most of them dark and rotting. A huge crater of excavated earth lay disturbed and uneven where the tree once stood, with vines of soil-covered roots still clinging to the tree base and some still embedded in the earth. The tree was so vast that the animals had to look upwards to see the top of the fallen trunk.

Streak wandered slowly past the tree on the solid, frozen ground. "Careful," Lyro said from behind as he joined the leader. Streak stopped and turned to his comrade. "Cliffside," the fox informed him. Streak returned his gaze forward. There, only a metre or so from where he stood, the frozen ground vanished and lead into a huge abyss of swirling fog. He wandered to the edge of the cliff and looked out. He had no idea how vast the hidden canyon was, and had no way of gauging how far it was across to the other side.

"The first test," he said to Lyro, who now stood beside him.

"If it's a test, there must be a way across," he replied.

"This tree is huge," Chance said, standing briefly on his hinds to have a closer look.

"What type of tree is it?" Checkers asked him as he stood in awe.

Chance scoured the barks and roots that he could see. "I don't know," he began thoughtfully, "I don't think I've ever seen such a type before."

"Maybe you haven't," came the deep voice of Brock, the warrior badger who emerged from the fog beside him with Danjo, their squirrel guide, and Selwyn, the brightly-coloured pheasant who completed this band of warriors. "The Forest of the Damned is indeed a strange forest, and many types of vegetation, flowers and trees may not be found anywhere else within Averon."

Streak wandered around the base of the uprooted tree, through the frozen earth where it once stood, and round to the other side. There, he stopped at the cliff-face again, looking out at the trunk as it stretched across the canyon and vanished into the fog. He was watched intently by Pairo and Makoto, their treacherous eyes giving no signs of their terrible plan. The rest of the animals settled as they watched their leader assess the first trial they would have to pass. He looked up, wondering if there was any way they could climb to the top of the trunk and cross the canyon on its side. The very fact that the tree was on its side across a huge open space suggested that its branches were resting on something both solid and strong. The trunk rested without even flinching in the harsh breeze that billowed around it, looking sturdy and strong across the canyon. The red fox with the dash of white fur through his left eye looked over the tree one final time before calling into action his plan.

Selwyn looked at the trees surrounding them. They reached up into the fog, reaching over them with their strange branches. "What manner of trees in Averon would harbour vines growing from them?" he asked, prompting Brock and Danjo to look upwards and note his discovery. There were indeed immense great vines that hung from their branches. Some were so long that they fell from the lofts above, and coiled in great length on the ground beside the trees they emerged from.

"None that I know," Danjo replied, as he looked upon his surroundings.

Streak wandered slowly to this small group of animals. "Selwyn," he said, drawing the pheasant's attention. "The trunk across this canyon is solid, but I don't know where it rests. The danger lies with where it leads. I don't want us to cross into a dangerous situation. Can you investigate it from the air and report back to us?"

Selwyn looked across to the fallen tree and the fog that engulfed it across the canyon. He knew that he would have to keep the tree in his eyesight at all times to stop himself becoming disorientated and lose his flight. He offered nothing but a simple nod in reply to Streak's question. He turned from the animals and began running to the cliff-edge. The air filled with the sound of his beating wings and, leaping from the cliff-face, he took flight and tracked above the fallen tree.

His brightly-coloured body was swallowed by the fog and he vanished into the abyss, the sound of his wings the only sign of his existence.

The animals gathered as the gentle beating of Selwyn's wings faded and vanished from their ears, leaving them to stand in the dulling fog in silence. They stood there for what seemed like an age.

"The canyon is indeed huge," Brock said as his distinct voice broke the silence.

"I hope it is indeed vast, and that nothing has happened to your warrior," Lyro added, surfacing the doubts that few had secretly kept to themselves.

"No, I have every faith in Selwyn," Streak replied, returning an anxious gaze out towards the fallen tree and swirling mist. Checkers looked silently towards Chance. Both otters displayed an expression of concern. Pairo and Makoto said nothing, their evil minds hopeful that the worst had befallen the pheasant. One less to slaughter would make their job much easier.

Danjo ruffled his grey fur and darted towards the base of the fallen tree. With nimble paws he leapt onto its side, catching grip of the deep grooves, and climbed rapidly the circumference of the trunk as he made his way to the top of the huge tree. Streak and Brock slowly wandered to the side of the fallen trunk.

"Is the fog breaking?" Brock asked the squirrel, who perched above him and out of sight.

"No," Danjo replied, "it engulfs the trunk fully. It is going to be extremely dangerous crossing, of that I have no doubt."

"Any sign of Selwyn?" Streak asked, hiding his emerging concern.

Danjo peered as best as he could out into the fog. It was moving naturally, drifting across the trunk and away into the unknown abyss. Danjo could see the signs of a branch across the distance, reaching upwards until it was engulfed by the cloud.

"None," the squirrel replied quietly.

Silence continued within the forest as the fog danced and swayed and passed silently by. Danjo kept his place atop the fallen log looking for any sign of his comrade returning from his reconnaissance mission. The fog swirled, a gentle breeze passed, and still there was no sign of Selwyn returning. Brock stood silently beside Streak at the edge of the cliff-face, looking out across the hidden canyon, looking for any sign of his friend. Chance and Checkers slowly approached them, their own concern now growing with every second that passed. Pairo and Makoto simply lurked in the background, their evil eyes watching the conflict that grew within Lyro. Would his allegiance change? Would he slaughter these animals after they had reached Stryder and his enchanted tree, as Akando their leader had ordered?

Slowly, Lyro paced to the opposing side of the trunk from Streak and the animals, his ears engaged as though he had heard something. Danjo had heard it too, and slowly stood upon his hinds as he looked out into the fog. There it was again. It grew louder and more rapid, coming closer and closer. Danjo smiled to himself. Streak sighed. The sound of Selwyn's beating wings filled their ears, and the flying pheasant emerged from the gloomy fog. He soared over Danjo as he began his descent. Danjo turned and watched the pheasant land on the dark ground beyond the trunk below him. The animals dashed towards the pheasant as he ruffled his feathers and came to rest in the small clearing.

"You had us worried," Brock said as he approached Selwyn.

"It's a long, long way," he replied as he caught his breath and relaxed a little. "I flew above the trunk thinking that the tree would have to end at some stage. It is huge, and rests in a clearing not dissimilar to this. The branches and leaves are so dense and vast where it rests, you will have to fight your way through them to continue along the trail as they fill the clearing completely."

"Can we cross in safety?" Streak asked him, hoping the pheasant had scoured the trunk.

"The trunk doesn't seem to become any narrower that I can see, although walking on a circular surface will be no easy task. It seems uneven at times, and shows signs of branches jutting from the trunk the closer you get to the end."

Streak looked upward at the fallen trunk. "This is it - our first trial. Let's hope that the forest is kind to us and that we all cross safely."

"Indeed. Let's hope for the best," a malevolent Pairo added as he drew towards the animals, his intentions known only by Makoto and Lyro. Lyro shot him a harsh glare, as though his words would compromise their situation.

"This is where our journey into the Forest of the Damned begins," Brock said, joining Streak in his gaze upwards. "Our first task is to find out how we climb up?"

"I have an idea," Danjo replied from atop the tree trunk. His small body leapt gracefully to the solid floor and ran around to the cluster of vines nestling beside the dark trees. "Help me with this," he ordered to no-one in particular.

"Clever," Lyro added as he followed Danjo's pattern of thought. The fox helped the squirrel find a sturdy thick vine, and carried it towards the trunk.

"If we can throw the vine over the trunk, you can pull yourselves up onto it," Danjo explained.

"Let me," Selwyn replied, and, moving the animals to the edges of the clearing, took the vine between his talons and flew across the trunk. It fell across the tree with a dull thud and uncoiled down its side, falling at the paws of Streak. Selwyn's wings fell silent as he came to rest upon the tree, looking now at his friends from its lofty height.

"This still isn't going to be easy," Streak mused as he gazed upon the dark, leafy vine in front of him.

"Nothing we do is ever easy, my friend," Brock added with a slight hint of amusement in his voice. "After you," he politely inclined.

Streak took one last look at the vine and the trunk, which now seemed to grow much taller with his anticipation. He grasped the thick vine in his jaws and tugged at it fiercely, ensuring it would not snap from the tree it was attached to during his attempted climb. Once happy it would hold out, he placed his front paws on the side of the trunk, released the vine and leapt quickly upwards, catching the vine in his teeth higher than before. All four paws had now left the ground and were pushing against the rough, uncomfortable bark of the unknown tree. Streak stayed there for a moment, wondering how he would be able to advance from here. Not even halfway up the side of the fallen trunk, he began to feel as though this would not work. Another idea then occurred to him. He slowly laid his red body against the knobbly bark, and found his paws become more secure within their grooves. A large green leaf protruding from the trunk tickled his left ear as he pushed against it, distracting him momentarily. Once he felt his paws were again secure, he slowly released the vine from its grasp, where to his surprise he clung to the tree without assistance. The vine now rested between his body and the tree trunk, and would be graspable for the next attempt. As he looked upwards into the foggy sky, the trunk circled outwards and slightly above him. He knew he would have to jump out further this time, but if he could clamber his paws over the circular summit and grab the vine, he may be able to drag his body over the top without needing the vine any more.

Chance and Checkers watched with the rest of the animals as their leader attempted to climb the huge trunk. "You know what?" Chance asked as he watched Streak clamber the uneven bark.

"What?" Checkers replied as he watched the fox ascend the tree.

"I never thought in my life that I would ever see a fox climbing a tree," Chance said, his gentle voice full of sincerity.

"Me either. I don't think any creature would believe us if we told them," Checkers responded.

Giving no further thought to the task, Streak pushed upwards with his four paws, and jumped. His muzzle smashed against the jutting tree, and his concentration was lost. Out of confusion he wildly clamped his jaws down and expected to hit the ground, but as his thoughts returned to him he noticed he was dangling from the vine, his hinds swaying freely, his front paws reaching up and over the trunk's summit.

Lyro looked on as the red fox rested momentarily, dazed by the hit he had taken during his leap. Slowly, Streak managed to paw himself to the top of the log. His hinds found the rough bark and eventually managed to push his body over the trunk. Streak scrambled upon the incline of the fallen tree, and when he saw Selwyn he released the vine and pawed his way carefully to the top.

Lyro looked towards Brock, and wondered how the short legs of a badger would cope with ascending the trunk. He smiled contently to himself. Brock made eye contact with the fox looking over him. "You're next," the fox stated.

4

The forest to The North was full of evergreens and pine trees, making it one of only a few places in Averon that kept natural colour all year round. There were no real clearings or open forest areas like the there were further to the south, but to the eye of an animal passing through its trees it would appear to be a hospitable and welcoming place. The forest was in the middle of the Big Thaw, the time of year that transitioned the cold season to the warm season, where the air was warmer, the days longer, and the sun brighter. The North held majestic sights when the sun was high and the weather humid. Bright shafts of sunlight would cascade through the trees on a clear day, and the multi-shaded leaves would glow with such an aura that it was almost too bright to walk through without shading your eyes.

Things within the forest had taken a turn for the worse, and now this beautiful landscape was tainted with the presence of the foxes that dwelled there. Former Great Council member and skulk leader Akando sat in the foggy dawn, overlooking his own community. Akando had betrayed the animals with which he served after a long, bitter feud with Shadow Oak leader Kedem. Believing he was the better fox to preside jointly over the Great Council of Averon with Rebus, leader of the badger sett, Akando had felt unjust and hard done by, resulting in his betrayal to Averon and his allegiance with Seerles and the Black Lands. It was by Akando's cruel paw that Kedem had fallen, beaten almost to death in a fit of rage when his nemesis defied his wishes and did not release the authority of the Great Council as he had wanted.

Akando reflected on this incident with little remorse. He felt pity for the animals who had chosen to follow the Great Council and who now defied his army. His followers had been tainted with the darkness and, under Seerles' influence, served him in any way he desired. Both Seerles and Akando now shared a common goal; to spread fear throughout the Great Forest of Averon, and destroy all those who opposed them. The more fear they spread, the easier it would become to overpower their foes. Those who would not join their army would die. And with such a huge amount of soldiers at his disposal, each one as vicious and unforgiving as those found within the ranks of the Dark Army, nothing could stand in their way.

The dawn of the Great War broke with the daylight on that dull, foggy morning within Averon, the war that had been foretold since an age long since past. Akando had taken a prize to tip the scale of war in his favour. Tali, the vixen sibling of the now mighty warrior Doran, had been taken hostage and was being held in a den not far from where Akando sat. If Doran believed harm would come to his sibling he would surrender without incident, Akando mused. He looked out upon the mass of darkened bodies gliding in and out of the fog, the bodies of the foxes he now controlled. Masses of them overwhelmed his dwellings, maybe even hundreds, and all of them awaited his next order. His army was huge. Akando smiled grimly. There was no way the Great Council could win the war that had now dawned.

No way at all.

5

The warriors stood on top of the fallen tree trunk - all except one. Brock, the badger who had been unable to use the vine and ascend the tree, stood on the solid ground, looking up at them. The otters and foxes had managed to climb the trunk, with the help of the vine being pulled by their comrades already above, and Danjo had gracefully returned to its lofts without needing any such assistance, but Brock had been unable to do so even with the full help of his comrades.

"It's no use," Brock began as he failed at another time attempting the climb. The warriors looked down, knowing he was fighting a losing battle. Streak did not wish to lose Brock at such an early stage in their quest, not a warrior as great as he, but time was pressing on and time was something they did not have the luxury to squander. "You need to go. The more you wait for me the more time you waste," he added, as if reading Streak's mind. Streak looked to the rest of the animals lining the bark of the fallen tree. He saw in their faces the truth, although it pained him to admit it.

Streak turned his attention to the badger below, looking glumly back at him. "Return to the clearing," Streak began, finally accepting the situation and issuing the only order the badger could follow. "Wait for us to return. I'm sure you'll be joined by more of us, although who I do not know."

"I'll keep the company of the eccentric hedgehog," Brock replied, the disappointment clear to tell. "I only hope you do not enter a battle without me at your side."

"If we encounter a threat, we will have to deal with it," Pairo interrupted, playing the game.

"We will deal with anything in our path as best as we can, Brock," Lyro began, in an attempt to reassure the great warrior.

"Yes, I'm sure you will," he muttered bluntly. Brock desperately wanted to keep going, to cross the tree and head deeper into the forest with his comrades; but the heeding voice of the hedgehog returned to his mind, warning him to turn back or face the consequences.

Brock sighed and finally gave in. "I'll return to the clearing and wait for you there," he said, turning away from the trunk. "Make sure you all return," he added, looking over his shoulder before beginning his walk back through the forest.

Streak watched as his friend vanished into the fog. Brock was a courageous warrior, and one who he set out with all those seasons ago to find Seerles during the threat of the Dark Army. This quest was much like that one, only this time it was much longer and far more dangerous.

"Streak," Lyro said, rousing the fox from his thoughts. "We must continue."

Streak nodded, and carefully turned on the uneven trunk. Their adventure would commence, with Brock the first warrior eliminated by the Forest of the Damned.

6

Loat glided nimbly over the forest floor. Along with Favradin and a handful of warrior muntjac, they attempted to follow the trail Akando had taken to his homeland in The North. They had undertaken the quest of rescuing Tali from her captors, unknowing whether this would lead to a battle and bloodshed. The darkness that swelled within the stoat was under his complete control; and although not as powerful as Doran, who he had helped to overcome the mystical force, he was still a great threat to any creature who may challenge him.

This group of animals had wandered off the beaten track, and pushed through large ferns and erratic bushes as they continued their journey onward. Their plan was going to take great execution if it was to be done as they imagined. They knew that success would be slim, but with Loat on their side they stood a chance.

The animals continued in silence as Favradin lead them through the forest and to the outskirts of Akando's jurisdiction. Having run the length and breadth of Averon as well as the Great Vast Open, he knew the direction he was heading and the best place to be to start their plan in motion. As Loat continued onward, chilled by the cold dew that had dampened his fur as he brushed through the foliage, he wondered if the plan they had hatched would lead to the first battle of the Great War.

Only time would tell.

7

Brock emerged solemnly from between the Twins of Despair. He paid them little attention, the once-foreboding landmarks twisted and construed, now serving as a reminder of his elimination. He wandered through the fog-covered trail back towards the clearing where they had stood together, listening to the warnings of the hedgehog who promised them doom and despair if they did not heed his advice. He walked on, listening to how silent and still this area of the Haunted Woods had become. Ghosts were said to wander these parts, having spent eternity gliding between the trees. Banafrits, the spirits of animals who had died or were close to death, were said to wander the Forest of the Damned, lost in its oblivion until they could find a way to pass to the spirit world. In truth, this wise, warrior boar did not understand the difference between the two. Averon was a huge forest - as old as the sun that shone down from above it, some believed - and with such a long history came tales of lore and legend. Most tales had been passed between many generations of animals, and Banafrits and ghosts were just two of them.

Brock emerged into the familiar clearing, and to his surprise saw the small, spiny body of Prickly the hedgehog foraging under an exposed tree root at a plump worm. Prickly began battling the worm from the soil, using his claws to drag it from its hiding place. Brock watched on as the small battle erupted, the hedgehog straining at the defiant worm as it clung to the earth to save itself from becoming the hedgehog's breakfast. Eventually Prickly won and chomped down on his meal with intense satisfaction. If only all the battles in Averon were so simple, Brock thought to himself.

Engrossed in his food, Prickly turned to return to his hollow, and saw Brock stood across the damp floor. He froze for a moment as he remembered Brock's vivid stripes. Suddenly the hedgehog remembered he was one of the warriors who had entered the Forest of the Damned. To his amazement, the badger was the first animal to ever return.

"I don't believe it," Prickly said in amazement, dragging the limp worm with him to the badger. "You returned! You made it back!" Brock sighed. He had made it back by falling at the first hurdle. "Where are your friends? Have they continued on?"

"They have," Brock confirmed as he gazed down upon the hedgehog, "I returned after failing the first trial."

For a moment Prickly seemed concerned, and then a look of joy passed across his spiny face. "Oh, never mind," he began rambling, seemingly unaware of the worm still clasped within his grip. "The important thing was that you made it out. If you have returned, your friends have a fantastic chance of returning also, as long as they remember my advice."

"They will," the boar confirmed.

"This is truly marvellous," Prickly began again, still surprised that a creature had emerged from the forest's grip. "Come with me. Rest a while. Wait for them all to return. The fox and the rabbits have only just entered, and -"

"A fox and rabbits?" Brock asked, his attention firmly upon the prickly body of the hedgehog.

"Yes. They passed through not long ago. In fact, I'm surprised you didn't pass them. Well, I suppose you wouldn't if you were crossing the plains. The rabbits

411

were Forest Guards, and the fox was a warrior from Shadow Oak. They were sent by the Great Council to enter the forest on a secret mission that even these trees do not know of. Maybe you know them? Doran and Wickett?"

"Doran? Wickett!" Brock shouted. "What are they doing in there?"

"I don't rightly know," Prickly began, relaying the information he had gathered to the boar, "but I don't think it was good. They seemed to be looking for a banafrit of whose name they didn't mention, but also to rescue your friends."

"Why? Why would they need rescuing?"

"Well, the trees seem to believe there is some treachery in your group. The foxes accompanying you were in fact sent to slaughter you after you had found out the information you needed."

Brock staggered momentarily at the hedgehog's revelation. "Oh no," he whispered, angry that he had left them in light of this terrible news. "Lyro and his soldiers?" Brock asked, looking to Prickly.

Prickly finally released the worm from his claw and spoke to the badger seriously. "Yes, I do believe it is." Brock snarled and smashed his paw to the ground in frustration.

"I did not know this until you had all passed between the Twins of Despair," Prickly said solemnly, almost embarrassed that he had not known. "I take it you do not know, then?" Brock gave Prickly a harsh stare. "Of course you don't," he answered himself, knowing full well he had no way of knowing.

"How could I have been so stupid," Brock pondered to himself. "I should have known. Akando set us up. This was his plan from the beginning."

The hedgehog sighed. "The Great War has been declared," he said, his voice echoing in the gloom that the foggy morning brought with it. "The Great Council has since united many of the animals within the forest to meet Seerles' forces in battle, although I fear it may not be enough to stand against the onslaught of his warriors. His armies are now a huge entity themselves, with various ranks and generals commanding them, and eclipse the animals aligned with the Great Council. But fight the Great Council will, in an attempt to bring peace to the forest."

There was much silence between the two as Brock processed the happenings of the forest in his absence. Finally he turned and looked back toward the track leading to the Twins of Despair, the gateway to the Forest of the Damned.

"I must go back," he said softly, and slowly moved his paws in that direction.

"No!" Prickly snapped, "It's madness, and certain death!"

"I have to. I must save my friends from those treacherous foxes and bring them back safely. They are the Warriors of Averon, and will be greatly needed in our battle against the Black Lands."

"But how will you do it? You did not pass the first trial?"

"Then I shall find a way!" Brock snapped, aware that the hedgehog was now ambling beside him.

"Re-entering the forest is extremely dangerous," Prickly warned, "and it is guaranteed that you will never come back. No creature had ever escaped its trees before you, not one. It will not give you another chance."

Brock slowed to a stop and looked down at the hedgehog following him. They had wandered from the clearing and were now on their way towards the gateway. "It is a risk I must take, not only for my friends, but for the Great Council and the forest as well."

Both animals looked at each other, Prickly resigned to the fact that the badger would not listen. "Thank you, my friend, for helping me," Brock said to break the silence, "but you will not dissuade me. I know the risks of entering the forest, and I do so of my own will. My friends are in grave danger and I must help them, no matter what the cost."

Prickly offered nothing more to Brock; no warnings, no advice, no nothing. He simply stood in the middle of the trail and watched Brock continue his journey back into the Forest of the Damned. As the boar vanished into the fog, he remembered the worm he had battled with. An empty stomach was an animal's worst enemy, or so he believed, and having emerged from the long slumber of hibernation not that long ago, he decided to take his meal back to his hollow and wait. Wait and see which animals returned. Or, wait and see if any returned at all.

Brock wandered tentatively towards the Twins of Despair, heeding the warning of the hedgehog in his mind. He had no idea how he would climb the fallen trunk, or even if he would even be to find his friends, who faced enormous danger. The two trees loomed from the fog once again. This time they appeared darker and more menacing, as if offering a final warning to the badger before he entered. A strange fluttering noise emerged from the fog behind, and Brock turned to see a dull gold aura looming above the trail behind. He stopped a moment as his curiosity increased. The golden light became brighter, and as it broke from the fog he saw Cyrius flying toward him. He watched as the barn owl glided past and banked around in the opening, returning to the badger stood in the cold air. Cyrius gracefully landed next to Brock as the aura subsided.

"Where are you heading?" Cyrius asked, knowing full well the badger's reply.

"Back to the forest," Brock began. "I have just learned of the danger that may befall Streak and the warriors."

"Indeed. They are in great danger, but you must not return there - it is far too dangerous."

Brock sighed. He had just finished the same argument with Prickly, and didn't want to explain his actions yet again. "I know of your bond with the warriors, Brock, but you must accept your fate and be done."

"Those are harsh words when you know of the danger they are unknowingly surrounded by," Brock replied scornfully.

"Harsh words, yes, but returning to the forest will almost certainly kill you. You have been eliminated, and your task now lies elsewhere."

Brock frowned at the owl. "Another task?" he questioned.

"Yes," Cyrius began. "Within Shadow Oak."

"Why am I needed there? Is the traitor Akando still lurking in its border?"

"No. Akando is long gone back to his own community in The North. There is a threat to the council members who dwell there, though. The beast is finally regaining her strength and will return to them soon. Four fallow deer have emerged from the Great Vast Open to offer protection whilst the Warriors are away, but they will need guidance from one such as yourself, Brock. You have the warrior qualities to help them in this time of great need. I ask that you return to Shadow Oak and help protect the council members."

It seemed to Brock that everything stood against him in his return to the Forest of the Damned, but with such a great threat upon Shadow Oak he felt no other choice. "And if I do return to the borders where the council is in danger, what will happen to those wandering the Damned?"

Cyrius turned to face the Twins of Despair. "I cannot assist in the quest to find Stryder, but I can help Doran and the Forest Guard. I hope that assisting their task will give them time to seek out Streak and the Warriors, allowing them to face the treacherous foxes with greater numbers and power."

"But why can't you assist them, Cyrius? Why go to all the trouble of assisting Doran and the rabbits when you can head to Streak immediately?"

"I wish it could be so simple," Cyrius mused. "Streak will be leading the Warriors through trials they must complete to earn a council with Stryder. If I do not complete those trials also, I will never find them. Doran's journey is different. Both he and the Forest Guard do not need to pass those trials. That will allow me to find his group within the forest, although it will be quite a task to do so."

"The forest is vast. How do you expect to find them?" Brock wondered. He knew even Cyrius would struggle to locate their friends in such a huge area.

"They are searching for banafrits, the souls of the animals close to death or who have died before their time. They wander a certain trail within the Forest of the Damned before leaving to find their way to the spirit world. I believe Doran and the rabbits will head there first, and that is where I intend to begin my search."

Brock looked back towards the clearing as a gentle breeze passed between them. Above the trees, some birds chirped as they navigated the fog and flew past. "I

416

will do what I can at Shadow Oak," he said to the owl after finally accepting his own quest, "and I place my trust with you, Cyrius. Help them, as I could not."

"I will do everything in my power," he replied, before opening his wings. "Now, return to Shadow Oak, where they need you more."

Brock watched as Cyrius took flight and glided above the trail towards the identical trees. He looked on as the owl's aura returned, only to be quickly diminished as he passed between the twins and into the forest.

8

The warriors wandered precariously across the huge
fallen tree as it crossed the vast canyon lost to an abyss
of fog beneath them. Its uneven surface made it
difficult to cross, and the though of a plummet into the
unknown unnerved some of them. Strange bird calls
could be heard echoing between the chasm's walls,
faintly away in the distance.

Streak led the pack as they crossed the tree trunk,
their vision impaired to only a few feet as the fog
thickened above the huge emptiness they were
crossing. He was followed by Lyro and his two warrior
foxes, then Chance, Checkers and Danjo the squirrel,
nimbly easing over the fallen tree at the rear. The fog
drifted across, obscuring and revealing the trunk as it
breezed past. From below the trunk came the noise of
the invisible wind carrying the fog through the canyon.
It whistled and screamed as it passed through the
emptiness, ruffling the furs of the warriors trying
desperately not to lose their footing on each gust that
swept beyond them and further away into the distance.
Checkers slowly slinked his long body over the trunk,
weaving around its occasional jutting branches with
more ease than the larger foxes he was accompanying.
For a moment, he wished he had wings like Selwyn.
The pheasant had flown ahead to scout for dangers, but
occasionally glided back to them to ensure everything
was okay. The inquisitive otter could not help but look
out over the side of the makeshift bridge he was
crossing, even though he could not see past the dense
fog.

Danjo wandered gracefully at the back of the pack. Being a squirrel he was used to the lofty heights of various trees and balancing along uneven branches high up in the air, and himself was unfazed by the whole situation.

Streak arrived at a thick branch jutting out from the middle of their path. It bore two further leafless branches reaching out on both sides, providing a potential hazard to those who would have to pass.

"Hold on," Streak ordered, coming to a standstill. The rest of the animals slowed down as their leader halted on top of the tree.

He examined the risk that now opposed them. The thick branch engulfed most of the width of the trunk they travelled across, and would require them to pass dangerously close to the edge if they were to continue on their journey. For the sake of the warriors he led, Streak hoped this would be the first and only danger on the natural bridge they were crossing. Looking to the left side of the branch there appeared to be slightly more room, but still not enough to pass safely.

"Be careful," Streak ordered over his shoulder at the following warriors, "slow and steady. Do not rush. Do not fall."

Streak slowly made his way to the branch. Focusing on his paw placement he found a secure groove in the bark, and pushing his body as close to the branch as he could possibly get, brushed his red fur around the branch and safely passed. He sighed with relief and continued onward to allow Lyro, who followed behind, ample room to move into, once past the branch. Streak then heard a strange scratching noise from behind. Lyro wandered slowly but did not see the knot of the tree trunk his paw hit. His leg buckled and paw slipped and in an instant, he fell.

Streak span round to see Lyro fall over the edge. "Lyro!" he shouted as he lunged to catch the fox with his jaws. Lyro swung his front paws at the trunk as he twisted and fell, embedding his claws into the grooves of the tree's bark.

"Lyro!" Makoto shouted.

"Help me!" Lyro gasped as he hung over the huge fog-hidden canyon, his hinds scratching at the side of the trunk, attempting to gain some grip.

Streak launched to the fox's aid, lying upon the trunk and stretching out as best as he could to the fox in mortal danger. "Hold on!" Streak began, seeing the fear grow in Lyro's eyes.

Chance and Checkers froze as the carnage involving the foxes unfolded ahead of them. Streak could not reach Lyro, as he maximised his stretch as far as he could to help him. Lyro perched solidly on the side of the trunk. Although unreachable, he was secure as long as he did not move and the tree bark held out.

Chance turned to see Danjo running back towards the clearing where they climbed the trunk. "Come on!" the squirrel ordered, appearing to have an idea.

"Come on," Checkers repeated to Chance. Both otters bounded over the log and gave chase to the grey squirrel.

"Hold on," Pairo said to his leader in a calm voice. Streak gave in on reaching Lyro, and slowly pushed his way to his paws. Selwyn appeared from the fog, his wings swirling the element as he flew towards them. Lyro attempted to pull himself up, but to no use. If he moved his paws he would most certainly lose his grip and fall.

"Don't move!" Pairo ordered, noticing Lyro's grip loosen as he attempted to climb up. Streak looked to Selwyn, who had landed beside him. He had no idea how to help Lyro.

"Danjo and the otters? Where are they?" Selwyn asked, looking beyond the foxes. Pairo and Makoto turned to see the trunk empty behind them. "I'll find them," the pheasant said, before taking flight with his radiant wings and heading in the direction they ran. Lyro began to notice his hinds slowly moving. The bark which his paws were embedded in slowly began to peel from the side of the trunk. Slowly, his red body shifted down.

"I'm losing grip!" he shouted to the warriors, who now seemed a million miles above him. Streak sighed with frustration and looked back into the fog where Danjo and the others had vanished. There was nothing he could do to help Lyro. He was too far away to reach and pull upwards.

Lyro attempted to adjust the grip with his front paws stretched out above him. If the bark under his hinds gave way, he would jolt down violently and fall if his paws were not secure. The bark was peeling, and in a matter of moments he would be in serious danger.

"Here!" Danjo ordered as they returned to the roots of the tree. He had remembered how huge the vine was that had helped the animals climb the huge trunk. The squirrel raced over, and with his small paws began tugging at the vine that still rested across the side of the tree and down towards the frozen ground.

"Quick!" Chance shouted, and both he and Checkers bounded over to the squirrel and began helping to pull the vine to the top of the trunk with their teeth. As they pulled, it began to pile behind them. Selwyn swooped down from the abyss to the forest floor, where the vine was rolling upwards. Suddenly, it got snagged as it dragged between the roots. The warriors yanked with all their combined might.

"Oh no!" Checkers shouted.

"It's stuck!" Danjo shouted down to Selwyn. The pheasant rushed to the tree's roots.

"Pull again!" he shouted back. The animals pulled once more, allowing the pheasant to pinpoint where the vine was held. It was snagged around a small, thick branch inside the roots. Selwyn reached high upon his talons and opened his wingspan graceful and wide, his vibrant colours impressive even in the dull fog. He took hold of the vine as best as he could in his beak and began pulling it out from the roots.

"Come on," Danjo whispered, his thoughts with the fox holding on for dear life above the canyon. Selwyn pecked and pulled at the vine, but his beak was not large enough to grasp it. He took hold as best as he could, and began beating his wings. If his beak would not free the vine on its own, he would attempt to use the power of his wings to pull it out. His wings battered the air around him, filling the air with the sound of rapidly beating feathers. He began chirping as he exuded all of his energy into freeing the vine. Selwyn jolted and fell back, his beating wings levelling out to keep him upright. The vine had finally been released from the thick roots and small branch it had become stuck against. Selwyn spat the vine from his beak.

"Go!" he shouted. The animals began pulling at the vine rapidly, and soon enough the vine began piling on top of the log once more.

Danjo saw the end of the vine rising quickly from the ground. "We're done!" he shouted.

Selwyn took flight into the chilly air. "Keep clear!" he shouted. The pheasant swooped down and took the vine between his talons. He rose rapidly into the air with the vine in his grasp, and vanished back into the fog.

Lyro tried pushing his body even tighter against the trunk, but was already as close as he could get. The bark beneath his hind paws had now peeled and was hanging on lightly. Lyro looked up at the foxes, who could offer him no help. The bark snapped and tumbled flakily down into the abyss, the jolt so big that Lyro's entire body fell with it. His front claws embedded into the bark as his hinds now swung freely. They began pawing rapidly at the trunk, but with no bark he could find no grip.

"Lyro!" Streak snapped. Lyro felt the bark under his front claws begin to break. Underneath the dog's weight the bark now began to crack, unable to withstand the strain.

Selwyn soared from the fog, and launched the vine towards Streak. It had unwound greatly as he had approached them, although there was still plenty to reach the fox in distress. Pairo grabbed the vine in his jaws and threw it towards Streak. He launched it behind the branch that separated them. For a heart-stopping moment Streak thought it was tumbling over the side, but saw it had stopped suddenly. He launched to grab it before it would have the chance to fall. He grabbed the dark vine, seeing that it was wrapped around the branch and would support Lyro if he could reach it. The bark was quickly breaking from the trunk, and Lyro felt himself slowly leaning back.

"Grab this!" Pairo shouted as Streak launched the vine down to the fox. Lyro snapped at it with his muzzle as the vine swayed gently. As hard as he tried, he could not grasp it. The bark peeled even further from the tree, and now his claws were completely free from the trunk and tightly grasped the breaking bark. He had one last chance. There was only one more thing he could do, and in his mind he knew he would either live or die. The look on the Streak's face showed concern and fear. The bark was breaking. He did the only thing he could...

Lyro launched upwards, pushing onto the bark and shattering it completely. In midair, he snapped his muzzle at the vine that hung beside him.

"Lyro!" Streak shouted. Lyro felt the air between his body. Slowly, his mind comprehended the sensation of falling. He had missed the vine and now tumbled into the abyss.

One last snap of his muzzle towards the vine, and suddenly he jolted. The sensation of falling had stopped. With an overwhelming sense of relief, he discovered that he had clamped down on to the thick vine.

Streak let out a sigh of relief as he saw Lyro hanging freely above the fog. The quick-thinking of a squirrel had no doubt saved the fox's life. He looked towards Makoto and Pairo, whose expressions said the same. "Come on," he said to both of them, "lets hoist him up."

Chance, Checkers and Danjo emerged at the branch next to Pairo and Makoto in time to see Lyro safely hoisted from the abyss where he so very nearly lost his life. The red fox dragged himself over the trunk and lay for a moment on top of the bumpy bark, panting heavily.

"That was close," Danjo said as he made his way nimbly over the tree. Lyro simply looked at him, his panting exuding a combination of both effort and relief. Pairo and Makoto looked him over dubiously.

"Okay?" Streak simply asked the rescued fox that lay beside him.

Lyro's breathing became less erratic, and within a moment or so he had risen to his paws. "Yes. I am now," he replied sheepishly, as he looked at the animals congregating around him. He looked towards the otters and the squirrel on the other side of the branch across from him. "Thank you," he said softly as the fog swirled about them. "I thank all of you for helping me." He looked down at the trunk below his feet, and sighed one final time.

"Alright. Crisis averted," Streak began as he once again took charge of the warriors. "We need to press on, and quickly," he added, thinking of the beast that would be prowling within Averon. Lyro nodded slowly, not wanting to bask in the thought of his near death. "Come on," their leader added, "and be careful."

The rest of the animals passed the branch, and with the exception of a narrow passage of bark that didn't pose a threat to the cautious animals, they crossed the foggy canyon in safety. As they emerged upon the cliff face they were heading toward the leaves of the fallen tree loomed from the fog with huge wild branches, reaching erratically in every direction. The trunk split into a series of thick branches and allowed the warriors to take various different paths down to the solid ground and safety. They all bounded down in different directions to place their paws on the safe ground, none happier than Lyro to feel the cold, frozen bracken beneath his pads.

The warriors assembled as the huge tree expanded its branches and leaves in every direction, hiding the next path they had to take. "Where now?" Makoto asked, marvelling at the sheer size and density of the treetop that blocked them.

"Through," Selwyn said answering his question. "Push through the branches and a trail emerges on the other side, I saw it when I scouted here before. Where it leads though, I am unsure."

"A trail is a trail," Streak added in the quiet gloom, "and we only follow one."

"Then that must be the way we continue," Danjo replied.

Streak and Lyro led the way, manipulating their bodies through the branches to form a path for those behind to follow - except of course for Selwyn, who simply opened his wings and flew above them.

Pairo and Makoto followed behind the rest of the animals. Both held doubt with their leader, Lyro. Having his life saved by this makeshift band of animals would play on his mind; of that they were sure.

"Lyro," Pairo whispered to Makoto as they fell back through the dense leaves, the sound of their fur pushing through filling their ears with each step.

"I know," Makoto replied as they passed through the dense branches.

"We have to do something," Pairo whispered behind to the following dog, "in case he goes cold."

"You mean -"

"Yes. In case he abandons our orders and refuses to kill these pathetic animals."

"What would you suggest?" Makoto asked, the pair slowing in order to keep their intentions secret.

"In the worst scenario, we take out those who pose the biggest threat to us. Streak first, and Lyro, if we must."

"After all we've been through, we have to turn on one of our own to see this quest through?" Makoto replied softly.

"Past conquests and brotherhood will mean nothing to Akando if we fail. If we must kill him, then we do it, and we do it as soon as we find out the information we need. If we clear the forest of the beast ourselves we seal a place amongst the elite ranks of the army controlled by Akando and Seerles. It will be us, Makoto, leading the assault against the Great Council. And when the forest is taken and the Black Lands victorious, we will have our own community to lead.

We will be the ones in control. But if we fail, we will be the ones to feel the wrath of Akando and Seerles."

"Then we have no choice."

"None," Pairo said slyly. "As soon as we find out what we need, we slaughter them all, and we find out exactly where Lyro's loyalty will lie."

9

"Do you think that Streak and the warriors came this way?" Blits asked as the Forest Guards and Doran stood at the edge of a dense, thick forest, in the ever-present fog. The trees grew slanted and twisted, forming strange shapes and scopes. Some reached into the sky and some twisted unnaturally over themselves, their tops and branches falling upon the floor. Some split at the trunk and reached out wildly in opposite directions. They grew between huge boulders and rock walls. There appeared to be little forest floor on which the trees could grow. The boulders were lined with dark moss at their northernmost edges, and gave further dissuasion to the animals gathered there not to enter. The rocks, as foreboding as they were, at least appeared to be natural, but the trees were so strange and contorted that none of the animals had ever seen them within Averon before. Their dark natural colours of the forest absorbed the little light there was.

"This looks worse than the Haunted Woods we travelled through to reach Seerles," Coinin said as he marvelled with apprehension at the forest which lay before him.

"In honesty, it probably is," Doran replied, looking over the strange, unknown trees. "Streak and the warriors may have passed through here, but their journey goes to a different part of the forest. Remember, this forest is a conscious entity that will take every creature who enters on a different path. There will be only one trail to those who enter, but I do not know if that trail will be the same for each."

"That's most certainly right," Apollo began as he stared at the contorted trees. "That's why you'll need me to stay right here and guard the trail. If the others come through, I'll keep them here."

Wickett turned to Apollo and smiled. "You don't get out of it that easy," he replied.

"Come on," Doran said to the rabbits as they stood on the edge of the ominous forest. "Let's get going."

10

Dark foxes surrounded Akando's dwellings to The North. The Great War was in its infancy, and the new dark alliance threatening the forest did not expect the Great Council to launch an attack. Still, sentries were posted between the trees in skulks of three, their dark fur looming in and out of the thick fog as it drifted by.

Akando rested within the safety of his army in an excavated den created from many hours burrowing into the earth. It ran deep and opened into a chamber much like those of Shadow Oak. After all, foxes still had the same habits, no matter what their differences in personality or belief. The bitter, ageing fox pondered what would happen next. He wondered who would take the first move in the strategic war they had now declared. Tali was not far from his resting place, being held in a den not too dissimilar to his own. As a political prisoner of war, he wanted to show her he could be compassionate, and ordered that she not be harmed. Capturing her was a great achievement, and should Doran attempt to rescue her it would almost certainly allow Seerles to...

"Control him?" A voice emanated from behind the resting fox. Akando turned in the gloom of the den, and saw two red eyes burning through the darkness behind.

The large, serpentine body of Seerles slithered into the dull light from the darkness beyond. There was only one entrance in and out of Akando's vast den, and Seerles had not entered through it.

"How did you enter here?" Akando asked, hiding a brief surge of anxiety.

"I can be wherever I need to, whenever I need to," the adder replied as he rowed his body around his coalition partner. Seerles stopped and raised his eyes to the level of the now-seated fox, as plumes of darkness evaporated into the open den. "No, Doran is beyond our control now," the snake began, his red eyes burning brighter with rage. "His mind was too strong to break down. He was far stronger than any animal in Averon who has been taken by the darkness. Only a few have ever resisted the darkness since the dawn of my creation."

"And he is one," Akando said with mild distain. "The one that I wanted," he then added. "The one I could have taken, had you not interfered."

Seerles hissed in offence, and Akando flew to the back of his den as though he had been thrown by a thousand foxes. He crashed into the earth, jarring some of the wall loose. Swirls of darkness erupted from the den and glided towards the stunned fox, nestling around his neck and midriff, pinning him firmly to the shaded wall of his home. Struggling but unable to free himself, Akando looked on helplessly as Seerles slithered towards him, his eyes glowing and fangs exposed.

"Remember who the strongest force within this forest is, and hold your tongue," the snake began as he approached the incapacitated fox. Akando looked on with fear. Seerles was the strongest, most unpredictable creature in the whole of Averon. Every creature knew of him and feared him - and here the legend was, inches away from his eyes.

"Doran is no longer within our grasp. He is a strong warrior, but his control over the darkness is nothing compared to mine," the adder said, his voice full of malice. "I can deal with him, and I will when the time arises. Until then, remember that you are only here because I allowed it so, and it would mean nothing to

431

me to kill you here and take your army for my own."
As Seerles spoke these words, Akando could feel the
rings of darkness that clasped him to the wall becoming
tighter, restricting his breathing. The fox released a
gasp as it tightened further. His eyes opened wider as
the threat to his life increased. Seerles leaned closer, his
face more menacing and demonic, seemingly taking
pleasure in Akando's demise. Akando squirmed as
much as the darkness would allow. It grew tighter still,
and now began to choke the helpless fox. "Remember
your role, Akando, or you will not live to see the fall of
the Great Council."

The darkness vanished from Akando's fur, causing
the fox to slump to the ground and begin panting. He
coughed to clear his airways, feeling the tickle in his
throat where he had been choked.

"Besides, we no longer need Doran in our ranks,"
the adder responded, his eyes dimming as the anger
subsided. "The Great Council is weak in numbers, and
whether he fights alongside them or not will be of no
importance."

"How can you be so sure?" Akando croaked,
snorting air through his muzzle to clear his throat.

Seerles paused a moment and slithered away
towards the tunnel leading up towards the den's
opening. He turned his scaly body to the fox that still
lay upon on the hollowed ground. "I have foreseen it,"
the adder whispered. "I have seen the demise of the
Great Council, and our victory."

Akando held his breath as he listened to what the
snake told him. "You've foreseen it? Are you sure?" he
asked after a moment.

"The darkness gives me many powers, foresight
being but one, and I have seen our alliance succeed in
victory. The darkness shows only shadows of things
which may or may not come to pass. The images I have

seen of the fall of Averon have been clear. Nothing I have seen before has been as clear as these. Averon will fall, and we will be victorious."

Seerles' eyes flashed and he was suddenly aware of something. "Intruders," he whispered.

Akando pushed his weary body to his paws and forced his way outside.

"Breech!" came a voice from beyond the thick fog.

Loat and the muntjac warriors had invaded Akando's community. They charged aggressively into their enemy's territory. The alliance of the Great Council had declared the first act of war.

"Charge!" Favradin screamed, as he led the muntjac into battle. Loat bounded over the sloping grass, ready to unleash the darkness.

Akando and Seerles emerged from the den, side by side. Seerles' eyes glowed. All around them the mass of unsuspecting dark foxes now turned their attention to the direction of the invaders, their own eyes burning red.

"They've come to rescue the vixen," Akando began. He knew exactly what the Great Council was doing, having sat amongst them once before. "Soldiers rally!" he then screamed at the top of his voice as he took command of his army.

The dark foxes looked upon their general as he issued the order, then out to the sound of the thundering hooves of the deer sprinting closer behind the fog. The muntjac weaved gracefully through the trees as they breached the fox's homeland. "Show no mercy!" Akando shouted as the impostors charged closer. "To battle!" he cried through the cold, oppressive morning. The dark foxes under Akando's control charged towards the border, their eyes glowing wildly in the dim light. "Protect our lands!" he ordered from his vantage point amongst the battle field. More foxes rapidly emerged from the fog behind the dark alliance's leaders, snarling and churning the ground as they darted past Akando and Seerles.

Loat gained speed, his eyes slowly burning as he darted through the fog at the mass of red eyes sprinting toward him.

Seerles sensed him. "Loat," he whispered, raising his body from the rough woodland floor.

"Show no fear!" Favradin screamed as the mass of bucks darted towards their enemies.

"Kill them!" Akando ordered as the charging animals ran into battle. "KILL THEM!"

Loat began welling the darkness inside as he bounded over the bracken and charged towards the enemy. He felt the force swirl and grow inside, his eyes burning with the anger of war. He held the power as long as he possibly could, and when he saw the dark muzzles of the approaching fox army only a few feet away, screamed out and violently unleashed the full rage of the darkness.

Two dark foxes flew back through the air as a wave of the swirling element exploded from the stoat. One muntjac jumped another fox charging towards him, allowing Favrad into smash it from his path with his small antlers. Pockets of dark smoke exploded in the fog as Loat hit the foxes with the darkness, knocking them to the cold floor. The dark foxes retaliated and launched at the muntjac. They leapt through the air and clawed at their bodies, smashing them to the ground and surrounding them in skulks to incapacitate them. Favradin smashed one skulk from a fallen ally and charged further into battle. Loat looked on as a dark fox leapt from the fog and bore down upon Favradin. With a flick of his nose the fox jolted sideways in the air and fell harshly to the floor, kicking up loose debris as he hit the ground. The remnants of the darkness that had smashed him from his pounce streamed away into plumes in the foggy air.

"The darkness?" Akando screamed, noticing the element drift across the battlefield on the chilly breeze and disband within the fog. "Is it Doran?"

"No, not him," Seerles replied, before lowering his head back to the ground. The adder contorted his body and began moving away from their perch and down into battle.

Akando watched the serpent slither away into the carnage that had befallen his home. "Let's see how strong you really are," he said quietly to himself.

A dark fox caught Loat off-guard and smashed him to the floor. It snapped its vicious teeth at the wriggling stoat, trying to latch a killer bite on his enemy. Loat's eyes flickered red, and the fox was launched high into the air. As it fell, it was smashed into the fog by a muntjac running past.

Loat hopped to his feet. He couldn't see a thing within the dense fog surrounding them. His fur ruffled as he commanded a breeze to sweep over the battlefield. The breeze he conjured exploded through the trees. Akando felt the huge gust surge through his fur and beyond his vantage point, as the breeze churned and momentarily cleared the fog. Loat released the darkness, and the breeze stopped. With the fog dispersed, he saw the battle in full motion. Bucks charged foxes. Foxes tore at their bodies with claws and teeth, their vicious pack mentality dragging their enemies to the floor and maiming them with huge wounds. Patches of blood soaked the woodland floor with blood shed from both bucks and foxes as they clashed in battle.

A buck charged in Seerles direction. With a flick of his tongue, an invisible wave of the darkness exploded from nowhere and smashed the deer high into the forest. His eyes ignited once more, and the bucks surrounding him exploded from the battleground and out into the dense fog that was reforming. Loat looked on as his comrades began crashing to the ground around him and out of battle. He dodged the falling bodies as they fell harshly to the dank ground around him. Loat then saw the unique body of the snake emerging from the newly-settled fog. The stoat froze momentarily, wondering what the dark one was doing here this far to The North. Not dwelling on it any longer, he quickly noticed a small formation of rocks not far from where he was standing. The bucks and foxes continued battle around him. He saw the bodies of enemies and comrades fighting, the fog unveiling and hiding them as it passed throughout the carnage. Seerles drew closer, and knowing that he could not match power with the adder, Loat took to a new tactic. The formation of rocks lifted gently to the air; five misshapen weapons that were jagged, heavy, and under his control. Without thinking twice, he launched them rapidly at Seerles. He watched as the rocks flew through the air and into the fog.

Loat stood there for a moment, realising that the battle around him was growing eerily silent. Seerles' eyes burned brighter, and he emerged fully from the fog. Swirling above the serpent were five rocks, each of them from the formation Loat had launched first in an attempt to catch him off guard. Seerles halted, looking over the stoat that had betrayed him and escaped from the Black Lands. With a cry of anger, Seerles launched the rocks past Loat and out into the fog behind him. With a powerful thrust forward, the adder launched across the debris and bore down upon the stoat in a second. He hissed wildly, his anger seething from every pore within his long body. Without time to escape, Loat suddenly found himself suspended in midair as Seerles engaged his control of the darkness and lifted him from the ground.

"Did you think you were strong enough to challenge me?" the adder screamed at him. "Did you think that your control of the darkness made you a powerful entity within these trees?" Loat began slowly twisting in the air as gravity took a hold. Favradin charged upon Seerles whilst his back was turned. As he bore down upon the adder, a shockwave of darkness smashed into him and sent him tumbling back out and across the battlefield.

"You are nothing! Nothing!" Seerles hissed, his attention still firmly upon the suspended stoat. Loat dropped to the floor and looked up to see his tormentor loom menacingly over him. "And now you will die, traitor!" he said coldly. Seerles opened his jaw, exposing the venomous fangs he used to kill and paralyse his enemies.

"No," came a voice from the fog. Seerles turned to see Akando approach across the now-silent battlefield. Dark foxes emerged beside him, their numbers too great for the muntjac to contend with. The deer lay battered and beaten upon the battleground. Akando had a plan for these enemies. His paws trudged over the freezing open ground. "We have Favradin, the buck's leader. If we take this stoat as well, we can spread fear even further within the Great Council." Seerles looked on as the allied fox joined him. "I bet you were sent to rescue the vixen, weren't you?" Akando then asked Loat, smashing his paw violently across the head of the fallen stoat. Loat felt the sensation of light-headedness, as though he was about to pass out. "If we keep him with the buck and the vixen, they'll undoubtedly send another rescue mission for them, which could play into our hands."

"A trap?" Seerles asked, the though not crossing his own mind.

"The Great Council is too predictable. They will launch another rescue attempt if they know these warriors are still alive. If we wait, they will bring the war to us. Ambush is the greatest way to take out our enemies. And as long as you can keep this one subdued, we can stay ahead in this battle."

"I can keep him subdued," Seerles replied, turning his attention back to Loat, "and when we no longer need you, I promise a slow and painful death."

At Akando's order, Loat was clasped within the jaws of a fox and taken to the den in which Tali was captive. The battlefield hung with the sense of victory, and as the foxes around them cleared their homeland of the fallen bucks, Seerles began to leave The North.

"What are you doing?" Akando asked as the adder began rowing away.

The snake stopped. "To increase our numbers," he replied, without turning to the fox behind. "It would seem that even though your foxes emerged victorious, they did so questioningly."

"You question their skills?" Akando asked with frustration.

"Many of the foxes we turned were not warriors, Akando. Many lived in peace within this forest and are not harboured to fight as strongly as your own. We may have the numbers to win a war, but we will need more warriors to utilise them fully. Had this been a battle lead by the Warriors of Averon, I fear we may have suffered greater losses than what we have sustained this dawn."

"And what would you suggest?" Akando asked sarcastically.

Seerles' eyes burned red momentarily at the tone of the fox stood behind him. "I have a plan," the snake replied, "and I will return to you when we are ready to wage war upon the Great Council."

Part 2

Search for the Lost

1

The beast charged from her resting place. She sped through the trees of Averon so quickly that no passing eye would see her, except the dark fur forming a shadow as she sprinted past. She had returned to her lair within the forest to tend her wounds and recover from the confrontation with Doran at Shadow Oak. Her mind filled with vengeance at the thought of the fox that had forced her retreat from the battle. No creature had ever been strong enough to stop her - not one. As she darted through the pines, she felt the chill of the fog engulf her muscular body. For many seasons now she had endured the cold season and almost became acclimatised to it, though she still felt the cold more so than any animal natural to the Great Forest of Averon. Her lair had been established within a hidden cave that bore deep into a small rock face surrounded by pine trees. Littered around her home were the carcasses of her prey, mostly deer she had taken from Flicar's contingency. Having time to heal and a safe place to rest, the beast now headed back towards the scene of her last battle to take revenge on the fox that had stopped her. Her paws thudded into the ground, launching any light resting bracken in her wake. The panther glided eerily amongst the fog like a silent shadow, her only sound the loud, thudding footfalls of the sprinting feline. She sprinted vigorously towards her last battlefield.

She sprinted towards Shadow Oak and the Great Council.

2

A fellowship of animals wandered through the mass of bodies seeking sanctuary within the safety of Shadow Oak as the Great War began. Rebus - the head of the badgers within Averon and joint council leader - walked with Jinx and Delfin, two senior foxes within Shadow Oak, and Achak, the fallow deer who had rescued a small fawn separated from the muntjac during an attack on their contingency from the beast. In a den underneath the huge oak tree which eclipsed the community and gave the land its name, rested the body of the fallen Kedem. Barely alive and in deep slumber, the only chance the sleeping fox had rested with Doran and the Forest Guards who were searching the Forest of the Damned to rescue him, before he found his way from the trees and into the spirit world.

"The survival of our forest rests within the paws and talons of a select few," Delfin said as they wandered to a quieter part of the community. "Is there nothing we can do?"

"I'm afraid not," Rebus began as they walked slowly away from the crowds. "The war has been declared, and we must leave it with those who have taken the first steps into battle. We must have faith in them," he continued as they made their way to the privacy of the council peninsula, where they knew they would be away from open ears.

"Sometimes faith is not enough," Achak replied, lowering his antlers as he passed underneath a low-lying branch.

"It is all we have," Jinx responded, his voice shallow and forlorn, "and until we know otherwise, we must believe that they are capable of completing their quests."

"Do you believe they can?" Achak asked the badger walking beside him.

Rebus sighed. "I believe that if each of the warriors in question should believe in their abilities, then we have a moderate chance of success."

"Self-belief is the key," Delfin added afterwards.

"Rebus! Quick!" came an unsettled voice from behind the wandering animals. They turned to see Dallie, the leader of the otter contingency and council member, charging towards them.

"Dallie, whatever is the matter?" Rebus asked, noticing the distress within the otter.

"The trees!" she snapped in an excitable voice. "Quickly!" she said once again.

Rebus and the wandering animals looked to each other, before following her quickly back to Shadow Oak.

"Oh no," Rebus whispered when he saw with his own eyes what was causing her distress. The animals had crowded into the circular clearing of the foxes community as fear swept throughout them. The trees surrounding them had begun contorting, bending and breaking in all different directions. Their barks turned black and their leaves shrivelled and fell in piles at their roots. Wind engulfed the now-vanishing fog and rattled the brittle branches of once sturdy, vibrant trees. Shadow Oak had turned into the decaying, dying landscape that engulfed the Black Lands. The wind settled and revealed the trees as nothing more than dead, lifeless, bark.

"The fear is spreading," Jinx whispered in dismay.

"Indeed it is," Rebus began quietly, "and as it spreads, Seerles becomes stronger."

They stood amidst the animals, looking at the oppressive surroundings standing sharp and foreboding.

"Only our warriors can help us now," Delfin said as the fog descended once again.

And indeed they were the only ones.

3

The erratic trees surrounded Doran as his mind flashed with images of the battle to The North, and the revelation of his friend Loat taken captive by Akando. His distress was clear as his mind wandered momentarily from the Forest of the Damned to the scene of the battle.

"Doran?" Wickett asked, noticing the concerns of the red fox.

Doran shook himself to consciousness. "What is it?" Blits asked as they came to a standstill within the thick fog and looming trees.

"It's begun," Doran whispered to them in the quiet forest. "The Great War."

"The darkness?" Coinin asked, wondering if he had seen a premonition.

Doran slowly nodded. "Yes," he began, his mind returning to his sister Tali and the muntjac who had accompanied Loat on their quest. "The raid to The North to rescue Tali has been unsuccessful."

Apollo turned away from the fox as he scouted the fog and trees for any danger. A strange noise drifted to the rabbit over the silence. He didn't know if it was a living creature, a ghost or a banafrit, or even just the sounds of the foreboding forest.

"What happens now?" Coinin asked quietly.

Doran paused a moment as the importance of their quest returned to him. "Nothing," he replied a moment later, firm in his decision. "There is nothing we can do for them except continue on our quest. The best thing we can do is to find Kedem."

Apollo looked into the fog and noticed what he thought was the shape of an animal drifting just out of sight beyond the fog. The puzzled rabbit frowned as it vanished, wondering what it was he had seen. He scoured the surrounding area for signs of it re-emerging, but found nothing.

"Well, we won't find him standing here," Wickett informed them as they stood within the forest, discussing the dawn of the Great War.

Apollo looked out once again and saw the hind of another rabbit vanish within the fog. A brief flurry of fear crept over him. "Wickett," he began in a noticeably shaken voice, "we have company."

Doran and the rabbits turned their attention to Apollo, who had now moved away from the pack and was standing on his hinds looking in the direction of the phantom creature.

Wickett bounded over to him and stood on his hinds next to his comrade. "What did you see?" he whispered without knowing.

Apollo felt his whiskers ruffle in the gentle breeze which had quietly emerged. The fog swirled in front of his eyes with every subdued gust. "A rabbit," he whispered back, his voice as low as his leaders. Both rabbits peered out longer as the forest vanished and reappeared within the fog. The grey shadow of a rabbit darted across their eye-line. "There!" Apollo said, directing Wickett's attention to some twisted trees further across the way.

"I see it!" Wickett replied as the shadow of the rabbit vanished behind a gnarly tree trunk. "Come on," he then added.

"What?" Apollo asked as Wickett slowly moved in the direction of the tree. "What if it's a ghost?"

Wickett turned to him. "We'll go and find out," he replied.

Apollo sighed and slowly joined his leader in heading towards the ominous, dark, oppressive-looking tree that the shadow was hiding behind.

"What if its not there?" Apollo whispered as they drew closer.

"Then you have nothing to worry about," Wickett responded.

Without making a single sound, the two rabbits reached the knotted bark of the foreboding tree. Wickett gestured for Apollo to slowly circle the trunk to the right. Apollo understood the order and slowly began creeping around the trunk. Wickett began moving around to the left, being careful not to make too much noise as he negotiated over the jutting roots and uneven ground. As he continued around, he expected to bump into the hiding body of the rabbit they had seen just moments ago through the fog. Slowly and silently he continued around the tree, so as not to distress their target. He continued silently around the tree until his eyes slowly found the whiskers of Apollo approaching from the opposite direction.

"Apollo?" he asked in bewilderment. "Did it run past you?"

"No, Apollo replied in his faint voice, "I thought it ran in your direction?"

"No, nothing came this way."

"Then how did it escape? I saw it. We saw it hiding here."

"It must have r-"

Apollo was smashed away from the trunk and sent sprawling across the damp bracken. Wickett was pinned instantly to the tree by a powerful force.

"Why are you hunting me?" a snarling voice questioned as he squirmed against the rough bark.

"We're not hunting you!" he replied instantly.

"You are," the voice replied, "so I will ask you again. Why are you hunting me?"

Wickett looked towards the grey rabbit pinning him to the tree. He was shaded, almost like a shadow, with a burning white aura dancing slowly around his body. Wickett studied the rabbit's features for a moment and suddenly felt his heart leap.

"Answer me!" the shaded rabbit snapped.

"Digby?" Wickett asked as shock set in. The rabbit's tense features suddenly relaxed. Its eyes looked Wickett over. As the rabbit stared upon him, its grip against Wickett relaxed.

"Wickett?" the shocked banafrit asked, releasing Wickett to the ground.

"Digby! It is you!" Wickett replied joyously. Apollo charged at Digby in an attempt to rescue his leader. "No, Apollo!" Wickett snapped, halting him instantly, "it's Digby!"

Apollo's eyes widened as Digby turned his attention from Wickett. "Digby? I don't believe it!" he said quietly.

"Wickett!" a voice shouted from the fog. The three rabbits turned to see Coinin and Blits emerge from the fog, with Doran in tow.

"We're alright," Wickett replied sternly as they bounded over.

Blits skidded through the debris when he saw the banafrit stood between them. He'd know that rabbit anywhere. "Digby?" he asked, just as the previous two had done so.

"Blits. Coinin," Digby replied as they came together.

Doran watched on silently as the Forest Guard reunited with their former scout, one who had met his demise in the jaws of a hound from the Dark Army. Being taken by the hound was far before Digby's time, it now seemed, and his banafrit wandered slowly through the trees of the heinous forest as he tried to find his way to the spirit world.

"I remember scouring the western border for signs of a breech with you," Digby said as he recounted his memories, "then being chased by a hound. Then I remember waking here in this forest, and I've been searching for a way out ever since."

"Do you know that you're -"

"Dead? Yes, I know that," Digby said, stopping Blits from continuing, "and I know that I'm heading to the spirit world, but I don't know how to get there."

Doran watched on as the rabbits spoke with their lost friend, allowing them the time to settle the banafrit.

"Digby, we're looking for another banafrit like you, but this one's a fox. His name is Kedem."

"Kedem?" Digby replied as though deep in thought. "Yes, I have met him wandering these trees."

Doran resisted the urge to jump in straight away and take control of the situation. Instead, he watched from a distance as Wickett and the Forest Guards did the work for him.

"Could you tell us where you last saw him?" Wickett asked his lost friend.

Digby looked into the distance, between the foreboding and terrible trees. "Across the Morgas Field, a trail lays that snakes its way through the entire length of this forest. It runs beside the field and vanishes into its depths. Many banafrits wander aimlessly up and down this trail, hoping to find a path they may have missed that will lead them out to the spirit world. Some, like me, wander the trail and then decide to leave and make our own way through the forest. I met Kedem on this trail. He told me of the Great War that has now begun across the plains of existence. He is desperately searching for a way back, but was yet to leave the trail when I last saw him. There is still a chance he is there."

"Digby, can you help us?" Wickett asked, his heart now full of sorrow for his wandering friend.

"Of course," Digby responded, glad to assist his friends one final time.

"Can you tell us where this trail is, where you saw Kedem last?"

The banafrit gestured with his head towards two trees jutting out from the fog. "Continue forward from between those trees. Eventually you will arrive at a huge field. That is the Morgas Field, and you must cross through it to reach the trail. The Morgas Field is extremely dangerous."

"How dangerous?" Doran enquired.

"Extremely. A colossus slumbers within the area," Digby said, recalling the danger that lurked within the recesses of the darkened forest.

"What's a colossus?" Wickett asked the glowing banafrit in front of him.

"We don't know for certain," Digby began as he relayed the facts to the animals. "Most creatures we lay eyes upon in this forest are ghosts or banafrits, and this is where we belong. We can wander safely through these trees without fear of being attacked. We are Damned, and that is punishment enough, but living creatures such as yourselves who have passed between the plains of existence are forbidden to be here. No creature that I have known has ever disturbed the colossus resting in the Morgas Field; it is only the paws of the living that will wake it." Digby leaned closer to his Forest Guard friends and glared a wild, intense look to all of them. "It will be you who will disturb it should you choose to cross the field," he whispered coldly, "and if you do, you will face danger unlike any within the living realm of Averon. Nothing can prepare you for it. Nothing."

"We have a great warrior with us on this quest, Digby," Wickett said to the banafrit, breaking the uneasy tension that had taken the animals.

Doran stepped forward from the background. "I will protect them, Digby; of that you have my word."

Digby looked over the fox standing before him. He sensed something different about him, something more powerful and more determined. The callous look vanished from the banafrit, and the features of the Digby they knew in life slowly emerged. "They are my friends, Doran," he said, welling pride with the Forest Guards. "Please take care of them. I do not want them to befall the same fate as I."

Slowly, he turned back to the Forest Guard. Apollo hid a tear welling behind his eye. "Remember, it is Kedem who will find you. You must do something to draw the attention of the banafrits on the trail; it is the only way they will recognise the living. Remember this. Remember it well. Goodbye my friends, and good luck."

"What about you?" Coinin asked remorsefully.

Digby shrugged and offered a wry smile. "I will find my way, sooner or later."

Digby turned, and without another word vanished silently into the fog. They had been reunited one last time, able to say their goodbyes and put to rest the sadness they had felt upon discovering Digby's body within the grass of the western border all those seasons ago. He was lost, but all banafrits found their way sooner or later. Seeing him wander the forest in safety gave them great comfort and put them all at ease. The Forest Guards gained their composure, and looked towards the direction Digby had suggested.

"That's where we're heading, then," Apollo began. "We head deeper into the unknown, and must avoid disturbing a colossus along the way."

They stood in silence for a moment and watched the fog swirl and dance around the trees. Their heading was now clear, and no longer were they wandering without direction.

"What are we going to do to draw Kedem's attention?" Coinin asked, remembering what Digby had said about the banafrits wandering the trail. If Kedem had strayed from this beaten path there would be no way they would find him, and his body within Shadow Oak would most certainly fade and die.

"Let's not worry about that now," Blits replied. "We'll find a way. We wander this forest with hope."

"If hope is all we have, then hope is all we need," Doran added as they began their journey towards the Morgas Field. "That's what Cyrius says. There's always hope."

4

Streak brought the warriors to a standstill. They had been heading along a frozen trail that had slowly become littered with stones and rocks. The path had led them down a gradual incline, and the passing trees and vegetation had slowly been replaced with boulders and rocks. As they had continued they declined further and further, and now trod upon uneven, grey stone. The path had turned into a channel, with cliff-faces jutting out on either side of the animals that towered high above them and into the thick fog. The element had shown no signs of letting up and dispersing, making their task harder as they continued on their journey.

Ahead of Streak a sheer rock-face emerged, its dull colour blending almost perfectly with the fog that engulfed it from above. The animals felt the rush of a breeze emerging from seven small dark openings within its surface. They looked to be tunnel entrances, and with the solid grey walls towering on both their sides directing them into the dead-end channel, seemed to be the only way forward. The tunnels entrances were jagged and tight, reminding Streak of the rock formation he had looked upon within the Black Lands where Seerles resided.

"Looks like another test," a voice said as Streak scoured the surroundings for other paths or trails.

"Yes, I think this is another," he replied, turning to see Lyro stand beside him. The remaining warriors were clumped together just behind their leader. "These look like tunnel entrances."

"That means we must go through," Lyro responded.

Streak took a step forward and peered at the openings within the rock. They howled as wind gusted through them from their gloomy depths. "I see no other way."

Lyro listened to the wind as it expelled from the entrances like a winter gale breezing through the trees. "The otters and the squirrel will be fine, but will the rest of us manage to fit?" he asked.

Streak made his way to one of the tunnels, his red fur and whiskers flickering in the emanating breeze. He peered into the deep darkness of a jagged entrance. Strange patches of mist exploded from the tunnels as the wind screamed from their depths. Streak turned his head and closed his eyes as the breeze engulfed him, chilling the fox to his bones. The cold quickly passed, and Streak turned his gaze to the tunnel once more as the breeze subsided.

"I don't like this," Chance whispered underneath his breath.

"Why are there seven entrances?" Danjo asked, his grey fur feeling the remnants of the cold blast that swept past Streak.

"Seven different routes?" Makoto asked.

Selwyn looked on. "Or maybe to eliminate one of us," he replied softly. The rest of the warriors looked at him.

Of course.

The forest would not make their task easier, and it had already eliminated Brock.

Selwyn wandered towards his leader. His usually vibrant colours now seemed to dull, as if the journey was taking an immense strain upon him. Streak noticed the pheasant emerge by his side. Selwyn's eyes pierced the darkened entrances, but even his sharp eyesight could not reveal anything other than the pitch blackness that screamed back toward him.

"Streak," he began in his usual, soft voice, "I cannot join you any further," he whispered.

Streak looked at him. "Why?" the fox asked, confused by his comrade's statement.

"Look," the pheasant replied, gesturing with his beak towards the open tunnels. "Each entrance is barely able to allow you foxes to pass through. You have paws to help drag you through should the tunnels become too difficult to navigate. I have only my talons. These wings will not help me through should it become too cramped. I will become stuck with no way to free myself."

"But we don't know that these tunnels are tight," Streak began. "They may widen out further inside."

"This is the Forest of the Damned, Streak. Do you think that these trials will become any easier?" Streak sighed. He knew that if anything, the trials would become worse. "I will follow you to the ends of the Great Vast Open, Streak, you know that - but what use am I to you stuck deep inside a mountain of rock?"

Streak looked beyond Selwyn to Lyro, who offered nothing but a mirrored stare back at him. "All right," the reluctant fox finally agreed. "Fly back along the path we came, across the canyon and out to the clearing. Wait for us there with Brock."

Selwyn looked at the tunnels. "Make sure you return," he said to his friend as they stood in the cold fog. "The Great Council needs you."

Without hesitating any further, Selwyn chirped and flapped his wings, taking flight over the warriors and back into the fog from where they came. The remaining warriors looked above as he passed above them and out into the deep fog. Pairo looked at Makoto, his eyes suggesting that their task had become slightly easier.

Streak watched as his comrade disappeared into the fog, listening to his beating wings vanish into the forest. His eyes finally caught a glimpse of the animals he was leading in this terrible place.

"We must split up," he ordered to them as they awaited instruction. Checkers' heart sank. "We must all take one tunnel through this rock and see where our journey takes us. There's no telling where we may emerge, but it is a risk we must all take."

"Why?" Checkers asked, his slinky body missing his homeland and the river water now more than ever. "Why can't we all head through one tunnel instead?"

"Because if we follow each other through the wrong tunnel we run the risk of danger, even death. The forest is eliminating us one by one, and so far no-one has been harmed. If we start bending the rules, we may be placing ourselves in serious harm," Lyro replied. "There are seven entrances. Now, there are seven warriors. We stand a better chance of survival if we play the game."

"Great," Checkers whispered under his breath. "I hope there's nothing in there."

"You'll be fine," Chance responded, knowing full well that they may not be.

"This is why we're the warriors. This is what separates us from the rest of the animals we protect," Streak said as he looked upon the wary otter. "We take these quests and place ourselves in danger so that no other animal has to."

"When the Great Council formed this guardianship, it did so knowing the risks that we would take. Risks that no other in the forest of Averon could face," Lyro added.

"Checkers, you and Chance were chosen for this task for a reason. You may feel afraid and vulnerable, but you will be vastly important our quest, of that I have no doubt. This is a fear we all feel, but all must face. Sometimes we all must do things we don't want to, or are afraid to do so. Completing these tasks is what makes us stronger," Streak lectured.

"Look at it this way," Chance began enthusiastically, "Brock and Selwyn were eliminated from this forest without coming to any harm."

Checkers sighed. He longed for the icy cold waters of his home. Otters surely shouldn't go this long without swimming, he thought to himself as the remaining warriors looked toward him. "Okay," he finally said. "Let's go."

Streak smiled as the otter faced his fear and wandered to the entrance of a tunnel.

Each of the warriors stood in front of an entrance, the wind gusting at their furs and whiskers as it emerged from the narrow depths. Danjo seemed likely to be the only animal small enough to navigate them with ease. Pairo looked toward Makoto, and nodded. Makoto returned the gesture.

"Keep advancing," Streak began as he stared into the dark abyss howling back toward him. "Remember. If you return to a place you have already passed, you are eliminated. Do not attempt to navigate again. Turn around and head back."

The air fell cold and the breeze sped past. The tunnels screamed back at the animals as if in warning. "Show no fear," Streak said, before starting his journey and heading into the darkness.

"Here goes," Danjo said, before vanishing into the darkness.

Slowly Chance and Checkers vanished inside their entrances, leaving Akando's clan to stand alone in the gully of rock.

"Don't forget -"

"I know," Lyro barked, interrupting Pairo. "We find the information, we kill them."

"That's all I wanted to know," Pairo replied. The sternness in Lyro's voice sat well with the two treacherous foxes. Finally, it seemed as though he'd accepted his fate.

"Get moving," Lyro then ordered, gesturing forward with his muzzle. "I'll see you on the other side."

Pairo nodded, and both he and Makoto entered their narrow tunnels.

When they had vanished, Lyro sighed and looked to the towering rock face on his left side. He then looked upwards and noticed how quickly it vanished into the fog. He knew that if he did not slaughter the warriors when their journey had finished he would feel Akando's wrath, but he now questioned whether he could go through with the order or not. All of them - Streak, Danjo, Selwyn, Chance and Checkers - all played their part in rescuing him as he clung to the fallen tree high over the canyon. If they had not helped him, he certainly would have fallen. They saved his life whilst Pairo and Makoto looked on.

The conflict grew within the red fox. What would he do? What should he do? Now was not the time to stand and think about his future actions. Now he had to reach Stryder and the oak tree he guarded, the tree that was believed to be the life source of the entire forest. Find the information, and then decide.

Streak navigated down a sharp decline full of stones and debris. The tunnel was indeed narrow, and extremely dark. His bearings were confused slightly until the incline narrowed out and he felt a level rock surface under his paws once again. He heard the wind gusting through the tunnel with a low growl. Strands of cobwebs flickered in the breeze about him. Somewhere in the distance the sound of water dripping echoed between the walls. Slowly the fox wandered on, becoming wary of something around him. His ears became more alert. He heard the sound of his paws trudging over the unknown debris on the smooth rock surface.

'Ahh...'

Streak froze. Was that the wind? He couldn't tell. His heart thumped in his chest as he stood motionless in the darkness. He'd heard something that sounded like a voice. A voice moaning somewhere in the darkness. He stood a moment longer. The wind moaned. Water dripped. His ears filled with the sound of his own heart beat. There was nothing there. Nothing.It's your imagination, he thought to himself.

He took one step forward, and stopped. The sound of his own paws seemed to thunder through the darkness, and would surely alert anything to his presence there. Still, the sound of his paws did not call to anything dwelling within the abyss of darkness. He was alone. After a moment or so Streak felt his courage return, and spurred himself onward and into the darkness.

Streak continued to wander along the narrow path. After wandering what felt like an age, he noticed the tunnel widen out and become easier to navigate. The fox remained alert as he continued his journey. His fur felt each breeze that bellowed through the tunnel. He noticed his breathing become somewhat laboured as he walked onwards through the black abyss. A touch of apprehension returned to the fox as he wandered through the tunnel. He stopped for a moment, and let out a sigh. He held his breath in an attempt to stop the apprehension taking over his body once more. Then he noticed it. The laboured breathing continued.

Streak span round out of instinct. There was nothing behind him. There was nothing in front of him. His fur stood on end. Fear took hold of the fox. Something was

461

there with him. "Who's there?" he shouted fearfully. There was no reply. The breathing stopped, leaving Streak with the sound of his own heartbeat. The wind howled.

'Streak...' Streak jolted at the voice that drifted to him from the dark recesses. 'Streak...'

Streak's heart hammered in his chest, ready to leap out at any moment. He closed his eyes. "It's just the forest. It's just the forest," he whispered to himself. Slowly, he opened his eyes.

Streak lurched back as a huge scream echoed through the tunnel. A ghostly white face filled his vision, causing him to fall backwards. The screaming continued as the red fox leapt to his feet. It pierced his ears with a high pitch and sent shockwaves through his mind. He looked around for his tormentor. The face was gone. The scream subsided. Streak panted heavily. His legs shook with terror. There was nothing there with him. "Ghosts," he whispered almost silently. "Get out fast."

Streak cantered as fast as he could through the tunnel. Strange moans and wails emanated from around his body as he rushed further down the tunnel. A wail emerged above him and a white mist rushed over his head, screaming ignorantly past and back along the tunnel he had slowly navigated. Low groans seeped from the cold tunnel walls. Streak saw white paws and claws emerging from the rocks around him. The ghosts of lost animals began emerging into the tunnel, forcing themselves from the walls and swirling wildly along his path. He saw the muzzles of foxes, badgers and weasels pushing themselves from the solid surface. He saw the beaks and feathers of birds emerge inside the tunnel. Suddenly, he was surrounded by a mass of ghosts screaming and dancing around him. They passed by at such speed that they caused unnatural breezes that ruffled his fur, some so strong that his eyes squinted to keep open. They shone in a vibrant blue glow, filling the tunnel with a paranormal, blue-tinted bright light. Each one of these the terrible beings bore bland, pupil-less white eyes and moaned and wailed horrendously, as though each was suffering great pain or terrible sorrow.

'Run, Streak!' came a soft voice from the back of his mind. 'RUN!'

Streak heeded the voice without a second's hesitation. He ran as fast as the tunnel would allow, the ghosts weaving around his body and screaming as they passed. The ghosts illuminated his path, allowing him to run faster. His stomach churned with fear. His heart battered his chest with terror and adrenaline. He sprinted as fast as he could through the tunnel, his paw-pads thudding mutely on the rock surface. So concentrated was he on escaping that he failed to notice the sudden drop ahead of him until it was too late. His front paws fell first, prompting his head and shoulders to follow.

Streak lost his footing and tumbled head first down a long, rough slope, yelping as his body crashed against the walls. He was tumbling so fast that he had no control over his limbs. Gravity took his legs and torso, throwing him around against his will and beyond his control. Streak rolled, tumbled and fell, until suddenly he lay motionless. His head still shook and swayed with the dizziness that accompanied his long fall, but now he lay still upon a cold, flat surface.

"Streak?" a familiar voice asked. Streak slowly opened his eyes and moved his legs and paws to check for injury. He felt a blunt ache in his right hind, probably from the tunnel wall it hit on the way down, but otherwise felt fine. Streak noticed he was in a huge area. The ceiling of the area towered high above him, its surface made of jagged rock. Dull light illuminated the area he was lying in, allowing him to see better than the glowing lights from the ghosts he'd fled from.

Ghosts!

Streak leapt to his feet, remembering the phantoms that had terrorised him. His eyes searched the entire landscape he had fallen into. The huge open area filled with shafts of daylight, cascading from hidden openings. He was stood inside a gigantic cave that reached far out into the distance. To his left, a huge rock-pool glistened motionlessly to the farthest reaches of the cavern walls. Groups of stalactites hung ominously from the roof of the cave, glistening with water at their long points. Stalagmites emerged erratically throughout the huge chamber, reaching high towards the top of the jaded cavern.

"Streak?" the voice asked once more from the cave.

Streak turned to notice the small grey body of Danjo standing close to him. "Danjo?" he asked quietly, "is that you?"

The squirrel moved closer to the fox. "It's me, Streak."

The fox sighed, and relaxed a little. The ghosts had vanished for now, and he hoped they would remain within the tunnel he had emerged from. "The tunnel. Ghosts," he said to Danjo through the crystal silence of the cave.

"I know," the squirrel replied quietly. "We appear to be safe here, at least for the time being."

Suddenly, the silence was broken by the sound of rustling emerging from somewhere. Checkers tumbled out from an opening, as did Lyro, both suffering a similar fall that Streak had endured. Streak noticed that the tunnels lay next to each other, much like they did at the entrance in the forest. This time, there were only five exits. Chance suddenly tumbled from the last, leaving the otters and fox to gain their bearings.

"Ghosts!" Checker suddenly snapped, leaping to his short legs. Lyro jumped to his paws and span around as though expecting danger.

"What's happening?" Chance said angrily.

"Okay," Streak replied, reassuring his comrades whilst still harbouring the dizziness that welled inside his own head.

The animals turned their attention to him. "Streak?" Lyro began, somewhat confused. He then noticed the huge cave reaching out into the distance. "Where are we?"

Streak followed his gaze out into the distance. "I don't know," he replied, himself marvelling at the size and beauty of the strange cave.

"Water!" Checkers shouted, and bounded over to the huge rock pool.

"Water?" Chance repeated, pushing himself to his paws and quickly following behind.

"Careful!" Streak warned the excitable otters as they ran past him and to their temporary salvation. The cave echoed with the sound of splashing water as the otters leapt gracefully into the pool's glassy reflection. Streak, Lyro and Danjo watched on as they swam without any fear.

"Do you think we're safe in here?" Lyro asked, remembering the ghosts he had encountered on his own journey through the tunnels.

"I think so," Danjo began, "as long as we don't stay here for too long."

"You encountered the ghosts as well?" Streak asked them both, his head finally settling from the dizziness.

"Yes," Lyro whispered over the echoes of the splashing otters.

Streak looked back toward the tunnel he had fallen from. "I think you're right, Danjo. I don't think we will be safe here for long," he said, remembering the speed at which the ghosts glided through the tunnel.

"Wait," Lyro added, turning around. "Pairo? Makoto?" he asked.

Streak suddenly remembered the remaining foxes.

"Where are they?" Danjo asked.

Streak remembered the five holes they each had fallen through from the tunnels. "Look," he began, turning their attention to their harsh exits. "There are only five openings," he informed them.

Lyro counted the voids they had tumbled from. Streak was right. Five. With each of the animals now present within the cave, five animals had emerged. Five animals from five tunnels. "That's it," he began slowly. "Five of us emerged from the tunnels. There are only five exits." He looked to Streak. "They have been eliminated."

"I believe you may be right," Streak replied.

"If they've been eliminated, where have they gone?" Danjo asked the two dogs.

"I have no idea," Streak replied, with a hint of concern within his voice.

They stood in the cave, surrounded by the echoes of Chance and Checkers swimming in the rock pool, watching the tunnels for any sign of the foxes they travelled with. Finally, Streak took charge of the situation and made a decision.

"We must continue without them," he stated. Chance and Checkers emerged from the water and bounded their soaking bodies towards them. "We have no choice," he explained.

Lyro felt a wave of uncertainty emerge within his body. He had been separated from his warriors, and

466

now he may have to take Akando's order into his own paws.

"Where are the others?" Chance asked, shaking his wet fur of excess water.

"They've been eliminated," Danjo informed them.

"We must press on," Streak ordered, and began walking in the direction of the open cave. The two otters watched him as he walked past, followed closely by Danjo.

"Come on," Lyro said to them, gesturing with his muzzle to follow them.

As they began their journey into the huge cavern, Lyro looked over his shoulder one last time at the tunnels. Now there were five.

Makoto emerged from his tunnel into a huge, dark chamber. It was circular in shape but housed a low ceiling that only just allowed him to stand upright. As he looked around his surroundings he heard a slight gasp, like the sound of a whimper drifting through the darkness. He squinted his eyes to help see through the chamber, and noticed a red fox cowering at a rocky wall.

"Pairo?" Makoto said anxiously as he wandered over to the curled dog.

Pairo looked slowly over to him, his eyes wide and fearful. "Makoto?" he whispered fearfully.

"What happened to you?" Makoto said, cantering towards his ally.

"They know!" he whispered frantically. "They know!"

Makoto frowned. "Who? Who knows what?" he questioned, unable to decode what the dog was saying.

"They're all around us! They know! There's no escape!"

"Calm," Makoto whispered, his own fear creeping upward. Pairo was a fearless and mighty soldier in battle, and had now turned into a quivering wreck laid in front of him. He looked around the chamber to see only two entrances, one which he had emerged from. "We can turn around and go back."

"No!" Pairo snapped, "they won't let you!"

"Who won't?" Pairo did not answer. "Who won't?" Makoto snapped.

"The ghosts," he whispered.

The two entrances began pulsing with a luminous blue light. Strange moaning began echoing through the tunnels. The moans turned into cries, and then screams, as though a thousand animals were suffering horrendous pain and grief. Makoto snapped his head around as fear swept through his body. His erratic movements looked for the creatures making these terrible cries. Pairo shot to his paws, panting heavily. He screamed as though his mind had been lost, taking Makoto by surprise and making him jump. The chamber filled with a bright, burning white light. Pairo leapt from his position and sprinted along the tunnel Makoto had emerged from.

"PAIRO!" Makoto shouted, his own voice terrorised and afraid. From the white light swirling mists appeared; mist in the form of lifeless animals. Rabbits, foxes and stoats swirled around him, their eyes pupil-less and dead. Weasels screamed from the light, as did owls and rats. They darted through the air gracefully, swirling around the terrified fox. Pairo screamed from the depths of the tunnel. His body exploded back inside the chamber as though he had been thrown violently. He rose to his paws and stood beside Makoto, both of them frozen with fear.

'We know your secret,' a demonic voice boomed.

"NO! NO!" Makoto screamed.

'We know of the lives you intend to take.'

"WE DON'T! WE WON'T DO IT!" Makoto shouted to the swarms of ghosts dancing around them. An evil laugh cackled through the chamber. Pairo felt his heart ready to explode.

'You belong in a world as evil as yourselves. You belong with us!'

"NO!"

The ground shook beneath them. Rubble shattered as huge cracks broke open in the gnarly walls. Makoto dashed for the tunnels, but was smashed back by an invisible force.

'Hahahahahahahaha...'

The cracks widened, and exploded with light. From the open rocks, a nest of lifeless snakes slithered into view. They hissed and coiled as they fell limply to the floor. Makoto and Pairo lurched to the furthest reaches of the chamber. Snakes continued to fall from the cracks, some huge, like prehistoric giants long forgotten, and began rowing their limbless bodies towards the foxes. Pairo sighed with terror. Around them, the ghosts swirled. A snake bit down upon Pairo's paw. He screamed with shock. The bite did not hurt, but clenched tightly. Around him more snakes bit down upon his fur, his struggling body being immobilised by the white ghosts. He screamed as they began dragging him across the chamber floor towards the bright light emanating from the cracks.

"HELP ME!" he shouted as he continued to fight.

Makoto clamped down upon his tail, and began to pull. The immense pain did not even register with Pairo as he battled with the serpents. More latched on to him. They continued to drag him haplessly toward the light. Makoto pulled at his tail forcefully. He felt a pop within his jaw, and the tail fell limp. Pairo screamed. A huge snake smashed Makoto from the side, clasping him tightly in its mouth. It thundered around the chamber with the fox struggling in its grip. Makoto struggled as he blurred past the ghosts tormenting him. Randomly, he realised something as he was speeding through the chamber. He still had Pairo's tail in his jaws.

Both foxes screamed as they entered the cracked opening. Makoto's vision was filled with blinding light. He turned as best he could and saw the darkened entrance sealing behind them. He screamed one final time as they both vanished from the chamber. The ghosts swirled from the darkness back into the light, as the cracks bonded together strongly.

The chamber was as dark as it had been when the unfortunate foxes stumbled into it. It rested silently, as though nothing had happened.

But something had. The two evil foxes had been condemned to damnation for planning to take the lives of innocent animals; a plan that had cost them their own.

6

Loat slowly gained consciousness. A faraway memory stirred in his rousing mind as his eyes opened into the dim light. He remembered Seerles and Akando towering above him, but nothing from there. The stoat stirred his long body and ruffled a patch of dry leaves he was lying upon. He rolled on to his underside and gently shook his head, trying to remove the fuzzy feeling that swirled within.

"You're awake," came a soft voice through the gloom. Loat turned his long body around and noticed a pair of eyes reflecting back at him. Slowly the eyes drew near, and from the darkness a bright vixen wandered into view. "I thought for a moment you had been taken, like the others," she said as she joined the groggy stoat.

Loat looked upon her vibrant red fur and feminine eyes, and another memory returned to her. "Tali?" he asked quietly. It was indeed Tali who stood beside him, the vixen he had been sent to rescue.

"Yes," she responded inquisitively. "How do you know my name?"

Loat suddenly felt a rush of consciousness sweep through him, forcing his mind into clearer thinking. "Tali," he began in a whisper, "I am Loat. I was sent to rescue you by the Great Council," he said, moving closer to the vixen as he spoke.

"The Great Council!" she whispered back. "What has happened to Shadow Oak? The Warriors? What about Wickett and the Forest Guard?"

"Settle," Loat began, instructing the excitable fox to calm. Tali sighed and sat down on the rough flooring.

"The Great Council has declared war," he said seriously, informing Tali of Rebus' decision. "It has been forming for an age now it seems, and there is no way it can be resolved. The division between Seerles and Akando and the Great Council is just too immense."

"Then the Great War has begun," Tali whispered to herself.

"The dawn of the Great War is upon us," Loat stated gently to her. "As for the Forest Guards," he sighed, his voice now a little more upbeat, "they escaped the clutches of the dark alliance and were on course to make the Forest of the Damned."

Tali closed her eyes, and smiled. Those rabbits were resilient. Perhaps the most resilient warriors within Averon. She knew deep down that Wickett would lead his guards to safety, and that her self-sacrifice to Akando had not been in vain. Then she remembered. "Doran," she asked softly, expecting to hear nothing of her sibling.

Loat leaned closer. "Doran has returned," he whispered.

Tali's eyes widened. "Doran?" she asked again, almost in disbelief.

"I returned with him to Shadow Oak. He has overcome the darkness that took grip of his mind."

A feeling of joy warmed through Tali. "He did it," she whispered.

"Indeed he did, and so powerful is he that upon his return, he repelled the beast as it attacked Shadow Oak." Tali looked on in amazement as Loat told her the story of her warrior sibling. "He is accompanying the Forest Guards within the Forest of the Damned. And with his help, the tides of battle will soon turn in our favour." Loat then began pacing around the den. He examined the earth, the debris and the entrance of the den he was stranded inside. "We were sent to rescue you," he said, whilst still examining his prison.

"You haven't done a very good job then, have you?" Tali replied boldly.

Loat ignored her remark and continue to look around the gloomy den. He saw the entrance to the outside guarded by two dark foxes on either side. He knew Favradin would be captive elsewhere in Akando's community, somewhere larger that would hold a muntjac. The deer who had been injured in the battle would be no use to the dark alliance as soldiers, and those who were still fit enough to run would have done so from the battlefield.

Loat smiled as the basis of his plan had begun to form. "Who said this plan wasn't working?" he replied confidently.

7

Achak patrolled the border of Shadow Oak. The fallow deer stood tall within the looming fog, still as relentless as it had been at dawn and throughout the entire day. Now, as twilight began to emerge, it settled again and showed no sign of disbanding. Katori patrolled alongside him, as the forest was vast becoming a dangerous and hostile place. The trees around them had shrivelled and died as fear had swept the resident animals of the forest, causing the darkness to become powerful and drain the life force from the vegetation as it grew.

"The forest is dying," Katori said as they wandered between the husks of once-fantastic and beautiful trees.

"This is such a terrible fate to a forest so vibrant," Achak replied, noticing the decaying landscape around him.

"Is there nothing we can do?" Katori asked. A small breeze brought with it a surprisingly warm feel that told them the warm season was quickly approaching.

"Nothing. The hope of this Great Forest lies with those who have ventured inside the Forest of the Damned, and those alone."

Achak caught the sound of something strange. First he thought it was simply the dead trees swaying in the breeze, causing a low, rumbling noise, but quickly established that the breeze was not nearly strong enough to move the branches in such a way. "Did you hear that?" he asked his comrade.

Katori looked into the fog around him. "Yes," he replied seriously, the concern clear within his voice. There.

"Where is it coming from?" Achak asked.

"From all around us," Katori replied.

The rumble became louder.

"It's moving closer," Achak whispered.

"What is it?" Katori whispered in return.

"I don't know."

"I can't hear any movement, though."

"It's..." Achak trailed away.

"What?"

"It's stalking us." Achak turned to Katori. "The beast," he whispered. The strange noise suddenly turned into a rumble, the rumble of a low growl.

"What do we do?" Katori asked.

They stood motionless in the fog. Somewhere, beyond their eyesight, lurked the beast.

"As soon as we move, the beast will be upon us," Achak whispered. "We must split up."

The menacing growl emanated from the fog once again, this time deeper and closer. "Return to Shadow Oak," Achak ordered Katori. "Order all animals there into safety, and wait for me to return."

"What are you doing?"

"I will lure the beast away from you."

Katori nodded. "Ready?" Achak asked. Katori nodded again. "GO!"

Katori sprinted into the deep fog. He heard the beast scream wildly in the fog behind as he darted between the dead trees and back toward Shadow Oak. The cool fog flowed between his antlers as he dashed rapidly over the damp ground and back inside the border of Shadow Oak. He leapt the natural obstacles about him and sprinted as fast as he could. Slowly, the shapes of animals loomed from the fog. "Back to Shadow Oak!" he shouted. "Get back!"

Rebus emerged from a den upon hearing Katori's cries in the distance. "What is going on?" he shouted to the approaching fallow deer.

"Inside your dens! The beast!" he screamed.

Concern swept through the animals, and suddenly a stampede erupted. "Quick! Get inside! Get to safety!" Rebus ordered.

Squirrels climbed the trees hastily. Foxes and badgers vanished inside the abundance of dens.

"To the tunnels!" General Lupus ordered the rabbits.

"Follow the rabbits!" Lisket ordered the hares.

"What is happening?" asked Glif, noticing her contingency of squirrels fleeing to the safety of the dead trees' branches.

"The beast!" Rebus warned.

Ciros and Tienos leapt into the clearing. The two fallow deer that ventured inside Averon with Achak and Katori had been returning from a patrol, when they heard Katori shouting. Shadow Oak cleared, leaving the fallow deer and Rebus out in the open.

"Retreat to safety," Katori ordered the badger as the atmosphere fell eerily calm. "We will protect these lands." Rebus stood a moment longer with the deer.

"You must leave," Ciros reiterated to the badger. "We will call to you, should we need to."

"Be strong," Rebus replied. He complied with the deer's request and retreated inside the hollow underneath the huge oak tree where Kedem lay, close to death.

The three fallow deer stood together inside the fog. The dead trees created brittle and open hollows, and in the silence the breezes howled menacingly through.

"Achak has distracted the beast," Katori informed them as the foggy light of day slowly began to fade. "He lured her away to give me time to get here."

"Then he is in great danger," Tienos added.

The wind howled, and in the farthest reaches of the trees a bird called and flapped away, hidden by the dense fog still laying across the forest. The loose bracken and woodland debris rustled in the breeze. The fog swirled in coils as it drifted lazily by. The three fallow deer stood together in the silence.

Below the ground, Rebus mused over proceedings with a nervous tension. "Where is Cyrius?" he snapped, his frustration clearly upon the barn owl who often appeared in times of distress to help the Great Council.

Outside, the herd of fallow deer scoured the fog for any sign of movement. A branch broke somewhere in the distance. A bird called. The branches swayed. A breeze howled. A creature exploded from the fog, causing the fallow deer to lurch back. Debris churned in its wake as it crashed into the clearing.

"Achak!" Katori shouted.

"Get back!" Achak snorted, his chest tingling with exhaustion. "It's close behind!" Achak joined his herd. "Stand tall," he ordered, between his gasping breaths.

The fallow deer separated at their leader's order. They spread around the clearing, losing sight of one another in the fog. "Remain vigilant," Achak ordered breathlessly. "We stand together. If you call, we will join you."

The forest stood in the grips of a wilder breeze. The branches shook as it powered past them, making them scream and wail horribly. The hollows they found howled like ghosts wandering the Haunted Woods. Ciros squinted into the dull light. A dark shadow passed quickly behind the fog. "Movement!" he shouted.

"Stand together!" Achak replied.

A rumbling growl drifted through the murk. It grew louder as it emanated from the dying trees within Shadow Oak.

"Where are you?" Tienos whispered, jolting his head back and swaying his antlers, ready for the battle that would commence.

The growl continued. Katori noticed the rumble subsiding into the distance. "It's moving," he shouted to the herd.

Ciros took notice. A thought struck him. "It's waiting," he replied quietly. The growl continued, but from a farther distance. "It's biding its time for the perfect opportunity to strike," he subtly added.

"Clever," Tienos replied.

"Then we wait," Achak ordered to his herd, each hidden from one another by the fog. "We wait; and when it attacks, we fight back."

8

Doran and the Forest Guard emerged, from the twisted trees and immense rocks, upon a huge open area. Even though the fog still lingered around them, it became much lighter and allowed them to see further into the distance. The area was huge, almost as daunting as the Great Vast Open, but away across its depths the tell-tale signs of trees shadily emerged from the clearing fog. A light dusting of mist lingered thinly above the grassless, muddy area.

"This must be it," Blits began as they sat a moment at the tree-line, looking out. "This must be the Morgas Field."

"It's huge," Apollo replied. "Almost like the Great Vast Open." They sat, in awe at the huge area they would have to cross.

A thought struck Coinin. "The colossus?" he asked, remembering Digby's warning from back in the forest.

"I don't know," Wickett said, his eyes still scouring the Morgas Field. "It must be lurking somewhere in here."

"But it's not here now?"

"Then now is the best time to cross," Wickett replied.

"Good judgement," Doran said, agreeing with the rabbit. "We need to be cautious and watch out in all directions. We cross together and quickly, and we do it quietly. We don't want to alert it to our presence."

Wickett looked to the rest of the rabbits in his guard. "Follow Doran's lead. He's in charge of this task," he ordered.

Doran nodded. "Come on. Less haste."

The animals quickly laid their paws out onto the Morgas Field. Wickett was surprised to find the mud hard underfoot, as though it had been baked day after day by the scorching sun during the warm season. They quickly moved across its surface, the mist breaking against them as they continued into the open air.

The animals passed quickly and quietly across the Morgas Field, their eyes peeled in all directions for any sign of the colossus. Digby had warned of a huge, giant-like creature roaming this immense field. As they continued across the mud they thought less of the foretold threat and more of the trees across the open, looming closer as they approached. They continued their silent journey for what seemed like an age, hastening across in silence and reaching far out into the huge, wide open area.

Doran halted rapidly, forcing the Forest Guard to follow his lead. Wickett looked at the fox with a questioning expression. Doran gestured to the ground with his muzzle. Through the light mist, Wickett noticed huge piles of bones scattered all across the field. There were so many that he couldn't tell to which animals they had once belonged. Many bones were small and fragile, many were huge and unbreakable. It seemed to be a vast forgotten graveyard of animal remains, and with the mist gliding eerily over them, seemed as though it had been taken straight from the lore of the Great Forest.

Wickett turned the attention of his Forest Guards to the bones scattered across their path. They knew instantly the danger he alerted them to. He gestured to one of the bones, and shook his head. They all nodded, as though some type of psychic connection existed between the four rabbits that allowed them to communicate silently. Wickett looked to Doran, who then looked at the Forest Guards. They nodded back, confirming their understanding. Slowly, the journey began once more. This time the animals weaved around the vast piles of bones in an attempt to keep the peace and keep the Morgas Field relatively undisturbed. They separated slightly as their path around the remains took them in different directions. They continued carefully across, thankful that the ground was solid and not damp as they had expected. If loose mud had moved under their paws, there was no saying how many bones they would have moved by now.

Coinin slowly squeezed between a pile of unidentified bones in his way. He cleared them quickly, but his light tail gently grazed a pointed bone protruding from the pile.

A huge low groan filled the air and erupted across the Morgas Field, so loud that it shook the ground they stood upon. Doran froze. The groan was immense, like a huge beast stood growling down upon them from a great height. Birds became spooked and launched from the trees immediately, cawing and croaking as they fluttered high into the dull sky.

Apollo noticed the bones around him begin to shake. They clattered together as they shook, filling the air with the morbid sound of reanimated bones swarming back to life. Wickett span around. All around them the bones were shaking, as though they would suddenly explode at any moment. The groan subsided, leaving the animals surrounded by the chatter of the shaking bones. Slowly they levitated, gently rising into the cold air. Across the entire field, broken and decaying bones rose from the mist, filling the sky full of dark debris. Suddenly they exploded through the air one after another, faster and faster into the farthest reaches of the huge field.

The rabbits stood on their hinds, half in terror, and half in amazement as the bones whistled high above them and across the sky. Huge, spiked bones jolted upright from the earth at the edge of the trees, rapidly sealing the animals within the Morgas Field. They followed one after another, slicing the air with precision as they shot from the ground. Doran turned to see them emerge from the mud and tower high above him, fencing them in and blocking their escape route.

"We have a situation!" he shouted with mild disdain.

The Forest Guards turned to see the rapid fence of bones explode from the ground and chase themselves around the entire field. "Pellets!" Blits shouted. There escape route was now entirely blocked. Not even the rabbits could run fast enough to reach the trees in the distance that the bones were sprinting to.

"What now?" Blits shouted.

A huge groan emanated across the field. The bones that flew through the air were bonding together. They flew into place and locked together with morbid precision.

"The colossus," Wickett whispered.

From across the distance, the animals could see a pair of hind legs rapidly building skyward by the bones that levitated through the air. They clasped together to form a huge pelvis. The bones continued to swarm around the emerging colossus and began forming the lower vertebrae of a spinal column. A shockwave surged through the field, knocking the animals to the floor. The ground near the forming skeleton began to crack and lurch, shaking the foundation on which the animals struggled to regain their footing. The earth exploded, sending soil searing high into the air. The spine formed completely, and reached up high above the treetops. The swarming bones, now dark specks against the dull sky, locked tightly to the towering column, and formed a ribcage of discarded remains. Clavicles formed and bonded on top of the ribs. Bones raced high in the air and created the shape of a humerus on either side of the colossus. They soared through the air and bolted firmly to a fully formed scapula. The remaining arms took shape as the ground beside the colossus presented a huge skull emerging from its depths.

"What is it?" Coinin shouted wildly as he regained his footing.

The skull levitated high above the trees. Soil and debris fell abundantly from it as it lofted through the air and latched on top of the theratic vertebrae, the final piece now firmly in place.

"Human!" Doran shouted through the carnage. "It's the form of a human!"

"Why human?" Blits shouted.

"Because..." Doran began, before realising exactly why, "humans are the greatest threat to any animal in the forest or within the Great Vast Open."

The eye sockets of the human skull flickered to life. Huge white flames exploded from their dark recesses, as the colossus became conscious. The flames roared loudly through the air, their edges flickering red as they emerged to life inside the skull. The colossus turned towards the animals standing in the middle of the field. It slowly stooped down and roared thunderously towards them, its mouth opening so wide that they could see its bony body through the gape.

"I think it's seen us!" Apollo stated fearfully.

"You think?" Coinin snapped, more from fear than sarcasm.

The colossus stood upright, its makeshift legs cracking with support. Shards of bone fell from the colossus as it turned away from them.

"How do we get out of here?" Blits asked.

Doran surged the darkness in his body. His eyes turned inky black, and a shot of the powerful element exploded from the fox and into the wall of bones blocking their escape. He heard the impact of the force strike the fence and watched as it dispersed into the air above. Across the field, the fox saw that his attack had been in vain. The fence still stood.

"We can't!" Doran replied.

The Forest Guard glared at him. "WHAT?" Coinin screamed.

"We're trapped! We can't escape!"

"What are we going to do?" Blits shouted.

The colossus leaned down once more, grabbing a huge tree from beyond the fence of bones. The animals heard the sound of the tree creak across the distance as it was dragged effortlessly from the ground in which it once rested. The colossus roared and clasped its trunk with long bony fingers.

"Whatever it is, make it soon! It doesn't seem very happy!" Apollo said, as the remaining animals attempted to find an escape route. The colossus turned back to face the animals, and with a swift, powerful throw, launched the tree through the air towards them. Apollo's eyes widened.

"INCOMING!" he screamed. The trunk smashed violently into the ground ahead of them, and bounded closely over the ducking animals. The colossus roared once more, and broke into a slow but immense sprint across the field.

"PELLETS! PELLETS! PELLETS! PELLETS!" Coinin shouted.

"DISTRACT IT! GIVE ME TIME!" Doran shouted.

"TIME FOR WHAT?" Wickett replied.

"JUST DO IT! SPLIT UP, NOW! RUN AS FAR AS YOU CAN!" Doran ordered.

The Forest Guard split in different directions and tore away from each other. They ran towards the colossus and split, Apollo and Coinin darting left, Wickett and Blits shooting right. Doran sat, motionless, where he was.

Slowly, he closed his eyes. A strange breeze began to ruffle his fur as he began calling upon the darkness. The colossus stooped down and thundered a clenched fist deep into the surface of the Morgas Field. Tearing the landscape apart, it drew a huge mace from the earth. The mace was forged of heavy stone and rang long and smooth in the skeletal hand of the colossus. At its tip, a huge stone sphere housed sharp stone spikes with which to skewer its enemies upon.

"WHAT DO WE DO?" Blits shouted to Wickett as they bounded over the misty field.

"KEEP MOVING!" Wickett shouted.

The colossus roared as the Forest Guard darted separately across the field. Apollo and Coinin approached the gigantic skeleton, weaving in tandem as they began the plan. They thundered across the ground, approaching the colossus quicker and quicker. The giant noticed them first, as they sped quickly toward it. It roared thunderously at them and raised the mace it clenched high into the sky. Through the darkened air the mace smashed violently to the ground, the aftershock sending Apollo and Coinin into the air. Coinin landed straight on his paws and continued the sprint. Apollo thudded on his side and rolled quickly to his front, before sprinting away uninjured. The colossus drew the mace from the crater, tearing the ground that had been impaled by the spikes and sending huge mounds of earth flying into the air.

Doran sat in a trance as plumes of dark smoke rapidly circled him in different directions. The breeze around him turned into a gale, and whistled about him.

Anger surged through his dull red body. Behind his closed eyelids, his eyes began to burn. Electricity slowly flashed and crackled within the darkness shrouding him. The edges of the darkness burned mauve. His body filled with rage. Never before had the fox felt so intensely angry. The raw power of the force within escalated to a level so high that he felt invincible.

The colossus raged, swinging the mace through the air as it noticed Wickett and Blits approaching from a different side. Slowly, it rose its bony foot from the ground, and smashed it down towards the advancing rabbits.

"SPLIT!" Wickett shouted. The rabbits darted in different directions as the colossal foot thundered into the ground. Wickett and Blits flew through the air as the surface below smashed into thousands of pieces. The impact of the attack launched the rabbits across the battlefield and harshly to the ground.

Across the field, Doran opened his eyes. Pure hatred burned bright red within his skull, his pupils replaced by a glowing rage. He screamed a huge, terrifying scream that echoed rapidly across the Morgas Field. The Forest Guards jumped from their positions, turning back across the field in the direction they had sprinted from.

The colossus slowly turned its head from the rabbits surrounding it. Its skull creaked and groaned as its attention drew to the fox far across the field. Doran rose slowly to his paws. The colossus turned its huge makeshift body to face him. The darkness swirled and engulfed its new master in erratic, excited movements, ruffling his fur as it danced and swayed around him. The colossus roared aggressively, its jaw wide open and eyes burning angry and violent. Doran screamed again, accepting the huge challenge he faced, and ran head-on towards the colossus, his head bounding up and down as his body navigated the hard ground. The colossus lurched from its position and gave chase. The darkness welled strongly within the fox as he sprinted, answering his call to the extreme.

Apollo pulled further to the left, the colossus ignoring him now and passing over the rabbit as it slowly sprinted towards the fox. He slowed down and turned as the colossus passed, noticing Doran sprinting across the mist away in the distance.

"What?" Coinin asked as he slowed to a stop beside his fellow guard.

"Doran," he simply replied.

The fox continued straight towards the roaring colossus with the power of a thousand warriors screaming inside him. Doran felt terrible anger. He felt the surge of emotion sweep through him as he bore upon his foe. He felt no fear. He knew no fear. Smoky darkness left his body and swirled around him, leaving patches in his wake as he ran. The colossus raised the gigantic mace high above his head as he bore upon the fox. Doran sprinted relentlessly toward it.

"Now!" Apollo shouted from across the field. "NOW!"

Before the mace came crashing down, Doran threw his head back and screamed. A huge flash of purple light erupted from the fox, and a huge wave of darkness exploded across the battleground, smashing the colossus violently in its sternum. The colossus lurched backwards at the sheer ferocity of the attack. Its legs buckled and gave way, forcing the gigantic creature to smash, knee-first, to the hard ground. The impact of the fall thundered through the mud, rumbling the ground beneath Apollo's paws. Doran's rage continued to attack the colossus as it fell to its knees and roared. Doran felt the power screaming through his body. His

487

muscles tensed as the darkness drove further and further into the colossus. The huge, skeletal, giant threw its skull skyward, and roared as the darkness drove through its morbid skeleton and weakened the attacking giant.

"YES!" Apollo shouted as the colossus lurched backwards and fell. Wickett and Blits stopped to see what had happened. "He's done it!" Blits shouted.

All four Forest Guards watched from their positions as the colossus became engulfed within the magic element that the fox had mastered. It groaned and howled in anguish as the element thrashed around it, through its bones and into the darkening sky.

The colossus screamed immensely as the Forest Guard looked on.

Slowly, the darkness subsided from the gigantic creature. It slumped further down and then crashed lifelessly to the floor, spewing mud and debris high into the sky.

The ground rumbled one final time and settled quietly, leaving the Forest Guards in silence.

Wickett watched on for what felt like an age as the debris rained down upon the carcass of the giant laying upon the tattered field floor. After waiting and waiting for any signs of danger to emerge, he decided that the colossus had indeed been defeated, and called Blits to join him. Both Forest Guards raced over the crater-filled field to the fallen giant.

Apollo and Coinin joined them as they approached the skull of the fallen colossus. It laid sideways, its jaw agape, smiling grimly at the approaching rabbits, as all human skulls do. Remnants of the darkness drifted from its eye sockets and jaws and floated thinly up into the air.

"Doran?" Coinin asked as the Forest Guards assembled at the head of the skull. Without response, the rabbits began searching for the fox that had destroyed the colossus. They foraged around the huge skeletal body of the fallen enemy for a sign of their comrade. Apollo noticed how grim the skeleton looked, itself created from thousands upon thousands of bones. As he wandered around the fallen giant he noticed a strange red flicker, much like the flames that had erupted from the skull of the colossus. Within the cervical vertebrae, behind the huge mandible that lay agape, a small bone glowed through the gloom. It pulsed slowly, gently growing brighter then subsiding as Apollo watched on, almost hypnotised by the strange phenomenon that pulsed from the depths of the morbid giant.

"Here!" came Coinin's voice, bringing him back to reality. Apollo hopped away from the colossus and over towards his comrade. The still body of the red fox lay in front of him.

"Is he dead?" Blits asked bluntly as he joined them.

"I don't think so - I think he's just exhausted himself," Coinin replied factually. Doran was indeed alive, and slowly regained consciousness with the rabbits stood looking down upon him. As he roused, he immediately remembered what had happened.

"Where is it?" he asked, as he rolled onto his front.

"Destroyed," Coinin replied. "You finished it."

Doran shook his head and pushed himself to his paws. He noticed the huge skull lying across the ground as he rose to his paws, shaking his fur as he did so. "We need to get going if we are to find Kedem," he said, almost unfazed by his amazing triumph.

The rabbits followed their weary leader as he began wandering across the solid ground. "That was amazing!" Apollo said, as they continued their journey.

"I didn't realise he was so powerful," Blits whispered as they fell behind a little.

"I know. Unbelievable."

The band of animals continued slowly across the ground, heading across the Morgas Field and toward the trees, where they hoped to find the trail and the lost banafrit of Kedem. A groan rumbled throughout the ground. The animals froze.

As they slowly turned, they saw red flames flicker to life within the colossus' eyes once more. Slowly its morbid body creaked and cracked, pushing itself up, laboured, from the ground.

"Oh no," Doran began, his legs trembling. He tried quickly to muster the power of the darkness once more. He felt a surge spark within his red body, but having exhausted himself already, he knew it would be nowhere near as strong as the blast he had hit the colossus with before. "My powers are weak," he began, filling the Forest Guard with dread, "I am not strong enough to stop it again." The colossus rose from the ground, roaring through the air with the low groan of immense movement from its huge limbs.

"What now?" Wickett said, with a sense of helplessness welling inside him.

"We're done for," Blits began, accepting his fate within the Morgas Field.

"The only thing that could stop the colossus is the colossus itself," Coinin mused.

Apollo watched as the colossus rose to its feet and towered high above them. The human skull roared to life once more. "Wait a minute," Apollo said to himself, "that's it! That's it!"

"What is?" Wickett asked. They watched on as the colossus stooped down and took the huge mace in its hand once again.

"Are you strong enough to direct its weapon towards me?" Apollo asked Doran frantically.

"What?" he asked warily.

"Can you keep its focus on me?"

Doran knew that physically he would be unable to assault the colossus, but he may just have enough energy to influence it.

"Yes," he said quietly.

"It needs to attack me, Doran. Make sure it does!" Apollo replied, and without a second thought dashed back across the Morgas Field and towards the colossus.

"APOLLO!" Blits screamed.

Apollo raced over the ground towards the gigantic skeleton. The colossus roared aggressively, its flamed eyes focusing upon the small grey speck racing towards it. The huge mace clasped tightly in its hand lofted high above its skull, as the colossus prepared to attack once again. Its arms creaked thunderously through the sky as it did so. Loose debris still fell from its bonded, decaying bones.

"WHAT IS HE DOING?" Coinin shouted.

"Leave him," Doran said, watching the rabbit hunt down the mighty creature. "He has a plan."

Blits looked at Wickett. "Apollo has a plan?" he asked.

Apollo sped across the solid ground, his ears flat against his back. This is it,' he thought as he ran closer to the colossus. I only hope it sees me.

The colossus roared and threw the mace down toward Apollo. Apollo leapt to his side and rolled as it smashed into the ground, destroying the earth, shaking the ground and sending the decaying landscape high into the air.

"APOLLO!" Wickett shouted.

Doran closed his eyes. He sensed Apollo still charging towards the colossus. "He's okay," Doran whispered. Wickett turned to him briefly, then turned back to the battle ensuing across the field.

The colossus drew its weapon from the ground, peeling huge mounds of earth with it from the crater it had just opened. Apollo still thundered towards the giant, his chest and legs aching with fatigue. He sprinted on, ignoring the pain his body was screaming through. Come on,'he thought, goading the colossus in his mind. Slowly, the spiked mace that the colossus held started emitting swirls of darkness. Doran began to feel anger surge within his exhausted body once again. The swirls erupted from the weapon as though a huge fire roared within its shaft. Apollo closed in on the left foot of the colossus, forcing his focus on the individual bones of the foot. The colossus lofted its weapon into the air once more, its gaze firmly fixed upon the rabbit charging toward it. The mace smouldered high above the colossus as it prepared to attack. A huge blast of wind emanated around Doran and the Forest Guard, ruffling their fur as the fox engaged his last ounce of energy to Apollo's plan.

The colossus tracked Apollo approaching closer. It roared with anger, its cry rumbling through the earth on which it towered. Apollo had reached it. The colossus cried out one last time, and smashed the mace down toward the rabbit. Doran took control of the weapon as it crashed down. He guided it towards the Forest Guard now darting beside the colossus' foot. The mace shifted in the air and jolted towards Apollo, who quickly launched with all his might from beside the colossus. The mace swung down and smashed through the giant's leg as it followed the rabbit. The colossus roared as the bones shattered into millions of shards, and forced it to fall. The colossus crashed to the ground, the impact so immense that it jolted the animals from their paws. It fell headfirst to the hard mud, destroying the earth that it crashed into. Apollo shook himself from the ground, and leapt to his paws. The colossus had crashed to the ground right beside him, its skull resting momentarily in a crater it had just created from the fall. Without thinking of his own safety, the rabbit sped in that direction, dodging the sharp shards of bone as they fell rapidly from the sky. There it was.

Apollo leapt onto the cervical vertebrae. It felt like a huge boulder rather than a bone. He struggled quickly to the top and found what he was looking for; the small red bone glowing gently from its resting place. The colossus still lay dazed upon the hard surface of the Morgas Field, paying no attention to the rabbit that now ran throughout its bones. Apollo reached the glowing shard, and began work.

He clasped the small circular bone between his teeth, and began to pull. The colossus screamed as Apollo began tearing at its life source. Its mandible opened above the rabbit as its scream grew louder, shaking the bones Apollo was stood upon, but still the rabbit continued. The bone became loose, but still clung on.

"He's doing it!" Doran shouted, the darkness baring an image of Apollo's struggle in his mind's eye. "He's inside the colossus! He's destroying its life source!"

Across the field, they saw the huge arm of the colossus raise. "We need to help him!" Wickett shouted. He knew the gigantic skeletal hand was heading toward the Forest Guard fighting inside. He knew that if they didn't help, Apollo would be in mortal danger. "We need a distraction!" he shouted.

A piercing scream echoed through the skies above them. A star fell, burning bright as it descended upon the Morgas Field, leaving a trail of glowing gold embers in its wake.

"CYRIUS!" Blits shouted.

From the burning white light, a barn owl emerged in the sky above them. Cyrius glided over the animals and headed straight toward the fallen colossus. Apollo struggled with the life force, jarring it as much as his small body would allow. The hand of the colossus began to fumble at its throat. Apollo swayed from side to side as the colossus struggled against him. His teeth bit down tighter around the bone as he attempted to stay latched on. Cyrius glided rapidly through the sky, jolting as he struck patches of warmer air on his descent to the fighting colossus. Apollo shook and swayed as the giant attempted to reach him, its huge fingers closing in around him. Cyrius soared faster, sensing the danger to Apollo. The owl reached the colossus, and screamed. An immense bright light exploded from the oracle, filling the sky with a blinding aura of white light across the entire Morgas Field.

Apollo closed his eyes as the light surrounded him. He felt the colossus settle momentarily, stunned by the light around them. With one final, forceful pull, he pushed his hinds down into the vertebrae on which he was standing and ripped the glowing bone from the colossus' spine. The colossus released a low, terrifying roar. Apollo was launched from the skeleton and thudded to the hard ground, far from the giant. The light began to die as the colossus writhed in pain upon the Morgas Field. Doran and the Forest Guard watched on as the colossus clasped at its throat, as though it was choking; and then slowly become less animated, and lay still. The bright light vanished, leaving them in the usual dull light they had come to expect from the Forest of the Damned.

Slowly, the ground began to shake underneath the animals. A rumble filled the air around them. "Get down!" Doran shouted. The colossus exploded upon the field, sending millions of bones flying through the air, all whistling sharply as they screamed through the sky. The fence surrounding the field burst violently. Large bones thudded loudly to the floor around them. Doran engaged the last ounce of energy he had to the darkness. A small shield emanated over himself and the rabbits, protecting them from the falling debris. The bones continued to rain down across the Morgas Field. As time passed, the heavier bones fell, and left the light, flaky shards to flutter down gently.

"Apollo," Coinin said, as the final bones came to rest upon the ground.

"Quick!" Wickett ordered, and the Forest Guard dashed from their protective shield. Doran followed slowly behind, his energy slowly regaining as he crossed the crater-filled field.

"Where is he?" Blits began, frantically scouring the bones around them.

"I don't know!" Coinin snapped.

"Split up! Find him!" Wickett ordered.

The Forest Guard scoured the field for their comrade. They searched in every crater that the colossus had created, and the farthest reaches of the tree-line that had been blocked from their escape.

"HERE!" came a cry across the open. The Forest Guards turned to see Doran beckoning them over. From three separated directions the rabbits sprinted through the bones to the red fox. Cyrius swooped low and landed beside Doran as the rabbits approached.

"Oh no," Blits whispered solemnly. Lying next to Doran was the grey body of Apollo.

"APOLLO!" Wickett shouted as he approached the animals.

"No, no, NO!" Coinin began.

The three Forest Guards joined Doran and Cyrius. There, lying lifelessly in front of them was Apollo. Apollo the Brave, the Forest Guard who fell whilst defeating the gigantic colossus. Each of the rabbits looked upon him with glassy eyes. Their ears lay flat against their fur.

"Apollo?" Coinin whispered, slowly making his way to the lifeless rabbit. "Apollo?"

Apollo offered no response. He simply lay motionless beside a pile of bones, his eyes closed tight and mouth slightly agape.

"No," Blits sighed, his voice shattered and emotional.

"Apollo," Coinin began. Coinin's mind flooded with memories of the rabbit that lay beside him. He suddenly felt guilty and remorseful. He had liked Apollo deep down, but never showed it. He had never complimented the rabbit, never encouraged him, and never even acknowledged him unless he had done something wrong. He felt that Apollo had never taken his duty seriously in the Forest Guard, and his bravery and heroics upon the Morgas Field had shattered his perception of the rabbit. He had never said anything positive to Apollo. Never.

"Apollo, I'm so sorry," he whispered to the lifeless rabbit. "I am so, so, sorry. I never meant to be mean to you. I never meant all those things I said. You aren't an idiot. You are brave. Apollo the Brave." Coinin felt tears begin to well within his eyes. Wickett and Blits joined him on either side. "You were Apollo the Mighty."

"Am I Apollo the Giant Killer?" a quiet voice asked the grieving rabbits.

"Yes," Coinin began, bursting into tears, "You are most definitely Apollo the... hey!" Coinin shouted. He looked down to see Apollo smiling at him.

496

"Did you call me Apollo the Great? Apollo the Mighty?" he asked enthusiastically.

"Apollo!" Wickett shouted, moving to his friend.

Blits sighed. A huge burden lifted from his body. His life-long friend was okay. Doran looked to Cyrius, and smiled.

"Yes I did, but only because I thought you were dead!" Coinin snapped, hiding his relief behind his usual grumpy persona.

"You called me a giant killer. What else would you like to tell me?" Apollo asked, knowing he was quickly grating on Coinin's nerves.

"That I, Coinin, of the western border Patrol Team, hate you more than anything or any creature within the forest of Averon!" he stated, throwing his nose in the air and turning from the rabbit. He looked at Doran, and after a moment or two smiled, thankful that his friend was okay.

"What were you thinking?" Wickett said, helping Apollo to his paws.

"I was creating my legend," Apollo began as he stood up. "Apollo, Master of Averon."

Doran turned to the barn owl perched beside him. "What are you doing here, Cyrius?" he asked, happy that he had swooped down in the nick of time when he did. "I thought you could not help us on our quest here in the Forest of the Damned?"

"Ah, now therein lies the question," the owl retorted, ruffling his bright feathers. "I told the Great Council I could not assist them on their quest to find Stryder within these trees." The four Forest Guards united together once more as Apollo rose to his feet. They all paid Cyrius their full attention. As they had now come to expect, he was a wealth of information and assistance in times of despair. "Your quest was, and still is, to find Kedem within these dark branches."

"Have you been with us the whole time?" Blits asked, perching himself on his rear for a brief respite.

"I'm afraid not. I have been watching events unfold within Averon," the owl replied.

"What news of the Great Forest?" Doran enquired.

"I am afraid it is not good," Cyrius replied, his mood dampening somewhat. "Akando and Seerles grow stronger each waking minute that passes. Fear spreads abundantly through the trees. Shadow Oak has succumbed to the terror they are instilling within the lands. The trees are dying. The forest is dying. Kedem lies restlessly in his den, asleep but alive. It is the beast, though. She is hunting on the outskirts of your community, Doran. The council members and remaining animals have been forced underground into the dens and tunnels for sanctuary. The community is being protected by the four fallow deer that emerged from the Great Vast Open. They are the only ones strong enough to repel an attack."

"Achak and his herd," Doran stated, remembering their safe delivery of the small fawn back to the muntjac. "What of Loat and his attack to The North?"

"And Tali?" Cyrius replied, remembering Doran's captive sibling.

"And Tali," the fox replied quietly.

"Loat and Favradin have been captured by Akando's army," Cyrius began, "but all is not lost. Loat has hatched a fantastic plan to ensure their escape."

"Are they okay?" Wickett asked, remembering Tali's sacrifice to ensure the Forest Guard's escape.

"For the moment, yes. They must wait for the right time to execute their escape, which may mean more days enslaved before they can set the plan into motion. All I can report is that Loat's plan is running as it should be. That, for me, is encouragement enough. My main concern now falls with Streak and the warriors, and their venture to Stryder."

"Then you need not worry, old friend," Doran said, sounding increasingly like a member of Kedem's advisory committee. "We encountered Brock on the trail leading inside this forest."

"He told us of a danger between Lyro and Akando's warriors accompanying him," Apollo added.

"Yes. It would seem that my prophecy was true. I saw blood and death on their quest, but to whom I did not know."

"Brock did," Blits smiled. "He was ready to tear them apart. He told us of Lyro's treachery."

"I did the only thing I could," Doran told the owl. "I helped him cross a canyon he had no way of crossing."

"A dangerous move," Cyrius began. "If the forest has eliminated him, it would mean certain death to return."

"Indeed it does - but the badger is wise, as well as strong in battle. We could not simply wander by, knowing that Streak and the rest were in danger, without assisting him. I gave him a shield of protection until he leaves this forest."

A look of frustration crossed Apollo's face. "You protected him?" the rabbit asked.

Doran turned to him. "Yes," he replied swiftly.

"You protected Brock? Why couldn't you protect us too? We had to destroy a colossus!"

"You don't need protecting," Doran replied, fairly amused at the rabbit.

"You defeated the colossus with your own bare paws," Blits reminded him.

"Yes, I know," Apollo began, "but still. I'd have liked to charge towards the giant with a shield or something."

"Legends are selfless on the field of battle," Cyrius said boldly, "and your actions would not been nearly as heroic if you had defeated the colossus using magic."

"Even I could not defeat the colossus, Apollo. It was your fighting spirit and bravery that defeated the giant," Doran added.

Apollo gave in, in light of his triumph. All around them the mist had formed fully once more, and shielded the craters that the colossus had created from its pound attacks upon the animals. Doran remembered the task at hand.

Kedem was somewhere near. Digby had told them the trail they seek lay just beyond the tree-line of the Morgas Field. With the colossus defeated, the next challenge would be to gain the attention of the banafrits. Digby had mentioned that Kedem was struggling to find a way back to help the Great Council as the war emerged. If they could only find him, persuading him to leave may be easier than if he wanted to stay.

"How can we get Kedem back to his body if he agrees to join us?" Doran asked the barn owl perched beside him.

"That is where I can assist. A banafrit can glide between the trees as fast as I can fly. I can lead him to the gateway, and when I pass between the realms he will disappear and immediately return to his slumbering body within the den at Shadow Oak. He could wander back through the trees with you; but I suspect there is one final event that will take place in this forest where you all will be needed."

"What will that be?" Wickett asked.

"Crossing a frozen lake to reach the Forsaken Island," the barn owl mused.

"That sound very dangerous," Blits began hesitantly.

"No, your quest within the forest will be complete. You will do so in safety - of that you have my word," Cyrius promised.

"Look," Apollo whispered, turning the attention of the animals to the tree-line.

"Well, your actions certainly garnered some attention," Cyrius said, turning his attention to the trees. The animals looked on as an army of banafrits slowly emerged from the murky depths. "You are safe," he told them as the burning aura of a thousand animals glided into the field. They watched on, as all about them it filled with the wandering souls of lost animals.

"Digby said it would be Kedem who would find us," Blits remembered. As they watched on, the banafrits glided across the field. At the head of the shades, a proud fox emerged at the head of the shadows.

Part 3

Reunited

1

Streak, Lyro, Chance, Checkers and Danjo emerged at the bank of a huge lake. Their journey out of the cavern had been swift and effortless, leading the warriors to a lake surrounded by strange trees twisting from the earth. The forest had yet again played games with the wandering animals. No longer did the thick fog swirl and drift across the forest; bright sunshine seared down from a hidden sun in the strange sky. From the horizon a bright, clear morning emerged. Crisp blue sky surrounded them, without a single cloud to see. As the morning rose into the sky, it merged with the dense darkness of night, and hundreds of stars twinkled brightly above them. There was no sun in the sky, and no moon in the stars. Still, light shone brightly down upon the animals, as though they were engulfed in the midst of a summer day. The lake itself bore the brunt of an immense winter, and glistened beautifully with a frost born of the cold season. The lake had frozen solid in entirety in the warm, bright day.

"Amazing," Danjo mused as he looked upon the strange skies merging together.

"How is this possible?" Checkers asked openly.

"The forest," Streak whispered. "It's nothing like we have ever witnessed in Averon."

Across the frozen lake, an island existed. Shrubbery and vegetation nestled at its edges, vibrant and colourful, not at all tainted by the winter that had taken the water. The island protruded into a hill across the distance. On top of the island, a huge oak tree sat. Even from this distance Streak could see it was larger than the tree that eclipsed the community at Shadow Oak. The tree seemed to be pulsing with a green, luminous hue from across the distance.

"That's where we are headed," Lyro said, noticing Streak's gaze far across the lake.

Streak nodded. "We're almost there."

A strange hoot emanated above the animals. A shadow glided over them as they stood at the bank, briefly shading them from the invisible sun. Streak looked up into the sunless sky. Nothing. Across the lake, the shadow of a bird glided across the frozen water and soared towards the island and tree. "That must be him," Danjo said, watching the shadow glide away gracefully.

"Do you think this is strong enough to hold us?" Lyro asked, slowly prodding the ice at his paws.

"There's only one way to find out," Streak replied, and slowly wandered out on to the glistening ice.

The animals followed warily. The foxes precariously crossed, their paws unused to the smooth, slippery surface on which they wandered. Chance and Checkers fared better, their low bodies closer to the ice than the foxes. If they needed to, they could swim in the freezing waters that lay hidden beneath the ice. Danjo wandered nimbly across the lake. He had crossed areas like this within the forest during the cold season, but never one as immense as the one under his paws now.

As they ventured further into the open lake, the frost subsided and the ice became clearer. Lyro checked the glassy surface with his paws. It felt as strong as it had by the bank, but still he led with caution. If the ice was to smash and the animals fall into the frozen waters beneath, with the exception of the otters there would be no way they could pull themselves to safety. Slowly, they crossed the natural glass with Lyro at the helm. Beneath the clear ice, a huge shadow swayed past.

"What?" Streak asked, noticing the fox halt in front of him.

"I just..." Lyro began, attempting to fathom what he had just seen. "I just saw something," he added after a moment or so. The remaining animals had also come to a standstill upon the frozen water. They looked on, bathed in an invisible warm sunshine from a sky that should not exist. "Something just passed by underneath the ice. Something huge," he said, continuing to scour the transparent ice for another sign of what had glided quickly by.

"It would have to be a fish," Checkers replied, his knowledge of rivers and lakes only matched by the other otter who stood beside him. "Maybe the warm weather has lured it from the depths of the water here. Most fish retreat to the bottom of their waters when the cold season descends upon the forest."

"It is true," Chance agreed, "most fish will begin to surface when the waters begin to warm."

"But we are walking across a thick ice," Danjo said questioningly, "and there is no sun within the sky. Surely the warmth must thaw this lake before any heat can penetrate the water?"

The two otters turned to each other. The squirrel made sense. "Why would a fish emerge?" Checkers asked.

"Perhaps," Streak began quietly, gaining the attention of the makeshift warriors around him, "this is a test."

Their leader could be right. "If it is a test," Lyro began, "then the fish must be-"

"A guardian," Danjo whispered.

The ice exploded in front of them, sending shards of shattered ice into the air. A waterfall of freezing water

507

cascaded down upon the animals, their footing failing as the ice beneath them began to crack and shatter. A huge striped tail-fin rolled in the exposed water, and vanished quickly beneath its glassy surface. The ice began to contort and submerge around the warriors.

"QUICKLY!" Streak snapped. All around them, the clear air filled with the snapping sound of cracking ice. Crooked lines appeared all around them. Lyro watched as the cracks ran out far across the lake. The ice shattered once more as the fish launched to the surface, creating another huge watery opening that forced even more lines to appear within the ice. A spotted flank vanished beneath the water's surface.

"Did you see that?" Checkers shouted. "Its a pike!"

"Get out of here!" Streak ordered. The animals began making haste across the flimsy broken ice, treading as lightly as they could.

"Another smash from that fish, and this will all shatter," Checkers said to Chance as they darted across the emerging lake. "If that happens, they'll all die. None of them can cope with the freezing waters."

Chance stopped. The lives of the warriors were now hanging greatly in the balance. The ice continued to break around them. Huge mounds broke away from each other and drifted apart, exposing the deadly cold water beneath. "We have to do something," he replied to his comrade.

Streak noticed the otters had vanished from his side. He turned to see them standing upon the ice behind him. "WHAT ARE YOU DOING?" he shouted back at them.

Checkers looked around, and saw a huge crater open close by. Pikes were dangerous. They could easily tear a limb from an otter or even kill them with their huge maw and razor-sharp teeth, plus they swam like lightning through the water. "We have to do it," he said, ignoring the fox yelling at him. He turned to Chance. "Are you ready for this?" he asked.

"OTTERS!" Streak screamed.

"Let's do it!" Chance replied.

The otters gave one last look towards Streak. Lyro and Danjo were now stood beside him, their concerned faces looking across the lake toward them. "What are they doing?" Lyro asked hesitantly. They watched on as the otters sprinted away from them across the ice and towards the newly-revealed water.

"NO!" Danjo shouted, watching as the otters committed themselves to certain death. They leapt gracefully into the freezing water and vanished beneath the surface.

"QUICK!" Streak ordered, turning the remaining warriors towards the island they were fast approaching. "They're distracting it! They won't have much time! We have to cross now!"

With heavy hearts, the animals turned and began running across the breaking ice. Powdery white frost seared around them as the ice cracked and shifted apart. Their path became unbalanced as the ice moved beneath their paws. The huge pike below the water darted through the depths, its long body unfazed by the freezing waters it glided through. With its high-set eyes it saw the shadows of the sprinting foxes upon the ice's surface. It thrust its powerful tail through its crystal-clear surroundings, quickly approaching the frozen surface and the animals that ran across it. It closed its maw, ready to explode through. The shadows rapidly approached. The sunlight cascaded down. The ice was there.

The pike veered away at high speed, changing its course from the surface to the depths of the lake. It felt a disturbance within the water. Somewhere, two creatures that did not belong glided within its domain.

The warriors sprinted across the lake. Ahead of them, the ice was already broken. Large pieces replaced the solid surface they had once stood upon. The island was close.

Streak leapt onto a cold floating surface that buckled under his impact. His hinds glided down its smooth surface and splashed into the cold waters. Streak yelped and leapt quickly to another one. Around him Lyro and Danjo transferred between the floating blocks, leaping the gaps of water and pressing quickly to the next.

The pike raced through the water, bearing down quickly upon the otters. Chance and Checkers glided side by side through the icy glass, bubbles escaping from their noses as they passed quickly through the water. The otters noticed the huge fish following behind. Chance dived, as it lurched forward and snapped at his hinds. Checkers darted sideways, confusing the fish that powered after them. The pike turned and gave chase to Checkers. They approached the shallows as the lake bed rose and merged into the land that formed the island. Chance knew that even if they built up a great lead over the chasing predator, it could still take them from the shallows when they had to return to their paws if not far enough ahead. He followed close behind the fish, the power of its tail churning the wake he followed in.

The pike opened its maw, and snapped towards the otter. Checkers darted upwards, avoiding its teeth as they snapped together in the water. The pike slowed. Chance launched at the fish's tail and latched his own teeth into its powerful tail-fin. The pike writhed and twisted in the water as the otter shredded its flimsy dorsal. He darted quickly away, and found his comrade. The pike seethed with anger. Its tail leaked cloudy patches of blood into the clear water. It felt stinging surges of pain in its tail as it swam, but still it gave chase to the otters. Chance and Checkers headed toward the island, hoping that their distraction had given their friends time to cross the ice.

Lyro leapt onto the muddy bank of the island, splashing water from its bank as he crashed down. He immediately turned. Danjo launched from further out, and submerged in the deadly water. Lyro leapt into the water, submerged his muzzle, and gently took hold of the squirrel in his jaw. Streak crashed down beside them, the freezing water so cold that it hurt his body. Lyro ran up the banks and released Danjo. The squirrel quickly shook his fur to remove the excess water.

"Cold, cold, cold, cold, cold!" the squirrel shouted as he bounded around the mud to raise his body temperature. The foxes both shook their red fur as they walked upon the banks. Danjo looked out upon the lake as the ice melted and vanished beneath the water. He noticed the dorsal fin of the pike gliding from the lake's surface. It gave chase to two swirling mounds rolling from the water.

"Look!" he said, turning the fox's attention to the water.

"Chance. Checkers," Lyro said, from beneath his water-drenched fur.

They watched as the fin gained rapidly upon the fleeing otters. It darted sideways and increased in speed. It gained quickly on them as they swam towards the bank.

"Quickly!" Lyro said, as though the otters would hear him.

"Come on!" Danjo added. The fin vanished beneath the lapping waves. The otters submerged.

Streak looked out into the water. The last pieces of ice were vanishing beneath the waves. The invisible sun was reflecting brightly from the water's surface.

The air was full of the gentle sound of lapping waves landing on the banks of the island where they stood.

Chance and Checkers launched from the water. Lyro jumped as they broke the tranquillity and splashed down into the shallows. Quickly, they scurried through the water, and emerged safely upon the bank. Streak watched on as the fin once more broke the surface of the lake and glided by. Slowly it submerged, and vanished from his view.

"You are both crazy," he heard Danjo say as the otters climbed the banks. He noticed that all of them had now been plastered in fresh mud - most of all Danjo, who looked as though he had emerged from the water with a completely new coat.

Streak wandered towards his comrades. "Indeed you are," he added as he approached the otters, "but your bravery almost certainly saved us from death. For that, I thank you."

"Yes. Thank you. Twice you have assisted in saving my life. I am in your debt," Lyro added. The otters had indeed played a most vital role in saving him on two occasions now, making his orders all the more terrible.

"There is no need to thank each other just yet!" a voice boomed from behind them. "None of you are safe, and none of you will be safe unless you can influence the Great War in your favour!"

The warriors turned slowly. Ahead of them, stood on the descent of the luscious hill and immense oak tree, loomed a huge Bengal eagle owl. His feathers merged into various shades of cream and pale brown, and across his plumage dark dashes of brown decorated him abundantly. His eyes burned deep orange. His brows tufted upward, forcing his brilliant eyes into a constant frown. Ears jutted sideways from the surface of his head. The owl looked foreboding and angry, and bore a necklace of rodent skulls and bones that hung limply around his plumage.

"You must be the one we have been sent to seek council with," Streak said quietly, turning fully to the owl stood ominously above him.

"I am Stryder, guardian of the Tree of Life and Protector of the Realms. You have ventured from the realm of the living, and passed the trials which measure your will and determination to seek my council. The land on which you stand is known as the Forsaken Island, and has never before felt the paws of living creatures wander its grass. You have shown courage and determination in your quest, and for your trouble I will reward you with my council."

Streak sighed, and finally relaxed. He had led the warriors through the Forest of the Damned, a feat which few had expected him to do. He had lost friends along the way, and overcome some truly frightening experiences. The ghosts within the tunnels had pushed him almost to the brink of sanity; but that small voice within his mind, the one that emerged in times of despair had forced him into action and pushed him onward. Now he stood with his remaining warriors, looking toward the owl he had journeyed so hard to reach. Behind him, the huge oak tree hissed with the sound of waterfalls. From the loftiest reaches of its top a waterfall cascaded down, hitting huge branches and drifting out into further streams of falling water. They filled the immense treetop and ran downwards into a stream that surrounded the tree. The water pulsed with a luminous green tint, giving the tree a sense of life as it ran freely through the branches and leaves.

"Amazing," Lyro mused, as he looked up into the amazing tree he could not believe.

"And I feel I have a surprise in store for you all," Stryder added. The animals looked on as a fox emerged from the fantastic oak.

"Doran," Streak whispered. Doran emerged with the four Forest Guards in tow. "Wickett!" he shouted.

"Streak!" Wickett replied down to his friend. The animals stood there in amazement. Neither had expected to see each other in the Forest of the Damned.

"I don't believe it," Checkers said to Chance as they looked towards their warrior counterparts.

"It seems that Cyrius had a trick or two in place for when your quests began," Stryder said happily. "Come, Warriors of Averon. We have much to discuss," he beckoned, opening a wing towards the tree. Streak heeded the owl, and soon the warriors were heading to the life-force of Averon to speak with its protector.

Rebus sat nervously within the huge den. He was joined by Jinx and Delfin, Shadow Oak's advisors, and Dallie and Glif, council members representing the otters and squirrels. Outside they could hear the nervous pacing of the fallow deer protecting the community from the lurking beast. They sat there in silence, knowing there was nothing they could do. They were at the mercy of the beast, and if the fallow deer should fall... it wasn't worth thinking about. They sat there, listening to the wind howl across the entrance to the den, and the trees creaking outside.

A huge breath engulfed the den. It sighed and began panting rapidly. Rebus jumped from his resting place. The sound of paws kicking against the chamber walls emerged. Something in the den was struggling. Rebus darted into its depths to find the answer. Kedem's body lay in a small chamber excavated from this one. He had been resting on his side with his paws stretched outward the entire time. He no longer rested on his

514

side. Kedem laid prone, his head finally lifted from the floor. He gasped as he took in breath, filling lungs that had only taken minimal air since Akando attacked him.

Rebus beamed happily. "I do not believe it," he whispered as he was joined by the council members. "They did it. Doran and the Forest Guard did it."

"Yes," Kedem croaked between the breaths of a second life, "they did. They found me inside that terrible forest."

"Quickly," Stryder said, beckoning the animals to squeeze inside a tunnel leading through the huge oak tree, "you do not have much time." The warriors followed the owl as he pushed through the glowing green bark, all still amazed to be reunited upon the strange island. The sound of the waterfalls falling around them hissed loudly in their ears, as though Seerles himself was only inches from them as they walked through. The trunk of the tree pulsed with the fluorescent light of the tinted water. A huge pool of water lived in the base of the trunk that the largest waterfall fell into. It branched into three tiny streams, running through the roots of the strange tree and out into the surrounding stream outside.

Stryder hopped the streams, and ventured to a clearing outside. The warriors followed, their awe clear as they passed through the fantastic oak. The owl led them into a grassy area, shaded by the thick leaves and branches. Large stones scattered around the grass, and strange purple flowers pulsed with the same fluorescent properties as the water. Strange buds poked from the branches above them, themselves appearing like stars as they glowed brilliantly above the animals.

"Does everything glow here?" Lyro asked, noticing the flowers as he walked out.

"It's life," Stryder replied quickly as he turned to his guests. "It flows through every leaf and every flower upon this island. Now, sit down," the owl then ordered, gesturing with an open wing for them to sit in a semi-circle.

Slowly the warriors grouped together and did as their host requested, sitting on the soft grass in the clear view of their host. Streak suddenly felt how achey and worn he was from the journey. He had not rested since they departed from Shadow Oak, and it now felt like an age ago since he had left behind his home and his friends. Apollo sighed and slumped towards Coinin, as his weary body felt the same. Coinin sighed and shook his head at the tired rabbit.

"Now, tell me what you seek," Stryder asked as their meeting began.

The Warriors turned to Streak. Even with Doran there, Streak was the one to whom they now looked. "We have ventured across the plains of life and death to ask you one question." Stryder's eyes focused upon the fox. "We ask that you inform us of how to defeat the beast terrorising our lands."

Stryder partially closed one eye, as a look of bewilderment crossed his beak. "You do not wish to know how to succeed with the Great War?" he enquired.

"The Great War?" Checkers said in astonishment.

"Yes," Stryder began, looking toward the otter. "Your war has begun."

"How? What's going on?" Danjo asked erratically.

"The nature of your Great Council is unclear to me, warriors. I do not know how or why, or by whom, but the very fabric of these realms is threatened to be torn apart should Akando and Seerles emerge victorious."

"Akando and Seerles are in league?" Danjo asked.

"I am afraid so," Stryder began solemnly. "The bones never fail," he said, reaching behind a rock and pulling an abundant amount of rodent bones and skulls from behind. "Akando betrayed your council, and fights beside Seerles in an attempt to bring darkness to Averon."

"But that means, if Akando is in league with Seerles, then..." Streak turned to Lyro. The traitorous fox returned a glare full of concern. "You?" Streak whispered.

"Streak! Wait!" Lyro replied.

Streak launched at Lyro, smashing him to the ground. He pounced atop the traitor, pinning him to the grass. "You!" he snarled, swiping Lyro's muzzle. Lyro yelped out. Blood poured from his laceration. "You're the enemy!"

"Wait!" Lyro screamed.

"What were you sent here for? To kill us!"

"Streak!"

"ENOUGH!" boomed Stryder's voice. A wave of energy separated the sparring foxes, freezing their movements before the fight became too intense.

"You lied to us?" Chance shouted to the bleeding fox. Lyro felt the stinging sensation of his fresh wound pulse along his muzzle. The damage that Streak had inflicted had been rapid, but only left a minor cut towards the tip of his nose. The Forest Guard and Doran looked on, having already been told of Lyro and his soldiers.

"You do not have time for this!" Stryder snapped, hopping towards the frozen foxes.

"Wait!" Doran shouted, turning the gaze of the battling foxes to himself. "Tell them, Stryder. Tell them what you told us."

"It is true," Stryder began, complying with Doran's request. "Lyro and the foxes who journeyed with you were sent to kill you once you had been here, but is thanks to Lyro that you all still live."

"What?" Danjo asked the owl.

"Deep down, Lyro has a kind heart. He never intended to kill you from the moment he joined your warriors. He has kept you safe from the two known as Pairo and Makoto. It was they who plotted your demise from the outset, and they who Lyro has thwarted in their attempts to slaughter you all."

A breeze gently drifted across the Forsaken Island. An atmosphere hung heavily across the animals there. Slowly, Stryder released the two foxes from his grip, allowing them to move freely once more.

"When?" Streak said softly as his breath from the attack slowly returned. "When did you save us?"

"He saved you by playing along with the plan the entire time," Doran answered in Lyro's place.

"They both had their doubts whether Lyro would follow Akando's orders from the outset, but realising they had to rely on themselves to do it they had to wait until the right opportunity arose. They knew if they intended to attack you that Lyro would fight by your side, and there was no way they could compete against two warrior foxes and the Warriors of Averon," Stryder confirmed to them.

"What do they intend?" Lyro asked sternly to the owl, his concern falling with his fellow clan members.

Stryder threw the bones from his clenched claw on to the grass. The tiny bones fell and bounced erratically to the floor. The owl hopped to the remains and studied them intently.

"Hmm... it appears they have already paid for their sin."

Lyro looked shocked. "How? What's happened?"

"It would seem they have... yes... they have become Damned. They were taken by the ghosts lurking within the tunnels. You are free from fear." Stryder paused a moment. "They will stay to wander the Forest of the Damned for eternity, unable to cross to the spirit world."

"Unfortunate," Danjo said, still feeling concern for those he had ventured with. The fate of the two foxes hung over the warriors like a dark cloud, all shocked, and some saddened at the news that the bones had brought with them.

Stryder continued without hesitation. He gathered the bones in his claw once again, and threw them across the open grass. "Now, to your plight with the beast." The bengal eagle owl hopped between the scattered remains once more.

Blits mused to himself. "Hope these bones stay where they are," he whispered to Apollo.

Stryder looked down upon the remains with caution. "This is bad," he said, sinking Streak's hope. "This is truly bad," he muttered.

Doran looked on. "What -"

"Hush!" Stryder snapped, his bright orange eyes glaring angrily at the fox. Doran shrank back, sorry he had spoken. Stryder moved between the bones some more. "Ah, there it is," he began, as he bore into the skull of a field mouse. He moved closer, as if finding something of interest within its tiny sockets. "There is a way." Wickett's heart lifted. All around, the Warriors looked to each other.

"You must create an ambush," the owl began, his focus still upon the skull. "You must lure it to the Great Vast Open. There, an ambush will take place should you succeed. If you do, the beast will trouble you no more." Stryder continued studying the bones. Checkers began to speak, but was hushed by his fellow otter. "It must be you, Streak. You must place your very life in danger to lure the beast out of the forest."

"Why Streak?" Doran interrupted. Stryder shot him a harsh glare.

"I do not know, or see why, but Streak is the one whom the bones have chosen," the owl responded. "If not he, then all will fall around you. You have no choice."

Streak nodded, although unsettled at the news. "Alright," he whispered gently.

"But you must leave quickly!" Stryder began as he peered into the bones. "The beast is about to attack your home!"

"Shadow Oak!" Doran cried.

Urgency swept through the Warriors. "How do we get back so quickly?" Streak shouted. "It has taken us an age to get here!"

"Stand back!" Stryder told them, removing his attention from the bones. The Warriors leapt back as the owl opened his immense wingspan. The grass ruffled as a warm breeze emerged across the island. Stryder closed his bright eyes.

A white orb of light appeared in front of the animals. They watched as it grew larger and flickered like lightning at its edges. As the orb formed, a hole appeared in its centre. Still the orb grew, and the hole opened wider and wider. The air filled with the sound of crackling electricity. The branches creaked as the breeze turned into a gale and rustled the leaves above them. The Forest Guards stood beside the otters, their fur attacked by the powering wind. The hole within the light grew huge, and within the hole loomed the unique oak tree within Shadow Oak. "GO!" Stryder shouted from above the gale. "Quickly, before the gateway closes!"

"Home," Doran whispered as he saw his community only metres from his muzzle. "Okay, quick!" he shouted, remembering where he was. The Forest Guard bounded through, followed by Danjo. The otters jumped in next, with Lyro passing close behind.

"Thank you!" Streak shouted to Stryder through the gusting winds.

"Go!" Stryder returned. "Save your forest!"

Doran and Streak leapt through the gateway together, their paws hitting the cold, sodden ground of Shadow Oak.

2

Brock bounded into the clearing. Selwyn soared above him. The fallow deer turned about quickly, wondering where these animals had suddenly emanated from.

"Brock! Selwyn!" Doran shouted, as they approached the deer.

The beast growled from the depths of the decaying trees. They stood in the dawn of a new day. No longer were they blighted by fog; instead, a clear sky and bright sunshine bore down into the cold morning.

"It's here!" Coinin shouted, hearing her growl.

The beast smashed into the clearing and thundered to the ground. She roared so loud that the earth trembled. The warriors stood reunited in the face of her threat, unflinching and strong. Streak remembered Stryder's words. It was he who would have to bait the beast into the Great Vast Open. He looked to Wickett, who looked back.

Streak sprinted into the decaying trees, swiping the beast as he tore past. She growled in anger and thrust a huge claw toward him. The fox darted sideways and vanished into the dead trees towards the Western Clearing. The beast leapt and gave chase.

"Come on!" Blits shouted.

The fallow deer sprinted with the Warriors as they gave chase to the pursuit. Streak ran as fast as his exhausted body would allow, darting between the trunks as he headed to the western border. The beast rumbled behind him, gaining rapidly as her muscular body powered through the forest.

"He's not going to make it!" Apollo shouted hysterically.

Selwyn soared through the sky and bore down upon the beast. His feathers bumped as he descended through the air and clasped his talons upon her muscular back. They bore deep into her flesh, causing her to roar. Selwyn felt the trickle of blood across his claws as he released and climbed the skies once more. He had slowed the relentless beast; although her focus remained with Streak, despite his attack.

Streak leapt the debris and thundered forward into the crisp morning. He was almost upon the Western Clearing, the place he had been rescued by Doran and Tali so very long ago. The beast roared behind him as she gave chase. He'd have to build up a lead inside the trees, as she would be much faster across the open ground. Branches fell across the path of the sprinting panther as Doran engaged the darkness to slow her down. His power still had not recovered enough to cease her attack, but he gave everything his weary body allowed to assist Streak with escaping.

Streak exploded into the Western Clearing, and darted rapidly across its soft ground. His body grew weary. His chest ached. His heart pounded. The beast bore upon him. His tail swayed in front of her jaws. She roared.

Achak smashed her from the fox's wake, veering her off-course and away from Streak. The panther roared in frustration but kept her focus up,on the fox sprinting away. Achak collapsed onto the damp ground, dazed by the ferocity by which he attacked her. Streak entered the tree-line once more and sped towards the Great Vast Open.

The Forest Guard emerged upon the stumbling beast, nipping at her dark legs as she stumbled. She roared in anger, but still kept her focus on the fox darting through the trees. She believed Streak to be the one responsible for her injuries during her previous raid on Shadow Oak. Quickly, she regained her bearing and followed Streak inside the trees.

The Warriors slowed as fatigue set in. "Come on!" Wickett shouted, noticing their decline. Brock huffed and puffed as he bounded through the woods, but slowed as he tired.

Streak was exhausted. He had nothing more to give. He could feel himself falter rapidly. Slowly, through the trees, he saw the Great Vast Open appear. He was almost there. Almost.

He gnarled his muzzle and charged toward the clearing. The beast gained quickly behind him. Almost there! he though to himself.

The fox broke the trees and sprinted into the Great Vast Open. The ground was wet as he navigated the slow decline of the land. There was nothing around him except open air and some trees scattered in the distance. Far away, he noticed the coppice where the hares once dwelled. He ran as fast as his tired limbs would carry him, his chest screaming in pain, begging him to stop. He ran with his head down, his efforts focused on his escape. The beast broke from the trees. Streak looked up. His eyes widened. He skidded as he thrust his paws deep into the slippery grass.

Streak threw his muzzle to the air, but kept his terrified focus ahead of him. He adopted a seated position as he slid across the wet ground. He attempted to turn and sprint back the way he came, towards the beast. Towards death.

A bugle pierced the clear morning. The sound of a thousand hounds filled his ears. Baal growled and smirked to himself. "HERE, BOY! BRING HER TO ME!"

Baal pounced upon Streak, smashing his turning body into the ground.

"NO!" Wickett shouted as the Warriors emerged at the western tree-line. The rabbit attempted to run, but was held back by his guards.

The Dark Army thundered past Streak as he lay immobile upon the floor. The mass of darkened hounds flooded past him and engulfed the beast like a living shadow. The warriors watched on as Streak and the beast became swallowed by the fox hounds, their numbers snarling and barking. The humans atop their horses pulled weapons, and aimed towards the roaring panther. Hounds flew through the air as she swiped them from her path, attacking them as violently as they did her.

"STREAK!" Doran yelled.

"LET GO!" Wickett ordered his Forest Guards sternly.

"No," came a calm, distinguishable voice. Cyrius emerged from the forest with Brock, and settled beside the rabbits. Blits felt Wickett give in, and his struggle subside.

"Oh no," Brock whispered as he watched the carnage across the Great Vast Open.

They heard the feline growl of the beast as she continued to fight the Dark Army, but slowly she succumbed to their sheer numbers.

A human pointed a weapon in her direction. The air filled with the loud pops it made when triggered, its end smoking as if on fire. More pops echoed across the field as another human joined with his weapon, and then they fell silent.

The Dark army barked and yelped, and the beast was destroyed.

3

The warriors waited on the edge of the forest for the Dark Army to clear. There were many slaughtered and wounded hounds that had fallen at the claws of the beast, but the humans seemed more interested in the dark panther than the hounds that they hunted with.

When the Dark Army cleared, the humans found a way of transporting the beast's carcass from the Great Vast Open using a monster they must have tamed. Its skin glistened brightly in the warm, clear day, and even allowed the humans to open it and place the beast inside. It sped away shortly after, roaring as it did so, leaving the dead hounds for another visit.

"Quickly," Cyrius ordered Doran. "The rest of you wait here. The humans will be back for the fallen hounds very soon."

"But -" Wickett began.

"Do not ignore me!" Cyrius snapped, forcing the rabbit back to his guards.

The owl and the fox left Averon and made their way across the Great Vast Open. Cyrius scouted the battlefield from the air, looking down upon Doran as he approached the fallen bodies.

Doran searched for any sign of his friend. He scoured the bodies of the hounds slaughtered by the beast, their bodies shredded and innards spilt. He trod through patches of blood as he looked for any sign of Streak. Slowly, he came to the body of a hound.

Cyrius disturbed the tranquil surrounding as his wings beat the air and he came to rest beside Doran. They both looked at the body at the fox's paws.

"I warned him," Cyrius said, noticing the milky eye of the dead hound.

Baal had fallen by the paw of the beast. So intent was he to kill Streak, that the beast had taken his life as he focused upon the red fox.

Doran thought things through in his mind. So much had happened that day; it was hard to fathom how this would affect the Great War. "What happens now?" Doran said to the owl as he stared with a morbid fascination upon the fallen general.

"We wait," Cyrius said quietly. "The Dark Army will rise with a new leader, and almost certainly seek retribution for this attack."

"What should we do in Shadow Oak?"

"We should allow time for Kedem to return to full strength. There is a war brewing in The North, although Akando and his army do not realise it yet. We should hold a full council meeting, and decide what approach we should take."

"The hounds will be outraged," Doran began, as he studied the body on the floor.

"Yes, they will, and they will look to Averon for their revenge. Streak was the one leading the beast here. It is the fault of our communities - or at least, that is how they will perceive it."

Doran sighed. "With Akando and Seerles fighting against us, and the Dark Army looking to seek revenge upon us, I fear our chances are bad. Very bad."

"They are, Doran, but there is always hope."

Doran's eyes flickered with rage as he turned to the owl. "What hope does our Great Council hold now? We could not match the numbers against the Dark Army before this, and now we face Akando's army, with which he was aligned with Seerles? There is no hope, Cyrius. None."

"If there is no hope, Doran, show me where the body of Streak lies."

Doran shook from his anger and looked upon the battlefield. There were many, many hounds that lay there, but one notable absentee. Across the entire field where the hounds had fallen, there was no sign of Streak. "Where is he?" Doran yelped, a feeling of hope now welling in his mind.

"There is always hope, Doran. Always."

4

"And tell me why it is should join you, Seerles?" a low voice echoed in the darkness. Seerles had ventured into the Forest of the Damned, his command of the darkness allowing him to do so safely. He was inside a cave so dark that even he struggled to see inside. Ahead of him, a cluster of red orbs burned through the darkness. A huge cobweb flapped in a breeze behind the entity he was conversing with.

"When Averon falls to us, there will be no plains distinguishing the realms of the living and the realms of the dead," Seerles hissed, his fork tongue flickering as he spoke. "You will be free to rule this forest in any way you see fit."

"Explain to me how this will work?" the gravelly voice questioned the adder.

"With the Great Council destroyed and the forest dead, we will rule ruthlessly. Any animal who does not pledge allegiance will die."

"You test my patience, Seerles," the voice growled. "How will you stop the animals from leaving?"

Seerles smiled evilly in the darkness. "There is a way, I assure you."

The cave filled with the sound of light tapping, as though thousands of twigs tapped upon its rocky surface. Clusters of red orbs grouped together in their hundreds, surrounding the adder within the dank gloom. "The gateway is open. I can create a portal of darkness to take you and your army to the Black Lands where you will lead my rodent army in battle. My general, Rogo, failed in his duties, and I will deal with him upon my return."

The air filled with the sound of light clattering as an army assembled. "You may leave the gateway open, Seerles. I will decide with haste whether I wish to align myself with you."

Seerles withdrew. "As you wish, Malok."

The cluster of orbs watched as the adder vanished into a corner of the cave, his darkness transporting him back to the Black Lands of which he spoke.

Malok thought about the offer the snake had made. Averon had never seen anything as intimidating as he. Even though his kin wandered its trees, they were deemed insects and unimportant. Malok mused at his thoughts. He was larger than a red fox himself, and thought of the fear he could spread amongst the world of the living.

Malok withdrew into his tangled nest, allowing his army to scuttle freely within the cave. What fear the arachnid could spread, should he emerge from the Forest of the Damned.

5

The warm and cold weather clashed violently above Averon. Thick clouds swirled and illuminated with brilliant flashes of lightning. The ground rumbled with every flash of the intimidating light.

The humans had returned to Averon to bury their hound, Baal. They never understood the fascination he had with the forest, always leading their army upon its trees instead of upon the Great Vast Open. It had been clear that the forest was where he had always wanted to go, and so they decided that his grave should be placed where he had always pined to be. A fresh mound of earth protruded from the Western Clearing, where Baal lay deep beneath.

The night above was terrible as the thunder crashed and the gales tore between the trees and their branches. The fear within the forest had not reached this far towards the Great Vast Open, and the vegetation shone with vibrancy even in the grip of the storm. The patter of rain fell rapidly down upon the grave as the clouds opened and released their waters. The leaves roared in the gusting wind above the clearing.

Slowly, a smoky plume of darkness wove eerily across the open grass. It did not disperse through the rain or the wind, and carried on its journey until it reached the fresh mound of earth. The thunder crashed above, and the lightning flashed right out across the Great Vast Open. The smoke suddenly drew down into the earth, as though something was draining the force from within the grave. The rain began turning it to mud, but the darkness still continued down.

A while later the grave lay motionless, the darkness long gone from its muddy surface. There it was. A twitch pushed from below the soil, forcing the mud upwards.

Seerles watched from the darkness of the tree's and smiled. "Welcome back," he hissed.

www.ingramcontent.com/pod-product-compliance
Lightning Source LLC
Chambersburg PA
CBHW021153030726
47493CB00029B/1409